D0364633

A Saving Grace

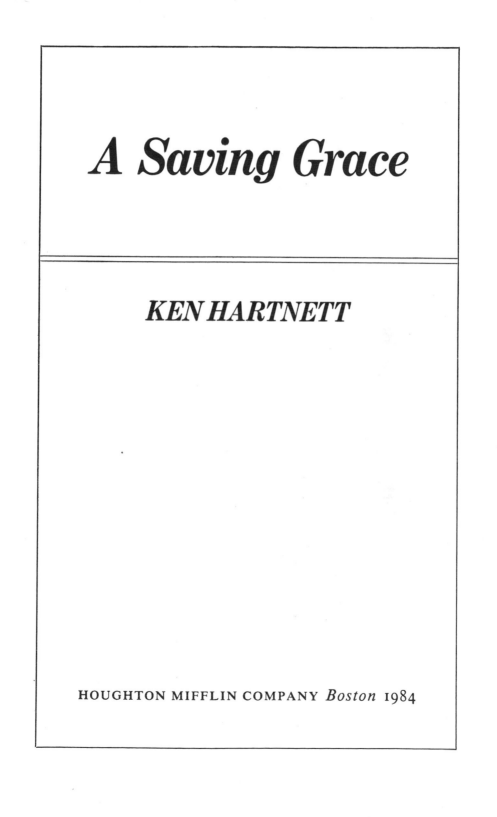

A Saving Grace

KEN HARTNETT

HOUGHTON MIFFLIN COMPANY *Boston* 1984

Copyright © 1984 by Ken Hartnett

All rights reserved. No part of this work may be reproduced
or transmitted in any form or by any means, electronic or
mechanical, including photocopying and recording, or by
any information storage or retrieval system, except as
may be expressly permitted by the 1976 Copyright Act or in
writing from the publisher. Requests for permission should be
addressed in writing to Houghton Mifflin Company,
2 Park Street, Boston, Massachusetts 02108.

Library of Congress Cataloging in Publication Data

Hartnett, Ken.
A saving grace.

I. Title.
PS3558.A7145S27   1984   813'.54   84-10749
ISBN 0-395-36298-9

Printed in the United States of America

S 10 9 8 7 6 5 4 3 2 1

To S.P.P. with love

A grouchy, suspicious, nasty, introspective monk,
a horrid, raggedy thing no faction would care to capture
— Nicholas von Hoffman

A Saving Grace

1

TONY OWEN DIDN'T SUSPECT she was angry until she practically hurled herself out of bed and stood in the dim light, swearing and stamping her bare feet as she groped for her underclothes and cigarettes. Then, her anger ignited his own.

"What the hell did I say?" he asked.

"It's that goddamn attitude of yours," she said, moving toward the chair by the window where the rest of her clothes were neatly folded.

He sighed and took one of his own cigarettes from the pack by the nightstand. He could feel her impatience scraping at him. He wished she would go quickly away.

"Where are my goddamn shoes?" she said, and as she spoke she found them half-hidden under the dresser. She slipped them on, then walked out of the room toward the apartment door. He could hear her swearing again as she fumbled with the array of locks. "This is it, Tony," she said. "The final straw. I've had it."

The door swung open and she was gone. He resisted the impulse to grab his own clothes and follow her down the single flight of steps to her car. Instead, he pushed himself out of bed and shuffled to the window. Her car was parked under the streetlight. As she opened the car door, she glanced up at his window and turned away. Tony hoped she hadn't seen him looking out. But she probably caught the slight movement of the shade and was cursing him for his gesture of protection. "That's all you're good for, Tony, gestures," she had said on more than one occasion. "Gestures are easy, Tony. The real thing, living, that's what's hard. I don't want your gestures."

He waited by the window until he heard the engine of her car respond. Then he trudged into the kitchen, polished off a tumbler of California brandy, and fell asleep back in his rumpled bed.

He slept lightly, awakening even before his clock radio stirred to life with the eight o'clock news.

He thought of Cynthia. She was getting to be impossible. Emotional incompetent, she had called him a few nights before. "That's E.I. for short. E.I., as in Ee-Eye-Oh."

"Don't take out your frustrations on me," Tony had said.

"What frustrations?"

"You hate your job and you expect me to compensate. Find your own compensations," he told her.

"At least I have a job," she snapped. "I wouldn't call what you have a job, working for that goddamn sinking ship. What you have is an ongoing nightmare."

"You are so gentle, Cynthia."

"Well, I'll tell you something, Tony. I'm the only girl you ever had who would tell you the truth."

"Someday I'll appreciate that," he said.

I don't care if it's over, he told himself now as he stared up at the ceiling and in the morning light traced the patterns left by the cracks in the plaster. But he wasn't sure. Ee-Eye. He wondered whether she was right.

His mind drifted in drowsiness. She could be so warm, then turn on him in an instant. Maybe it was something he triggered. He concentrated on trying to reconstruct what happened before she stalked out. They had spoken about Malachy. It was a subject Tony generally avoided. But they had just made love and Tony was feeling comfortable, so he brought up Malachy, mentioning that his brother was learning to speak in tongues.

"Do you know what speaking in tongues is?" he had asked her.

"It's babbling, right? Like when you're stoned?"

"Right," he replied. "Malachy's learning to babble."

"Are you worried about him?" she had asked.

"No more than usual."

"He embarrasses you, doesn't he?"

"You might say."

"I could tell something was bothering you. You were distracted. I wish you wouldn't make love to me when you're like that. I start wondering where you are, and I forget who I'm with, and it throws me off."

"I thought you had a good one," he had said.

"It was all right."

"You didn't act like it was only all right."

"That's as much as you know."

"Damn, Cynthia, stop playing games. You piss me off."

"Hey, it was fine. It just would have been better if you were all there. That's all I was saying."

"Shit."

"Oh, God."

Then there was silence as Tony tried to settle into sleep. But Cynthia by now was wide awake.

"What else is bothering you?"

"Just Malachy."

"Are you sure?"

He had suddenly felt the need for a drink and he noted her annoyance when he padded into the kitchen to get one. Always, she kept count of the number of drinks he'd have in any one night. This would be his fourth, she had told him, as if he didn't know himself. But she wouldn't confront him directly. Instead, she'd attack him indirectly, pointing out that he was getting a paunch or that he was neglecting his apartment. Last night, she honed in on the lack of curtains, which she saw as a symptom of incipient alcoholism.

"I don't know why you bother with candles," she had said. "We have all the light we need in here from that goddamn streetlight."

And he had told her as he had told her a hundred times before that if she felt the need to decorate someone's apartment, she could redecorate her own place. She had said, as she had said a hundred times before, that if Tony Owen wanted her to sleep in his apartment, he ought to do something to make it more comfortable because she needed her sleep if she were to look even halfway presentable on camera and it was impossible to sleep with northern lights searing her eyelids all night.

He tried to make a joke of it. She wasn't amused.

"I'm testing you," he had said. "Do you want to sleep or do you want to be with me?"

"I think you're just cheap."

"No, I'm just indifferent," he said, wearily.

She turned her back on him and tried to settle her head into the pillow. But she kept twisting and turning. "Please, try to go to sleep," she finally said to him. "I can't stand you just sitting there and thinking."

"In a moment," he said.

She sighed and rolled back toward him. "Well, at least tell me what you're thinking about."

"Same old things."

"You mean the paper?"

"Yeah, and the rest of the crap."

"O.K., let's talk about it," she said, and she, too, sat up, pulling the blanket up under her chin.

"But I don't want to talk about it, Cynthia. It has nothing to do with you."

"What am I, then?" she asked, suddenly angered. "Some goddamn slut you picked up in Cleveland Circle?"

"Well, you're not my wife, either," he snapped. "I didn't drag you in here by the hair."

"Oh, Jesus, did you ever hear of fucking intimacy?" she said.

And then there was silence and Tony retreated into his head, and soon he lost the sense that Cynthia was in the bed beside him. His mind rambled amid the debris of the day past and finally seized on a tiny scene glimpsed from the window of a taxi as Tony was riding back to the paper. The cab had stopped for a light at the corner of Commonwealth and Mass. Ave. Tony happened to look at the Harvard Club before the traffic began to move again. As he did so, out of the front door popped Bill Raleigh and Sean Dugan and the mayor himself. Someone must have said something very funny, because they were all laughing and carrying on and holding on to each other for dear life. As Tony's memory toyed with the scene, anger began eating at him. He hated the idea of newspaper people behaving like politicians, sitting in the same box with them at ball games, swapping stories at cocktail hour, behaving as if it were the most natural thing in the world for the mayor to be laughing in public with the two top news executives of the most powerful newspaper in the city.

He thought of turning the scene into a column. He had built columns on smaller stuff. But he knew Bobby Bantam wouldn't much like it. You'd lose the reader, he'd say. He'd think you were taking a cheap shot at the opposition. Sour grapes. He'd say it would look as if we were jealous of those fuckers in their $300 suits with the sense of entitlement they wear like cashmere. But it's reality, damn it. It's the reason the mayor is screwing this town so royally and getting away with it. Editors are getting off on power, not stories. Arrogant assholes.

Cynthia stirred. He realized she was still awake. He decided to have one more moment of safe, comfortable conversation. So he began talking to her about a fight he had had a few days before with Senator Cramer. The fight had ended with him calling Cramer a bastard for lying to him about the way the votes were falling on the rules fight. Cynthia had stayed silent as he told the story.

"You should have seen the look on his face," he had told her. "It was like I had smashed an egg in his pocket. And you know something, Cynthia, I loved it. That's the beautiful thing about our business. Imagine being an insurance man and telling Cramer that he was a shitbum. He'd have your house, your wife, your kiddies. But he couldn't lay a finger on me and he knew it. It was beautiful."

That's what must have ripped it with Cynthia. He saw that now as he got ready to push himself out of bed to face another day. She just couldn't deal with Tony as he was, as a guy who loved his job even if it was killing him. There he was, trying to share a basic personal value with her and she didn't want any part of it. His reality was not her reality at all. He had better start facing up to that. She thinks all I'm doing is hiding behind my newspaper and what I'm actually doing is being who I am. "And Cynthia," he said to himself out loud now as he swung his legs onto the floor, "you had better accept that fact because I'm not changing, lady, and I'm not apologizing, not now, not ever."

Twenty minutes later, he was sitting at a stool inside the Corner Deli, reading the newspapers: his own, the *Morning News,* better known to all its readers not by the name on the masthead but by the name it had been called on the streets of Boston as long as he could remember — the *Bruise*; and the rival paper, the *Daily Mammoth,* the paper with the odd nineteenth-century name no one ever dared to modernize but which at one time conveyed the Bunyanesque gusto that tamed a continent. Now it was indeed mammoth, gigantic, overwhelming in size and in profitability.

He turned to his own column in the *Bruise* first, looking for typos, which irritated him almost as much as Cynthia's pleas for commitment. This morning's column was letter-perfect.

"Sooner or later," it began, "someone is going to do something for Grace Garrison besides force her to move to the suburbs. It would be too much to expect that that someone prove to be the traffic commissioner. He has spent the last eighteen months making Garrison's life a living hell because he can't make up his mind whether traffic should flow north or south or in both directions outside the Garrison grocery store on Concord Street."

"That will teach the son of a bitch," Tony muttered to himself as he drank his second cup of coffee. He rarely ate breakfast. As Tony finished that second cup, the owner, Mike Goukas, came over to talk.

It was a ritual Tony enjoyed. Mike, a large man with an expansive stomach and a handlebar mustache, was a news junkie wired to the city's politics.

As usual, Mike began with a critique of Tony's column.

"What the hell you bothering with the flunkies for? Anybody can hit the flunkies. When you going after the big guy?"

"Hey, I haven't whacked him in two weeks."

"That recently? It seems like longer than that. Well, it's all right, then. I'll forgive you. That traffic situation is a mess, too. Even around here. You know I'd double my business if I had a place for people to park. What do I get now but the walkers, the college kids. A few big spenders like you. Hey, why don't you try some of these muffins? Have a bran muffin. Good for you. I baked them myself this morning."

"You wouldn't know how to bake a potato." Tony turned back to the paper.

Mike placed his own cup of coffee down on the counter in front of him. "Hey," he said, "are you guys going to make it? You're getting smaller and smaller, and the other guys are giving me a hernia picking them up at the doorstep every morning."

"Mike, we'll never die."

"You sure look sick to me."

"Mike, don't worry. We'll make it."

"I sure hope so. I like your little rag. It keeps everybody honest. Well, almost everybody."

Tony scanned the *Bruise,* looking for column ideas. The lead story detailed a gang rape just a few blocks from the deli. The front-page headline, bold and black, told it all: SEX FIENDS TORMENT COED.

"Neighborhood is going to hell," Mike said.

"Hey, this is one of the good neighborhoods."

"Hell it is. We still got poor people. And what are you talking about? How many times have you been broken into in the past year?"

"Just twice. And that was before I got my special locks. Now my place is like a vault . . . And you haven't had it that bad."

"That's because I close up as soon as it gets dark. And you know something? I'm never comfortable. Even in broad daylight, I can never relax. You never know when some maggot is going to come in here looking to clean me out. I'm selling, Tony. As soon as I get a decent price, believe me."

"Then what will you do?"

"Well, what I won't do is open another joint in this town. The only place you can make a buck is in the chichi neighborhoods, and I can't afford the rents and I'm not going anyplace where I have to worry about maggots. Who knows? Maybe I'll buy myself a farm somewhere."

Tony was now in the back of the paper, where he often found nuggets that with enough hard reporting could lead to his best columns. He scanned an item on the bottom of the obituary page. It was only three paragraphs long and concerned the identification of a body found three weeks before in the ruins of a burned-out apartment house on Duncan Avenue. He filed the name away in his mind: Bernie Kremenko, fifty-one, no certain address.

He picked up the *Mammoth.*

Its lead story was a long account of a currency crisis in Australia. Its off-lead story was another economic piece, this one on the Federal Reserve Board and its tight money policy.

"As big as this paper is, I can never find anything in it," Tony said.

"Nice piece on the Red Sox. They're going to put luxury boxes right into the left-field wall. Build them right in there."

"No kidding? Can they do that?"

"Money talks. They can do everything but buy a pennant, the bums."

8

Tony turned to the editorial page of the *Mammoth.* The lead editorial praised the mayor for a speech he gave last weekend to the Chicago Board of Trade on the importance of subsidizing big cities with heavy infusions of federal money. Said the mayor, as quoted by the *Mammoth*: "Although our city has weathered the worst of a crisis that has brought some of our sister cities to the edge of despair, we cannot rest, smugly content with our glittering downtowns, rising like jewels in the midst of past devastation . . . We must turn our attention from downtown to our neighborhoods and bring the same energy and imagination to their renaissance."

"The mayor is looking for more federal money for his machine," said Tony. "And you know something, he's going to get it — just in time for the campaign."

"He's a piece of work," said Mike. "And here it is an election year and we're going to be stuck with him for another four years. I think you ought to do a column on him. People will think you're getting soft."

"What am I going to say that I haven't said a hundred times before? The city is a fucking jungle and he's the guy who watched as it went that way and everybody's suffering and they're going to re-elect him because nobody can beat him. Besides, he's got the *Mammoth* in his pocket."

He left two dollars on the counter and jumped aboard the Green Line trolley across from the deli. The train was half-filled with students heading for Boston University, Emerson, the New England Conservatory, and the Berklee School of Music. He clutched the two newspapers in his lap, felt his head ache as he tried to read them on the swaying car, closed his eyes, and tried to think. A small sense of nausea gripped him for a moment. He couldn't keep doing what he was doing. It was insane . . . Five columns a week. The pressure never let up. Yet, he felt his own impact on events was slipping along with the power of the *Bruise.* The paper was too obviously in trouble, too obviously failing, and yet it was, and had been for so long, the bedrock of his life. Cynthia didn't appreciate that. It wasn't that he was running away. He knew who he was and what his life was all about. He was a columnist for the people's tabloid, and that's all he had to be as long as the paper survived.

It was his vocation, what he was meant to be even before the moment he walked in the door after his graduation from UMass in

1963 and talked his way into a copy boy's job. Bobby Bantam liked him immediately, or as soon as he told him that his brother was a priest and that he had grown up in Brighton, right behind St. Elizabeth's Hospital. "I'm from Allston myself," Bantam told him.

"Oh, I didn't know that," Tony said, telling a lie no one could detect. He had learned all he could about Bobby Bantam before he ever called on him for work. And it wasn't long before the chief was giving him little assignments — like running down to Filene's to pick up a pair of shoes. "You know the kind I like. Make sure they're seven-and-a-half C."

The shoes he liked were alligator, narrow in the toe, with inch-and-a-half heels. The chief was the only one Tony knew who wore shoes like that.

The chief also liked wide ties with exotic floral patterns that seemed phosphorescent, and dark, sometimes even black, shirts. His suits were smartly tailored. In the summer he wore linen; in the winter, a heavy dark wool with thick shoulder pads that exaggerated the narrowness of his hips.

It didn't take Tony long to understand that the chief was far from indifferent to the attitudes of the old city, which dictated the proper way to speak, dress, and run a newspaper. He knew them as well as the most ossified Brahmin snoozing in an Athenaeum armchair. He just deliberately turned them upside down out of both instinct and anger.

Once, the powers that be called a meeting of all the city's media barons to discuss the need for affirmative action to hire more minorities. A pledge card was passed around and signed by everyone there, including Bobby Bantam, and within a month he tripled minority representation on the newspaper by hiring a Malaysian, an Indonesian, and the Cherokee Indian he ran into at a bar across the street from the paper.

Bantam built his paper as a fun-house reflection of the old city and its voice, the *Mammoth*. But he also made sure he reflected the concerns of what he considered the only real city, the city peopled by working-class families with names like Antonacci and O'Brien and Sobolowski and Hanratty.

Those were heady days for Tony, who, only months after he was hired, was promoted to a neighborhood beat, then to City Hall, where his writing flair and capacity for finding stories that drove the

Mammoth crazy got him a shot at a column. Years later came the yellow school buses and the rocks and bottles and tear gas, the protest marches, the boycotts, the hardening of racial hatreds, and the opening of the floodgates to the suburbs, where gradually the Antonaccis, the O'Briens, the Sobolowskis, and the Hanrattys began to lose interest in what was happening in the old town and where the ancient slights and insults didn't seem to sting as much, or not enough to make them keep up their subscriptions to their Boston paper.

Bantam's paper continued to reflect the old neighborhoods, but now it was becoming like them — ignored, abandoned, crime-consumed, blighted, marked for demolition and death.

Tony got off the trolley at Park Street and switched to the Orange Line at Washington. He rode to the South End, getting off two stops from his paper. He wanted to walk. The streets were the one place he could be alone to think. The sun was now high in the sky and the springtime heat surprised him. If the Red Sox had been playing an afternoon game, he might have sought a column idea at Fenway. The sense of having to escape gripped him. It was odd, he thought, how it came on him when he was alone and how it usually disappeared once he plunged into his work.

He walked down a wide sidewalk and began noticing the makes of the cars outside the braces of rehabilitated row houses. MGs and Saabs and BMWs and Peugeots. The Fords and Plymouths belonged to the workmen tearing up the interiors. He passed one BMW, then another with signs propped up on their dashboards. THIS CAR HAS NO RADIO, they read. He also noticed the steel bars on the windows of the first-floor apartments. A knot of black youngsters clustered on a street corner outside a variety store. They glared at Tony as he passed. He looked down at their footwear. All had on sneakers. The all-purpose shoe. Good for games; good for getting away. With growing breathlessness, he walked on, listening for the soft footfalls of potential pursuers. He heard nothing but the sound of traffic and his own breath. He came to a commercial block. A few years before, it had been listless except for a couple of beauty parlors and liquor stores and barbecue stands. Now, the block stirred with new restaurants and health food stores and boutiques where before only the charred hulks of another generation's enterprises gaped like ruined spaces in an aged mouth. Young white males with short hair and compact bodies could be seen through the new plate glass, busy with small details of menus and window displays.

Two blocks down, his paper began to loom like an unwelcome relative. First one saw the giant emblem on the chimney — the young newsman, striding purposefully forward, topcoat open, notebook in hand, fedora thrust to the back of his head, moving into a mass of red letters that read: WE GET THERE FIRST. Once the sign was outlined in neon lighting and at night with each wink of the sign, the newsman seemed to be goose-stepping forward and back, ever determined. The lighting system had long since broken down and no one had bothered to repair it.

One of the old-timers on the desk, Arnie Johnson, suggested the newsman sign when he was a cub reporter forty years ago. Now Arnie spent most of his nights nodding sleepily over copy for the suburban-zone pages. He, too, had broken down, and no one bothered to repair or replace him. It was easier to let things remain where they were until they fell of their own weight.

The building itself stood like a giant pillbox, a squat mass of unpointed red bricks that seemed, except for the chimney, to be seeking refuge in the earth. In the parking lot, the asphalt was breaking apart and the chain link fence was ripped open, giving winos access to the comfort of unlocked cars. The sidewalk, as Tony approached the front door, was littered with beer cans and wine bottles. All was desolation except for a thin strip of turf at the edge of the entrance where Jim the janitor kept a flower garden.

Tony barely noticed the ambulance from Health and Hospitals pulling away and driving rather slowly down the street toward City Hospital.

2

AN HOUR EARLIER, while Tony Owen was still scouring the morning papers at the Corner Deli, Molly Minton, newly appointed as assistant city editor, was contributing another chapter to the lore of the city's feisty tabloid.

The *Bruise* hit hard, it left marks, it wasn't pretty. One didn't have to buy it, or even read it, to feel it. It was a force, a factor in the city's everyday reckoning. When aroused, the *Bruise* could turn on the outside world like the armies of Attila the Hun. It could also turn on itself. Fistfights were common in the newsroom until recent years, when the chronic waves of layoffs thinned the ranks of potential combatants. And once, back in the glory days before Bobby Bantam's ascendancy, an unpopular city editor had been hung from his heels outside the second-floor newsroom window, while half the newsroom staff urged that he be deposited on the concrete sidewalk below. That might have been the editor's fate had the publisher not chanced by and, in a memorable appeal to employee loyalty, reminded everyone how the story would play on opposition pages should the mutiny be carried to its conclusion.

"Those days, it was a man's business; now, it's nothing but college fucks," the old-timers would complain, and hurl cold, hard glances at the stiff back of the unyielding Molly Minton.

Sonny DeLoughery surely shared those sentiments, and he may well have been articulating them to himself that very morning when

Molly Minton, clipboard in hand, approached him with his assignment. She made her advance as she always did, first fixing her target with her wide brown eyes from across the cavernous room, then, smiling broadly, zeroing in on the defenseless reporter like a heat-seeking missile about to lock onto a jet exhaust.

"Wouldn't you like to go to New Hampshire today?" she would ask in a singsong voice that suggested a counselor at a camp for overweight adolescents. As often as not, the reporter would flatly refuse, sometimes shouting his disapproval in a stream of curses and kicks directed at the nearest inanimate object. Immediately, whatever staffers were in the room would gather round, egging on the pocket rebellion while tossing their own insults onto the head of Molly Minton.

On this morning, Molly Minton wanted Sonny DeLoughery to journey to a black neighborhood and interview the man on the street about the coming of spring. "Don't you think it would be a good change of pace? All we ever write about in Roxbury is murder and rape. Black people like flowers, too, you know, Sonny."

Sonny seethed. "You're out of your mind," he said. Then, when it dawned on him that Molly Minton, under her little girl's manner, was hell-bent on getting his tires slashed or his wallet snatched, Sonny DeLoughery exploded. He stamped his feet, he stormed, he cursed, and then he collapsed in a reddened rage, pitching face-forward onto the soiled carpet by a busted water cooler.

Another person might have backed off and let well enough alone while calling for medical help from the nearby hospital, but Molly Minton was not about to let Sonny DeLoughery slip so easily from her grasp.

She bent down and began administering mouth-to-mouth resuscitation, using a technique all her own, one that involved a lot of hopping on her knees from the right of Sonny's torso to the left. When she wasn't hopping, Molly was pushing her ear into Sonny's chest, listening for a heartbeat.

When John Walsh, the city editor, came out of his office to investigate the source of the commotion, he recoiled at the sight of the hopping Molly with her backside jutting in the air.

"What the hell do you think you are, a goddamn praying mantis?" he sneered, and tried to push Molly away and apply his own resuscitation techniques. But Molly wasn't to be moved, even by the city editor. When John Walsh pushed her, she pushed back, ignoring for now Sonny DeLoughery, who lay inert beneath and between them, his eyes staring up sightless into the dim yellow light cast by overhead lamps nobody ever bothered to clean.

The shoving match ended with the arrival of the medical technicians summoned, by whom it could not be determined, from the hospital down the street.

But the shouting match continued, even as the EMTs wheeled the lifeless body of Sonny DeLoughery out of the building.

"You killed him, you dumb bitch," yelled Walsh, who made no secret of his displeasure with Bobby Bantam for "foisting that bimbo on me." "You didn't even know what side of his chest his heart was, you idiot."

"You ruined it. I was bringing him around," she yelled before dissolving into sobs. Snatching up her purse from beneath the city desk, she ran out of the building.

"Molly Minton killed Sonny, don't you think?" asked Stella Ferral, the gossip columnist, as Tony walked into the city room shortly after Sonny's unscheduled departure.

"I don't think until I get the coroner's report," said Tony curtly, as he tried to push past Stella to get to his own desk across the room.

But Stella blocked Tony's escape route by clambering from behind her desk, positioned just inside the entrance to the city room, and standing squarely in the aisle. She moved forward as if to speak in confidence. "Tony, you know something? That bitch is going to kill all of us if somebody doesn't get rid of her soon. Things are bad enough around here without killers sitting on the city desk." She noticed he wasn't listening. She dropped her confidential tone and spoke directly. "Bobby wants her there, doesn't he?" she asked quietly.

"Why don't you ask Bobby?" he said.

He tried once more to pull away, but she grabbed him by the sleeve. "She tried to get me to find out last week what Connie Haydon gave his girlfriend for her birthday. I told her I didn't even know he had a girlfriend. She says to me, with a voice as snotty as can be, everybody knows the mayor has a girlfriend, and if I didn't like the assignment, I should go see Bobby because it was Bobby's idea. I told her she was just trying to set me up, and she laughs at me. Can you believe that bitch?"

Tony just nodded. It would be pointless to disagree. That would only guarantee placement in what Stella called her Book of Slights. Somehow, those whose names Stella recorded paid the price for having been on her wrong side. Seeing only neutrality in Tony's eyes, Stella relented and moved back behind her own desk. Tony seized the moment to effect his getaway.

He moved as quickly as he could without breaking into an actual run, hoping that he would be unnoticed long enough to get to his telephone and the thin pack of messages wedged under the plastic dial. But the city room was long enough to land a jumbo jet, and for all of Tony's dispatch, colleagues were lying in wait, eager to discuss with him the latest death in their ranks. Twenty feet from his goal, Doc D'Amato, the medical writer, stopped him cold.

"Now the question is, will the *Bruise* go under with some of its crew still alive, or will it be the death ship, the Flying Dutchman of the newspaper business, sailing along with a crew of ghosts? I think that's the big question, don't you, Tony?"

"No," said Tony. "I think the big question is whether I'm going to come up with an idea for my column tomorrow."

He resumed his journey toward his desk, now some fifteen feet away across an empty stretch of carpet. D'Amato, a plump man who walked around the city room with a perpetual frown as though he'd just read a computer print-out from the laboratory confirming that the disease was terminal, dogged his heels.

Tony finally reached his desk and scooped up the messages. Before he could focus on them, his eyes caught a bloodstain shaped like a quarter-moon on the carpet by the cooler. The reality of Sonny's death suddenly hit him and he shuddered inside. Death was getting close. Now, it was actually within the gates.

Long before Sonny's demise, *Bruise* people saw the signs of doom. They felt the hand of death, and each day they pored over the pages of *Editor & Publisher,* the industry weekly, looking for job openings and writing letters to papers large and small around the region and the nation. Every few weeks, one of the reporters too young to look for a job with the state or city would land something. Then there would be a going-away party, hugs and kisses in the newsroom, and another empty desk. In the past year, ten staffers had resigned and five had died. And while the number of empty desks mounted, so did the *Bruise*'s losses as the *Mammoth* consolidated its hold on the advertising market.

"He couldn't have died any faster if he'd been shot," D'Amato was saying. "Something gave way and he hemorrhaged. He was dead before he hit the floor. Painlessly. Like a bullet in the heart."

"That's a consolation," said Tony. "You ought to let his wife know how quick it was."

"I'll let her know. I think it was a massive embolism. The way the blood came out. It must have torn the artery wide open. Nothing could have saved him."

Tony looked at the water cooler. "What do you think he was doing over there? That goddamn thing has been broken for two years."

"Confusion, Tony. Probably at the moment of the attack, just as he was getting ready to kill Molly, he felt this sudden sense of disorientation and he just instinctively reached for the water cooler."

"Well, maybe now somebody will at least get the water cooler working again, so the next time somebody is about to drop dead around here, they can at least get a drink for the journey. And maybe they'll do something now about this carpet. The rag hasn't been cleaned in ten years. I don't blame those young guys." Tony glanced over to the far corner of the room, where a knot of young reporters was gathered, talking quietly. "If I were one of those fellows with fast feet and a nice J-school diploma, I'd be knocking on the doors down in the sunbelt. I'd be getting off on bee pollen and SMU cheerleaders, I would, and I wouldn't be breathing this crap for another day."

He looked up at the ceiling, where asbestos and plaster clung malignantly to the steel beams supporting the business offices upstairs. Last year, a chunk the size of a hand grenade splattered beside Tony's coffee cup while he was locked in his nightly combat with his column deadline. He had the fragments gift-wrapped and mailed with his compliments to Wichita — the headquarters of Gridlock, Inc., the corporation that owned the *Bruise.* Gridlock bigwigs were not amused. They reminded themselves of what they knew all along — that Tony Owen was a pain in the ass. Just to protect themselves, they dispatched a scientific team to determine whether the *Bruise* ceiling was lethal or just slightly so. The team's findings were not announced, which was a signal to the *Bruise* staff that they had reason for alarm. Wichita, the staff deduced, was keeping quiet because the situation, if publicly confirmed, would require remedy at considerable cost. The folks back in Kansas were not about to put an extra nickel into the *Bruise.* It would be money wasted with no hope of a return. As big-city newspapers go, the *Bruise* was a dog. It had neither pedigree nor promise and it cost millions of dollars to keep it alive. Logic dictated that it be put to sleep, but that solution posed a serious public relations problem for Gridlock.

Despite the loss in circulation, the *Bruise* still had a quarter of a million subscribers who were vociferously loyal. They would squawk to the heavens if their paper was shut down. At least that's what *Bruise* staffers liked to tell themselves when they debated the paper's future.

"On top of everything else, we have to live with this over our heads. I'd like to take a look at Sonny's lung tissue," said Tony.

"I don't think it would prove much. I don't think the asbestos has a lot to do with anything, I really don't. Besides, it takes as many as twenty-five years before that stuff can kill you."

"Well, I've been here twenty years," said Tony.

"So what are you worrying about? You've had a good ride. Besides, dying shouldn't bother anyone around here. We live on it, for Christ's sake. It's our stock in trade."

D'Amato was right. Death was the stuff of the *Bruise*'s life, especially violent death. A slaying in a love nest was always a tonic for circulation. But the *Bruise* reveled in killings of all kinds: gangland slayings, multiple hits like the card game in a downtown tavern after hours that somebody broke up with an AK .47; mercy killings like those in the North Shore cancer ward where the orderly ran amuck; cop killings; insurance killings; teenage death pacts; sex killings, especially when the killer repeated himself and eluded police for weeks on end; mad-dog killings where the murderer ignored his victim's pleas for mercy and blazed or hacked or knifed or squeezed away. Death not only sold papers; it solved some of the *Bruise*'s internal problems, like the chronic lack of reporters, especially reporters smooth and sophisticated enough to cover more complicated aspects of city life. Every reporter on the staff could cover death, be it on the highway or in a bedroom. It was as easy as writing an obit or covering a fire. All it took was a name, an approximate cause, and the rough circumstances, and the most inept reporter had a story and the *Bruise* a headline. Had anyone ever bothered to ask the chief whether he preferred the living or the dead, he would certainly have opted for the latter. The living complained, they wanted favors, sometimes they even sued. The dead could care less whether they were libeled.

"O.K., you're right, Doc. Another day on the death ship. Let's get cracking. I've got work to do."

Tony turned away from D'Amato and began looking at his messages. Call Cynthia at work. Call Stanley, the mayor's press secretary. Call Senator Timpson. Call your brother. He looked again at the last message. No number. "Good God, that's all I need, him again."

He was about to reach for the phone to call Stanley when Bobby Bantam bounced out of the corner office into the newsroom.

"What the hell is going on around here, for God's sake? Hey, you guys over there, what is this, a social club? Come on, get back to your desks. We got a newspaper to put out today, remember?"

He spoke in his best wise-guy manner, standing in the middle of the newsroom, waving a cigar the size of a small cannon. The reporters began to untangle and move toward their desks, not too quickly lest they seem cowed, not too slowly lest they seem defiant. Satisfied that his mission was accomplished, Bobby took Tony Owen by the arm and nudged him toward the corner office.

"Come on, let's talk," he said. "O.K., Tony. What you got going for tomorrow? Now I don't want anything about what happened here this morning. The sooner people around here forget about that stiff, the better."

"He wasn't so bad," said Tony.

"He was a stiff. He didn't do anything for this paper since the Cocoanut Grove burned down. He was a shitbum. Forget him. Besides, he croaked because he couldn't take a direct order."

"You're all heart, Bobby."

"I got plenty of heart, but I don't spread it all out like mayonnaise. I save it for the deserving."

He was a small man, no taller than five feet four, but he was compact and solid like an old-fashioned second baseman. Once, a few weeks after he became the editor, a reporter in the heat of an argument over story play jabbed him in the chest with his forefinger. The chief didn't hesitate. He shot a left-right combination into the reporter's midriff, doubling him over and firing him before he could straighten up. Reporters ever after were wary about how they approached the chief. He had been editor now for more than twenty years. He knew the newspaper from the basement where they stored the tall stacks of papers dealers couldn't sell to the publisher's penthouse where, years ago, an executive dining room had been planned, then abandoned by Gridlock as an extravagance. The room was now used to store junked typewriters and adding machines until they could be repaired or sold for scrap.

Bantam knew the city the same way. He recognized the people on their way up and the first signs of sure descent. He knew all the subtleties of the political landscape. He knew about personal lives, too, and not just the stuff that titillated the town's gossip mongers. He surprised Tony on this morning by asking him about his drinking.

"Hey, what are those little red circles around your eyes? You been up all night crying?"

"Cut the crap, chief."

"Hey, you're at the dangerous age. A lot of guys tumble over the edge when they're about forty-five. How old are you now?"

"Got a ways to go. I'm forty-two."

"Forty-two, forty-five, what's the difference? Just a word to the wise. Booze can get you, especially in this business. That's what got that poor bastard out there this morning. That and Molly. A good girl. She does as she's told."

Tony tried to change the subject. "What do you hear from Wichita?" he asked.

"Never hear anything good from those cheap bastards. They never understand that to turn this paper around for good, they've got to spend money, real money. Not the five million they're losing here every year. They got to be willing to lose twenty million, twenty-five million before they'll be able to turn the corner. They don't understand. So forget them. We'll just do our thing and not worry about them unless we have to."

"Do you think they're going to shut us down?"

Bobby stared at the man he had come to trust more than anyone who ever worked for him. It was not a total trust. Bobby Bantam could never forget that everyone who worked for him, even the few he considered close friends, stood apart, that only he was the chief, and some things could not be shared, no matter how deep the loyalty.

"Tony, I never thought so before. Now I'm not so sure anymore. There's a limit to the amount of dough you can pour down a rathole, and we're getting close to it. These people want to see a little hope, and I don't know what to tell them because, between you and me, I don't have much myself and I don't trust old Elmer, our publisher. He's already thrown in the towel from what I can see."

"Something happen I don't know about, chief?"

"Hey, Tony, a lot happens that you don't know about, and I don't know about. But I just have a feeling that something's about to give. And do you know something? This city just isn't the same place anymore. You know it, and I know it, and maybe old Elmer and Gridlock know it. It just doesn't work the way it used to. We got readers, all right. Not like the old days before busing, but we got readers, lots of 'em. But Tony, let me tell you, I think they're the wrong kind of readers for us to make it with the advertisers."

"You may be right, Bobby. We're wrong for the people who want to sell designer jeans to poodles."

"Would you believe that? I saw that ad last week in the *Mammoth* and I almost threw up. Yeah, we're on the wrong side of the tracks. Our people don't count anymore. They want to go out and buy used Chevies, and they still have Sunday breakfast after church and vote for politicians with the old Irish names. And there just aren't enough of them anymore in this town. Nah, it's a new kind of city these days, and to tell you the truth, I don't much like it. But let's face it, the *Mammoth* has the formula. It gives these people what they want. And it gives advertisers what they want."

Bobby was becoming more animated as he talked. He got up from his desk and looked out the window and down at the potholes in the parking lot. "And do you know what they want?" he said. "I'll tell you. They want women who wear Puccis and Guccis and Tuccis and who go to church to hear recorder music. They want people who'll buy their fucking dog designer jeans with a little hole in the back for him to take a crap in the park and who'll pay a thousand bucks a month for an apartment in the North End that's got butcher block in the kitchen. And the poor little Italian who paid ninety a month for the same place before it had butcher block is out on the street or living with his son-in-law in Medford. I think the situation sucks, Tony. And I don't think it's going to get any better."

Bobby's office was bare except for three framed front pages. One proclaimed the end of World War II in a screaming headline that read: JAPS QUIT. Another featured a giant photograph that captured the precise moment the wall of a downtown hotel gave way, trapping a dozen firemen beneath the rubble. The third was a routine *Bruise* that appealed to the mind of Bobby Bantam precisely because it projected excitement and action on a day when nothing exciting happened. The page featured a puppy picked up on a South End street and taken to the Animal Rescue League. YOU CAN SAVE HIS LIFE, the headline read. The caption explained that the puppy would be put to death within ten days if no one came forward to adopt it. The caption didn't mention that scores of dogs are picked up on the city streets daily and all face the same fate. To Bobby Bantam that didn't matter. What mattered was that the switchboard couldn't handle the flood of calls that poured in the next morning.

"Tony, why don't you write a little something about the governor for tomorrow? We've been letting that bastard get away with murder lately."

"I think I'll do something else," Tony said.

"What?"

"I don't know."

"You don't like the governor idea, huh? I got a good tip about phony expense accounts in the Department of Environmental Affairs. Doesn't that grab you?"

"No."

"You ought to go after him. At least once in a while. It will get your mind off the mayor."

"Bobby, I'm not obsessed with the mayor. He's a faker, that's all. You know it and I know it, and I have to sit back and watch the *Mammoth* doing his public relations for him. Makes me sick."

"I haven't noticed you sitting back lately."

"I haven't written about him in weeks."

"That's 'cause he's been away."

"So now he's back. And I'm still not planning to write about him. As a matter of fact, I saw him last night with the *Mammoth* honchos, all of them feeling no pain, about nine o'clock. Doesn't that piss you off?"

"No. I'd get drunk with him, too, if it helped this paper any. He's a proconsul, anyway. Connie Haydon and Bill Raleigh run this town. We're part of the chorus. Occasionally, when we get way off key, people notice us. But I wouldn't mind being proconsul, too. It would mean we were big, fat, and successful. There'd be no more of this death ship talk every time somebody drops dead."

"I don't think that's our job. People read us because we're not that way," Tony said.

"Maybe," Bobby Bantam said. "The ones who still do, maybe . . . How's it going with your girlfriend?"

"Fine."

"Nice looking. I saw her on the news last night. Nice looking."

"Is that all you can say about her, Bobby? She's not a bad reporter."

Bobby Bantam smiled and began picking at the papers on his desk, a signal that the conversation was over.

"She isn't a bad reporter, Bobby," Tony repeated.

"Maybe, but she got a little mixed up on the news last night. I didn't know what she was talking about."

"Maybe you weren't listening," said Tony, defensively.

"Oh, I was listening. She was going on about a South Shore stolen car ring, and I could swear she was reporting from Lynn."

"She probably meant North Shore. She gets mixed up sometimes when she isn't concentrating. Gets bored easily."

"Better she's on television, Tony."

Tony stood up to leave. He turned as he neared the door and said, "Bobby, Molly Minton is a disaster."

"She's not a disaster, Tony. She's just doing her job. Better people get on her ass than mine or Elmer's. Elementary management."

"She's still a disaster," Tony said.

3

SCOOTER CONROY was in trouble. Tony realized it seconds after he answered the telephone and there was Scooter, sounding as if he had just climbed three flights of stairs after a lifetime of Camels and VO. "Got to see you, Tony, right away. You got to get down here."

"What's up, Scooter?" Tony asked, surprised that a man who took professional pride in never accidentally betraying emotion seemed suddenly unhinged. "What happened? Your wife finally catch up with you?"

"Tony, I don't know what I'm going to do. He's trying to stiff me good."

"Who?"

"You know who. The mayor. Would you believe it?"

"Offhand, I'd say no. You know too much. On the other hand, nothing he does would surprise me."

"He's stiffing me, all right. So you'll be down right away, right?"

"Wait a minute. I'm not sure I can. This place is like a wake today. Another reporter just dropped dead."

It was a line that would ordinarily stop Scooter in his tracks. Among his assorted duties for the mayor was the job of representing him at wakes and funerals, and he kept up to the minute on the news of the newly departed. But today his only response to the news of a death in the *Bruise* family was a lame "Who died?"

"Sonny DeLoughery."

"Too bad," he said. "Nice man. You going to see me?"

"Oh, Christ. Where?"

"Don't do me any favors. I'll call the *Mammoth.*"

"Where, Scooter?"

"Usual place. Right away, O.K.?"

He hung up. Tony slipped the receiver back into its cradle and thought for a moment of calling Cynthia. No, he would wait for her to call. He had had enough grief already for one day and here was more coming. He gazed around the city room. It was all but deserted now at the lunch hour except for a cluster of editors sitting around the city desk. Someone had sprinkled sawdust from the pencil sharpeners onto the bloodstain by the water cooler. Once more he was seized by a sense of his own mortality. Tony lit a cigarette, his first of the day, and headed toward the exit. He stopped by the city desk to tell Walsh he would be back in two hours.

"What are you writing about for tomorrow?" Walsh asked.

"Too early to tell."

"Nothing like planning."

"Yeah. Too bad we're not a shoe store. You'd be in charge of the inventory."

Scooter Conroy — building inspector, bagman, and direct descendant, at least in his own mind, of the immortal James Michael Curley, who had recognized the talent in the Dorchester stripling and given him his first city job — was a heavy man, but he was more sturdy than fat. And it wasn't until recent years that his belly had begun spilling over his belt and his jowls had begun their descent in veiny pouches toward his collarbone. Had he consulted a doctor, and Scooter would have sooner asked a blind man for the time of day, he would have been advised to alter his lifestyle radically. And that would have meant, among other things, giving up the table reserved for him daily in the rear of Andy Kerr's chophouse in Charlestown. There he took not only his major meal of the day, and as a point of pride paid for it, but there he conducted his office, doling out small favors that Scooter's people believed were strictly up to politicians to provide. Scooter knew, of course, and some of his people may have begun to suspect, that there was in reality little he could provide that they couldn't obtain themselves. Yet he spent each day arranging to deliver teenage boys in trouble from the arms of juvenile authorities into those of the U.S. Marines. "You're going to be proud of your baby," he would say to parents counting off the days when their son the thug would report to Parris Island. "We're lucky to live in such a great country. Wait until you see what a man your little baby is going to become. And you won't believe what the Marines told me about your kid. They said, 'Scooter, if you got any more like that, let us know and we'll send a limousine out to pick them up.' A limousine, mind you. And they weren't kidding."

A call from Scooter might also trace that lost social security check or get the cops to come around and talk to the owner of that noisy dog up the street. A call from Scooter and a little medical insurance might also get a relative into a nursing home, or he might arrange an interview down at the personnel office of Jordan Marsh or Filene's or Bradlee's.

But only occasionally could he deliver a real favor — a city job such as the one Curley had provided Scooter when he was sixteen years old. Those jobs were becoming rare. Poor white kids from Scooter's neighborhood were no longer a top priority at City Hall unless the kids were willing to settle for temporary jobs on the back of a garbage truck. The real jobs free of heavy lifting were doled out by the mayor's office directly, and they were going to kids from the black neighborhoods.

Those were the neighborhoods that were growing, the mayor himself had explained to Scooter the summer before when he went down to see the boss himself with a laundry list of musts for his people. Everybody was cutting back, from the feds on down, and it was a question of spreading what was available to where the jobs would do the most good. All Scooter could do was shake his head when the mayor explained that it was more important to give a job to a black kid than a white kid because the white kid was less likely to bang an old lady over the head when he was broke than a black kid was. "You put a poor kid to work and you cut down on the crime rate. It's a two-fer, Scooter," he had said.

Scooter saw through all that talk. He knew, better perhaps than did the mayor, that his people had lost their clout at City Hall, that the power was passing to the black neighborhoods and to the well-heeled whites, who had as much contempt for Scooter and his politics as the blacks did. He knew that the mayor could take his people for granted because they had nowhere to go but out, if they could afford to move to the South Shore. He also knew that, as much as the mayor might ignore Scooter's neighborhoods, the neighborhoods would be with the mayor in any showdown with the blacks and the liberals. So all Scooter could do was listen and look for the crumbs from the table.

As for Scooter himself, he was still valuable. Though the number of votes he could deliver was dwindling, they could still affect the outcome of an election. And he could still play the good soldier when it came time to fill the campaign coffers. He was of the old school, and what he lacked in finesse he more than made up with persistence and loyalty.

Tony found him at his usual place in the rear. A half-empty coffee cup was on the table in front of him and a copy of the *Bruise* open to the gossip page.

"You ever write any of this crap?" he asked Tony.

"My column keeps me busy enough. What are you, on the wagon?"

Scooter pushed the coffee cup aside. "Hey, the way I feel, if I start drinking I'll be on a toot that will carry me into next Wednesday and by then I'll be indicted."

"Come on, Scooter. Who would ever indict you?"

"Tony, it sounds like a fairy tale, but he's throwing me to the dogs. I'm gone."

"How is that possible?"

"He's letting the feds nail me."

"You can ruin the son of a bitch. He wouldn't dare."

"He doesn't believe that. He doesn't think I can hurt him at all. The way I look at it, he sees me as a used-up old hack and he's putting me on the ice like I'm some old Eskimo without any false teeth. He forgets that I used to know his father, that I pulled his kayoones out of the frying pan on more than one occasion. He's Mr. One Way and I'm going down the street the wrong way. You know him, anyway. His friends are all the uptown people who check the silverware whenever I walk through their living room. As far as he's concerned, I'm gone, Tony."

Tony looked at Scooter's massive face and saw how the veins in his nose had darkened and widened. The old hardness persisted in his red-rimmed eyes, but there was also a hint of childlike vulnerability. Yes, Tony thought, Scooter is going down. "Well, what can I tell you? He's a scumbag. You worked for him all these years. You knew it. Now you're getting your payoff."

"You hate the guy. That's one reason I called you."

"Scooter. Let's get something straight. I don't hate the guy. He's a politician, like you. I try to stay objective. I try not to get personal. There's some politicians that make that easier than others. And there's some that make that damn hard. He makes it hard because he's always working to undercut what I do, which is . . ." Tony broke off. "I was about to give you a lecture about telling the truth. But fuck it. I don't have to tell you what I'm all about. You probably wouldn't understand if it was in black and white on this menu."

"You want something to eat?"

"Yeah, get me a cheeseburger with bacon."

The waitress had materialized by Tony's side. "Scooter's not paying," Tony told her.

"You having the usual, Scooter?" she asked.

"Just the soup."

"It's cream of mushroom."

"Good. Just a cup."

Tony suddenly felt sorry for the hulk of a man sitting in front of him, his hamlike hands toying with the now empty coffee cup. "O.K., Scooter. What did you do to get into the soup?"

"This goddamn liberal. That's what he was. I should have known better than to try to talk reason with one of those birds. But I should have known better. Just to look at him was enough to know the kind of guy he was. Anyway, he was referred to me in the usual way."

"By your boss?"

"Stop playing reporter, will you? I'll tell you what I can tell you and no more. Anyway, this guy was trying to get all the permits he needed to open up that movie complex off Shelby Road. So he comes to see me. He was sitting right where you're sitting right now. So I offer to help him in the usual way and I lay out the terms. You know, Tony, I've been doing this for years and everybody in town knows it. It's the way the boss operates."

"You mean the mayor."

"Whoever."

"Maybe we ought to set some ground rules here, Scooter. Are we on the record or off? 'Cause you're telling me one helluva story and I'm going to go nuts with it."

"We're talking like we always talked for years. We're off the record unless I tell you we're on, and I don't remember saying anything about you being free to write anything. Should I continue?"

"Continue."

"Anyway, I lay down the terms. It ain't a bribe. It's a fee for services for me, and it's a way for the mayor to have some walking-around money like he needs whenever he has to buy a suit or a pair of shoes or help out some bum in trouble. O.K. You know all this. So why do you keep interrupting me? Anyway, this guy gets really pissed. So he tells me, O.K., it's a deal, and we shake hands and he comes back the next week with his little envelope. Except this time, he's wearing a wire."

"The second meeting happen right here?"

"No. In the Hotel Congress. The bar."

"You get busted?"

"No. Not yet."

"Then how do you know he was wearing a wire?"

" 'Cause the mayor told me. I took the envelope. This was two days ago. And I put it in the bank, in my safe-deposit box. And I go home and the mayor calls me. He tells me to look out my front window. I look out and he says did I see a tan Plymouth parked outside. And I said I did, and he says did I notice the two guys sitting in the front seat. And I said I did, and he says they're FBI agents and they're tailing me and I'm all through. That my transaction with the developer was all on tape and they tailed me to my bank and have a lock on my safe-deposit box and the envelope that I put in there. I asked him how he was so smart to know all this, and he says he was the guy who called the FBI, that I tried to muscle a developer and he didn't play that kind of game and I was all through. And I asked him if this was some kind of joke, since when didn't he play those kinds of games since it was his kind of game I was playing, and he says talk like that will make me look not only like a thief but like an ingrate, trying to bring down the guy who let me play Mr. Big around this town for the last twenty years. I couldn't believe I was hearing Connie Haydon talking, the kid I helped make in this town. He sounded so cold, like he wanted to croak me."

"Amazing."

"Amazing? See those two guys sitting at the table by the door? Guess who they are."

Tony turned to look. He wondered how he had missed them on his way in. They might as well have been wearing uniforms.

"They're going to bust me this afternoon. They would have done it sooner, but the U.S. attorney was out of town and he and Connie want to have a joint news conference to show how tough they are on corruption."

"I don't see how he can get away with it."

"Of course he can. I can't talk without fucking up a lot of my friends, and I never talked money with the mayor. I always knew where the envelope was going, but I couldn't prove it. He knows I'm not going to talk. I'm boxed. I know he's a bloodless son of a bitch. But in a way I can understand what he's doing. That developer was headed for the feds, come hell or high water. Connie knew it, so he played it the only way that was open to him. This way he gets credit for fighting corruption, puts the U.S. attorney in his pocket, and all he's got to sacrifice is me — and all that does is send out a message to everybody in the organization to mind their p's and q's. I might have done the same thing myself."

"No you wouldn't."

"No, I wouldn't."

"So what do you expect me to do? I can't write that you were a bagman for the mayor. I have no proof. And all the *Mammoth* guys are going to write that you're a relic from the old days of the Irish mugs. I might be able to offset that for you. But I don't see what you expect me to do."

"I want you to fix that cocksucker."

"O.K. How?"

"He knows I haven't got anything on him, except a lot of pigeon-shit crap like fixing parking tickets and that sort of thing. But what must make him nervous is all the things I hear about the reason why so-and-so gets a job or a contract. Things I hear, you know? Nothing hard. But there's one thing I hear that's pretty good. I mean I hear it from people who don't usually shit me. I hear there's a mess over on Duncan Avenue. A real mess. Remember the bum they found dead in that basement? There's an item about it in the paper this morning. Your paper. Here it is. The bum."

He flipped through the *Bruise* and found the item on the obituary page.

"Here it is. Bernie Kremenko. I hear there's a helluva story in this fire. I can't guarantee it. But I'm told this could be one helluvan embarrassment for the mayor." He put away the eyeglasses he used to read the item in the paper, and he seemed more old and beaten than he had before. "You know, Tony, I never ratted on anybody in my life. This is the closest I ever come to it. And it's probably all I'm ever going to say. But I hope you get the prick. I know you hate him. You do hate him, don't you?"

"I'll look into it, Scooter. And let me know where I can call you."

Tony shook hands with Scooter, wished him luck, walked out of the chophouse, and headed down the street to a cigar store. He walked into the phone booth and called Bobby Bantam.

"You got a good one going for tomorrow. Get some guys down to the U.S. attorney's office. The mayor is going to be there about four o'clock for a joint news conference. They're going to bust Scooter. They got him cold on an FBI wire."

"A shakedown, huh? They get the mayor, too?"

"No, of course not. Just Scooter, and Connie is throwing him to the wolves. That's why he's going to be there. He's the guy who turned him over to the FBI."

"You're kidding me. And the feds are standing still for that? I can't believe it."

"You better believe it. Connie's going to come out of this smelling like a rose. Mr. Clean, the leader of the goo-goos."

"Hey, you're still tight with Scooter. Grab him and don't let anybody else near him."

"Chief, calm down. I just left him and there's not much we can do with what he told me unless you can get old Elmer to agree to call Connie a crook. Anyway, Scooter isn't talking for the record."

"Well, you better put the whole thing into perspective. We'll get Rosen and Baker down to the feds. You write your column from here. Hurry up back. Hey, is there any angle we can grab from Scooter? That son of a bitch owes us plenty. We could have put him away ourselves years ago except you liked him, Tony." Bobby paused, waiting for a reaction.

Tony let the moment go. The chief knew as well as he did the reasons for never getting tough with Scooter. Tony and every other reporter in town found it difficult to look too closely at a man who never lied to them, even when he couldn't answer their questions, and who for all his skill in extracting money from developers and contractors, gave dollars away as freely as he doled out fifteen-cent cigars. Besides being the easiest mark in town, he was always ready with a quote that would rescue the sorriest story assignment. He was also a folk hero to the people who read the *Bruise*. He was with them on the front lines during all their losing campaigns to save what they considered their city. If he was scarred and banged up in a hundred different battles, he was never cowed, never apologetic. And if he was a crook, he was the people's crook. The *Mammoth* could attack him, and did — although as long as he was the mayor's man, it never investigated him. As for the *Bruise*, it would sooner go after Gridlock, Inc.'s internal finances than take too intimate a look at Scooter Conroy.

"Yeah, I may have an angle, but it won't be for tomorrow. I'll explain it when I see you."

□

Between stories, Tony Owen was like an alcoholic between drinks, a man half alive, his emotions all but buried under the weight of an ordinary day. A good story, one that sent little shock waves of wonder or outrage or empathy out over the city, changed all that abruptly. It dissipated, as no amount of alcohol ever could, the sense of despair and dread that stalked his waking hours. A great story that he had to himself did even more; it lifted Tony into a state of euphoria beyond his power to explain either to intimates like Cynthia or to himself. A major scoop meant not just a triumph over the *Mammoth*. It was also a triumph for that part of Tony that longed to be connected to something vital and human. Breaking the news was a source of joy for Tony and always had been, from the time he was a boy and his aunt would send him around the neighborhood with the news of births and deaths in the parish. His aunt, as president of the Rosary Society, would be among the first to know, and Tony would be the emissary to the ladies of the parish without telephones. "Mrs. Maloney," he would shout up the steps of the tenement, "my aunt sent me around to let you know that Mrs. Green has passed away." There would be a shout from the top of the stairs and a torrent of "Glory be to God," and Tony would be off to the next stop, flushed with a sense of power at being able to evoke such undeniably honest emotions from women who usually considered him just another punk from the neighborhood. And so it was that even now, after a quarter of a century in the news business, he could still be transformed by knowing what was generally unknown. When he was about to pass that precious bit of knowledge along, his mind and senses snapped to attention. The years, the weariness, melted away. He became the young warrior on patrol, poised for combat and victory.

He walked past the cabstand and headed up the slope toward Bunker Hill Monument and sat on a bench at the edge of the grounds. A charter bus filled with tourists pulled into the parking lot and Tony glanced at them as they disembarked. Automatically, he checked to see if there were any blacks. There weren't. A few years before, a group of black tourists had been beaten with baseball bats on the monument grounds. The tourist office had been insisting ever since that the incident could never be repeated. Still, few blacks were willing to put the official assurances to the test. He leaned his head back and closed his eyes, feeling the midafternoon sun on his face, and thought about his column. Bernie Kremenko. Wonderful name. He knew Scooter didn't just drop it in desperation. He couldn't be sure how long it would take to ferret out, but he knew the story was there. He knew the way he always knew. His gut told him. He could picture the mayor's news conference.

The mayor was a magician under the television lights, always thinking three questions ahead of the reporters and always trying to recognize the dimmest-witted members of the news corps and then seizing on fragments of their questions so it always appeared that he was being responsive and candid despite media harassment. Yes, he would say, he had done the most painful thing he had ever been forced to do in his public life — turn in a friend, a man he had trusted for more than twenty years. He had no choice. Scooter had betrayed him and depended on him all those years. And someone would ask whether the mayor was being a stand-up guy and he would reply that there was something wrong with the reporter's ethical values if he meant by standing up for a friend that he would allow him to compromise his entire administration. And then someone else would suggest that it would be impossible for a man to work directly for the mayor all these years and shake down a contractor without the mayor knowing about it, and that it was common knowledge that Scooter was a bagman. That would be the question the mayor was waiting for. He would turn in fury on the reporter and berate him for not reporting Scooter himself if he knew he was doing something wrong, or at least reporting him to the mayor. If it was common knowledge, the mayor would say, he didn't know about it. And then he would challenge the entire assembly to provide one scrap of evidence that Scooter had ever turned over a dollar to him or to anyone in his administration, and when no one came forward to accept his challenge, he would close the news conference by insisting that no such evidence existed and that he himself was being victimized by their lack of imagination. He was, he would tell them, what they couldn't conceive of because they were too cynical. He was an honest politician surviving in a dishonest age, and he would so glower with indignation that all who heard him had to admit in their hearts that quite possibly he was a man of honor after all and they were knaves for not acknowledging what was before their eyes.

Tony himself was not immune to the mayor's magic, and he made it a practice to avoid his news conferences. He knew the man from his works and preferred it that way. People like Scooter gave him a good idea of what the mayor was like. So did the cast of characters he kept around him — a curious mixture of leg breakers, manipulators, and female devotees. And so did the city, which he had transformed into an El Dorado for a handful of developers and a wasteland for the Irish, Italians, and blacks too poor to live inside the bastion of condominiums and town houses enriching the downtown.

The tourists began heading back to the bus. Some stopped to snap pictures of the monument. Stetsons and Florsheims. Must be Iowa or Nebraska. Texans would have cowboy boots. An idea for a column began to form itself in Tony's mind. "The day Connie Haydon shot down his old pal Scooter Conroy, the WHITES ONLY sign was still out at Bunker Hill Monument, the streets of the South End were littered with last week's, or last month's, garbage, and the old ladies out in Roslindale stayed locked behind their lace curtains, prisoners of fear. The mayor had struck a blow against corruption. Maybe now he'll start taking on reality."

It's a start, Tony thought to himself. He stood up, stretched, and headed down the hill toward the cabstand, passing by the chophouse just as the two FBI men, with Scooter in tow, were getting into their tan Plymouth to drive toward the Federal Building.

Malachy was waiting for him in the lobby when he got back to the *Bruise.* The sight of him was a shock. It always was. Tony felt pity, then embarrassment, then anger as he looked at the man smiling vacantly before him, his long, lean frame lost inside a worn and outsized black suit, his feet encased in a pair of pink running shoes worn through at the toes. He wore no socks and the big toe on his right foot was dark with grime from the street.

"I was going to keep him out," said the lobby guard. "But he said he was your brother."

"That's all right," said Tony.

He turned back to the derelict and said, "Malachy. They let you out. I can't believe it."

Malachy's eyes hardened with anger. "That's all you care about, that they let me out. You didn't care much when I was inside. You didn't visit. You didn't call me. You didn't know what I went through. You're the conscience of the city, and you don't even care what's happening to your own brother. You're a fraud, Tony. I bet you're ashamed to have me standing here. People will see me and know what a fraud you are. You're embarrassed. You should see yourself. It's comical. What are you ashamed of?"

Malachy moved forward and reached out as if to embrace Tony, who pushed him away. "Come on," Tony said. "Let's go to the cafeteria and get a cup of coffee."

It was late afternoon and the tables were empty. Tony got a Coke out of the machine and set it down before his brother.

"Things aren't going well, are they Malachy? They could get better. I could help you, you know. I've been talking to the people at the chancery. They tell me they have a wonderful place where they'd love to have you. All I have to do is lift the phone. Saint Joseph's out in Weston. Just for priests and brothers. No pressure. No drugs. Just a place to rest until you start to feel like yourself."

"No," he said.

"What do you mean, no?" Exasperation was starting to build in Tony, who looked up at the clock and realized at once that Malachy had caught the gesture. He bit his lip and settled back into his chair. To rush Malachy was invariably a way to prolong his visit.

"You can't handle feelings, Tony. I understand that. I know that's why you're in the newspaper business. And that's too bad. You could be a much happier person and a much more effective columnist if you didn't get yourself so uptight. You'd also be a better human being. You really are a shit, you know."

Tony kept his patience. He would not let Malachy provoke him. He asked again, gently, "What are you going to do, Malachy?"

"I'm a priest, Tony. I'm going to live like a priest. I'm going to feed my flock. You were a Christian once, you son of a bitch. You ought to understand." Malachy was becoming agitated. He kept tapping the can against the table, faster and faster. The Coke began to spill out over the dark hairs on his wrist. "You're trying to put me away for life. You want them to lock me up. You're a coward, Tony. You really are. That's been your problem all your life.

"And you won't do anything about the most important story in the city today. It could win you and your joke of a newspaper a Pulitzer Prize, and you're too uptight to even consider it. It's that great man in the hellhole out in Mattapan. It's like Jesus and the Pharisees all over again and you don't have the imagination and the balls to see what's right in front of your eyes."

Tony stared at his brother's hand. He did not want a scene. Once he had had to call the police, and the sight of the blue uniforms drove Malachy into a frenzy and half a dozen men were needed to get him into the wagon. He didn't know whether Malachy wanted to create an uproar, but he could never be sure. Malachy veered in and out of madness, like a child climbing in and out of a sandbox.

"Malachy, tell you what. I'll make you a deal. If you're talking about the same guy you've been talking about for the last five times I've seen you, you know how I feel about it. You know that he's not the guy you're talking about. Old Tarzan is dead. So if your guy is telling you he's Johnny Weissmuller, he's putting you on. But as I said, I'll make a deal. I'll go halfway, more than halfway. I'll try to get someone from here to go up to Mattapan and look for himself, and while I'm doing that I want you to consider that maybe it's God's will that you take the deal the chancery is offering you and get off the street. I mean, open yourself up to the possibility that maybe it's you who's not seeing what's before your eyes."

Malachy slammed the Coke can down hard on the table, splashing the contents into the air. A few drops hit Tony in the face. "No deal . . . Damn it. You do your job. That's all I'm asking you to do, and you let me do mine."

"Malachy, don't you try to Mau Mau me," Tony said, his voice quiet out of a forced calm. "I've offered you a good deal, a chance to get your guy's story out to the public. Nobody else in this city is going to give you that chance. But I'm not going to fight you. If you change your mind, just call me and leave your number with the operator. I'll get back to you as soon as I can."

Malachy grew silent and drew into himself. He closed his eyes and tilted his head back so far that his Adam's apple pushed hard against the skin at his throat.

"Borromeo and excelsis in in suum dignum, señor meum amicus. And Manny, Moe, and Jack. And all the ships at sea. Barco veniat in Barcelona. Rocco in sancto padua in warm water. Three times a day. Do you get the drift?"

"No."

"The jungle is dark and dense. A bisha can condulla in the medulla oblongata and the hypothalamus is equidistant on all three sides."

He began to chant. "A busha ka da, a bush ka da in omnipotens terra. Lux mundi. A bush ka da. A bush ka da."

"Jesus Christ, you're exasperating, Malachy. You really are a pain in the ass."

"I'm learning to play the spoons. Would you like to hear me?"

"Maybe next time."

"Johnny's teaching me that, too."

"He must be one helluva guy."

$$\underline{\underline{4}}$$

CORNELIUS J. "CONNIE" HAYDON was in the foulest of moods as he left the Federal Building ahead of two aides, Stanley Blum, press secretary, and Corinne Daniels, special assistant. The anger had been growing in him from the time seventy-two hours before when he sat in silence and listened to the developer howl about Scooter. Anger was a weapon Haydon had long ago learned to rely on. It had always been there, black and implacable, a force stored deep within his psyche. Harnessed, his anger could intimidate, punish, overwhelm; unharnessed, and Haydon had long ago learned the dangers posed by his unbridled fury, it could kill. "He's got a temper like his grandfather," his mother used to say. "It's Black Irish. That's what made them such great warriors. The hot Spanish blood mixing with the Celt. Watch out."

Haydon had not known his grandfather, a Railway Express dispatcher run over by a truck before Connie was born, and he had barely known his father, a carpenter who joined the Seabees in World War II and died when his bulldozer plunged off an Iwo Jima cliff. Whether a father's restraining hand would have softened young Connie's temperament was a debatable point within the Haydon family as he grew up. His mother, Margaret, a social worker, accepted Connie's temper the way she accepted his dark eyes and declined to punish him even when he used a baseball bat to smash the nose of a boy who taunted him during his seventh birthday party.

Connie regarded his temper as a weapon of personal power. He had no apologies to make as he slammed the door of his limousine, almost catching Blum's hand in the back door. "Wake up, Stanley," he said. "Go sit in the front."

Corinne opened the opposite back door and slid in, taking care to keep a cool distance in public from where the mayor sat, taut and glowering against the soft leather upholstery. She said nothing and stared straight ahead. Finally, the mayor spoke.

"Stanley, I ought to fire you, you incompetent . . . Oh, what's the use. You'll never learn."

Stanley said nothing but stared straight ahead out the windshield. Corinne could see that a patch of skin between his collar and the edge of his hair had turned crimson. She was unsure why the mayor was venting his spleen at Stanley. The news conference had gone off like clockwork, she thought. But obviously she had missed something and she wasn't going to reveal her ignorance.

"Stanley, I'll bet you're so dumb you don't even know why I'm furious at you. Turn around and look at me, Stanley."

Stanley twisted in his seat and looked at the mayor, his face full of fear and confusion. Corinne was never sure when she saw that look whether Stanley would be able to hold back a rush of tears.

"Stanley, can't you talk?"

"I don't know," he said. Corinne was surprised by the amount of control in his voice. She looked at Haydon to see if he was also surprised. His face reflected nothing but anger.

"Well, I'll tell you. When you arranged that goddamn news conference, you gave the store away. You let Dwyer handle the whole show. You let him open. You let him close. You made me an afterthought. Don't you ever do that again. You also didn't get Hornblower over from the *Mammoth*. Now you have no sense how they're going to play the story."

Stanley didn't answer. It would have been useless to tell the mayor that the friendly reporter Henry Hornblower was out sick that day and there wasn't sufficient notice of the news conference in any case to get him there. And Haydon wouldn't have bought the explanation that since the conference was on the U.S. attorney's turf, his office controlled the ground rules.

"The play will be good. You stole the show anyway. Nobody had any questions for Dwyer. You'll see. Wait till we get back. You'll see what's on the tube. It will be all you," Stanley said.

Corinne finally spoke. "I thought that this one might have brought out Tony Owen. He stayed away again."

"Better to knock my block off tomorrow, the bastard. That's all right. Nobody pays attention to that rag anymore. He can say what he wants."

"He was with Scooter this afternoon," Stanley said quietly.

"Good. They deserve each other. How do you know that?"

"Dwyer's guy told me. They had a long talk at lunch."

"There's not much he can write no matter what Scooter told him," said Corinne as the limousine crept along in the rush-hour traffic in a slow arc toward City Hall. It would have been easy for Connie to walk from the Federal Building back to his own office, but the walk would have exposed him to a peppering from reporters who would stalk him every inch of the way. Better to drive from subterranean garage to subterranean garage and avoid further questions.

"Everybody's in the same boat," said Stanley. "Nobody laid a glove on you in the news conference."

"Nobody ever does in this town. The reporters here are all a bunch of turkeys. Lazy drunks who have no concept of this city or how it's run . . . Those TV guys are a joke. If they had to concentrate for more than a hundred and twenty seconds, they'd be atomized. All that would be left would be a little puddle on the floor. Who was that girl from Channel Four, the one who kept asking me about how I felt? 'But tell us how you felt inside when you had to turn in your friend; didn't you worry whether you were doing the right thing?' " He mimicked the reporter's singsong voice.

"That's the famous Cynthia Stoler, Tony's girl," said Stanley. "One of Tony's girls, I should say."

The angry edge had begun to fade from Haydon's voice, but with the new mention of Tony Owen, his tone turned venomous again. "Nobody's going to remember his name in five months. You wait and see," he said. The mayor's face suddenly softened. "Why is she wasting her time with a broken-down bum like Tony Owen? You figure that one out," he said.

They returned to the mayor's "communications center" just in time for the six o'clock news. Three television sets were fixed into the wall right behind Stanley's desk. The mayor and Corinne sat on a leather sofa while Stanley took a chair off to the right. All three local stations led with the story of Scooter's arrest and shots of him arriving at the Federal Building and being whisked to his arraignment. Scooter stared straight ahead, making no effort to hide his face or duck the cameras.

"Look at him," said the mayor. "He loves the cameras. My God, he could be arrested for child molesting and he'd still be right there hogging the cameras."

The voice-overs were just what Stanley had predicted. A bombshell in Boston City Hall. Mayor Connie Haydon, in a dramatic attack on corruption within his own administration, blows the whistle on the colorful Scooter Conroy, turning him over to the FBI to answer bribery charges.

The cameras zoomed in on the news conference and there was the mayor, looking stern and righteous, his brow furrowed, his dark eyes flashing, explaining the pain of meeting his public responsibilities. "As much as I love Scooter Conroy, and I do, I love this city even more," he said.

"Wonderful," said Corinne. "Just wonderful."

Channel 4 panned to Cynthia Stoler outside the Federal Building. "Let's see how much Tony Owen is influencing her," Stanley said.

"The real story," said Cynthia, "is what went on inside the heart and mind of Connie Haydon as he debated whether to throw his longtime aide to the wolves or to try and cover up a glaring example of public corruption. We asked Mayor Haydon about his emotions in the hours before he went to the FBI and this is what he said:"

"I told you that this was the most painful moment of my public career, perhaps the most painful moment of my entire life. What more can I tell you? I'm hurting inside." Once again the mayor's face was on the television screen, the look of pained virtue in his eyes, the voice softer and halting as if hinting at emotions under the surface that no real man could express in public.

"Hey, she played it straight," said the mayor.

Once more the camera was on Cynthia. "One question the mayor did not address," she said, "was whether the alleged shakedown of the hotel developer was the first instance of misconduct on the part of Scooter Conroy that has come to his attention in their more than twenty years of association. If that is so, then what happened to

Scooter Conroy that he so suddenly strayed from the straight and narrow path? If it wasn't the first episode — but only the first episode that has come to the mayor's attention — then Haydon must explain how he so seriously misjudged a close associate over the years he has occupied City Hall."

"Hey, that sounds like an editorial," said Stanley.

"No, it sounds like Tony Owen," said Corinne.

"What's that 'close associate' garbage? I think I've spoken to Scooter five times in the past two years. Call the station and tell that broad's boss to set her straight. When they run an editorial, they'd better label it. And make sure you talk to everybody writing at the *Mammoth* tonight. Remember you need proof. I never had proof. This was the first time. I go by the book. Anybody who doesn't think so better have evidence to show that I don't. I'm going to head over to the *Mammoth* myself tomorrow and see Raleigh. But you better control the damage tonight, Stanley. Get going. Corinne, you come with me. We've got to talk."

He walked briskly ahead of her down the thickly carpeted corridor into his private office. He sank into the sofa, which like the other furnishings in the chamber was dark brown as if to match the color of his eyes. "I'm exhausted," he said. "I can't remember the last time I've been so tired."

"Lean your head back," she said, and walked behind the sofa. She took his head in her hands and slowly but firmly began to knead his scalp and the muscles of his neck and shoulders. Her hands moved rhythmically and surely and possessively.

"Are you afraid?"

"Yes," he said. "A little . . . I'm not sure why. I mean, I think everything is under control that can be kept under control. And you never know how this will play in the long run. Scooter has nothing on me and I'm not sure even if he did that he'd use it. But he's got to be hating me right now. He's got a lot of friends in this city and it's never helpful to stir things up like this. Everyone will be looking for other bagmen and interviewing all the people dealing with the city for the past hundred years or so and . . . Well, it becomes another thing to manage and I have my hands full already. But Scooter should never have put me in this situation. I really can't forgive him for being so goddamn careless."

He reached up and grasped her hands with his own, squeezing

them down harder onto his neck. "And Eileen is getting impossible. She's threatening to leave me, you know."

"As long as she's just threatening, nothing's changed," Corinne said. She moved from behind the sofa and sat down beside him, still holding his hand. "She has nowhere to go. And you haven't embarrassed her."

"No, I haven't done that."

Haydon stood up and walked to the big picture window looking down on Faneuil Hall Marketplace. For a man of almost sixty, with a shock of thick white hair, he was in mint condition, as lithe and trim as a man nearly half his age. He moved with the grace of the shortstop he was in college. "Slats" they called him then, because of his long, lean build. The years showed only in the lines of his face, most notably in the creases that slashed in twin lines from his nostrils downward to the edges of his lips, stamping his face with a frown that deepened whenever a dark mood was upon him. The fixed frown vanished, of course, before a smile that seldom failed to disarm because it seldom failed to surprise as it broke across his face. Corinne had learned that the only reliable way to read Haydon was to study his deep dark eyes and to recognize that when they clouded over, it was best to stay clear.

His eyes were soft now as he turned away from the window and looked at her and said, "The only things I've ever feared in my whole life are the things I can't control, and I've spent my whole life keeping those things at a distance. That's why I love my job. Jesus, that's the problem right now. Damn imponderables. All let loose by stupidity. My stupidity, too."

"Come on, Connie. You didn't shake that developer down."

"You don't understand. That doesn't matter. I let Scooter have too much room to run. I should've reined him in years ago. I just didn't get around to it. And people after a while are going to say to themselves, like that Stoler bitch was saying a few minutes ago, where was the mayor? Where was he when all this was going on? And I have to blame myself. I've been telling 'em for years that this is my city. And in a way it is. People believe, and it's true, that you can't turn a spade of earth in this town without my O.K. That's right. I'm on top of every detail. Put up a skyscraper and it's *my* skyscraper. I want to know what it's going to look like, and if I don't like it, it doesn't get built."

"Come on, Connie. That's the way it should be. That's why you're so good at what you do."

She moved toward him as if to take him in her arms, but he pushed away. "This is a true story. I heard it from Stanley the other day. A restaurant closed on Beacon Hill — you know the place. Martha's. Right. The place off Cambridge Street. Anyway, Martha was losing her shirt and Stanley dropped in there. Did he tell you? Anyway, she tells Stanley that the only reason she's closing is that the mayor didn't like her quiche. He passed the word it was too custardy. Now would you believe that?"

Corinne smiled. "Well, it was, wasn't it?"

He smiled back. "As a matter of fact, it was. But I didn't say that to anyone. At least not that I remember."

"Oh, Connie," she said. "You are King Tut — admit it."

This time, he took her in his arms and embraced her, kissing her gently on the top of her head. "Yeah, I am," he said. "I'm the king, all right, of a second-class city populated by a collection of apes and pygmies. Look at those people." He pointed out the window back down to the marketplace, which was filling now in the twilight with tourists from Peoria and Topeka, advertising men on the make for legal secretaries from the downtown law firms, sailors on leave from the ships berthed at the waterfront. "Look at 'em. Everybody on the make, wearing the same kinds of clothes, the same kinds of shoes, the same kinds of hairdos, all thinking they're the top of the class, first-rate, top drawer. All after the same sensations, reading the same books, going to the same movies, buying the same furniture, singing the same songs. Nobody down there is thinking for themselves. And tomorrow, if one of their chichi writers tells them the mayor is a crook, they'll all believe it and they'll all look up at this window and say, 'There he is. There's Connie Haydon, the crooked mayor.' And I'll be down the chute. And all the years I've spent pulling this city out of the garbage dump are forgotten. They won't be talking about electing me president. They'll be talking about sending me to Walpole. And do you know something, that could happen. I'm the best and most honest mayor this town has ever had. And you know something, I could end up in Walpole. What a world. What a city."

Corinne felt flushed with love for Haydon as he spoke. It thrilled her to hear him speak directly of his power. It especially thrilled her because she knew she was the only person in the world he spoke to so candidly. He trusted her with his life and she loved him for it. She wasn't convinced that he loved her; she suspected he did. She knew he needed her, and for now that was enough.

She knew his feelings toward Eileen were deeper and more complicated, and she never picked at them. It would never do to force a showdown with her. He had traveled a long way from his Irish heritage, but it was still a part of him, and she feared that by brushing against the roots of his tribal loyalties she would arouse reactions in him that she could neither comprehend nor control. But she was certain that Eileen was unworthy of Connie Haydon, that she was part of the working-class past he had rejected in his mind and heart, just as he had rejected the neighborhoods where men like Scooter Conroy were admired. He was better than the people he came from, she thought, a superior being.

He seemed to be reading her mind. "Corinne," he said, "Eileen is getting out of control. She really is. This Scooter thing infuriated her. She said I was cutting my last ties to my own people. That I'm a turncoat. That I've forgotten who I am. That I'm turning this city over to creeps, like the ones down there." He pointed once more out the window. "She says I'm turning my back on her as well, and her family."

"You certainly haven't done that. If you ever walk out of here, her family's going to have to go to work for the first time since they got off the boat."

Her tone was too sharp and he looked at her crossly for a moment. "I mean she has some talented relatives," she said quickly.

"They're good people. Well, some of them are. Tommy Mannion, my God, he practically grew up in my house. He still practically lives there. I didn't realize when I married Eileen that I was marrying a small army. A pretty powerful one, too. They'll all be up in arms over Scooter."

He was trying to tell her something. She wasn't sure what. She studied his eyes. They seemed tender. Suddenly, she grasped his possible message and felt a sense of alarm.

"It would be the end for us, wouldn't it, if Eileen walks out."

"Why do you say that?"

"I thought that possibly you were trying to tell me that. If it looked as if she left over me, then I would have to go, or you would have to get out of politics, isn't that true?"

"You've been thinking that?"

"No, it just occurred to me."

"You're awfully bright, Corinne."

"Then it's true."

"It would be awkward, wouldn't it? But she's not going anywhere, not if I can help it. And who knows? I don't. Maybe I will get out of politics. Maybe I'll have no choice."

Corinne glared at him. "Don't be dishonest with me, Connie. I love you too much."

Corinne Daniels had been a Connie Haydon assistant for the past two years. The mayor had always liked women around him, young, attractive women with flouncy skirts and competent eyes. He had precise specifications for those he would admit to his inner circle. They should be bright. That was a given. They should be loyal, too, and their loyalty tested. He wanted no woman around him who would prefer to be home with husband or baby. They must be discreet. Gossip, unless it was calculated, was forbidden. But the most important qualification was the look: they must be lean, like their boss. That way the mayor was certain they were disciplined. He detested fatness. It offended his eye. But it also offended his moral sense — it was evidence of a defective character. Spare women also caused less talk. A woman of obvious sexuality set tongues wagging. Connie Haydon's women — with the exception of Corinne — were flat-chested and asexual. They had one other quality in common: they adored Connie Haydon. They adored him as totally and uncritically as his mother had adored him. Corinne adored the mayor, but she was a full-blooded and full-bodied woman who happened to be competent.

As Haydon grew older and more established in his sense of power, he began to rely on his women more than on his men, who began to irritate him with their need for arm-twisting and cajolery and their barely disguised competitiveness. He began to realize why it was that, long ago, eunuchs had been in demand as courtiers. One wasted little emotional energy dealing with rival male egos after the ego had been neutered. Women served as Connie Haydon's eunuchs. Choose them with great care and define their lines of authority to minimize conflict, and they are the most trustworthy and trouble-free aides a man can find.

He loved the look in their eyes when he walked into a room and smiled and began bantering and teasing them about their work, their husbands, the movie they may have seen the night before. All the while he kept his eyes fixed fully on them, forcing them to break off the contact or return the boldness of his own gaze. He was aware of the sexual nature of the game and he pushed it, not to draw the women into bed but to confirm his sense of mastery over them. It was the testing that he relished, especially when the woman was new to City Hall and unsure of her own standing in his eyes. His approach was consciously cruel. He would learn that a woman had to be at home that night, perhaps for a dinner party or to care for her baby. He would summon her to his office within a few minutes of the time she was planning to leave City Hall. He would advise her that something important had just come up, that the problem could not wait until the next day, that she would have to change her plans. He would then study her reactions, note the degree of vexation or the composure with which she hastily rearranged her life. An expression of extreme annoyance was fatal; a refusal to remain, unheard of.

Usually, he could predict the reactions: the biting of the lip, the slight fidgeting of the fingers, the shadow of distress that flickered in the eyes. Sometimes, he wasn't sure. Had he known how Corinne Daniels would react, he might never have tested her. His trivial game had upset the balance of his life.

"You know, don't you," she had said, "that I have a dinner date tonight."

"I can't run a city according to your social calendar," he had said. "The feds need that finished application by nine A.M."

"I don't think the application has anything to do with your asking me to stay tonight. I think you're asking me something else, and I wish you would ask me directly."

"What do you think it is I'm asking?"

And so their relationship had begun. As they grew closer — during working days and nights when they were inseparable — it made little difference to Eileen that her husband's ties to his new aide were still not overtly sexual. Had it been sexual from the start, Eileen might have understood, believing as she did that no man, not even her husband, was immune to the charms of a young and pretty woman. As for Connie, he soon realized that his relationship with Corinne would be easier to handle if it were sexual. Sex has a way of defining relationships and keeping them within bounds. But Connie held back because he despised men who took women the age of their daughters to bed. He was also frightened by Corinne's sexuality. Before he met her, he thought of sex as something simple, devoid of mystery. Sex was power. It was a way to keep women under control. But Corinne was different. To take her to bed would mean a surrender of his own authority. She would see in the sexual act not her own surrender, but his, and that would make him an equal in her eyes. In all his life, Connie Haydon admitted to only one equal. And his mother had been dead for ten years.

The intercom buzzed. Haydon picked up the telephone. "I've got to see you immediately. Major news."

"Come right in."

Within seconds, Stanley was in the office, his face pink with excitement. "The pope is coming to town. Just heard it from Monsignor Foley in the chancery. The date isn't set, but his security people will be in town within three weeks to check things out and talk to the police. There won't be any announcement from Rome for a while. But I'm sure we can leak it." Stanley spoke breathlessly, and as the words gushed out of his mouth he bounced delicately up and down on the balls of his feet.

"The Lord moves in mysterious ways. Here goes Scooter right off page one. Terrific. Let that Tony Owen write whatever he wants. Leak it to the *Mammoth* tonight. Get on the horn right now," exulted Haydon.

"I'm not so sure that would be wise," said Corinne. "It's almost seven o'clock. You know how the *Mammoth* gets whenever they have to break up their front page. And they might not get the necessary confirmation in time. Is the chancery fully informed, or is the monsignor the only one who knows the details?"

"She's right, Connie. If we leak it now, the *Mammoth* might just make it a box on one. They won't get anything out of Rome and the cardinal will be all over Foley's ass if we don't give more time for the rumor to spread. If we wait a day you can drop the story on Raleigh when you see him in the morning. They can plan for it the whole day. And you don't have to worry about the *Bruise*. They won't have a thing. Wait till you see Bobby Bantam's face. He'll be ready to kill."

The image of an enraged Bobby Bantam amused Haydon, and for the first time that day, he smiled. A look of deep contentment came over his face. "That bastard will be suffering and so will Tony Owen. Another nail in their coffin."

He sat down in an armchair by the window and looked out over the marketplace crowd. "What a city!" he said. "Everybody wants to come here, even the pope. We've got to get going on the planning. Corinne, head out tomorrow and see the cardinal and arrange a private luncheon with him for next week. We'll make this the biggest bash in history. What an honor! Can you think of anything better that could happen to us? Stanley, what more do you know about this? Why is he coming here? What's the agenda?"

Stanley looked confused. "I don't know," he said. "Foley said something about a personal mission. A saint or something. I didn't pick up on it all the way, and he wasn't sure himself. I think he's probably going other places, too. A national tour or something."

"You think or you know?"

"I think. I don't know because Foley didn't know. He said it was strictly pastoral. Then he said something about personal reasons. Somebody who lived here. I'm not sure."

"It sounds incredible," said Corinne. "Do you know of any saints from this place? I can't imagine."

"Find out, Stanley. That's an intriguing idea. A saint from Boston. That's something to sell. Whoever it is would have to be dead for a hundred years. Jesus Christ, we could have a religious revival around here. The pope himself coming to Boston to honor one of our saints. The cardinal himself would be levitating. I'll bet he'd think the pope was coming to canonize him. Piety finally pays off in the big one. Get cracking, Stanley. This is wonderful news.

"Corinne, once we confirm this visit with the cardinal, I want you to draft me a personal message to the Holy Father. You'll know what to say. Make it courtly and correct but warm and personal. I hope we'll have time for a long conversation. There's a lot we could teach each other. He's a helluva politician. Do you know much about the man?"

"No," said Corinne. "Do you?"

"Just what I hear in church, just what I hear in church."

His eyes glazed over and he retreated to a lonely place somewhere within his head. Corinne frowned. She knew that for now there was no reaching the mayor, that he was already locked in a profound and touching conversation with the pontiff, a conversation that would spin on and on in his head until the magic day when the pope would actually arrive at Logan Airport. She knew, too, that when he did arrive, the magic would soon evaporate as the mayor found himself jostled aside by luminaries of greater status, the president himself, perhaps, or maybe the governor or Senator Kennedy. No, there would be no tête-à-tête, no soul sharing, no signal of any kind that Connie Haydon was something special. The pope would be polite, correct, cordial, and distant, and Haydon would spend weeks after his visit trying to reconcile himself to still another demonstration that the greatness he was born to embrace had somehow, somewhere eluded him.

5

ACROSS TOWN, *Mammoth* editor Bill Raleigh was pleased. A brief moment of self-satisfaction was all he allowed himself. Genuine excitement would never do. To exult in triumph was as déclassé as whimpering in defeat. It was a way of displaying what must never be shown. The nature of one's goals and hungers and ambitions must never be made explicit. Always, it must be expressed in a cloak of selflessness and public service. Still, the news this day was sweet. It should be discreetly shared with the publisher.

Smiling, he set sail from his office for the publisher's quarters on the other side of the building. It was easily a five-minute walk, even at a brisk pace. But today, Bill Raleigh moved leisurely, pausing to chat with whatever editors or reporters he found in his path, making small talk, dropping a few words of encouragement here and a note of displeasure there, and giving no one even a hint of the portentous news he was carrying.

The placement of the publisher's suite so far from the news operation was deliberate. The news side was Bill Raleigh's domain; the business side belonged to the young publisher, Walter Griswold. They communicated, of course, but each observed the line of demarcation, which, in Raleigh's eyes, was sacred. The publisher might own the newspaper, but he, Bill Raleigh, ran it. Raleigh had made that clear from the day Griswold came out of Columbia Journalism School, his head brimming with new ideas.

Young Walter, as Raleigh referred to him then and still referred to him now, fifteen years later, had no future in the newsroom. If he wanted to play newspaperman and get out of the business office, he could take a job on a paper in Hartford or Minneapolis or Sacramento, where he wouldn't be in Bill Raleigh's hair. Raleigh didn't think much of Columbia J. School graduates, and he wouldn't hire one, even with the pedigree of a Boston Griswold. Board members, of course, had their own ideas, and now young Walter was the publisher. And though he didn't test his authority by challenging any of Raleigh's prerogatives, Raleigh's territorial rules rankled young Walter's proprietary instincts. Besides, he didn't like Raleigh's paper. He found it boring and complacent and, worst of all, self-indulgent. It was, he believed, a ripe target for serious, well-heeled competition. One day, he would move against Bill Raleigh, when the timing was right. Meanwhile, he avoided confrontations. He found them ugly and a waste of energy better spent on enhancing the *Mammoth*'s profits.

Raleigh, as was his custom, entered Griswold's office without knocking or being announced, knowing, of course, that with his breach of protocol he was reminding the publisher that they weren't really equals at all, that the publisher — board favorite or not — worked for Raleigh like everyone else at the *Mammoth*.

"What's up, Bill?" said Griswold, who was sifting through a pile of computer print-outs piled atop his massive oak desk. "As you can see, I'm terribly busy."

"Oh, I can come back some other time."

Raleigh turned to leave, but as he expected, the publisher summoned him back and invited him to take a seat.

"I hate to interrupt such a busy man. Here we are, it's seven-thirty and you're still at it. My, you are a determined fellow."

Griswold, despite his youth, was a man of limited patience. He hated it when Raleigh hesitated getting to the point. And Raleigh delighted in adding to his irritation, which showed itself in the slight drumming of his fingers on the top of his desk. "Bill, what's on your mind?" he said, smiling thinly.

"I thought I'd let you know that we've won another Pulitzer. It's Hawkins this time."

"How did you arrange that?" Griswold asked.

"You give me too much credit. Hawkins is a damn good man. Fine reporter."

"Sure, but last week I heard we'd been shut out."

"Well, you know what happens. Well, maybe you don't."

"Maybe I don't want to, either."

"There's nothing not to want to know, Walter. I hope you're not suggesting anything improper. People go through a lot of soul-searching before awarding those prizes, in case you don't realize it."

Griswold sighed. He had walked into one of the little traps Raleigh loved to set.

"I'm not suggesting anything, Bill," Griswold said.

Raleigh leaned forward now on his chair. "I'll tell you what I know about the deliberations. Hawkins got screwed last year by those people down in Miami. You know those folks would do anything to get a little respectability, and they worked the territory pretty hard. They knocked poor Hawkins out in the review process and got one of their own guys in for a series about cotton pickers in the new South or some such claptrap. This year, the tables got turned, and for a number of good reasons. You know how sympathetic everybody is down in Washington. I'm sure that helped. And Chicago took an interest. So merit was rewarded and Hawkins has the prize."

The more Raleigh talked, the more uncomfortable he made young Walter feel. Griswold was aware of the backroom politics that Raleigh played as well as any newspaper editor in America. He didn't for a moment underestimate its value. But he preferred to stay as ignorant of the details as possible. Yet Raleigh always insisted on laying the details before him like a soiled tablecloth, and he sensed that the insistence was calculated to make him a co-conspirator. He opted to get on firmer ground.

"What did Hawkins do, anyway? I can't recall his story."

"Remember that great series on hazardous waste in Middlesex County, and how all those bandits from New Jersey were trying to poison us? A corker. Great public-service stuff. A natural. You can't do enough on the environment. And we have the field to ourselves around here."

Griswold did remember the series. And he remembered thinking at the time that it was a perfect issue for the *Mammoth* because it was the kind of series that best expressed the civic spirit of old New England. "That was our kind of piece," he ventured.

"I don't follow you, Walter."

"I think we're better at it than some other people."

"What do you mean, 'we'? Do you mean you and me, our kind, or the *Mammoth?* I'm not sure I follow you."

"Well, let me put it this way, Bill, though God knows, someone who didn't know us wouldn't understand. But can you think of a single Italian environmentalist?"

Raleigh paused and closed his eyes as if to concentrate. "You may have a point," he said. "I can't think of an Irish one either, for that matter, and they're probably the major source of the beer can problem. But I wouldn't push it."

"Nor would I. Just speculating. Please see to it that we give Hawkins a decent bonus."

"You'll be signing the check, Walter." Raleigh got up to leave. "And there's one more thing. But maybe I'll save it for another day when you're not so busy."

"What's that?" Griswold asked.

"Gridlock has decided to shut down the *Bruise.* From what I hear, if they don't pick up their circulation by twenty thousand within a month, they're going to lock the door. And they're not, in the meantime, going to spend a nickel on promotion. So there you have it. It'll take a miracle to keep them going beyond the first week in May."

"Twenty thousand. That's not so impossible, if they get the right stories breaking for them," Griswold said matter-of-factly. He wouldn't give Raleigh the pleasure of seeing him react to the prospect of ruling the roost all alone.

"Without promotion, it's impossible," Raleigh said. "And they haven't got a staff left that could break a story even if they got the Second Coming. Of course, we can speed the inevitable by spreading the word around to the advertisers, giving them ample time to get off the death ship."

Griswold frowned despite the secret delight he felt and said, "I'm not sure this is altogether welcome news. We seem to be having enough trouble right now getting our people to work hard. Without the *Bruise* pushing them a little, they'll really get complacent."

"I'm not sure I share that assessment," Raleigh snapped. "I think we have a crackerjack crew out there. I'm not sure who you've been talking to who told you otherwise."

"Complacency is always a problem with any successful enterprise," Griswold said, skirting argument.

"I'm quite capable of combating complacency," Raleigh said.

"You'll have to be," Griswold said.

"We're near the end of an era. My, that sounds pompous, doesn't it?" Raleigh said. "But it's true. Eight papers in Boston when I started here, and soon we'll be all alone in the market."

"Well, I hope you're right," said Griswold, standing. "That they'll be gone and we'll be stronger than ever without them. But I'm not convinced. The *Bruise* has been at death's door for a long time, and Gridlock just can't bring itself to pull the plug."

He stood up and stretched, as Raleigh moved toward the door. Then he picked a fountain pen out of the antique inkstand on his desk and circled the date on his calendar. "O.K., Bill," he called to Raleigh. "I've marked the spot. The *Bruise* is dead. Bill Raleigh said so. If you're right, I'll make you vice president."

"Don't do that," Raleigh replied. "Anything but that."

"If you're wrong, I'll definitely make you vice president."

"It's a deal," Raleigh said, and headed back to his own office.

□

Bill Raleigh scooped up a handful of telephone messages from his secretary's desk as he went by. He closed the door and sat back in his chair, the same worn leather that had supported the backside of every *Mammoth* editor in an unbroken succession since 1832. He was only the eleventh in the venerable line. All but the first, Jacob Vandermint, were Harvard men, and all but the first were Boston men. All, after Vandermint, suspected from the moment they walked into the *Mammoth* that they were destined to lead the newspaper in its unique mission, which was to disseminate the news without fear or favor — up to a point. The special gift of a *Mammoth* editor was to know when that point was reached and when the uncontrolled rush to print generated side effects that would never do, not if Boston was to remain what it always had been: a community where civilization mattered and where the people who guarded tradition could keep it forever fresh. Raleigh understood, as did his predecessors, that the

Mammoth was more than just a newspaper; it was also a social gyroscope that kept Boston from teetering into the wrong hands. It had kept its leverage, despite the changing tides of population, by the prudent exercise of power. The Irish could take control of City Hall; the Jews could dominate the city's commerce; but the *Mammoth* held the city's soul in its grip, forcing the upstarts of whatever questionable breed to adhere to the *Mammoth*'s agenda, the *Mammoth*'s values, and ultimately the *Mammoth*'s view of reality. Vandermint, way back before the Civil War, had been the only *Mammoth* editor who had not understood the uniqueness of a city that held a special niche in the universe, and his failure had cost him not only his job but his newspaper as well.

It was a lesson that was never forgotten. What the misguided zealot Vandermint had done was to insist that the *Mammoth* crusade against the carefully crafted statutes that kept Irish immigrants confined to the overcrowded ships that carried them across the sea to the New World. A Dutch immigrant himself, Vandermint knew at first hand the menace posed by a voyage of eight weeks or more in steerage. He also knew that few immigrants could afford the hundred-dollar disembarkation fee to guarantee they would not become public wards. As he agitated for repeal of the anti-Irish laws, he also stirred the emotions of the Irish who had already settled in Boston's tightly packed waterfront neighborhoods. Rioting broke out that only hardened the hearts of the native population and the Know-Nothings in the legislature.

The people guarding the city's traditions turned on the *Mammoth* as an alien force. Even the Irish failed to support him, seeing in his crusade the hand of an opportunist seeking the main chance at their expense. It was Vandermint they blamed when a mob broke into the Ursuline convent, roughed up the nuns, smashed crucifixes, and burned the building to the ground. And it was Vandermint the natives blamed when the Supreme Court of the United States overturned the disembarkation fees. Left with no constituency and no hope of merchant support, Vandermint had no choice but to sell the paper to a group of wealthy Brahmins, who saw to it that the Vandermint error would never be repeated. Henceforth the board would see to it that *Mammoth* editors would be men of prudence, schooled in the ways of Boston but cannily wary of the ways of the world. They would understand that although a newspaper was in the business of news, it was also and primarily in the business of power, and maintaining power meant keeping Boston the way it was — no matter who lived there.

Over the generations, the *Mammoth* had become ever more skilled in the power game, ever more subtle in playing off the incoming waves of settlers while adeptly shrouding the face of the authentic elite. Of all the men who led the *Mammoth,* Bill Raleigh was supreme at the game. Now, as he sat back in his chair and surveyed the candid shots that all but covered his office walls, he enjoyed a rare and fleeting moment of smugness. There he was with Haile Selassie and Pius XII, with Nasser and Mobutu, with De Gaulle and Maria Callas. A whole section of the wall recalled the days when John Kennedy was in the White House and Bill Raleigh was close at hand, at Hyannis and in the Rose Garden, and there was a delightful shot of the two men by the window in the Oval Office. Under Bill Raleigh, the *Mammoth* meant something in New England and the nation. But it also stood for something in the world.

Life had been good to him, he reflected. Of course, he had learned his lessons well, becoming a competent newsman despite a singular lack of either news instinct or writing skill. What he could not do naturally, he learned to do mechanically, painstakingly assembling a file index of virtually every conceivable news lead. As a young reporter, he had managed to compete with more gifted rivals by pulling the appropriate card, be his assignment a four-alarm fire in Chelsea or the dedication of a new library at Harvard.

But if he learned his journalism by rote, his political skills came naturally. At home in the Brahmin world that produced him, he was quick to learn the ways of the Irish, the Italians, and the Jews by choosing his friends with an eye toward their ethnic background. Tom O'Hara, who joined the *Mammoth* on the same day in June 1935 as Raleigh, was his entrée to the Irish. O'Hara taught him not only how to drink but how to hide one's intent behind self-deprecating laughter. He was also Raleigh's guide to judging political horseflesh.

Andy Panacheo educated him in the Italians, after elaborate precautions were taken, leading him into a police-protected private club in the North End where he sat quietly and watched swarthy men play hearts until dawn. His Jewish mentor was Al Goldstein, who gave him a limited but serviceable Yiddish vocabulary that allowed him to sprinkle his conversation with words like *shtick* and *schmuck* and *zaftig* but also taught him what Raleigh took as the wisdom of the ages: "Steal with your eyes, never your hands." "Dress British; think Yiddish."

He glanced down at his messages. The first was from the mayor. Raleigh picked up the phone and caught Connie Haydon just as he was leaving his office for his home in Back Bay.

"Connie, great time last night. That Dugan is something. My, that guy can drink. You'd think that after all these years I'd learn to stick to my own pace instead of trying to keep up with him. And you're not bad either."

"Bullshit, Bill," the mayor replied. "You Yankees can drink any two Irishmen I've ever met right under the table, as you proved again last night."

"Proved nothing. You ought to have my hangover. I hope we got some business accomplished."

"Of course we did," said the mayor.

"I hope you're right. We'll see how the editorial board reacts when I run the plan by them. But you already convinced Dugan. Best reorganization plan he ever saw. That's what he told me."

"He never even read it."

"Doesn't have to. Dugan never reads. He just absorbs things through his pores."

"That's my kind of guy," said the mayor. "But Bill, let me get back to you on that. I've got something else on my mind I'd like to share with you."

"Fine, what can I do for you?"

He had a good idea why the mayor had called. It was to make sure that nothing went wrong in the coverage of Scooter's arraignment and the news conference — but he waited for the mayor to be more direct.

"I've got a helluva story for you, Bill. I can't talk to you about it on the phone, but I'd like to see you as soon as possible. Like tomorrow morning."

Raleigh had two standards in dealing with the mayor: one social and one professional. This was a professional call, and Raleigh didn't like the idea of the mayor setting the agenda by designating the time. "I'm at your disposal, Connie. But tomorrow morning is awfully jammed. I have a delegation coming in here from the Jewish Defense League."

"You're still backing those Arabs, huh? Don't you realize that there aren't that many Arabs around here? You'd make a lousy politician."

"Could we do it some other time?" Raleigh said, ignoring the mayor's banter. "Maybe the beginning of next week." He wanted him to mention Scooter.

"Hey, if you don't want the story, I can always peddle it to Bobby Bantam," Haydon said. "Tomorrow morning it's got to be, or you could lose it."

"Too bad about Scooter," said Raleigh, finally opening the subject himself.

"Yeah, it is too bad. He's in many ways a wonderful man, but he's from another era. He didn't realize in time that you can't play by the old rules around this town. He hasn't been reading your paper, Bill."

"So, we can't do it next week?"

The mayor was getting impatient. "Bill, this has nothing to do with Scooter. I could care less about Scooter. This is important. Do you want to hear about it or don't you? I don't want to get in the way of the Jewish Defense League, but this is hardly of the same order of importance."

"Well, I hope you don't mind talking to me about Scooter. I think it's a pretty interesting story. We're going to give it a good bump in the morning."

"I'm sure you will and I'm also sure you'll be fair. I'm glad we have one responsible paper in town, which is why I want to see you. Ten o'clock, your place?"

"Okay, ten o'clock. And I'll be looking forward to it."

"See you, Bill."

"See you, Connie. Love to Eileen."

□

Elmer Granger knew what he wanted to do with the rest of his life. The revelation had come to him about twenty-five miles out of Garden City on the Kansas Turnpike on a July afternoon three years ago. He was riding in his Lincoln Continental — a present he had just picked up at Gridlock headquarters where the high command decorated him for his courage in not spending a nickel more than he had to on the *Bruise* — and now he was heading westward toward the sunset, his air conditioner going full blast, his wife, Edith, beside him on the front seat, and all the publisher could see were the waves of golden wheat shimmering off toward the horizon. The tears came to Elmer Granger's eyes and he turned to Edith and said, "God, I love this country. This is America. What the hell are we doing in Boston?" and he began to sing "God Bless America" in a voice that reminded him of the way he used to sing when he was a lad in Osawatomie. He pledged there and then that he was going to force the folks at Gridlock to see the situation back in Boston the way he saw it and shut down the *Bruise*.

Boston was not America. He knew that from the moment he arrived to take over the *Bruise* five years ago. It was an alien place, too filled with foreigners, too hobbled by rules that didn't apply in the part of the country where he grew up, the great state of Kansas. That was the real America where people were straightforward and square dealing and could care less whether you went to KU or Winfield State. No, the time he spent in Boston was time he'd never spend looking at wheat fields and grain elevators and the Grand Canyon and Mount Rushmore and the great rain forest of the Northwest and Disney World and Hap's Alligator Farm and everything else that wasn't the East and Boston. And on that hot July afternoon, in the cool of the Continental, he vowed to Edith that once they finished their work at the *Bruise* they would take off for Road America and not stop until they had seen every rick and gulley of this great land and their joints were too creaky to climb in and out of the front seat. Deliverance Day, he called it. That would be the day they shut down the *Bruise*.

Now, three years later, he was sitting happily at his desk, deferring the call to Edith, who would exult with him. Deliverance Day. It's here, sweetheart. Start packing.

Granger had driven Gridlock to the inevitable conclusion. While proving to Wichita that a newspaper could get by with the very barest maintenance, without spending a dime on promotion, without hiring telephone operators to take new subscriptions, without bothering to do small humane things like fixing the water cooler where Sonny DeLoughery died dry, he had imprinted the *Bruise* with the stamp of death and kept it from generating fresh advertising support or expanding its readership. He had also argued unceasingly in memos, letters, and telephone conversations with Wichita that the age of the newspaper war was over and that what had happened in Des Moines and Philadelphia, Chicago, New York, and Buffalo had also happened in Boston. There was no point in further rear-guard action. The *Mammoth* had won and that was that. Accept the inevitable and save a few dollars for investments that had some promise.

Now, his fellow Kansans had made the decision they had deferred for so long. And it was time to be a man about it and play out the hand. He summoned Bobby Bantam to his office.

☐

"What horseshit, Elmer. These fucking guys . . ."

"These guys are businessmen who afforded you a good living for the past twenty years, so don't dump on them. It's their money they're pouring down this rathole and they've said 'enough.' So it's enough."

Bobby kept silent. He detested Granger and felt certain that it was the publisher who was keeping the paper from turning the corner. But a part of him suspected that perhaps Granger was right and that no amount of money or energy would help the *Bruise* survive. The *Mammoth* was too overwhelming, too established, too far ahead.

"We'll be closing the doors. Let's face it, Bobby. It's time to consult your options. Meanwhile, stay on course and do your job the way you've always done it. You have nothing to be ashamed of, and of course, there will be a handsome settlement. You can count on that. I've already advised Gridlock that with you they should be extraordinarily generous. You deserve it, Bobby, you really do. There's no quit in you, and that's about as American as you can get."

Bobby's contempt began bubbling. "I'm not an American," he said. "I'm a Jew and I don't know what the hell you're talking about, except that you don't seem at all upset, and you know as well as I do that when this paper goes, this town is gone, too — at least it is for the people who supported this paper all these years. But you're not from here, so maybe you don't understand."

The publisher smiled, stood up, and moved around the desk toward Bobby. He put an arm around his shoulder and said, "I do understand."

"Maybe you do. But I put a lot of myself into this fucking rag, and well, maybe it's news to you but I gave up a marriage for this place, and two girlfriends. One of them I really hated losing. I also developed a duodenal ulcer and I probably have lung cancer from the asbestos you wouldn't take off the ceiling."

"Hey, you're getting upset, Bobby."

Bobby smiled and sat down in the chair that he had avoided since he entered the office. "No," he said. "I'm not upset. I just got the idea that you were almost pleased by what they told you this afternoon."

"No, I'm not pleased," Granger said. "But I am a realist. And you, for all your cynical front, are a romantic who doesn't understand what's happening in this city. The people who read this paper, in case you don't know it, don't count anymore. They're beside the point, Bobby. Totally. They don't even count politically, which is why the mayor could care less about what he did to Scooter this afternoon. You know who reads us better than I do, and you won't let it sink into your head that they're the wrong kind of people and the right kind of people don't want you or your newspaper near them, unless it comes in a plain brown wrapper. And that ain't no way to sell a newspaper."

"You're wrong."

"Am I? Well, you had plenty of years to prove it. Why didn't you? I'll tell you why, because you're selling the past and it doesn't make any sense. People want quality. They want to read quality and sell quality and they feel — whether they're kidding themselves is another point — that they are quality. There is room for one quality paper in this town. And that's not us. It's the other fellows. As for our people, they can get what they need from the television, and all they want from us anyway is a little news about this city, which is going down the tubes, too — you mark my words on that — and some used car ads and some ads for hemorrhoids. And they can get that from the TV too."

Bobby Bantam didn't respond. He got up to leave, then turned to the publisher and said, "I want you to know that I'm not giving up. If it takes a twenty thousand circulation jump, I might buy twenty thousand papers myself every day or call twenty thousand people on the telephone or sell my stock in IBM. But I'm not giving up."

"You'll fail."

"So what? I'm going to try."

□

Bobby Bantam's first move on returning to his own office was to summon Tony away from his typewriter and lay out the situation. "The son of a bitch acted almost happy. You should've seen the look on his face. Would you believe it, Tony? Five hundred people will be out of work and this town will be owned by the *Mammoth,* and he sits there feeling pleased with himself. That, in my opinion, is what evil is all about. That is being evil."

Tony studied Bobby's face for signs that he, too, might be relieved that the end was in sight. He knew the muddle of his own feelings and that at the core of them was the hope that somehow the treadmill would stop and he could escape into a new life. But he also felt that his own salvation was somehow tied up in the fate of the *Bruise* and that he could not survive its demise. Bobby, he suspected, felt the same way. He was the *Bruise;* his was the vital energy that kept it going when it should have simply lay down and died; his was the passion that kept the staff caring, even after it was clear that the front office could care less.

"I'm sorry, Bobby," he said.

"Hey, I don't need your sympathy, Tony. I need your ideas. What are we going to do? You're not giving up on me, too, are you?"

"No, Bobby," he said. "I'm not giving up."

Tony looked out the window of the editor's office across town to the neon sign above the Hotel Congress. Vandals had demolished the C, the N, and the S. The sign now read, OGRES. He wondered idly if the hotel management noticed or cared. A long-standing city room joke was that when all the lights went out on the Congress roof, the *Bruise* would die, but not before. The lights were going fast now. Some days he felt as if he should hire some strong-arm kids to take out the final lights. He looked at Bobby, who was waiting to hear if he could spin out one of those Owen originals that even if it failed might enliven the final days of the paper. There was the time he dreamed up the Mickey Mouse award, inviting readers to nominate the people in their lives most deserving of a prize for pettiness and misery-making. Thousands of readers nominated bosses, wives, teachers, cops on the beat. The contest was the kind of thing that united Tony Owen's column and the *Bruise* with their readers. The *Bruise* recognized the fact that most people lived under petty tyrannies in their lives, and rarely if ever had a vehicle to express their frustration. The *Bruise* was that vehicle. The Mickey Mouse award went to the owner of a waterfront restaurant who fined his waitresses five dollars each time they failed to refill the salt shakers and ketchup bottles after their tour of duty. The prize was a Mickey Mouse T-shirt.

"I don't know what we can do to grab twenty thousand more readers . . . unless we buy the circulation. I suppose we could appeal to the public. Turn the paper into one of the animals we saved from destruction. It's not too dignified a way to go, though. Maybe nobody will come forward and we'll scare away the people we've always had. Nobody likes to be around a walking corpse."

Bobby grimaced. "No way. I want this paper to go down with dignity, with the band playing on the deck. I don't want to beg for our miserable existence. It wouldn't work, anyway. No. I want us to go out with a string of good stories, stories they're going to remember us for. And who knows, if we get really hot, maybe we'll get a circulation run that will bail us out. I can't see it happening, but I'd love to see the look on everybody's face, that Granger especially. That son of a bitch. How I'd love to keep him around here another six months, just to see him twisting in the wind."

Tony shrugged. "We got a good one from Scooter. I don't know what it's about yet. But something is there and that could help."

"It won't be enough. No matter what it is."

"We'll have to wait and see what it is. Right now it's just a dead bum, a two-bit fire in a run-down neighborhood, and a hint of Connie Haydon involvement without any evidence to support it except the word of a guy with a king-size ax to grind. But it's the best thing I got, and if Scooter is on to something, we might get lucky. And you never know when you start whacking the mayor. He reacts like a crazy man. He might do something stupid and we'll be on a roll."

"You're dreaming."

"It's the best thing I got, unless you want me to get undignified. I could come up with some undignified idea, like a hit list of advertisers who won't support us. Let the folks know who's really croaking us."

"Great idea," said Bobby. "But Granger won't buy it. Let's stick with Bernie the bum. That's his name, right, Bernie? Wonderful. What a way to go, writing about a bum killed in a tenement fire. Maybe we deserve to die."

Tony returned to his typewriter, walking past the rows of empty desks, his feet falling heavily on the soiled carpet. He was tired now, the elation of his meeting with Scooter long since extinguished by a steady stream of bad news. He looked up at the city desk clock. He had forty minutes left before his deadline and he felt tight and tired. He picked up the telephone and caught Cynthia as she was going out the door.

"I'm sorry about last night," he said.

"It took you long enough to call," she said. "I don't see any future for us, Tony."

"So you're not accepting my apology."

"I didn't say that," she said. "What did you do today?"

"I worked a little on the Scooter story."

"Is that what you're writing about for tomorrow?"

"Yeah."

"I covered the mayor's news conference. It was some show."

"I know. I caught you on the six o'clock news. It was pretty much what I expected."

"You have him pegged."

"You're not doing bad yourself."

"Will I see you tonight?"

"No, I don't think so. I don't feel good. My brother was around today."

"Jesus, you are having a run."

"I still haven't gotten my column together."

"What are you going to do later?"

"I want to be alone to think. I've got a project. I'll talk to you about it later. Not tonight, though."

"You have another honey."

"Nothing like that."

"Then why so mysterious?"

"I don't want to talk now. I'll call you tomorrow. You were good on the six. Haydon is going to hate you, too."

"He already does."

"See you."

"Good night."

6

IT WAS NINE O'CLOCK — forty-five minutes past deadline — before Tony finished his column with an out-of-patience Bobby Bantam hanging over his shoulder. Tony was not happy with the column, nor was Bobby, but in Tony's view, for all its failings, it was serviceable and, under the circumstances, a decent piece of work. Tony had been all but immobilized as he sat before his typewriter, groping for a column line in the chaos of ideas and feelings the day had visited upon him. Malachy's sudden appearance badly unnerved him, and he had barely regained his composure when Bobby dropped the news about the future of the *Bruise*. Tony's column rode on his grasp of the here and now, but all he could think of as he sat down to write was the wretched vision of the past that enveloped his brother like a tattered overcoat and the frightening companion thought of a world without the *Bruise*.

He had to get out of there. Yes, Malachy was right. Cynthia was right. Working for the *Bruise*, being a newspaperman, was his way of avoiding life and all the pain it brought. It was the reason he was sane and that Malachy was mad. Yes, he was a coward and he preferred it that way. He could not abide life on the other side of the screen through which he viewed reality. Take away the screen, and he was alone and unprotected, as vulnerable as the next man to love and the death of love. Behind the screen he had all the freedom he could ever use and would ever need. He could live life entirely on his own terms. As long as he could judge others, he had no need ever to judge himself.

Without saying good night to anyone, he slipped on the jacket that had been draped behind his chair and walked out the door. Instead of turning right toward the parking lot, he turned toward the left and Chinatown, walking briskly, with his head down, not noticing the derelicts slumped in the doorways of boarded-up shops, the clusters of Chinese kids gathered on the corners in their designer jeans, talking football.

A few blocks into Chinatown, Tony reached the medical center that was pushing out on all sides into the neighborhood, squeezing the housing at the edges. Once he did a column on the tough housing conditions in Chinatown and got a big yawn from his readers. "Hey, Tony, you forget who lives in those places," one reader had called him to say. "Ten years ago those people were living on junks floating on the shit in Hong Kong Harbor. Who you think you're kidding?" And the truth was that for all the Americanization of the Chinese young, the elders were just as pleased to hide behind the stereotypes. That way City Hall left Chinatown alone and so did the Police Department and the health inspectors and the Building Department. Sweatshops could flourish, so could the gambling dens and bordellos, and rare was the restaurant kitchen subject to scrutiny from the Board of Health.

A cluster of young women dressed in white passed by. Years ago, they would have been nurses; now they were interns or residents. On other days, when Tony spotted a beautiful young woman with a stethoscope in her pocket, he wondered what it would be like to be treated by a doctor who looked like that. Tonight, his fantasies took no fire. He felt disconnected from mind and from body as he headed toward Tyler Street, moving like a driverless truck ponderous and freighted. He walked as fast as he could, hoping that the strain would reunite body and mind, but his mind floated above him like an obscure flag. An elderly woman carrying shopping bags brimming with leafy vegetables turned a corner in front of him. Tony cut smartly to his right to avoid her. The near collision slowed him down. He was at an entrance to an alley. In the darkness at the alley's midway point, the lights of the Grotto Inn beckoned. Except for the lights, the alley was in darkness. Tony felt a surge of excitement as he looked into the shadows. He began moving toward the lights, half-daring someone to leap at him from the darkness. A fight would do nicely, perhaps a fight to the death. He picked his way through the broken glass. No one challenged him. He felt disappointment, tinged with relief.

He had never been inside the Grotto before, but it was as he thought it would be — dark and smelling of urine. An old woman, dirty and toothless, smiled at him from her place at the bar. Tony tipped his cap and moved to the far end of the bar. He felt easier enveloped in the darkness. The bartender approached him. He was a corpulent man with a bald head and yellowish eyes that bulged as if from a rare disease. He wore a purple T-shirt that read: I LOVE NEW YORK I HATE THE YANKEES. Tony ordered a bottle of beer. He didn't specify the brand. He didn't care. The bartender gave him a bottle of Miller's and a glass. Tony ignored the glass and drank from the bottle after wiping its mouth with his hand. He stared about him as his eyes grew accustomed to the darkness. He saw two men, thin as skeletons, sitting at a table playing dominoes. They ignored him. A cat as thin as the domino players sniffed his trouser cuffs. He dropped two dollars on the bar and tried to think. He wondered whether Malachy came in here in search of souls and a glass of Wild Irish Rose. He tasted the beer and remembered why it was he hated Miller's. It left the taste of cream soda in his mouth. He called to the bartender for a shot of bourbon. The bartender reached for a bottle of Four Roses and poured it into an outsized shot glass. Tony downed it in one swallow. The old crone moved down the bar toward him. She asked Tony for a drink. He told the bartender to take care of her, and he dropped another two dollars on the bar and turned his back on her. "O.K., you got your drink; now leave the man alone," the bartender said. The hag took her whiskey and moved back to her perch near the door.

He looked to his left at a part of the room he had not examined before and saw the dim outline of a tall, angular man, smoking a cigarette. For a moment, Tony thought it was Malachy and was about to head for the door. No, he didn't really want to see him. He wanted to see himself as Malachy, to try to feel with him, to share the rotten smells, the fetid air, the darkness, the despair. No, this couldn't be him. He remembered the day of Malachy's first Mass and how they posed for pictures outside St. Catherine's and how Malachy looked in his white vestments and how happy he had felt. No, not happy, really, but relieved. No one to care for now. The archdiocese and God himself had Malachy now. And there he was on the pulpit, wearing a smile like a cassock, preaching his first sermon, a learned lecture on unselfish love, but reserving the final words for Aunt Jenny and her old-fashioned devotion to duty. Tony had watched his aunt as the sermon closed, and he smiled as he saw the tears running down her cheeks. It was better this way, he had thought then, that his father had run away, better for all of them, even Aunt Jenny, who had given a "son" to God despite her virginity, and better for himself because he had learned to be his own father, and better for Malachy, who could never be this happy in ordinary life. Now, Tony could live in comfort behind the screen: Tony the reporter, Tony the columnist, Tony the voice of the city, the guy who cared as long as the caring meant good copy. On that day at St. Catherine's he did care for something outside himself. He cared for Malachy. Hell, he raised the kid. How many guys from Brighton put their kid brother through the seminary? For what? Maybe the old man was the same way, and maybe that was why he ran away, trying to head off the craziness because he knew that once you started falling through the chute, there was no way to stop until you hit bottom. Better to run and hide than end like this.

The tall man pushed back his chair, swayed to his feet, and moved across the room toward Tony. "I know who you are," he said. "You're from the welfare, ain't you? My wife sent you to track me down. Well, I ain't got nothing to give her and I ain't got nothing for you either."

"I'm not from welfare. I'm just drinking like you," Tony said, trying to stay clear of the man's breath, which was thick with whiskey and sickness.

The man seemed not to hear him. He reached for the lapels of Tony's jacket and said, "I don't want you tracking me anymore. The welfare can go shit in the hat. That bitch is trying to ruin me and she can't keep her pants on. You know what a whore she is. You probably been visiting her yourself. Oh, you're sly. You are the sly one."

He leered at Tony. The teeth were missing entirely from the right side of his mouth and he had a three- or four-day growth of white beard. Tony pushed him away and said, "Sorry, Jack, you got the wrong man."

"Leave the man alone, Sailor," the bartender said, "or I'll kick your ass out of here."

Sailor put his hands down at his sides and tilted his shoulder in a half shrug. "You sly boots bastard, poking my old lady. Buy me a drink."

The bartender opened a bottle of beer and came around the bar. He took Sailor by the shoulder and sat him back down at his table. "Now drink your beer and leave the man alone," he said.

Tony wanted to leave, but his feet stayed glued to the floor. That could've been his brother, that could've been his father, that could've been him. He ordered another whiskey for himself.

"You a cop?" the bartender asked him.

"No," Tony said.

"I didn't think you were. But I've seen you somewhere."

Tony stared back at the bartender. His was the kind of ugliness that did not diminish as you studied his face.

"I'll bet you read the *Bruise*," Tony said.

"Yeah, I read it. You work for them? What's your name? Do you know Cliff Daniels?"

"Yeah, I work for them. And I know Cliff. A nice guy and he does a good job with the Red Sox."

"Jeez, I hear him on the radio program. The dugout show. You listen to the dugout show?"

"No."

"What do you think the Red Sox are going to do? They gonna win it?"

"No, they'll blow it, as usual."

"You a sportswriter?"

"No. I'm a columnist."

"Yeah, what's your name?"

"Tony Owen."

"Oh, I've heard of you. What you doing in here, looking for a story?"

"No. I just came in out of the rain."

"Is it raining?"

"Kind of."

"No shit."

"Yeah, I'm kidding you. It's a nice night. I was in here looking for someone."

"You probably won't find him in here. We only have bums, especially at night. During the day, we get steelworkers and some warehouse people from up the street. The rest is Chinks and they don't drink. I don't know what they do. So at night what we got is bums. They're harmless, though."

"Where do they get their money?"

"Are you kidding? Most of them get checks from somebody — the welfare, social security — and they panhandle. A good panhandler can make twenty bucks a day, easy. Every time they make a hit, they come running in here, have a couple of pops, and I let 'em. Otherwise we'd have to close."

Tony stared into the bartender's eyes. He was tempted to ask him about Malachy.

But he didn't want to know. He didn't want to talk anymore, either. He suddenly wanted to be with normal people in a comfortable place. He wanted to get out. He reached for his drink, tossed it down, then set the glass back on the bar. Again, he looked into the bartender's eyes as if to say good-bye. Instead, he heard himself asking, in a voice that seemed to him that of a stranger, the question that he had come into the Grotto to ask.

"Any priests come in here?"

"Any what?" the bug-eyed man said, as if he didn't understand the question.

"Priests. You know, Catholic priests," said Tony, listening to himself with dismay at the effect of a couple of whiskeys. "You're a Catholic, aren't you?"

"Yeah, sure," he said. "But no, we ain't got no priests. You're quite a joker, ain't you? We got bums, no priests."

"Any bums who act like priests?"

The hag by the door had been stirred into animation by the conversation, and she had slid closer to hear what was being said. "Al doesn't know what he's talking about," she said. "Sure a priest comes in here a lot, but only in the afternoon before it's time to go to the shelter. You know the guy, Al. He's always wearing black like he's some kind of Sicilian. Ain't he a priest?"

"Sure, he's a priest," said Al. "And I'm fucking Minnie Mouse."

"He is a priest," said Tony. "So you better take good care of him the next time he comes in."

He left a ten-dollar bill on the bar and plunged back into the night, rushing through the alley as if demons were at his back. When he hit Tyler Street, he stopped to fill his lungs with the night air. "God almighty," he asked himself, "what's the matter with me?"

He hailed a cab outside the medical center and directed the cabbie to Larry's in South Boston. He got out four blocks from the place, in front of the Broadway housing project. He wanted to walk more and lose the smells of the Grotto that lingered in his nostrils. He also wanted to absorb the scene before he took it with him into Larry's. He needed lightness and gaiety and escape, but mostly he needed to get back in touch with himself. He felt aware of his own breathing. His breath seemed shallow and labored. Sonny, you son of a bitch, I'm next, man, he said to himself. As he walked down the street toward Larry's, he tried to envision his life without the column, without the *Bruise,* and all he could see was emptiness. As the depression took hold, he decided he would hail a cab and head for home. But as he walked toward the curb to look for a cab in the street, he felt a tug at his arm.

"Where you headed, Tony? Come on, I'll buy you a drink."

Joseph Kennelly, a Larry's regular, had just closed up his law office in Andrew Square. Now he was pulling Tony toward the tavern.

"Come on, one more will never hurt you. And I got to hear what happened to old Scooter."

Tony nodded and walked passively along beside Kennelly.

"It was quite a day, quite a day, for a newspaperman," Kennelly said.

"It was quite a day," Tony agreed.

They walked into the bar, a glittering and gleaming place of deep mahogany and shining brass. The bar was all but filled by young men in three-piece suits. Some had leather attaché cases on the floor by their feet. A few had wives or girlfriends sitting nearby. In the middle of the bar were four women in their late thirties, early forties. The youngest stood holding a glass of white wine while her friends sat or leaned against barstools. She was the widow of a firefighter killed the year before in a warehouse fire down the street.

Tony had known her for years through her public relations work for a Southie civic group. And a month before, he had driven her home from a neighborhood meeting, one of many he attended to keep in touch with the grassroots. They had fallen into a clinch outside her apartment house, a clinch that ended with her rushing from the car when things began taking a more serious turn.

Tony was greeted by everyone as he walked past, still in Kennelly's tow; they were headed for two empty seats at the very end of the bar. The firefighter's widow, a plump woman of about thirty-five, had clear blue eyes and perfect teeth. "How's everything at the *Bruise?*" she asked Tony as he squeezed past her in the narrow aisle.

"Nothing ever changes, Louise. And how are you?"

"I'm fine. I'm sorry about last time."

"I'm the one who's sorry," Tony said.

She smiled and Tony settled into his seat next to Kennelly.

"I can remember when this was a workingman's bar," he said. "Jesus, now everyone is gentry, wearing three-piece suits. I guess everybody in Southie these days is a lawyer or going to law school."

"Or working in City Hall."

"Yeah, you're right," said Tony, as he looked around at the faces along the bar and sitting at the tables. "City Hall annex."

At one table a man in a gray flannel suit was slumped, face cradled in his arms. He had a bottle of beer in front of him. Tony couldn't make out who he was.

"What's the deal with Scooter? I can't believe the balls on the mayor. Jesus. His own guy."

"Survival, baby. He's just trying to survive."

"But Scooter, Jesus. He was in here just the other night."

"What can I say? Read my column tomorrow."

"You gonna rip the man?"

"Read it."

Hal Boyland, the bartender, approached. "Hey, Tony, you know what's an Irish ménage à trois?"

"No, Hal, you tell me."

"I'll tell you. It's a man, a woman, and the bartender."

"Hot shit," said Kennelly. "That's hot shit. You know the one about the Polish cavalry?"

"Yeah, forget it," said Boyland. "I heard it a hundred times. Let me tell you the one about the Polish hooker who starved to death."

"Jesus, give me a Molson's," said Kennelly. "And take good care of my friend from the fourth estate. What are you having, Tony?"

"I'll have a John Jameson, straight, with a Bass chaser."

"The drinking man's cocktail," said Kennelly.

"What's new with the *Bruise?*" Kennelly asked. "They going to turn off the tap?"

"The paper's unsinkable, Joe, you know that. It'll be here long after we're gone."

"Jeez, I hope so. I'd miss reading you every morning."

"Me too."

Boyland returned with the drinks. Tony barely got his into his hands before he polished off the whiskey and took a deep draught of the Bass. "Hit me again with the Jameson," he said to Boyland.

Tony took a glance toward the table where the man in the flannel suit had been resting. He thought he recognized him.

"Hey, who's that over there? Isn't that Eileen Haydon's brother, Tommy Mannion?"

"Yeah. Looks like he's half in the bag."

"He sure is. He's also staring at us."

"Ignore him," said Kennelly. "He's an asshole."

Tony called Boyland over. "Hey, how long has Eileen's brother been in here?"

"He's been going hot and heavy for three hours. But if you hurry you can catch up, Tony."

Kennelly glanced over his shoulder at Mannion. "That guy is trouble. You should see the crowd he's running with. Heavy-duty types. I don't know what happens to some guys. They go along like they're going to be all right, then all of a sudden you see them in here smoking big two-dollar cigars and talking rough and throwing bills around like they own the world."

"Is he still selling real estate out in West Roxbury?"

"He's still got his office out there somewhere," Kennelly said. "But lately, he's into bigger stuff. No more triple deckers and suburban Cape Cods. He's a developer. Get him going and he'll tell you all about it. A real big shot."

"I didn't know that. What's he developing?"

"A big line of bullshit, from what I can gather. But he's got the dough to throw around. I can tell you that."

"Maybe he's into cocaine?"

"That would be nice for Connie Haydon, wouldn't it? No, he's fucking around with real estate."

74

Tony made a mental note of Kennelly's remarks and savored the Irish whiskey. He was halfway through his second drink when Boyland arrived with a third.

"Your money's no good in here, Tony," the bartender said.

Tony glanced down the bar to where a cluster of men in three-piece suits was standing. He waved his glass at them in thanks.

"I don't think I know our benefactors," he said to Kennelly.

"It doesn't matter. You're among friends."

Tony looked once more to his right and caught Louise staring at him. Again, she smiled. Tony smiled back and drank.

He was now at the point where the whiskey and beer were working on him. A few more drinks and it wouldn't matter who he was or what he did for a living. He'd have no past, no future, only the moment of pure drunken freedom, a moment when he might say or do whatever came into his mind. For a time, he could slip out of his skin, lay aside the weight of all the years, escape the menace of the feelings buried within. Tomorrow he'd pay for it, of course. But tomorrow could be placed at a safe remove if he drank enough. Perspective. That's what he was getting, he told himself, as he downed his third drink and reached for his fourth. He had to get above his situation, to see what it was that was happening to him. Cynthia was too insistent. He wasn't ready for the life she wanted him to live.

"What'sa matter, Tony? You're looking depressed," Kennelly said.

"I'm sorry. I was just enjoying the booze. It tastes particularly good tonight."

"It's the company. You should come around more often."

Louise walked down the bar, carrying a gin and tonic with her.

"Do you mind if I join you?" she asked.

"I'd be delighted," Tony said, putting his arm around her waist. "You know Joseph here, of course?"

"We're old friends," Kennelly said. "How are you, Louise?"

"I'm doing fine, Joe, thanks."

Tommy Mannion looked up from the table. Tony thought he was glaring at him as he embraced Louise. He lifted his glass in Mannion's direction.

Mannion looked away, then stood up uncertainly and lurched past them toward the men's room.

"I don't think he likes you," Louise said.

"Family loyalty. I'm sure he takes his cues from Connie," Tony said. "But he's an ugly bastard, isn't he?"

"Tony," Louise said, "if something happens at the *Bruise,* maybe you could go to work for the *Mammoth.*"

Kennelly snorted. "And maybe the pope can become the archbishop of Canterbury."

"Nothing's going to happen to the *Bruise,*" Tony said. "It's a sturdy old tub and there are those who love her."

"I love her," said Louise. "It's the only paper that cares about us."

"That's easy," said Tony. "We're all cut from the same cloth."

"Well, I really hope everything turns out all right."

"Things will turn out," said Tony. He was becoming conscious of her breasts, big and matronly under a white blouse. He squeezed her waist once more and told her how pretty she looked.

Kennelly ordered another round, including a drink for Louise.

"Please, Joe. One more of these and I'll never get up in the morning. It's hard enough for me to get out of bed as it is," she said.

Tony thought of Louise in bed, and in a disconnected way he felt angry at Cynthia, as if she were standing in the way of what he wanted. He became aware that his arm was still around Louise's waist and that she wasn't pulling away.

Kennelly and a gray-haired man three stools away got into a conversation about whether Haydon would run again, and Kennelly moved off so he could talk without shouting.

Tony turned directly toward the bar and Louise stood alongside him.

"I've been thinking of the last time a lot," she said. "I just wasn't ready. I hope you understand."

Tony turned toward her, and in her eyes he saw that she was frightened by her own daring.

"I understand," he said. "I hope you weren't upset. It was no big deal."

She winced. Tony tried to make amends. "I mean, it was nice, as far as it went. I wasn't expecting anything more."

"I was," she said quietly. "I just got scared."

He patted her on the hand. She still wore her wedding ring.

Kennelly returned to his stool, and Louise got up to move away. "No, dear, stay where you are," he said. He started talking about a case he was handling involving a trucking company in trouble with the ICC.

Tony was surprised to see that his whiskey glass was empty. He sipped his ale and ordered another round. This time, Louise offered no protest. The pain of the day had evaporated now. He felt as if he were flying high above all the dead ends choking his life. Louise's face was flushed. Kennelly had fallen into a sodden silence.

He felt a hand on his shoulder. He turned around to see Tommy Mannion confronting him. His eyes were red and his face seemed oddly distorted. He was in his early thirties and built like a nose guard who had gone to fat.

"I don't like the way you were looking at me," he said.

Tony was serene. "I didn't know I was looking at you, chum. I thought I was watching that fly on the wall behind you."

"Well, you're a fucking asshole, and your paper is a piece of shit."

"Hey, Tommy," said Kennelly, who was a bear of a man, "cool it. This is a nice place."

Boyland had come over and was about to leap over the bar, but Kennelly moved quickly behind Mannion and squeezed him, and began walking him out the door. For all Mannion's size, he offered no resistance, but kept glaring at Tony.

"Good night, folks," Kennelly said. "It's time young Tommy here went to bed."

Louise marveled at Tony's control. Tony only smiled. He knew, even in his unsober state, that all it would have taken was one punch to bring the police running. And how Connie Haydon would love to have Tony Owen in the drunk tank, witnesses or no witnesses. His controls had broken down, but not all of them.

□

An hour later Tony was in Louise's kitchen, drinking a glass of milk and eating a fried egg sandwich. It occurred to him shortly after he arrived in the apartment that he was very drunk and that he hadn't eaten since his meeting with Scooter. "You need someone to take care of you," Louise said, and he winced.

"I thought you were a sophisticated lady," he said.

"No, I never said that. But is it so unsophisticated to point out the obvious? You need a manager."

"Don't be so sure I don't have one."

"You go out with that reporter from Channel Four, don't you? I heard that. One of my friends saw you with her downtown."

"Yeah, Cynthia Stoler."

"Is she your one and only?"

"Not yet. But I like her. Right now I like you."

"Are you in love?"

"What's love?"

"Good Lord, maybe I'm not sophisticated. Are you talking to me in code? Answer yes or no."

"I never answer questions like that on the first date," he said, his voice slurred. "I don't want to deceive you. So think the worst, and take that as true, and nothing I say can fool you."

She sat on a kitchen chair by the window, looking tired and worn under the harsh light from an overhead fixture. A calendar from St. Anne's Church was on the wall by the refrigerator. A boy's baseball glove was on the floor in the corner.

"You haven't slept with anyone since your husband got killed, have you? So you pick me and I'm the worst possible choice. Besides, you're too serious. You couldn't just accept a roll in the hay for what it is. You'd look at your son in the morning and you'd hate yourself unless you could say, 'Hey, I met the most wonderful man last night.' And the next thing you know you'll be dreaming of me taking him to Red Sox games and off to the museum and around the newspaper office and picnics in the summer and all the stuff I've spent my life trying to avoid. You see, in a way, I am a married man. I'm married to the *Bruise*. That's what I live for. I don't have any room in my life for any more."

"Do you see everyone in categories?"

"No, just Irish women like the girls I grew up with, women like my aunt and her friends . . . I know them."

"You don't know me, and I suspect you don't even know them, or you wouldn't have if you were the same generation."

"Irish women are like Irish men."

"Bullshit."

She stood up and stared at him, kissed him on the cheek, and walked him into the bedroom. An ornate crucifix, like the one his aunt had in her room, was over the big bed, and a picture of her

78

firefighter husband was on the bureau. She unbuttoned the white blouse, dropped her skirt, and stood in her underwear before him. She was full and round, so like a mother, Tony thought. He knelt before her on the floor and buried his head in her belly. "I love you," he murmured.

She pulled away and said, "Don't turn this into something other than what it is. That's how things get mixed up. Let's keep it simple."

She stepped out of her panties and unhooked her bra. Tony's cheeks brushed against her hair. She reached down and pulled him to his feet and climbed into the bed.

"Tony, don't think of anything but doing it to me, please. That's all I want, believe me. It's been a long time for me. I just want it."

She reached for him and they were together. He felt as if he were floating in cloudy softness, floating without any sense of his own controls. "Oh, it's so good to screw again," she said.

□

It was almost 7:00 A.M. when she shook him awake. "I don't want the boy to know you were here," she said. He fished through the bedclothes for his underwear, and his head throbbed.

"I'll see you again," he said.

"You don't have to, you know. It was just what I wanted. I don't need more."

"Was it good?"

"You mean did I come?"

"No. I mean was it good, for you. Are you going to be able to look your son in the eye today?"

"Yes," she said. "Why shouldn't I? The only reason I'm hustling you out of here is that I don't want him to be confused by seeing a man's face he might not see again. Little boys like to think their mothers are mysterious and aloof. Strangers in the morning don't help that. Think of your own mother."

"She died when I was little."

"I'm sorry. But you know what I mean. So you better get going now . . ."

"You didn't answer my question yet."

"Which was?"

"Was it good?"

"I don't know yet. It's too early. I'll have to see when I get horny again. Please go."

"I'll call."

"You don't have to, Tony. I wish you'd understand that . . ."

He kissed her good-bye and left. It was a beautiful morning. He hoped it would be a decent day.

7

ORDINARILY CONNIE HAYDON was crisp from the instant he opened his eyes, but on this morning he awakened a distracted man who could barely drag himself out of bed. Eileen was on his mind. She was out of control, that's precisely what she was, he told himself, and if he wasn't careful, she could bring down his whole house upon his head. The thought of their encounter the night before still vexed him, and it was a listless Connie Haydon who took to the floor for his calisthenics. Each day his regimen was the same: fifty push-ups, followed by twenty-five sit-ups, then twenty-five more push-ups before he headed for a cold shower. Silence would then prevail until he had finished selecting his clothes from a wardrobe stocked end-to-end by J. Press and Brooks Brothers. Silence was easier now that Eileen had abandoned the master bedroom for one down the hall, and Connie could concentrate on his own thoughts, which inevitably extended no further than himself. But today he wasn't enjoying the stillness. He wished that Eileen were here, so he could continue the argument and perhaps convince her this time that for the good of the family as a whole it was imperative to stick together.

It's over, she had told him, after their late supper in the kitchen. He had come home after dropping off Corinne to find her sitting in the kitchen, sipping wine with the detective assigned as her body-guard and chauffeur. "At least he talks to me," she had told him after he sent the detective home and reprimanded him with the coldest of glances. The detective, he knew, wasn't important. The attitude of defiance was. Corinne infuriated and humiliated her, and she had no idea how to handle it. The mayor's dependence on his young assistant was so public, so undisguised. "You'll never have to worry about who your husband is bedding down," her mother had told her before she married Haydon. "You have to worry about who he's kissing. It's the kisses that's dangerous, and the confidences." But she had never confronted him about Corinne. Women were becoming as competent as men in politics now that they were being given a chance, and she would be the last woman in Boston to try to stand in the way of women's advancement. And she had no evidence, except the feeling in her gut, that more than efficiency was behind Corinne's rise to the top. She could sulk and brood and even move out of the master bedroom, but she would not ask her husband to fire Corinne. That would be the end if he refused, and she wasn't sure enough of her ability to read his mind to risk putting her feelings to the test.

The Scooter case was another matter. She would take her stand on the Scooter case. She could look at that objectively. That was a matter strictly of values, the values both she and her husband had been raised to believe in.

"Have you ever heard of loyalty?" she said to him. "I can't believe it. You're not the man I married. The man I married would never turn on a friend, especially someone like Scooter. Whose side are you on if you can't stand by your own friends?"

He told her he was surprised that Scooter meant so much to her. And she bristled and said that she knew where she came from and that she'd not forget that, no matter how high in the world she happened to be.

"I would never for a minute kid myself into thinking I'm one of them," she had said. "I remember who I am, where I come from, and who the enemy is, and it's the same enemy it's always been."

And he told her that the world had changed, and the city had changed, that he himself had helped to change it, to break down the old attitudes. "For Christ's sake," he had told her, "it isn't the Irish against them anymore. The Irish *are* them. The war is over. It's been over a long time. Do you honestly think Bill Raleigh down at the *Mammoth* looks at me as an Irish politician? Jesus Christ, I could be president of the United States."

"Connie, I feel sorry for you. How the hell do you think Raleigh and all those other people look at you? Do you really think you can belong by becoming like them?"

He tried to tell her that he hadn't turned in Scooter because of the *Mammoth,* that he had done it for purely pragmatic reasons, that he had no choice once it was clear that the developer was headed for the FBI.

"You could've tipped Scooter off," she said.

"And how long do you think that would've been kept a secret?"

"You could've finessed it."

"That guy wasn't going to let me out of his sight till after I called the FBI. One false step and it would've been me in the soup right alongside Scooter."

"Maybe that's where you belong. I guess you would've done the same thing to your own flesh and blood."

"I don't see the point."

"You'd turn me in, too, to save your skin."

"You're on the same plateau as Scooter. I hadn't known."

"You would've turned on your own family."

"You've had too much to drink."

"No, I haven't. You have no loyalty. You'd turn on Tommy. I know you would."

"Why? Is Tommy up to something?"

"No, he's not, but I can tell you he's upset about Scooter. You hate your own kind. They aren't good enough for you. I know what you really think. You're too good for me, for my friends, for my family. And if we had children, you'd probably be too good for them," she said.

"Always it comes back to that, doesn't it?" he said.

"You hate everything except the crazy idea of whatever it was your mother raised you to be," she said.

"You are so drunk."

"I'm not drunk enough, or I'd tell you what I really think."

He tried to change the subject by telling her about the pope. The news of the visit only touched off another tirade about his hypocrisy. "What do you care about the pope? You aren't a Catholic anyway. You're . . . I don't know what you are. Just one of them."

He tried to help her up the stairs to her bedroom, but she resisted him. "I don't want you touching me," she said. "Save your touching for that young bitch with the big tits."

"At least I've given you a new complaint," he said.

And then in a moment of what seemed to Haydon utter sobriety, she told him that she planned to leave as soon as she could find a proper place to stay, and she didn't care that the pope was coming or that he needed her for re-election or anything else. She no longer respected him and no longer cared. "The bitch can take my place," she said.

Now, in the morning light, he still felt threatened. The timing was all wrong. He had enough to deal with without this, too. Usually he spent this time each morning plotting the day. He would tick off in his mind the names of those he would see and consider how he would approach each person. Haydon distrusted spontaneity. Without a preconceived approach, each meeting would begin even, and he had learned long ago that to have an edge, even a thin one, was infinitely preferable to starting even, especially when the edge could be attained with just a little preparation. Now, he could not concentrate on the day ahead, even when it promised to be a critical one, perhaps the most critical of his career.

Haydon found the kitchen empty, with Eileen nowhere in sight. His place was set at the breakfast table and the morning newspapers were folded neatly alongside his plate. Haydon was a man who liked to get unpleasantness out of the way as quickly as possible, so he reached first for the *Bruise,* approaching it warily, the way a man might stick his hand into a gopher hole. The front page contained a big picture of Scooter with the immense headline: STUNG!

Inside, there was a straightforward account of the day's events and Tony Owen's column. It could have been written by Eileen. "For more than twenty years, Cornelius J. Haydon has been undoing brick by brick the Irish city of his forefathers. Yesterday, he ran out of patience and reached for a two-megaton bomb and set it off under the man who symbolizes Irish politics in this city. Now there's one Irish politician left in Boston and he isn't even Irish. He's Connie Haydon, and he wants to build a city not for Irish, Italians, or Danes, but for people like himself, with little sense of history, loyalty, or themselves.

"Haydon says it was duty that forced him to turn in his long-time ally Scooter Conroy. It was duty all right: duty to save his own skin . . ."

Haydon was relieved. Tony Owen hadn't laid a glove on him. All he did was equate a little bit of corruption with Irish politics. Wonderful. Wink at the Irish rogue as he reaches for someone's wallet.

He ignored the tone of mockery. He had long been conditioned to a *Bruise* that delighted in his every embarrassment while gibing at his cultivation.

It was the *Mammoth* that understood him and recognized his dimensions as a man. The *Mammoth* seldom surprised him. In fact, Raleigh and his assistants made it a point to contact him personally in advance on those occasions when the *Mammoth* was planning to publish a story critical of Haydon's administration, and Haydon returned the favor by giving the *Mammoth* a head start, whenever he could, on stories he knew they'd relish, stories that, for the most part, would glaze over the eyes of *Bruise* readers, stories on the workings of a new architectural committee, on bond ratings, on the cultural commission's fund-raising drive, on cemetery restoration, on the condition of the nineteenth-century sewer system, on anything to do with the city's early Brahmin mayors.

He reached for the *Mammoth* each morning with utter serenity, knowing that he'd be in for no rude awakening. He smiled as he looked at its front-page display on Scooter. It was right down the middle. An interminable story on turmoil in Pakistan led the paper. Scooter was the off-lead story, commanding a two-column hole down the left side of the page under the headline: MAYOR BLOWS WHISTLE ON LONG-TIME ALLY.

It was just the right focus, stressing the mayor's action, not Scooter's shakedown.

But Haydon could barely read the piece. He noted that it was a win, which made it a two-win morning (he always counted it a victory when a *Bruise* story did no serious damage), but the gravity of the Eileen situation weighed too heavily on him for small satisfactions.

He wanted to speak to her again and walked to the foot of the stairs and called her name. There was no answer, but Elizabeth, the maid, walked into the kitchen and told him that Eileen had left shortly after she arrived for work. "She didn't say where she was going, Mr. Mayor. Should I try her at her brother Tom's?"

"No, I'll see her later," he said, and began to scan the papers, reading them with only half his attention. He returned to the Tony Owen piece. "Loyalty," Tony Owen had written, "is just one of the virtues prized by the Irish in Boston and abroad. But, as often as not, it's the distinguishing virtue. Talk to Scooter Conroy about Connie Haydon, and to this day he'll defend the mayor for being man enough to do what he had to do for political survival. That's loyalty. Talk to Connie Haydon about Scooter Conroy, and he'll sound like a civics textbook, not like a man who's done in one of the people who made him. That's not loyalty. That's sin. Mortal sin."

He sounds like a theologian, Haydon thought . . . Mortal sin, what an idea. Eileen will probably send him a letter. Mortal sin. Loyalty. All that Irish crap. When do people ever grow out of it and define themselves along more realistic lines? The Irish weren't going to save the city; they had practically wrecked it until he came along and tried to slowly change the way the game was played. The idea that Scooter Conroy helped make me!

Mortal sin. Someday he would sit down with some of these professional Irish Catholics and tell them what a mortal sin really was. He'd tell Eileen, too. Do you know what a mortal sin is, you drunken drone? I'll tell you what it is, and you can tell your soul brother at the *Bruise* the same thing. A mortal sin is when you lose what you've fought for. When you get soft and let sentiment stand in the way of the hard choices you need to make to grow and advance and maintain what you've spent your life trying to build up. No, Eileen, you can't leave me. You can't leave me because I need you, and you need me to keep what we have. That's our mission, our personal mission, and that's the reason why you have to put up with people like Corinne. No, she's not a rival, you fool. She's someone I need to grow, and if I don't have her, if all I have is you, then I'll get like you and your brother because you'll be the bounds of my existence. I think you understand that. You'd be nothing without me, and I'd be nothing if all I had were you.

The doorbell rang. Stanley walked in.

"Good morning, chief. You ready for Raleigh?"

"I haven't given it much thought yet. What did you think of the papers?"

"Not bad. Tony Owen was vicious but just what you'd expect. People don't take him seriously anymore. Such a hater."

"A Johnny one-note. That's what he's become. Anything new with the pope?"

"No, just what I told you last night. I'll have a full package for the *Mammoth* by this afternoon. I'm heading for the chancery myself at noon. Foley will have a full briefing."

"Just what in blue blazes is the pope hoping to accomplish by coming to this place? Maybe Foley will let you in on that little secret. I would like to think he's coming here to help me get re-elected, but I'm sure he has other items on his agenda. The pope. By Jesus, the next thing you know we'll be getting the Queen of England."

The idea of the papal visit dispelled some of Connie Haydon's gloom. If the timing was right, he would be in town sometime within the six weeks before Election Day. But even if he arrived after the election, the mayor would benefit from the preparations for the festivities.

"You know, it's an amazing thing, Stanley. For the better part of a century, this was a Catholic city and the pope never so much as flew over the place. Now, I don't know what the place is . . . It certainly isn't Catholic anymore, and here he comes on some kind of mission. What kind of mission should we call it, by the way? What should we tell Raleigh it's all about?"

Stanley looked intently at the mayor to read his meaning. A misreading could lead to a temper tantrum. As a result, Stanley waited before speaking, a hesitation that sometimes infuriated Haydon more than an answer to an unasked or misunderstood question.

"I'm not sure," he said.

"What do you mean you're not sure? Be sure. I pay you to be sure."

"Well, I don't know if we should do any more than tell him what we know. That he's coming, sometime soon, on a mission the nature of which has not yet been disclosed, and let it slide at that."

"Stanley, try to bend your mind a bit to think with me on this. I know the *Mammoth* will run with this story. But I want them to go with it on page one every day until the pope gets here, whether that's a month from now or three months from now. Whenever. So let's feed them a little angle. Give them a mystery trip. What do you think? Would we get blown out of the water?"

Again Stanley hesitated. Then he blurted, "Yes. I mean, no. I mean yes, if we planted it in the *Mammoth* and it was wrong. No, if we let the *Bruise* have it."

"You want to give that angle to the *Bruise?*"

"No, not give. Give a hint of it to the *Mammoth* and let the *Bruise* pick up on the hint. That way, no matter what happens we won't get blamed."

"And the *Bruise* is off our backs until the pope comes and goes. Not bad. What do you think they would do?"

"Who?"

"The *Bruise,* meathead."

"Why, I think they'd probably run a contest. Find the mystery behind the pope's visit. Is he coming to find a saint from Boston?"

"The pope might pull out if he thinks we're exploiting the trip."

"No, he would understand how tabloids are. He wouldn't understand if the *Mammoth* did the same thing. Then he might cancel, don't you think?"

The mayor was getting excited. "This is beginning to sound like something. Just great. The only hitch I can see, if we move right, is if the pope announces prematurely that his visit to Boston is strictly pastoral and in conjunction with a trip to half a dozen other places. Then the bloom is off the rose."

"I don't know if that will happen. Monsignor Foley told me that the pope won't even announce his itinerary officially until a few days before he leaves. As long as it's not official, he can pull out."

The mayor was struck by an unpleasant idea. "What if he decides at the last minute not to come, or what if he gets sick and doesn't show, or just decides he'd rather be in Seattle or Chicago than here? Then we're left with egg on our face."

"Yes, but the worst that can be said is that he changed his mind because of the press of official business. It happens all the time. Meanwhile, you'll have won a lot of good ink over an extended period of time."

"But what if I'm blamed for his not coming? Could that happen?"

"I don't see how," said Stanley. "I really can't see how. Who would believe it?"

"It's perfect. O.K., Stanley. I'm off to see Raleigh. You check with Corinne and make certain that everything we talked about last night is in process, especially the cardinal. No foul-ups. Now everybody will be trying to hit me over Scooter and they won't get near me. The politician's dream — the pope's coattails. How can I lose?"

☐

Connie Haydon was ushered into Raleigh's office, the door was shut, and the blinds were drawn. The two most powerful men in the city sat down side by side in twin chairs that once belonged to John and Abigail Adams. The chairs were placed at right angles, and Haydon had to keep his neck turned to face Raleigh, who relished this slight and seldom consciously noted home-court advantage over visitors, who came, invariably, with a complaint or to seek a favor: a job, a favorable editorial comment, or some attention in the news pages.

"That's Abigail's chair you're sitting in," Raleigh said after the two men settled down. "Treat it gently."

"I'm always gentle with Yankee antiques," said the mayor.

They sat in silence for a few seconds before Raleigh asked the mayor what was on his mind. He knew he'd get no direct answer. The rituals had to be observed and the rituals of their meetings seldom changed over the years. Raleigh would be blunt and direct; the mayor, ever evasive and looking for the right opening to deliver his message. Their encounters rarely ended in stalemate. Invariably there was a winner and invariably it was the mayor.

"Nothing really pressing, Bill. It's important to keep in touch. The two of us have been friends a helluva long time now," the mayor said, all the while staring straight ahead so that Raleigh could read the mayor only in profile, as if his face were engraved on a coin.

"You came down to see me about Scooter, so cut the baloney. We're both busy men," Raleigh said, finding himself slightly disconcerted by the mayor's refusal to twist his neck.

"Bill, what can I say? You're a man who cuts through to the quick of things. And you're right. Scooter is on my mind. You know me well enough to realize how that decision cut. Jesus, Scooter has been like a brother to me over the years, and he's my guy. He's — as the Jewish people like to say — he's of my tribe. It's like you blowing the whistle on a Salstonstall or a Sargent. Hell, you couldn't do it. You'd probably sooner quit the paper. But you wouldn't. You know you wouldn't. You'd do what I did, and do you know why?"

"Tell me. You're going to anyway."

"Hey, come on now. You know I'm talking about home truths

here, as much as you might not want to face it. But I'll tell you why, Bill. It's because you and I are so much alike. We both are primarily Bostonians. You're a Yankee; I'm an Irishman, but I'm — and don't you dare ever print this or I'll never speak to you again — but I'm a Bostonian before I'm an Irishman. I've got to do what's good for the city — beyond ego, beyond family, beyond tribe. To some people, that would sound corny . . ."

"Or disloyal."

"Or disloyal. But it's me. It's my nature. It's your nature. They talk about power corrupting. Well, I'll tell you, it hasn't corrupted you. It hasn't corrupted me, either, and for the same reason. Because it toughened us. It taught us to make the hard decisions."

"How's Eileen?"

"She's just fine."

"I'll bet she wasn't happy with what you did to Scooter."

"Jesus, how do you know my wife so well? Well, you're right. She wasn't happy. She isn't happy with a lot of the things I do. She isn't happy, as I suppose you know — everybody else in town seems to know — with the idea of a young woman as my special assistant. She knows that the relationship is above board. Come on, now, Bill, we're both a little too old for the cooing and the kissing. We're at the looking stage. That's all we can afford to do, just look. What she doesn't like is that it makes people talk, and they put her down and make her the object of a lot of vicious backbiting, and, well, you know how this city is. It's like a little village with everybody thinking they know everybody's business. And you have to fight that all the way."

"I'm not sure I liked what you did to Scooter, either. You know, for all his stage Irish bullshit, he isn't a bad guy. In fact, he's kind of smart, too smart, I always thought, to get caught doing what he obviously did . . . unless."

"Unless what?"

"Unless."

"Say what's on your mind, Bill," the mayor said. He still refused to look at Raleigh.

The editor paused to consider his words. Just a hint of the Haydon anger was in his voice. Raleigh had seen him explode before and hated confrontations where the rage was out of the bottle.

"All I was going to say is that Scooter has been working for you for a long, long time, and it sure seems odd to me that all of a sudden he goes off the rails for no apparent reason. I mean, he isn't the kind of guy who seems to change his act much."

The mayor stood up and walked to the window. He said nothing, but his shoulders were taut and Raleigh could sense the hostility. The mayor wheeled around from the window and for the first time looked directly into Raleigh's eyes.

"You know, you're unbelievable. The suggestions you're making are suggestions that I resent, I deeply and personally resent. And after all we've been through together over the years, for you to sit there and indicate that you think that I either encouraged or profited . . ."

"Wait a minute now, Connie. I suggested no such thing. You're going too far," Raleigh said.

"Don't interrupt me. I didn't come down here to talk about Scooter. I came down here to give you a news story that now I think I'll hustle across town, where I think they'll appreciate it more. But all you want to hear about is Scooter. Well, I'll tell you about Scooter, and I didn't want to because you're going to be thinking it's one harp out there trying to protect another harp, and you'll have gotten it all wrong because you're so fucking smug. I don't know why an Irish Catholic would ever buy your paper, you have so many assumptions that are insulting to them."

"Now you really are going too far," said Raleigh.

"All right, I am. But looking into your eyes, I can see the face of prejudice, the same face my great-grandfather had to confront when he got off the typhoid ships."

"And you really believe it?"

"At this moment I do."

"Well, I'm sorry. I thought we were close enough friends."

"I did, too," the mayor said, his face softening by degrees. He stared at Raleigh and he smiled, an almost kindly smile. "The pope is coming," he said.

"What is that you say?"

"The pope is coming. Give Stanley a call. He'll fill you in on all the details. But don't call the chancery unless you want to share the story with the *Bruise.*"

"You're kidding me. The pope is coming to Boston? When?"

"No definite date from Rome. No definite reason, either. A hint of something, though, about a mystery objective. A local saint, maybe. I really don't know. I hope Stanley has all the details. He was scurrying around last night and early today, trying to nail everything down."

"You mean it isn't nailed down?"

"Oh, it's going to happen all right, but it isn't Vatican policy to make it official or to set the exact timetable until the last minute. Security reasons, you know. But the cardinal probably has been briefed, and I'll see to it that you get everything we get as soon as we get it."

"Let me bring Tom Curtis in here, the city editor. Will you tell him what you told me?"

"Yeah, but remember, this is exclusive. Absolutely. It's all yours."

Twenty minutes later, the mayor walked out of the *Mammoth* building, and he could barely restrain the smile on his face. He never did have to tell anyone about what went wrong with Scooter Conroy.

8

DUNCAN AVENUE had its moments. Babe Ruth lived at number thirty-four. That was during the 1916 season when Ruth and the apartments were new to Boston. By the time the Babe departed for New York in 1920, the neat brick row houses tucked away in a stubby stretch behind Huntington Avenue had already begun their slow descent toward slumdom. The little neighborhood, so close to the city's commercial center yet so hidden from its daily traffic, had since colonial days been a magnet for brothels, and it wasn't long before that special commerce began to spill over from the adjacent streets onto Duncan Avenue. A spectacular police raid in 1919 netted two aldermen and a Unitarian divine and front-page attention in the city's newspapers. It also rubbed away the respectability the new apartment complex had conferred on Duncan Avenue. By the time the Great Depression struck, the developers of the London-style project had long since gone bankrupt and the housing had become the plaything of slumlords milking the property for every cent in rent receipts and for every tax advantage.

By the mid-1970s, not even slumlords were interested in the buildings. Fines for code violations exceeded what could be squeezed from an ever poorer class of tenants in rent, and property taxes offset the breaks offered by the federal tax code. Meanwhile, the neighborhood remained as isolated as ever, seemingly immune from the boom that was transforming neighborhoods nearby. Now most of the apartments were either abandoned or occupied by squatters or turned into trick pads for hookers, who in the age of automobiles, worked the sidewalks instead of the genteel parlors of the old-fashioned brothels.

Tony Owen, unshaved and unshowered, stepped out of a cab at the middle of Duncan Avenue shortly before ten o'clock. In another two hours, the girls would be on the sidewalk, preening for their lunch-hour trade. But at this time of the morning, it was deserted. Tony, notebook in hand, stood there, studying the buildings on both sides of the street. In the middle of the block, directly in front of him, fire had swept four buildings, which were boarded up, hiding the ruin inside. In the areaway outside, debris was scattered. The fire had smudged the red brick with black scorch marks. On the lower level, some of the boards had been ripped away, perhaps by vandals, perhaps by squatters.

Tony sketched the pattern in his notebook, noting each address, including number forty-two, where Bernie Kremenko had perished. On the east side of the street where he faced, nine attached buildings were left standing. Two at the end seemed to be occupied. Three others showed no sign of fire damage but appeared to be abandoned.

Across the street, two of the nine buildings were burned out, the rest abandoned, except for one building at the corner.

For almost five minutes, Tony stood on the sidewalk, filling out his diagram of the block. Then he walked around the corner onto Holgate Street, past empty lots and a once stately apartment building that still retained a bit of turn-of-the-century charm, and turned onto Burnham Road, directly behind Duncan Avenue. There a revival was under way. Several of the old apartment buildings were being restored, and a stretch of four empty lots had been cleared of rubble.

Tony noted the sign slapped on the brick face of one of the buildings under renovation. ARTICULATE, INC., DEVELOPERS. He pulled out his notebook and sketched a diagram of Burnham Road. He then rounded the corner and headed back toward Duncan Avenue and the corner building where he could see plants hanging in a window.

As he crossed Duncan Avenue and headed for number seventy-one, a blue Plymouth approached. The driver stuck his head out the window and shouted at Tony: "Hey, ace, what you doing down here, slumming?"

"What are you doing, looking for a low-calorie lunch? And what the hell are you doing out of the cage without your keeper? What happened? You quit?"

Stanley, the mayor's press secretary, smiled. "You son of a bitch, you're making me work overtime trying to keep track of you."

Stanley pulled the car over to the curb and Tony stood by the driver's window, peering in at Stanley, a slight and almost girlish-looking man, who, when he was away from the mayor, spoke in a high-pitched staccato that under pressure escalated into a whine. "What are you doing down here? I've been watching you for the last fifteen minutes and I'll be damned if I see much of a story."

Tony scowled. "Don't tell me the mayor has you spying on me. That I can't believe."

"Don't flatter yourself, Tony. I came by the paper looking for you and somebody told me I might find you down here. I was hoping we could grab a quick cup of coffee."

"Who told you?"

"I forget. John Walsh or somebody."

"O.K., but I can't have a cup of coffee. I'm busy. What is it you want?"

"Well, get in the car for a few minutes. It's hard to have a conversation with you so uncomfortable."

Tony walked around the car and climbed into the front seat. The lights on Stanley's police radio blinked like the bulbs of tiny flashlights. "Tony, if I were tailing you, I wouldn't have let you see me. I wanted to talk to you about Scooter."

"What about Scooter?"

"I hear he gave you an earful yesterday."

"You are well plugged in."

"Don't trust him. He's all fucked up."

"You think so. I wonder why. O.K., I'll take that into account."

"And if he's the guy who sent you down here, that really proves he's fucked up. Nothing ever happens in this neighborhood except a few businessmen get their ashes hauled if they're willing to take their lives in their hands."

"O.K., Stanley. I heard you. Is that all you have to talk about?"

"Look, Tony, I know how you feel about Connie and that you'd do anything to get him. If that's your trip, fine. It's O.K. with me. I don't care what you do. But I don't want to see you get hurt or look bad, and that's what you'll be doing if you take the side of Scooter the martyr. He's no martyr taking a fall. I could fill you in on a dozen times that the mayor could have bagged him and he let him go with a warning, and I'll tell you why. The mayor likes him. He likes him as much as you do, and you must know how tight Scooter has been over the years with Eileen."

"Fill me in."

"O.K. I will. Not today, though. I have to check with Connie to see if it's O.K. If he says go, it's a go. I mean that."

"Why doesn't Connie do something about this shit?"

"What shit? Duncan Avenue has always been this way."

"I don't mean the whorehouses. I mean the fires. Look at the fires, for God's sake. What's he doing about them?"

"I don't even think he knows about them. He doesn't exactly hang out around here."

"Well, somebody should know about them."

"I don't know why. They look like vandal fires to me. These buildings are all abandoned, most of them, anyway, that I can see." He paused, then looked hard at Tony and said, "Is that what Scooter told you? That the mayor is burning down Duncan Avenue?"

"Cut the crap, Stanley. I'm not going to tell you what Scooter told me, and you know it. But I think it's fascinating that you're so concerned about whatever little secret Scooter had to share that you feel compelled to follow me."

"You're not back on that track again?"

"Jesus Christ, Stanley, Walsh isn't even working today, and I didn't tell a soul I was heading to Duncan Avenue."

"O.K., believe what you want. Make a fool out of yourself. I was going to give you another story. That's why I tracked you down. But you're not interested."

"I'll bet you have another story. Let me see. Let me guess. I got it. The mayor is going to retire. He ain't going to make a run and he's going to give back the two million bucks he has in illegal contributions with a note of thanks to all the people he squeezed dry."

"You're impossible, Tony. Really. You don't take help even when you need it. O.K., have it your way."

"I don't want your help, Stanley. I really don't."

"Fine. But don't come crying to me tomorrow."

"I won't come crying, ever."

Tony opened the car door, waved, and without looking back headed for the building on the corner.

The apartment with the plants in the window was on the second floor. The bells downstairs had long since stopped working, and the security door leading into the building itself was off its hinges. The stairs up the dark passageway seemed fragile beneath his feet. He knocked on the door. He heard the shuffling of feet, the scraping of a slipper over a linoleum surface. The door opened just a crack. He saw an old woman's face.

"What do you want?" she asked, her voice aged in Boston. "Are you from the housing? If you're from the housing, I don't want to talk to you. You can just go fish."

"No, I'm not from the housing. I'm a reporter. I just want to talk to you."

She opened the door a crack wider to get a better look at Tony, then stood back and let him come in. The door opened on the kitchen, which smelled of cats and airlessness. "Hello, my name is Tony Owen. I came by to see how you're doing."

She shuffled back toward the kitchen table and sat down. She wore a short-sleeved housedress, and the white flesh of her long, thin arms jiggled like an empty sack. He judged her to be eighty.

"I'll talk to anyone but the man from the housing. I'd talk to a robber in the hall before I'd talk to those people, trying to push me out on the street like I'm some kind of stray animal."

"Who do you mean, the people from housing? You mean from City Hall?"

"Well, where do you think the housing people are from? Sure they're from City Hall. They want us all out of here so the mayor can build his retirement hotel. That's what Rosie says."

"Oh, of course," Tony said. "Do you mind if I help myself to a glass of water?"

The woman said nothing, just stared at Tony, who stood up and walked to the sink, all the while studying the room for signs of the woman's identity. By the back window, there was a little telephone table and chair. He approached the window as if to look out, and on the table he saw two letters. The first was from St. Ignatius Church, addressed to Mrs. Mabel Sloane. The second was from an attorney's office. He looked out the window into the back yard. Two spruce trees stood side by side near a fence that held back a wall of debris tossed from the alley that ran behind Duncan Avenue.

"Are you the Mabel Sloane who used to run a hardware store over on Mass. Ave. up from Symphony Hall?"

"No, and it wasn't anybody named Sloane who ran that store. That was Johnson's Hardware. The colored drove them out, and if you're from around here you should know that, young man. My husband wasn't in business. He was a craftsman. A tool and die maker. He's been dead for thirty years."

Tony finally edged his way back to the sink, got his glass of water, and sat down at the table.

"Is that lawyer from City Hall?" he asked.

"What lawyer?"

"The lawyer who sent you the letter that's on the table by the window. I happened to see it when I looked out at the yard."

"I don't know. I didn't open the letter. It just came the other day."

"Do you mind if I look?"

"What business is it of yours?" she asked, her voice flat with disinterest.

He didn't reply and her mind skipped to another track. "Tell me what the lawyer's letter says. I can't seem to find my glasses. Rosie comes in to see me every afternoon and she helps me find my glasses. Do you see them?"

"No," Tony lied. The glasses were on the windowsill by the table. Tony got up from the table and picked up the letter. It was from a lawyer he had only vaguely heard of: F. X. McGivern, 50 State Street. He opened the letter and began to read it aloud: "Dear Mrs. Sloane: This is to advise you that eviction proceedings will be initiated against you as a result of the serious delinquency in your payment of rent unless you vacate your apartment by April twenty-fifth. According to our records, you are twenty-eight hundred dollars in arrears. Interest and penalty charges totaling four hundred fifty-six dollars are also due. To avoid further liabilities, including the costs of legal action against you, I suggest you vacate forthwith."

"What foolishness," Mrs. Sloane said. "Nobody's been around here to collect rent in two years, and even then they didn't always come. How can I pay someone I don't know? I wouldn't even know where to send the rent if I had it to pay."

"Well, who's this guy McGivern?"

"How do I know? I've never seen him. The only one I ever see is this man from the housing who tells me I have to get out by May first and he doesn't care where I go. He says the mayor needs the building. He wants to knock it down. He says you can't fight City Hall and that he's trying to get me in the project, but I don't want to live in the project. I don't have anything against the colored people, but people should always stick with their own kind. There's trouble if they don't, and I don't want to live with colored people. I'd rather be here by myself with Rosie looking after me."

"Mrs. Sloane, did the man who said he was from the housing tell you his name, or show you his card?"

"Maybe," she said. "I just don't remember."

Tony pulled out his wallet and showed her his press card. "You see, I'm from the *Bruise*. But the other man may not be from housing after all. He might just want to scare you out. That's why they sent you this letter from the lawyer. You don't have to go. All you have to do is go to the housing court and nobody will bother you."

"But Rosie told me I had to go, too, and she lives downstairs. She said it isn't safe anymore around here."

"Because of the fires?"

"The fires are terrible. A poor man died just a few weeks ago right across the street."

"Have they told Rosie she had to go, too?"

"Oh, she's going. She'll be gone."

"So I guess you'll be moving to the project after all."

She stared straight ahead as if she hadn't heard the question. Tony got up and looked into her refrigerator. He saw a bowl of congealed soup and a tin of condensed milk. There was nothing else he could identify.

"Do you want me to call the welfare for you? They have some nice people who would be happy to come by and take care of you."

Again, there was no answer. Tony stood up and fetched Mrs. Sloane's glasses and placed them in her hands.

"Next time the fellow from the housing comes by, make him show you his card, O.K.?" he said.

She nodded and fell back into her private world.

Tony said good-bye and walked down the stairs. He knocked at the door of the first-floor apartment. Rosie answered. She was a heavyset woman with dark hair, plain except for her eyes, which were brown, deep set, and lustrous.

"You're too early," she said. "Come back in an hour."

"I just want to talk to you."

"Come back in an hour."

"Hey, it's about the old lady upstairs. I'm a reporter. Don't give me a hard time or I'll ruin your act." He displayed his press card.

"You people are worse than cops, for Christ's sake. What do you want?"

"Let me talk to you for a moment."

She opened the door. The apartment was totally bare except for the front room, which contained a bed, a worn easy chair, and a black-and-white television set. Rosie had been sitting, watching television and reading the *Bruise*. She flopped down on the bed, her back against the wall, and lit a cigarette. Tony sat in the frayed easy chair.

"Just tell me what's going on in this neighborhood."

"The same old shit."

"Why are they trying to force people out?"

"I don't know. I'm leaving because I'm going to go into another line."

"Rosie? That's your name, right?" She nodded. "Tell me, why are they pushing the old lady out?"

"They want to take the building down, that's obvious."

"Who?"

"What do you mean, who? There's only one 'who' in this town. Either him or his people. And that's all I'm going to say and I wish you would go, because pretty soon you're going to be costing me money, mister."

"Why did you tell Mrs. Sloane to get out? Do you really think she could get hurt?"

"Hey, you don't stand in the way of progress no matter how old you are without running a chance that some bulldozer is going to knock you down along with the building. I just told her that. I wasn't meaning to scare her."

"Look, if you tell me one thing, then I'll leave you alone. Who's scaring you out and how?"

"Hey, nobody scares me out of any place. You kidding me? I've looked death in the face more times than I can count, and I'm not going because I'm scared."

"Then why are you leaving?"

"Why face a hassle you can avoid? That's all."

"That's really all?"

"That's it."

"Did you know that guy killed in the fire across the street?"

"Sure, he was a regular. What? Are you kidding me? He was a bum looking for a place to come in out of the rain."

"And he got killed."

"He was in the wrong place at the wrong time. That's life, isn't it?"

"O.K. If you ever change your mind and feel like talking, you can reach me at the *Bruise*. I'm Tony Owen. You read my column?" He glanced at the *Bruise,* which was within reach of her hand.

"Yeah," she said. "You're the guy who hates the mayor."

"Not you, too," he said.

He stood up, fished in his pocket for a twenty-dollar bill that was crumpled there, and handed it to her. "This is for your time. Thanks."

"Thanks," she said. "You're getting away cheap. My minimum is forty."

"Thanks for the bargain."

Tony walked out of the building, spotted a police car parked across the street, confirmation that he was being watched, and headed for Mass. Ave. He hailed a cab near Symphony Hall.

He made a quick stop at the *Bruise,* where he telephoned the State House man, Arnie Albanian, and asked him to check the list of officers of a company called Articulate at the secretary of state's office. Then he telephoned the courthouse reporter, Sally Train, for a reading on a lawyer named F. X. McGivern.

"You mean the little fat guy who used to represent the porno shops down the Combat Zone?"

"Maybe. I don't know the guy. I can't place him."

"A vicious little bastard. Likes to hide behind the leg breakers."

"Well, he's moving upscale. He's got a State Street address now, if it's the same guy."

"Let me check him out. I'll let you know. You going to be around for a while?"

"No, I've got some checking to do at City Hall. I'll be back about four. You can get me then."

"O.K., I'll call with what I can find out."

Cynthia called just as Tony was about to head out of the building. She caught him by surprise and his defenses were down.

"Where were you last night? I tried to reach you until two o'clock and you never answered your phone."

"I got into a card game."

"Bullshit. You hate cards."

"I'm trying to learn to love them. Why, was something happening?"

"Tony, I can't abide liars."

"O.K., I wasn't playing cards. I was working on a story."

"What was the story? It must be terrific to keep you out all night. I don't believe you, Tony."

"It is terrific and I'll tell you all about it tonight. You want to get together tonight?"

"I don't know why I bother," she said. "I can't depend on you. I really can't. I don't know about tonight. I'm working on a story, too. Maybe I'll be out all night. You probably wouldn't care anyway. You wouldn't, would you?"

"What are you working on?" he asked, trying to steer her away from the anger he felt building in her. "I guess you're following up on Scooter."

"As a matter of fact, I've been chasing Scooter all day. And I finally got him at his house and he told me he won't talk to anybody else in the media except guess who? He says he'll talk to me if you say it's O.K."

"Come on, Cynthia, what are you trying to do to me? We're competitors, for Christ's sake."

"Well, let's talk about it."

"I don't see the point, but sure, I'll talk about it. See you at my place. We'll bring in Chinese. About eight. No, make it nine. I'll see you at nine."

"O.K. Nine-thirty, your place."

Bobby Bantam was standing by his desk as Tony hung up the phone. "You got a good follow going?" he asked. Then he looked straight into Tony's eyes. "Jesus, you must have had one hell of a night. No Jewish girl left you looking like that. Christ, can't you even change your shirt? Jesus, I can smell the pussy from here."

"Hey, Bobby. You're reaching. I've been working round the clock, haven't had time to change. The story is cooking."

"O.K., Tony, anything you say. But you ought to take a look in the mirror."

"Actually, I feel pretty rested."

"Well, isn't that nice? Well, before you continue on your appointed rounds, I suggest you run into the men's room and shave. You look like you're identifying with your victim — what's his name, Bernie Kerensky?"

"Kremenko."

"Kerensky, Kremenko. What's it look like?"

"Hard to say. Somebody is buying up a lot of buildings in back of Duncan Avenue and there's pressure on the people still living there to get out fast."

"What the hell, nobody lives there but hookers and pimps anyway."

"Not quite true, Bobby, but hey, do me a favor. Get the city desk to check out the number of fires on Duncan Avenue in the past year and the causes, O.K.? I got to get down the Hall to check out the properties down at the Building Department. I think it's a pretty good story."

"It would be better if we knew the mayor was involved."

"That would be too much. But Stanley was down there this morning checking me out."

"Stanley on Duncan Avenue? He was probably getting laid."

"No, really, he was there to see what I was up to. I think they followed me right from here, or they came over after somebody spotted me walking around down there. I toured the block."

"What a waste of tax dollars. Isn't that something. They pay that creep Stanley fifty grand a year to tail a broken-down old reporter like you. Well, actually, if he was tailing you he wouldn't've let you spot him. That wasn't too slick if you saw him."

"Oh, he came right over to me. He wanted to find out what I was looking for. It really bothers them that Scooter took me into his confidence yesterday. Hey, maybe they're running scared."

"Wouldn't that be something. Here we are dying by the day and we're scaring them. I love it. I hope we get that bastard by the throat and take him right down with us. Imagine Connie Haydon with only the *Mammoth* in town. Jesus, I can't believe what it would be like to live here. I'd split myself. I'd even take a job in New Orleans at the *Picayune,* for God's sake."

Twenty minutes later, Tony Owen was in the office of Richard Hummell, the building inspector, asking to see the names of the landlords of record for all the properties on Duncan Avenue and the streets abutting.

"Sorry, Tony, can't help you," said Hummell.

"What do you mean you can't help me? That's a public record."

"Yeah, but I don't have them. They're being used."

"What are you talking about? You can't take them out of the building."

"That's right, and they're not out of the building. Somebody else is looking at them right now. You'll have to come back tomorrow. They should be available for you tomorrow."

"Hey, Dick, I'm going to knock your block off in print tomorrow if you don't let me have those records and right this minute. This is crazy."

"Sorry. Can't let you see what I don't have, and I don't have 'em. Hell, you can go back and look for yourself if you don't believe me. They've been borrowed."

"Who took 'em?"

"Not going to tell you, Tony. It's none of your business."

"O.K., Richard, we'll see whose business it is."

He turned on his heels and took the elevator to the eighth floor, where Stanley and his Communications Department were encamped. "Stanley is in conference, Tony," said the receptionist outside Stanley's office. Tony ignored her and walked in. Stanley was huddled with Henry Hornblower of the *Mammoth.* "Hey, I'm busy, Tony. You wait outside."

"Like hell, I'll wait outside. What're you doing with those records?"

"What records?"

"You know exactly what records I'm talking about, and I better have them in ten minutes or your ass is going to be sizzling in the morning."

"Hey, you better spell out what you're talking about. On second thought, you'd better clear out of here or I'll get a cop to throw you out. I'm in conference, Tony," he said, his voice rising near the whining point.

Tony stared coldly at Hornblower, a reporter he despised for his craven coverage of the mayor. "Call a cop. Let's give Hornblower a chance to write a story he hasn't been spoon-fed."

"You want me to tell him where you were this morning?" asked Stanley.

"He wouldn't know what to do with it, so go right ahead."

"Maybe I should get out of here," said Hornblower.

"Maybe you should," said Tony.

"I'll call you later," said Stanley, speaking as calmly as he could.

Hornblower got up and left, taking care to gather up his notebook and a handful of what looked like press releases from Stanley's desk.

"O.K.," said Tony, after he and Stanley were finally alone, "why are you trying to keep me from seeing legitimate public records?"

"I'm not keeping you."

"Cut the crap, Stanley, or so help me, I'll strangle you."

"All right. They're being studied. It's a matter of investigation. The records have been impounded."

"By court order?"

"Maybe."

"What do you mean, maybe?"

"An internal investigation is under way. You cannot see the records, if they're the records I think you're talking about, until after the investigation is complete."

"Then I'll go to court myself."

"By then the investigation will be complete, I'm sure."

"Oh, Jesus. I'm telling you I'm going to cause a blood bath tomorrow. Wait till you see my column."

"You're going to embarrass yourself."

"I suppose the Tax Department books are closed, too."

"I'm sure they are."

"All I can say, Stanley, is you're giving me one helluva column for tomorrow."

"Tony, let me tell you something. I don't give a damn what you write tomorrow."

"We'll see."

"Won't we?"

The bitchy note in Stanley's voice surprised Tony, who expected to find, as his anger rose, the customary defensive reactions of the public relations man. He was reminded at once of their conversation that morning and the story Stanley seemed to be offering him then.

"You're feeding a whopper to Hornblower, aren't you? I could see it in the wimp's eyes. He just took it up the ass, didn't he?"

"Tony, I'm really busy. And I guess you are, too. I mean, you have to try to get to court, don't you? Why don't you try Judge Doyle. He's always good with freedom of information cases."

"Fuck off, Stanley."

Once Tony left — and he headed not for the courthouse but for the *Bruise,* just as Stanley knew he would — Stanley rushed into the mayor's office, where Connie Haydon was in conference with Corinne and the corporation counsel, Harold Hooper.

"Christ almighty, you should see Tony Owen. He's fit to be tied. He'll come out smoking tomorrow."

"I can hardly wait," said the mayor.

"Do we have anything to worry about?" asked Stanley.

"Not up against the pope, we don't," said Corinne.

"God bless the Holy Father," said the mayor.

Both the Tax and Building Department records on Duncan Avenue were on the coffee table in neatly folded computer print-outs. "What the *Bruise* is looking at must be the turnover rate in these properties," Hooper said. "Look at this. Four different companies buying up every piece of property in a three-block area over the last two years."

"Somebody's putting together a nice parcel," the mayor said. "What's Articulate? Find out who's behind that right away. They look like the umbrella group."

"I'll get right on it," Hooper said.

"Have there been fires down there?" the mayor asked.

"Yeah. Tony was mouthing off about that this morning. I'd say about a quarter of the buildings on Duncan Avenue have some fire damage."

"Find out what the Fire Department is up to," the mayor said. "See if they have any arson cases going."

"I'll take care of it, Connie," said Hooper.

"That's a funny neighborhood," the mayor said. "I wonder why Scooter steered him onto that. I know goddamn well I never even heard of anything going on down around that block. You know, I wouldn't be at all surprised if Scooter led him down a blind alley on this one. What do you think?"

"That I would doubt, Connie," said Corinne. "It's possible

Scooter didn't say a word to him about Duncan Avenue. Maybe he was working it before the Scooter thing broke."

"Maybe. But I doubt it. Scooter is what's hot today. Tony goes with the heat."

"Right into the fire."

"Let's hope so. Now, let's talk about the pope. Is everything set with the *Mammoth?*"

"Hornblower has as much of the story as I can get right now," said Stanley. "And here's the latest word from the monsignor." He pulled a note from his shirt pocket and glanced at it, then returned it to his pocket. "The visit is definite. The cardinal will meet with you sometime next week to discuss particulars. The timing is vague. It could be soon; it could be late August or September. A blowup in Poland could wipe it out altogether. He has a definite agenda for Boston. He is visiting other cities, but Boston is his first stop and the most symbolic. Foley doesn't know the precise nature of his visit but suspects it's primarily pastoral. I don't think we're off base by selling it as a mystery. But I wonder how hard they're going to hit that angle at the *Mammoth.* Too speculative for those folks."

"They'd better hit the hell out of it or the *Bruise* will be all over it, believe me," Haydon said. "Raleigh's turkeys will let the *Bruise* stay in the ball game. Wait till you see what Bobby Bantam does with this story."

"Once he gets over the apoplexy after he reads the papers tonight," said Corinne.

"Oh, he'll be steaming, and all we have to say to him if he calls is we tried to feed the same story to Tony Owen and he was too occupied with his witch-hunt. You should've heard me trying to sell it to him on the street today, but all he wanted to do was ask why you haven't done anything about the situation down there."

"He's so hungry for a story, he can't see one when it's dangled in front of his eyes," said the mayor.

"It's a good thing he didn't grab it," said Corinne. "Or we'd have two papers all over us."

"Corinne," Stanley said sternly, "I wouldn't have offered it if there was the slightest chance he would've taken it."

The press aide looked to the mayor for approval, but Haydon was paying no attention to the by-play between his aides. "This Duncan

Avenue business bothers me. I want a full report on that whole situation by tonight. I don't like things happening in this city I don't know about. I hope I don't learn about a new mess on my hands when I pick up the *Bruise* tomorrow. I certainly hope I don't, Stanley."

"You won't," he said, feeling proud of the way he was on top of his job. "And even if there is a mess, nobody will notice. Not with the pope."

"I'll notice," said the mayor.

□

A message from Scooter was waiting by Tony's telephone when he returned to the *Bruise,* still fuming from his encounter with Stanley. And a memo from the city desk was on top of his typewriter. No official determination of arson in any Duncan Avenue fire during the period requested. Instead, all fires attributed to electrical malfunctions as the likely cause, except for the fire at number forty-two. That was attributed to "suspicious origin" and was under investigation. Tony snorted. "Lazy bastards," he muttered.

"Who you talking about?" asked Doc D'Amato.

"The arson squad. Bunch of political hacks taken off the trucks so they'll be available for Connie's organizing. Lazy whores."

"Hey, you are in a good mood. Watch your blood pressure. You'll end up like Sonny," said the medical writer.

"We'll all end up like Sonny," Tony said.

Scooter left a number and a one-word message: "Call." Tony glanced at it and headed for Bobby Bantam's office and privacy.

Bantam was out, so Tony eased himself into his chair, padded to raise Bobby's stature so he wouldn't be swallowed behind the big oak desk. The desk was bare. Bantam hated disorder. Tony took out his pen and a few pieces of copy paper from beside Bantam's typewriter and telephoned the number Scooter left.

Scooter answered the telephone, almost immediately.

"Where are you?" asked Tony.

"Can't tell you. Been trying to duck reporters all day. Somebody might tail you if you tried to find me."

"O.K.," said Tony. "Tell me, how are you holding up? Family fine?"

"Things are just about what you'd expect. They're awful. My

wife and daughter can't stop howling. You'd've thought I died."

"Well, hold on, old scout."

"Hey, I'm holding. Nice piece you did this morning. And that was a nice piece on Channel Four last night. That Cynthia, is she your girlfriend?"

"Hey, is that why you're calling? I thought maybe you had something to tell me."

"No, I'm calling to see what you can tell me. Been down to Duncan Avenue yet?"

"Yeah, this morning. Interesting."

"Yeah, what did you find?"

"Fires, abandoned buildings, a few other things, hookers and old ladies and some rehab work over on the next street."

"So, what do you think?"

"I don't know what to think. And the mayor's office already pulled all the records."

"No kidding? They got their spies. Jesus, that was fast."

"Yeah, I'm going to have to wait a while before I find out who owns all that shit, unless you can fill me in."

"I can't do that. You have to find out by yourself."

"But you can tell me if I'm warm. Who the hell is F. X. McGivern?"

"A creep. I can tell you that."

"How do you know him?"

"I know all the creeps."

"Is he connected with an outfit called Articulate?"

"Jesus, you are working."

"Am I getting warm?"

"You are a good reporter. Remember, McGivern is a bum, a regular maggot. I kid you not."

"How come I never heard of him?"

"He's been around but in the background. He's an ozone player, Tony. You never know he's there until you run into him."

"Do I have a story?"

"You're getting there. That's all I wanted to do was check in on you. You're on track. I gotta run."

"Hold on a minute. That Cynthia from Channel Four?"

"Yeah, I just asked you about her."

"Do me a favor, will you? Talk to her. Don't tell her anything. I mean, don't get her going with the stuff I know about. But give her some hearts and flowers. You know. Set her up so she's happy. Tell her about how you can't eat or sleep, whatever. You know, how a man's life can be destroyed by his friends, that sort of thing. But nothing hard, O.K.?"

"I got you. Just enough to keep her off your ass, is that right?"

"Maybe someday I can return the favor."

"Maybe you have already. O.K., let her have this number on condition she doesn't give it out to nobody. And I'll talk to her, but not on camera, not in person, just over the phone."

"A deal."

He immediately called Cynthia, who was grateful for the favor but still a bit cool. Then he called Albanian at the State House, who had a few facts about Articulate. Its officers of record were all women, probably secretarial help, all listed at the same office address on Main Street in Dedham. Its legal counsel was also listed at that address. His name was Otto Otlowski.

He called back the courthouse reporter. "Sally," he said, "any luck with McGivern?"

"Not much. He's bounced around a lot. Had a drinking problem or a drug problem. Don't know which. But he almost had his ticket pulled. Got in a jam with a client over commingling and got off with a reprimand. Did some mob stuff down the Combat Zone. But I think somebody was trying to do him a favor, from what I hear. He ain't the mob lawyer type, a little too unreliable."

"What do you mean he bounced around a lot?" Tony asked.

"He's had two or three different partners."

"Can you find out who they were?"

"I can't tonight, not if I'm going to write anything for tomorrow."

"You got anything good?"

"Fuck you, Tony. You think I should drop everything just to do your legwork."

"Hey, Sally, don't you get on my case, too. All I wanted was an answer, not a frontal assault."

"O.K., yes, I have two good trials, including the murder-rape in the Back Bay. They're hearing the appeal today."

"Jesus, I won't stand in the way of a good murder-rape. O.K., but when you have a chance, if you have a chance, try to track down anything else you can get on McGivern and one other guy, a lawyer in Dedham named Otlowski, Otto Otlowski, O.K.?"

"O.K., I'll get it when I can."

"Great." Tony hung up the phone, dialed information for the office number of F. X. McGivern, then dialed the number. "Is F. X. there?" he asked.

"Yes," said the young woman who answered. "Who's calling?"

"It's Otto," he said.

"Otto who?" she asked.

"Otto Otlowski," he said. There was a pause.

"Excuse me," she said and laid down the phone.

Tony could hear the echoes of conversation, then the clatter as the woman picked up the receiver. "I'm sorry," she said. "There must be some mistake. Otto Otlowski is dead."

"Oh, of course," he said. "I'm sorry I didn't make myself clear. This is his son."

Again the woman put down the receiver, and again he could hear the voices conferring in the office. This time, they were more animated. Finally, he heard a male voice grumbling and drawing closer to the phone and finally saying into the receiver: "Otto Otlowski never married and he had no son, and who is this calling, please?"

Tony had learned enough. He hung up the phone without speaking. He didn't want to give his voice away to McGivern the way McGivern had just given his voice away to him: it was gruff, and bullying, and memorable. He would recognize it when he heard it again.

Tony's anger was now assuaged. It always pleased him when an old reporting trick worked so well. Otlowski and McGivern knew each other. It would be easy to learn now whether they ever worked together. His instincts told him that they had. He telephoned the library and asked them to pull the files on Otlowski and McGivern. Then he hung up the phone and sat back in Bobby Bantam's big chair and smiled.

"Don't smile like that when you're sitting in my chair or somebody will think you own it," said Bobby Bantam as he walked into his office. "I'm the only one entitled to sit in that chair and smile, and I haven't done it in twenty years."

Tony somewhat awkwardly stood up. Although Bobby Bantam allowed Tony to sit at his desk and use his telephone, he didn't necessarily like it. And had Tony not been so intent on trying to track down McGivern, he would have sat more tentatively in Bobby Bantam's chair.

"Here, take your job back," said Tony, moving to the other side of Bobby's desk. "This is a good one I've got going."

"You've got the mayor burning down Duncan Avenue?"

"No, I've got a lawyer named McGivern possibly linked to Articulate. That's a company redeveloping in the neighborhood. And McGivern is a goon lawyer trying to force an old lady out of her apartment on Duncan Avenue."

"That may be good, but it doesn't sound so good to me. Where's the mayor?"

"I don't know yet."

"You mean you don't know at all."

"Not at all, yet. I do know that son of a bitch has pulled all the Duncan Avenue records. Even the Tax Department books."

"And the Building Department?"

"Yeah."

"That's illegal. We ought to go to court. You talk to the lawyer."

"No use. By the time we got a court order, the books would be back. Stanley says there's an internal investigation and that's why we can't have the books."

"The son of a bitch. You got to watch out they don't alter the records. These bastards will do anything."

"I'm not worried about that. They may just want to get some idea of what's in there so they can pull a Scooter all over again. Get in front of any monkey business."

"Well, doesn't that mean the mayor doesn't know anything about any monkey business on Duncan Avenue?"

"It could. But it could also mean they're trying to cover their ass now that they know we're onto the story."

"All I can say is I hope there is a helluva story there. We're like the cavalry trapped at Fort Comanche. We got only twenty bullets left in our guns and there are two thousand Indians out there. No misses, Tony."

"Hey, Bobby. There's no guarantees, either. Come on now, don't all of a sudden get unreasonable, for Christ's sake."

"I know. I just don't like this Bernie bullshit. I have a feeling we should be concentrating our attention elsewhere. But my mind is open. You better get back to your desk and start writing."

□

It was five-thirty in the afternoon before Tony started writing and it was almost seven o'clock at night before he got the lead he wanted. His column began like this:

"Somebody killed Bernie Kremenko.

"Somebody is trying to kill Duncan Avenue.

"Nobody seems to care who killed Bernie. And nobody, least of all the administration of Mayor Connie Haydon, seems to care who is trying to kill Duncan Avenue.

"But Mabel Sloane cares, and so do the handful of other people who are trying to hold on to their homes on what is surely the saddest, most vulnerable and dangerous block in all of Boston — a block in the path of the forces of greed rapidly turning the city into a mecca for tourists and parvenus (that's French for fast-buck artists, pal) and a wasteland for the rest of us folks who happen to have been brought up here.

"Haydon's Fire Department didn't get around to counting the number of buildings that have burned on Duncan Avenue over the past twelve months (the number is six) until asked yesterday by the *Morning News,* and it sees nothing sinister in the fact that all but one of the blazes was attributed to an electrical malfunction. They really ought to talk to some of the torches around town about how easy it is to make arson look like an electrical accident.

"They haven't even gotten around to a definite cause in the fire that claimed Bernie Kremenko's life. None of this is at all difficult to understand. Bernie, after all, was a nobody, a bum, a squatter, a drifter who came in out of the cold and met his death in a building that somebody happened to be torching.

"We'd like to be able to tell you a little this morning about who might be responsible, but public records, basic public records that are routinely available, not just to reporters but to anyone who wants to examine them, weren't available yesterday.

"Mayor Haydon, knowing that the *Morning News* was interested, had them pulled out of their files and brought to his office. An internal investigation, his minions are saying. We have a better word for what's going on. We call it a cover-up."

"Not bad," said Bantam as he looked over Tony's shoulder. "I'd get pretty quickly to the way property is being snapped up around that block. And I'd get to some calculations on the real estate value, too."

"That's coming, that's coming," said Tony. "This should shake them up pretty good, don't you think?"

"Yeah. It'll give the mayor something to worry about. What are we getting on the shyster McGivern?"

"You better shake up your pal down the courthouse; she doesn't seem too anxious to dig into this."

"I'll talk to her, but if you want to get something quick, you'd better handle it yourself."

"Why is it, Bobby, you can never lean on the pretty young things around here, only the crones and the cranes?"

"Don't you hate to see a pretty girl cry? I know I do. Besides, I'd love to fuck her."

"That's what I like about you, Bobby, you're so suave."

"Tell me about it, Tony."

9

"REPORTERS are so full of self-delusion, Tony. They really are. Myself included, when I let myself go on a story," Cynthia was saying as she sat on the sofa in Tony's living room, artfully arranging a mound of moo shu pork onto a Mandarin pancake, then folding it delicately into a compact bar that seemed almost machine-made.

She ate with small bites that barely disturbed the concoction. She was a nibbler rather than an eater. Like most everything else she did, it was considered. The smaller the bites, the more bites she would take and the less she would eat in relation to the energy she expended. It was one of Cynthia's many methods, this one aimed at weight control. She also had her own method of walking, leaning forward on the balls of her feet as a way both to offset her distinctive height and to save the wear on her heels — the most vulnerable part of the shoe. She had her method of sitting — with shoulders thrown back as a way to strengthen her stomach muscles. Yet for all her deliberation, Cynthia remained ever natural, and her artifice struck those who knew her as a reflection of her distinctiveness, not of the gnawing insecurity of a woman who grew up tall, rawboned, and Jewish in the Waspish world of the Massachusetts North Shore. If she was going to be noticed, she would be noticed for her style, not for her size, and she brought her sense of style to everything she did — under the rubric of method.

"It's the letting go," Cynthia was saying. "That's the scary part.

Everything other people see as vital to their lives, reporters can just discard: friends, family, their own health, their chances of ever having money, life, everything. Once we're on the trail of something really good. And when is anything really good? I mean, there was Watergate. The Kennedy assassination. Wars. Patty Hearst."

"Bobby Thomson's home run, don't forget that."

"You know what I mean. We're like Pavlov's dogs. And for what? Here you are, ready to jump off a cliff over Scooter and that crook Connie Haydon. And who'll remember anything about it two years from now?"

"And you? Aren't you ready to jump, too?"

"Why do you say that? Because Scooter is going to talk to me, thanks to you? He won't tell me anything, or else you wouldn't have arranged it. I know you."

"And I know you, too. You can worm a secret out of a stone. I've seen you do it."

"I haven't had much luck with you. Where were you the other night?"

"Forget it."

"I'll forget it, but if I turn up with herpes I'll know who to come after."

He laughed and hugged her. She pushed him away. "I'm not joking," she said.

"O.K. You're still sore, so I'll tell you. I'm onto a helluva story."

"Where? Down on Duncan Avenue?"

He sat back and slapped himself on the forehead. "Isn't anything secret in this town? How the hell do you know that?"

"I heard today from Stanley that he saw you down on Duncan Avenue. That's where Scooter sent you, isn't it?"

"Come on, Cynthia. This is why I shouldn't have set you up with Scooter. You're going to try to grill him on Duncan Avenue, aren't you?"

"There've been a helluva lot of fires down there. I happened to pass through the other day. Bombed out. Tough."

"Christ, Cynthia, stop riding my coattails, for God's sake."

"Riding your coattails. You have a lot of nerve. You know that's what people think. Oh, here comes Cynthia Stoler, Tony's girl, not a brain in her head except what he puts there. Listen, Tony, I know as much about covering this city as you do, except I work in a different medium, where everybody thinks a pretty woman is a fluff-head. And I don't need that brand of bullshit from you."

He threw a chicken wing down onto the paper plate he was eating from. Tony hated to wash dishes. "What are you saying to me?" he asked.

"Nothing, except I was thinking of going down to see what was happening on Duncan Avenue anyway, even before I heard you were down there. And I think I'll head over there tomorrow."

"Goddamn it, Cynthia. That's bush, for Christ's sake."

"No, it isn't. I really had it in mind, I did. I don't care if you believe me. I know it's true."

"Well, good luck. I hope you find something. I'm not sure you will."

"You said it was a hell of a story."

"Hey, I was talking about my story."

"We'll see. Anyway, if I can't trust you, why should you be able to trust me?"

"I can't believe you."

She laughed and threw herself into his arms. She was delighted to find him, for the first time in weeks, free of the great weight of the *Bruise.* All sense of time slipped away, like the sense of separateness, and they were together like old friends, laughing and touching and squeezing, toying with their lust as if it were kited to a spring breeze. After a time, they moved to the shower, where she soaped and scrubbed him and took him into her mouth while the water teemed down around her dark head. Finally, they dried each other and headed to the bed. The telephone rang as he was poised to enter her. Instinctively, Tony reached for it. She was quicker. Bounding from the bed, her breasts bobbing under the mass of water-soaked hair, she seized the phone and hurled it against the wall. "Goddamn it," said Tony, rushing to retrieve the receiver. "It could be something impor-tant."

"Oh, no," she said. "I don't believe it."

"Tony," Bobby Bantam said into the phone, ignoring the clatter that Cynthia created. "We won the hoople of the year award, so help me. The goddamn pope, you hear me, the goddamn pope is coming to town and we haven't got a line; we haven't got a word. What the hell have you been doing all day, trying to sink me? I can't believe it."

Tony, sandwiched between two furies, listened without comprehending at first. Cynthia had thrown herself on the bed and was beating her fist into the pillows.

"Bobby, I can't handle this. Calm down, please," he said.

But Bantam's voice just grew more strident. "Calm down?" he thundered. "The *Mammoth* is leading with the pope bigger than life, and we're out front like the *Christian Science Monitor* with some crap about a bum dying in a fire in a whorehouse of a neighborhood."

"The *Monitor* doesn't cover death, Bobby," he said, speaking with deliberate obtuseness as a way to smother Bobby's rage. It didn't work.

"Tony, you don't understand what I'm saying. Wichita isn't going to wait after they see this one. They're likely to close us down at once for gross incompetence. What are you trying to do to me?"

"Bobby, I don't know what I did to you. I don't even know what the hell you're talking about."

Cynthia kneeled up in the bed and bellowed, "Hang up on the bastard, or I'm leaving, you hear me?"

"I hear you, Cynthia, keep quiet."

He glared at her. Then, turning toward the wall, he said quietly to Bantam, "Bobby, now very slowly, tell me what you're talking about."

"The pope is coming to Boston, that's what I'm talking about. It's all over page one of the *Mammoth* and we haven't a clue, not a goddamn clue, and I just called up that little creep Stanley and he tells me he tried to give you the story this morning and you weren't interested."

"He's a lying son of a bitch."

"Maybe he isn't. Maybe you just weren't listening, you being so intent on that Bernie Kerensky crap."

"Hey, I'm not going to stand here and argue with you. I'm not even sure what you're talking about, but I'll bet you even up right now that it's a phony."

"Tony, they're quoting the chancery."

"Do they have a date?"

"No, they don't have a date. And we don't have a story. We're out there bigger than life with 'Who Killed Bernie Kerensky?' And we could have had the same thing."

Cynthia was now sitting back on the bed, her head in her hands.

"I can't believe it. I can't believe it. Give me that goddamn phone."

"Get away, Cynthia. Bobby, I got to go."

"Listen, Tony, what are we going to do?"

"You're the editor. Replate. Don't ask me."

"Replate. Great. Thanks a lot."

"Good night, Bobby."

He hung up the phone. Cynthia was up on her feet now, putting on her bra. "I'm going. Being with you is like being caught in a nightmare that never ends. I'll see you."

Now Tony was in a fury. "If you go, never come back, Cynthia. Goddamn it. Do you think I asked Bobby to call? The pope is coming. Stanley fed the *Mammoth*. He told Bobby he tried to feed me today and I wouldn't take the story."

"And Bobby believed that?"

"He believes it now, just so he can get mad enough to get the paper replated for the second edition. He won't believe it tomorrow. But what a game they're playing, and now you want to walk out of here."

"Tony, I want us to have a life like two human beings. You should never have answered the phone. You don't care about me. You care about news, and if I stay with you I'm going to become the same way. I'm becoming that way already. I don't want that. I really don't."

Tony glared at her. "Take your clothes off and get back in bed."

"No," she said. "I'm going."

"No, you are not," he said. He grabbed her and began wrestling her back onto the bed. She was half-dressed now, with her skirt on over her panties. He began pulling at the skirt.

"Are you going to rape me?"

"I will if I have to," he said.

"Take the phone off the hook and leave it off," she said.

He walked over to the phone, which was on the floor by the bed, and nudged the receiver off the cradle with his foot. He then climbed into bed where Cynthia was ready. He took her without preliminaries and within seconds she shuddered. "I love it when you're like that," she said.

"You love it or me?" he asked.

"I don't know," she said.

Moments later Tony was asleep.

□

The energy was moving in Tony Owen long before he woke up and felt for Cynthia, who had left for her own place shortly after Tony fell asleep. Without a trace of grogginess, he began girding for the day. All his senses were alive and his mind was totally free of the fog that cushioned it whenever the guilt began to rise in him. He awoke as if cast into a fresh reality where he played a golden hero, young and strong and certain of victory. It was the way he felt in the old days when the outlines of a story broke before his mind as he slept, and while his body rested, his brain plotted the way for him to seize the quarry: the clean, sure hit that would shock the reader into seeing what was obviously true now laid bare in print in the *Bruise*. The story was there, perhaps the story of his life, there in front of him; now he had but to grasp it. He had completely forgotten about the pope until he got to Mike Goukas's deli and spotted the big headlines:

POPE JOHN PAUL II PLANS
TO VISIT BOSTON SOON

The *Mammoth*'s sober headline ran four columns over the top of page one with a story that began:

"Pope John Paul II will visit Boston on a spiritual mission shrouded in mystery, the *Mammoth* learned yesterday.

"Vatican sources would neither confirm nor deny the pontiff's plans, but sources close to the Catholic Archdiocese of Boston said security arrangements were already being drawn up.

"Sources said the visit does not appear to be part of a U.S. tour but a trip limited to Boston itself. But just why the pontiff has singled out Boston for the trip was unclear. 'He has a specific purpose in mind; that's all I can tell you because that's all I know,' one source said.

"His Eminence, Cardinal James Michael Flaherty, declined comment."

The replated page one of the *Bruise* read like this:

POPE JP II
HUB BOUND

The *Bruise* story, for all its verve, was a rewrite, with some license, from the *Mammoth*. It began:

"The globe-trotting Pope John Paul II will embark on a spiritual mission to Boston within the next few weeks, but his sacred agenda remains a closely guarded secret within the Vatican, the *Morning News* learned last night."

A small box on the bottom of page one teased to Tony Owen's column with the headline: WHO KILLED BERNIE KREMENKO?

"What the hell is the pope coming here for, Tony?" asked Mike as Tony studied the two papers, glancing first at his column, then skimming the pages of the *Mammoth* for a reference to Scooter. He found a short story back on the Metro page. It had no new information.

"The pope? Who the hell knows."

"It says here he has a special mission to Boston. Maybe he's coming to bring Christianity," said Mike.

"More likely he's coming to drive out the snakes," said Tony. "Or to give a campaign speech for Connie Haydon."

"So you think he's running?"

"With the pope in his corner, what else is he going to do? Of course he's running. The pope will probably knight him, make him a Knight of the Holy Garter Belt. It's depressing."

Mike poured hot coffee into Tony's cup. "I wouldn't be too depressed. It gives us something to think about. Something a lot more interesting than the mayor's race, especially when no one is going to lay a glove on our man Connie. Though I see you got a whack at him this morning."

"Well, I'm glad somebody read it."

"Good piece. But you know something, Tony? Who cares about Duncan Avenue, really? I mean that's the only way neighborhoods get upgraded. That place has been a sewer as long as I can remember."

A customer at the other end of the counter was waving his coffee cup in the air. "Hey, Mike, for Christ's sake, give me some service."

"Coming right up."

"You know, you sound like my editor, Mike. You're a helluva pal."

"Hey, you may be on to something, but the mayor isn't going to get involved in that kind of stuff. He's got too much class to fool around with property on Duncan Avenue."

"I didn't say he was involved."

"I know you didn't, but I can read between the lines. You think there's something rotten there."

"We'll see."

"You know what makes me laugh about this whole thing?" Mike said. "It's that Haydon is such a lousy Catholic. I mean he's such a lousy Christian, and look at the break he's getting. O.K., I dumped on your column just now. I mean a little. I thought it was interesting and all that. But if the pope wasn't coming, I might have had a different reaction to it. It just looks so much like small potatoes. You know what I'm saying, Tony. I mean I'm talking about the mayor, not you."

Three motormen from the T walked in and sat down alongside Tony. Mike pushed mugs of coffee in front of them and yelled at the waitress at the other end of the counter. "Hey, Helen, get down here and wait on these gentlemen, will you? I'm in a deep conversation with Tony."

"We better continue it later on," said Tony. "I've got to run."

□

Bobby Bantam was waiting for Tony as soon as he entered the newsroom. Tony had a good idea what was coming, that Bobby had swallowed the bait.

"You've got to drop that Kerensky story for now," he said, after pulling Tony into his office. "You can get back to it in a few days, but there's only one story in town right now and that's the pope."

"What do you have in mind?" asked Tony, who knew from long experience that it would be futile to fight Bobby on the general direction he wanted to travel. The only chance for a win was on the specifics. Bobby wasn't always strong on specifics.

"I want you to find the saint," he said.

"What saint?" asked Tony.

"The saint the pope is coming to honor. You know there must be a saint somewhere. Popes don't travel just to see ordinary people. There's got to be a saint around here, a Mother Theresa or a Saint — what the hell is the name of the guy who talked to the birds?"

"Yeah, Bobby. You don't want me to find the saint. Have one of those kids on the city desk find a saint. And when they get him, I'll interview him."

Bobby Bantam frowned. He disliked fighting with Tony, but he was plainly unhappy with Tony's Duncan Avenue obsession. He shrugged, stood, and edged out from behind his massive desk. He walked to the window, surveying the skyline sliced here and there with the ochre steelwork of new buildings awaiting a shimmering skin of metal and glass. Then his eyes locked on the Hotel Congress. "My God, Tony, would you believe that?"

Tony joined Bantam at the window and the two of them peered in the direction of the Congress. "I can't believe what I'm seeing," said Bobby. "But that's got to be a scaffold up there by those letters. Am I right or wrong?"

"Bobby, it's enough to make believers out of us."

The sight could not be denied. A work crew was erecting scaffolding on the long-untended sign.

"Those fuckers are fighting back at long last. They're fixing the sign. A portent. Maybe we'll be saved after all, Tony. Jesus, after all this time."

He rushed back behind his desk and picked up the phone. And banged out the number of the city desk. "Walshie, you there? Great. Look, Walshie, get a reporter over to the Hotel Congress right away and find out if they have new owners or whatever the hell has happened. They're fixing the sign. Hey, I don't want to hear your troubles. There's got to be somebody breathing in the city room. I don't give a damn who you send. Get somebody over there. Now. O.K. O.K."

He hung up the phone. "Walsh is flipping out. He can't even cover miracle stories anymore."

"He really doesn't have any reporters out there, Bobby. The city room is like a morgue."

Bobby frowned. "You think I don't know that? Of course I know that. You have to make do. You have to go with your best shot. We're down to the last few days or weeks, and people know it and they're already giving up. That's what has got to be resisted. That's defeatism, Tony. That's no way to go out in style. That's going the easy way. There's always somebody to send. I ought to dump him and put Molly Minton in that job. At least she'd go out blazing."

"Bobby, you got to be kidding!"

"No, I'm not. She does what I tell her to do and she doesn't give me any excuses. So the reporters hate her. So what? Walshie says we haven't got any reporters anyway. And it would make me feel good."

Tony winced. For all the years he had worked with Bobby, he never learned to anticipate his traps until he had fallen into one. Now, he recognized once again too late that Bobby had cut the ground out from under him. Yes, it was clear, he had conceded the point himself, that there were no reporters available to do what had to be done: to find the object of the pope's visit, to find the saint in their midst.

"I know I have a helluva story going, Bobby. I know it."

"Will it save our necks?"

"Probably not."

"Would a campaign to find the saint save our necks?"

"Probably not. There's probably not even a saint to be found. Where did this saint business come from anyway, City Hall?"

Bobby ignored the question. "But which would help the most? Which would get the energy running and keep us in the ball game longer?"

"I'm not sure."

"Ah, Tony, but I am. It's the saint. It doesn't matter if he's real. I can see the whole campaign. We can start tomorrow with a readers' poll. Name your saint and why. A hundred and fifty words. The winner gets a set of specially blessed rosary beads and a chance to meet the pope."

"Cash would be better," Tony said.

"Cash would be crass, a sacrilege," replied Bobby.

Bobby spoke with a tinge of solemnity that Tony felt at first was deliberately ironic until he looked into Bobby's eyes and saw no hint of mirth. The seriousness in Bobby's face and voice touched something in Tony and he smiled. And when Bobby noticed the smile and remarked on it, Tony laughed out loud.

"Hey, old buddy, we're fighting for our lives. I don't see what's so comical."

At that, Tony laughed louder and then became convulsed as the idea of a search for a saint took hold in his mind, and the imagery of the *Bruise*'s final crusade and the final failure of Bobby's own sense of absurdity began to double him over. He laughed until the tears came and then he began to cough, in great rasping waves, until his ribs hurt and he reached for a handkerchief in his back pocket, all the while looking away from Bobby for fear that a fresh wave of guffaws would sweep over him. And then he screwed up his face into the most sober look he could muster, and he asked with solemnity that matched Bobby's own:

"And what should I do about Bernie Kremenko?"

As soon as he said the words, he began to laugh again, and when he looked at Bobby he could see the anger filling his face. Bobby sputtered: "I don't give a shit what you do, just find me a saint." Saying that, he walked out of his office, the steam almost rising from his back. Tony sat in the chair opposite the now empty desk and laughed for a moment longer before he followed Bobby back out into the city room.

Bobby was over by the city desk, talking to Jack Walsh.

"Hey, Bobby," he said. "Maybe it's Bernie the pope is coming to canonize. Maybe they'll have a special ceremony down on Duncan Avenue."

"You're not funny, Tony. You're not funny at all."

☐

Malachy Owen sat in the rear of a delicatessen around the corner from the *Bruise* and stared at the replated headline with reverence and awe: POPE JP II HUB BOUND. At first he couldn't believe it, then his doubts gave way to a sense of wonder at the workings of God in the world of men. But he must be careful, he told himself, lest he give in to the sin of pride. Perhaps his prayers had been answered, but he must not presume, he must not allow himself to presume on God's intentions. But a pattern seemed to be unfolding. The pope would receive him — of course, he would. Tony would arrange it. It would be part of the deal. He would free Johnny Weissmuller. That would be for starters. But there was so much more to be done, so much to be said. He would need time, not just a few minutes. It would be difficult, even for Tony, to get him all the time he needed. Ah, but he had to trust in God. He was already on the case. That was for sure. But he had to do some planning, some hard, detailed thinking about how he would proceed. Tony would exact a price, of course, a big price. Maybe going into the chancery's home. If that was the sacrifice required, so be it. Still holding the *Bruise* in his grimy hands, he put his sneakered feet up on the bench, where he sat and leaned his head against the wall and dreamed of what he would say. He would tell the Holy Father about his trouble in the order, and that no one had understood the uniqueness of his mission, and that it took a special kind of person, a special kind of priest. Oh, the things he had witnessed that no priest had ever witnessed, except maybe back in pagan days when they forced Christians to watch the most degrading spectacles as a way to rip them away from their inner vision.

Malachy could see the look of profound sadness in the Holy Father's eyes as he heard his story. He could even see the tears begin to brim there as he called his secretary over and ordered him to take down all the essential information. Then he would turn to Malachy and ask him the question he had been waiting all his life to answer. Yes, the pope would have the question that would confirm the meaning of all the misery he ever encountered anywhere in the world. It was what he had learned from Johnny W. locked away in that dark hell of a place in Mattapan. "Yes, yes," he would say as he fell on his knees before the pontiff, and he would exclaim: "You see, we are matched; we are brothers. The answer is here. It's poetry. Don't you see? It's what Johnny says it is. It's poetry. Poetry, that's the answer." And the pope would sit there, dumbstruck, and when he regained his senses, he would say, softly, and from the heart: "Do you know I was a poet once?"

□

"Get your feet off the bench, you bum," the proprietor boomed, and reaching down, he clutched Malachy by the heels and roughly swung his feet back onto the floor. "And now that you've finished your coffee, you can beat it."

Malachy stood up and threw his shoulders back and said: "The Holy Father is coming; you should be looking into your heart for the wellsprings of charity and try to see Christ in everyone you encounter."

"Don't talk mumbo jumbo to me, you little cockroach. Get your ass out of here."

He grabbed Malachy by the shoulders and shoved him through the doorway into the street. Malachy almost fell forward onto his face, but he caught the stanchion of a traffic light and stayed upright, then spun back toward the deli entrance and shouted, "It's a man of God you are roughing up."

Momentarily bewildered by the violence, Malachy took a few steps back toward the shelter. Then he paused, retraced his steps, and headed back to the deli. The owner spotted him as he came through the door and came rushing from behind the counter. "I thought I just threw you out of here."

Speaking quietly, Malachy replied, "I left my paper behind. I hadn't finished reading it."

He picked up the paper and walked outside. He thought for a moment of where he might go to sit in peace and read the paper. He was desperately anxious to find out all he could about the papal visit. But he also wanted to read his brother's column. Sometimes, he found messages there for him, messages that Tony didn't realize he was transmitting. Lately, however, the messages were not apparent, if indeed any messages were being sent, and Malachy felt a growing concern for his brother. He was, it seemed to Malachy, becoming increasingly closed, more remote. Something was killing his spirit, drying up his soul, choking off the poetry in his vision.

Malachy walked down the street. As he passed the Do Drop Inn, he spotted Sailor, one of his street companions.

"Fadder, come here. I got dough." The words whistled out of his mouth as he pulled Malachy into the dark doorway. "I got almost three bucks. Come on."

Malachy followed Sailor up to the bar. It was barely nine o'clock, but three street people were already inside the tavern, which was dimly lit and smoky. The bartender was sitting by the beer taps, scanning the *Bruise*. Sailor ordered two shots of Old Forester and a bottle of Ballantine. He tilted the bottle and poured all but an ounce down his throat before handing it to Malachy. Malachy drained what was left and tossed down his shot of whiskey. He then walked over to a table that caught the morning sun and opened his *Bruise*. He turned to his brother's column on page six and read the headline: WHO KILLED BERNIE KREMENKO?

It took him several moments before his eyes could focus on the small print. Then he read:

"His name was Bernie Kremenko and he never hurt a fly. All he wanted out of life was a dry place to sleep, a crust of bread, and a little booze to kill the pain. He was a little guy who got in the way of the big guys, and now he's in potter's field.

"He's there because he walked into a building on Duncan Avenue March 6, walked down a flight of stairs into the basement, found a cozy spot near the furnace where the coal bin used to be years ago, and fell asleep with his pint of muscatel. He didn't realize that the abandoned building he selected was the very same one the big guys had picked to torch that night. The arsonists didn't even bother to look for him. They just sprayed their gasoline down the basement steps and threw a match, and Bernie never knew what happened to him.

"The administration sees nothing out of the ordinary in the fires on Duncan Avenue. 'It's a slum area and slum areas have fires' is the way one of Connie Haydon's aides put it the other day.

"Besides . . . nobody has died . . . nobody but Bernie Kremenko, an old bum society threw away years ago. . . . I personally think that's the kind of heartless reasoning that is turning this city into a province exclusively for the well-to-do. What would have become of our forefathers if they came to this city after the Famine and found only the rich could live here? They would have perished. They lived because this city was what all great cities should be — places where there is room for all kinds of people — the rich, the poor, the unfortunate like the Bernie Kremenkos of this world."

Malachy suddenly felt suffused in the light of grace. His doubts about his brother melted away, and he was convinced that the pope's visit was tied to his own mission, to the search for sanctity on the streets. And Bernie Kremenko was another aspect of the same reality that kept Johnny Weissmuller a captive in the madhouse. Perhaps he was a great man, too, a political prisoner, a martyr put to death by the new Romans. The pope would understand that. Surely, he did understand that, or he wouldn't be coming to this place.

Folding the paper, Malachy got up and walked stiffly to the bar, where Sailor was trying to bully the bartender into letting him have another shot on the cuff. Malachy interrupted. "Sailor," he said, "did you know Bernie Kremenko?"

"I don't know no Bernies. You got a quarter?"

"No."

"Then let's get out of this place."

"Not today. I've got to be alone. I've got to think. Something important is happening. I've got to be ready when needed."

10

MAYOR HAYDON'S staff was waiting at the round conference table for fully fifteen minutes before the mayor arrived, walking sprightly from his main office into the antechamber, his lips pressed in a small smile. He had just read the morning papers, and though it was not a complete triumph, it was a victory. Were it not for the annoyance of the Tony Owen column, the results were precisely what the mayor had hoped and bargained for. The *Mammoth* was gushing with news and excitement about the papal visit, and the *Bruise* had all but swept Tony Owen under the rug in its final editions — the only editions Haydon cared about because they were the ones sold in the city. The Scooter story was buried deep within the Metro section of the *Mammoth,* and except for Tony Owen's column, the *Bruise* skipped the corruption subject entirely. The television stations, taking their cue from the *Mammoth,* as they did customarily, concentrated entirely on the pope.

"Score one for the white hats," said the mayor as he sat down at the head of the table. "Now we have to keep up the campaign until the pope actually arrives. Stanley, you dig up the names of every holy person who ever set foot in this city, and keep feeding them to the papers, both papers. I don't care if you have to invent people, just come up with them. I'm sure there must have been a Jesuit or two burned by the Indians, or the Pilgrims or somebody. Anyway, dig up the data. Head out to BC or Holy Cross. I don't want anybody running dry on these things. And stay in touch hourly if you have to with the chancery. Marry those bastards over there. Jesus, I can't get over the *Mammoth.* Christ almighty, did we ever score!"

"It was almost too easy," said Corinne. "I'm afraid we aren't out of the woods yet. The Tony Owen column was a little nasty."

The mayor's tight little smile dissolved. "The hell with Tony Owen." Then, turning to Stanley, he said, "If you get any inquiries about anything in the *Bruise* or in the Tony Owen piece, I want you to say to anybody who asks: 'All that is, is desperation crap from a dying newspaper.' I could care less what the *Bruise* or any of its rum-dum hacks have to say about me."

The corporation counsel sat with a manila folder in front of him. "I have information for you on the matters you requested yesterday. Do you want to hear it?"

"Is it good news or indifferent, Harold?"

"It's inconclusive, to a degree. But it could be quite bad," said Hooper.

"Lay it out."

"O.K. What's happened, apparently, is this. A company called Articulate, Inc., incorporated in Dedham, with office help listed as the officers, has been buying up every piece of land they can get hold of on Duncan Avenue and the adjacent streets. It's a pretty impressive parcel, if you lay it out. Take a look at this."

He pulled a plot map from the folder and laid it out on the table in front of the mayor. "The properties shaded in green are owned by Articulate."

"Hey, they own practically the whole neighborhood," Stanley said.

"This is amazing," said the mayor. "And I don't know anything about these people. How the hell did this happen?"

"I'll get to that in a moment, Connie," said Hooper. "That's the part that's inconclusive."

"How long has this been going on?" Corinne asked.

"For at least three years now, they've been buying up properties."

"Jesus, they must have six acres there, enough for a goddamn hotel and a parking garage."

"They have precisely seven acres right now, or they will have as soon as they can get title to about four more pieces on Duncan Avenue. The pieces shaded here in blue," Hooper said.

"How is it zoned?" the mayor asked.

"That's very interesting. The zoning has been changed, or it was changed about two years ago. Here it is. March 8. The Zoning Board of Appeals approved the change to A4-CR. They could build a hotel, with your approval, of course."

"You mean that, they could go through the Zoning Board without me knowing anything about it? That's incredible."

"And that's part of the problem," said Hooper. "I called Alan Arnold last night, and he said the Zoning Board approved it on the assumption you wanted it."

"And how the hell did that happen?"

"Well, Alan said your brother-in-law came to see him and told him he had discussed the matter with you in detail and it was O.K."

"That son of a bitch."

"I take it he didn't discuss it with you," said Hooper.

"You're goddamn right he didn't."

"Well, that's how the approvals happened. People just assumed."

"I'll give you 'people just assumed,' Holy Christ. Is Tommy Mannion behind Articulate?"

"That's what I don't know for sure. It's hard to say for certain, but it appears that one of his close friends is involved."

"Oh, Christ. You should see some of that guy's friends. Which one of them is it?"

"F. X. McGivern."

"Francis Xavier, that shyster. Hey, get this cleaned up right now. If McGivern is involved, it's crooked, and we've got a helluva mess on our hands. I told Tommy I didn't want him hanging around with people like McGivern. Christ almighty, the old neighborhood strikes again. They grew up together. I can just see how this happened, and he never says a word to me, just uses my name and people are assuming all over this town that I've got a secret piece in this big deal on Duncan Avenue."

"Well, it is a big deal," said Hooper. "The Real Estate Department estimates that the parcel right now is worth about fifteen million bucks, especially with the zoning break. Even without it, it would've been worth plenty, just for condominiums. Now they can put up a Symphony Hotel. And it's a gold mine for somebody."

"And this is why Tony Owen was down on Duncan Avenue. He'll croak us all. Jesus, he could have me sent to jail."

"Don't get ahead of the problem, Connie," said Hooper. "I have no evidence that he has a piece of any of this. I don't even know for sure that McGivern is involved, except that the preliminary work was done by a now deceased Dedham lawyer named Otto Otlowski. McGivern used to work out of his office."

"Is that all you have?" asked Haydon, his tone somewhat relieved.

"Officially, that's all."

"And unofficially?"

"Unofficially, the word is that it's McGivern and Tommy who set up Articulate as a straw and that they are the principals."

"The principals acting in my behalf."

"Yes, that's the word on the street."

"And that's what Scooter fed to the *Bruise*. O.K., we've got a helluva problem, counselor. What's your advice?"

"Well, there are options, of course, assuming that what seems to be the story is the story. And I think the fastest way to determine the truth is to talk to Tommy Mannion. See just how deep his involvement goes. If it's just McGivern . . ."

"McGivern doesn't have a pot to piss in," said the mayor. "He's fronting for somebody. I know that."

"You don't know that, Connie," said Corinne. "You feel it."

"I feel it to a certainty, then," said Haydon.

"Assuming you're right, Connie, here are some suggestions, if you care to hear them," said Hooper.

"Go ahead," said the mayor.

"You can go public with the story, assuming that if you don't, the *Bruise* will. You do, in effect, what you did with Scooter. You go to the FBI or the AG. The AG may be the better bet. He'd be more sensitive to the political nuances here. You lay out the whole story. You insist you knew nothing of what was happening down there, that you just learned through your internal investigation into the death of that derelict. You beat the *Bruise* to the punch and you walk away with minimal damage, as a man who trusted too much."

The mayor frowned. "That'll play beautifully at home. Here's a guy so squeaky clean he'd turn in his own kin."

"That, Connie, would depend entirely on the scope of your kin's involvement. He may be peripheral to it; he may be smart enough to have kept things at arm's length, at least legally."

"We'll soon know the answer to that. But let's stick to the worst-case scenario: that he's in this up to his eyeballs. What else can we do?"

Stanley sat uneasily at the edge of his chair, as if terrified that he might be called upon to offer advice. Corinne leaned forward, her elbows on the table, her head resting in her hands, her brows furrowed in concentration.

Haydon leaned back in his big leather chair, playing with a yellow pencil. Hooper was cool and crisp. He had anticipated most of the mayor's questions, most of the mayor's responses, and he was prepared and assured.

"Here are some other options," he said. "Tommy could deny categorically he has any involvement in the deal, destroy any evidence, if any exists, linking him to the straws, blame the *Bruise* for embarking on a vendetta to get you, and then disappear."

"What do you mean 'disappear'?" asked Corinne.

"I mean get the hell out of town, lay low, until the whole thing is over."

"And if it's never over?" asked the mayor. "Remember, a man has been killed."

"That doesn't mean there's been a homicide. The arson squad only said it looks suspicious. They didn't say it was arson. They could rule it out. That would minimize the criminal responsibility."

"This is a political problem," said Stanley.

"It's both," said Hooper.

"Keep your mouth shut until I ask you to speak," said the mayor, turning to Stanley.

"An important aspect of any option is to make sure there is no finding of arson," said Hooper. "And that's delicate."

"The Fire Department is no problem," said Corinne. "The problem is the *Bruise.* They could call for an inquest and the DA would have to grant it."

"The boys at fire headquarters wouldn't stand up," said Stanley.

The mayor glared at him but said nothing.

"Everywhere we turn there's the one problem," said Hooper. "And that leads me to a third option. Dealing with Tony Owen and the *Bruise.*"

"And how do we do that?" asked the mayor.

"You're not totally without resources to do that," said Hooper. "Gridlock needs help. You can help them stay in business by giving them a tax holiday. In return, they're unlikely to knock your block off."

"Hey," said the mayor, "they want to go out of business in this town. The last thing they want is for me to come up with a way for them to keep losing dough around here. Then they *will* knock my block off, for putting them in a public relations bind. No, forget Gridlock."

"Well, if you don't want to deal with Gridlock, you can deal with Tony Owen. If he's not going to break the story, no one is."

"We can get Raleigh to give him a job," said Stanley.

"You know how that would play out," said Corinne. "Besides, there's his girlfriend. She's probably on to it, too."

"And there's no reason to believe she's an independent player."

"Which means what?" said the mayor.

"Which means," said Hooper, "that if Tony were out of the picture, there's no reason to believe she'd get anywhere with the story."

"That's ridiculous," said Corinne. "She's a good reporter. She was good before she knew Tony Owen."

"Yeah, but he gave her that special edge she's been using on us," said Stanley.

Haydon sat silently. "How do we get Tony Owen out of the picture, short of hiring a leg breaker?" he asked, finally.

"That's the real problem, silencing that guy," said Hooper. "And the way to silence him most effectively is to close down that paper, once and for all. Get Gridlock to pull the plug before he can fill in all the blanks on this story. That's what we should be concentrating on. Gridlock and that publisher of theirs, what's his name?"

"Elmer Granger," said Stanley.

"Elmer, that's the guy. I'll pop in over there today and have lunch. I want to see if we can do some business. Meanwhile, let's see if the pope has the kind of impact on Bobby Bantam I think he will. If I'm right, Tony Owen is going to be up to his ass in Holy Rollers. O.K., counselor, I'll be talking to you after I have a family conference. Stanley, get going on the other stuff. And Corinne, hang in here a moment. I want to talk to you about another matter."

The mayor stood up and watched Hooper and Stanley walk out the door. "Close it after you, Stanley," he said.

Once the door was closed, the mayor moved to the sofa. "Corinne, this is a disaster. You realize that?"

"Of course," she said, and sat on the sofa beside him, her hand patting his knee as if to reassure him. "Do you think Eileen knows?"

"I don't know," he said. "But I do know she'll expect me to do all I can to protect Tommy. And I don't think she'll be too pleased with anything short of a cover-up, which at this point looks almost impossible."

"Connie, you shouldn't get out ahead of the facts on this. It's like Hooper says. It all depends on the degree of involvement and the deniability. It could be there. You know that."

"No, I see the whole picture," he said. "It's as clear as a bell. Tommy, playing the big shot, uses my name behind my back. Everybody bends over, thinking they're doing me a favor, and the next thing you know I'm in the soup for something I didn't do. It's almost laughable."

Corinne reached over and rubbed his neck. "Connie, you may be misreading Eileen. She has as much right as you do to be furious at Tommy. He's messing with her life, too, you know."

"You don't know Eileen," he said.

The mayor stood up abruptly and moved to the window. Corinne remained poised on the sofa, studying his back and the way he arched his neck as he looked down at the crowds moving in the marketplace below. He finally turned back to her and said:

"You realize she'll use anything she can get her hands on to destroy me if something happens to her brother. He's precious to her. She could care less about his principles. It's all flesh and bone. That's all that counts with her, and she thinks I'm something less than human because I don't feel the family in the same way she does. She'll try to destroy you, too, Corinne."

"You mean she'll go to Stella Ferral?" she asked, almost abstractedly.

"She might. She might. She has no evidence, of course, but she wouldn't need it. It would be blind rage. And anything could happen. I'm telling you this to prepare you. There may not be much time after we talk tonight, especially if it blows up in my face. Then, if I were you, I'd be ready to leave."

"You mean go on a vacation? Maybe I could travel with Tommy. Just disappear."

"I'm not kidding, Corinne. You might have to leave abruptly, for your own sake."

"You sound so cold, Connie."

"That's because I'm scared."

She lurched to her feet and moved to his side by the window. Pulling him out of view by the people below, she embraced him. He did not respond, but stood stiffly, his body bristling.

"I'll go home now, Connie," she said. "And wait for you to call."

He looked back toward the crowds below and said nothing. She moved quickly out of the room, and it wasn't until she reached her own office that she gave way to the tears.

□

It wasn't fear that Corinne had felt in Haydon; it was fury. Once alone in his office, he let the rage flow into his shoulders and arms and hands. Then he walked over to the sofa and began to rain down punches and kicks into its padded contours. The blows fell for a full minute but served only to fuel his anger because the sofa was so soft it merely absorbed them. He looked for something to smash and seized upon a porcelain lamp that was more decorative than practical (it cast only a soft glow, too soft for reading), and taking it in both hands, he lifted it above his head and hurled it against the cinder-block wall. The crash brought his bodyguard running from the adjacent room.

"Forget it," Haydon said to him. "I'm doing some redecorating. Get the hell out of here."

The bodyguard retreated and Haydon sank into the sofa and tried to think of a way out. But everywhere his mind turned, he saw himself facing a blank wall. "Duncan Avenue," he said to himself, "who would believe it?"

Perhaps, he thought, it would be smart to contact Tony Owen directly, concede to him that, yes, for the most part over the years you have been right in what you said about me: yes, I have cut corners, yes, I have even made some money, none of it illegally, mind you, although there were some dubious transactions to be sure. Give the devil his due. Tony, you have read me right. But on this one, I don't care what you've done in the past, on this one I am 100 percent in the clear. I know nothing about it. Nothing.

And then it hit him. Oh, my God. He remembered a conversation. Jesus, it was two years ago. A Belgian development team wanted to know about building a hotel on Duncan Avenue. What did I do? I sent them to see somebody down in zoning. Jesus, it was Alan Arnold at the Zoning Board. Did I ever talk to Tommy about that? Oh, Christ. Maybe I did, just in passing, about underutilized parts of the city and what might go good there. Could Tommy have known about the Belgians? I'll have to ask. But I'd lay it out to Tony. On this one, there was no intention to cut any corners, to make a killing, to build a retirement fund. None at all. It just looks that way. Tony might go for that, especially if I tell him about the family problem. He's got one, too, with his crazy brother. He knows you can't be responsible for what your relatives do. Look at Jimmy Carter. Oh, Jesus, he'd croak me.

The intercom buzzed. It was his secretary. "Bill Raleigh is holding. Do you want to talk to him?"

"No," he snapped. Then he caught himself. "By all means. Put him through."

The phone rang and he picked it up. "Bill," he said. "You guys looked awfully good this morning. You pushed the opposition closer to the brink."

"Thanks, Connie. You were a big help. This is a helluva story."

"Yeah, it is. What are you going to do about finding out the purpose of the pope's visit?"

"We're not exactly sure. I think we'll have our man in Rome try to work the Vatican and see if we can get some more definite clues. I'd rather not go out on a limb with the pope. But it's a helluva story in any case. The town will be hopping."

"It's the only story in town," said the mayor. "I guess the *Bruise* will be climbing all over it from now on."

"You can bet on that one. They'll go after the saint angle. We might, too, in a more hypothetical way. If there were a holy man or woman in Boston history who would be likely to draw the pope, who would he or she be? We might do something like that, an historic overview, so to speak."

"The *Bruise* will be knocking on convent doors all over town, I'll bet," said the mayor.

"Or they'll be trying to find out more about that bum on Duncan Avenue," said Raleigh. "That might be a pretty good story, too."

"Hey, they're making a mountain out of a molehill. That wasn't even arson out there, believe me, Bill. It's a nothing story. Tony

Owen has got this compulsion to come after me and he'll seize on anything."

"Well, that was a tough piece. We're probably going to look into it ourselves."

"Hey, Bill. We had this conversation the other morning. I guess we haven't progressed anywhere since then. If you want to pump up a nothing story from that dying rag trying to compete with you, then go ahead."

Raleigh paused. "Connie, please don't be offended, but I think you are overreacting. You're working too hard again. Maybe you should take a few days off in the mountains or someplace. The Scooter business may have you unhinged."

Haydon almost slammed the phone down in Raleigh's ear, but caught himself just in time. Instead, he said, "Bill, if you weren't my friend, I'd take what you just said as an insult I would never forgive. Since you are my friend, I know that you meant nothing but concern by the remark. But lay off, please."

"O.K., Connie, but keep in mind that it is a newspaper that I'm running, and as much as I like you, I have a certain responsibility that can, at times, transcend friendship."

"It hasn't before, has it?"

"That's because you were more understanding of what a newspaper is all about than you seem to be right now."

Connie sighed, just loud enough for Raleigh to hear it, then apologized. "Go ahead," he said. "You're right. I'm telling you that what Tony Owen is writing about Duncan Avenue is garbage, but you're right. If you think it's your duty to see for yourself, put somebody on it. Put a reporter on it and see what he comes up with. He'll come up with just what I'm telling you. See for yourself. But I didn't want to get bogged down in this conversation. I wanted to find out from you when the two of us could have lunch with the cardinal on the papal thing. You interested? Just great. Have your girl work out a date with my girl, and we'll set it up today or tomorrow."

The mayor hung up the phone and sat back in his big leather chair. He could see clearly what was happening this very moment at the *Mammoth*. He could see Bill Raleigh reaching for the phone to make another call, one that would put a reporter on to the Duncan Avenue story. The mayor already knew who that reporter would be, and despite himself, he smiled at the thought of Henry Horn-blower.

□

Cynthia Stoler was a menace in the newsroom. Not only would yawning holes appear in her stories, but inaccuracies would pop up as well. She was capable of making a mess out of a routine identification. Once, she even reported from the wrong town. Having been in Hingham to cover the raising of a new church steeple, she told her viewers later that afternoon she was still in Hingham, when in reality she was covering a hazardous-waste story in Weymouth.

But once excited by a story, the bored, spacy Cynthia evaporated, and in her place would be a reporting machine that relentlessly swept aside every obstacle in the path of the story, gathering and sorting each detail with the eye of a diamond merchant. It was this Cynthia that seemed to emerge each time a news director grew exasperated enough to consider summoning the other Cynthia to his office and advising her to find a more suitable occupation.

It was the turned-on Cynthia Stoler who broke the story about the housing project where more than half the girls between the ages of fourteen and sixteen were pregnant. It was this Cynthia who led a camera crew to the secluded spot under the Mystic River Bridge where policemen on the graveyard shift slept to be fresh for their moonlighting jobs in the morning. Cynthia found the Boston man who had been married nine times. She found the city's most burglarized apartment house: twenty-five break-ins in less than a month in a building with twenty-eight units.

But it had been three months since her last hit, and she could detect the looks of grumbling disapproval in the eyes of her superiors. She needed a hit. She also needed to teach Tony a lesson. He was so smug about his own role in the city, so condescending about hers. Only rarely would he concede that television reporters were also journalists, with a craft and style and professional standards. He applauded her when she broke the policemen-cooping story. But he rode her ragged for a week when she misidentified the town. "Cynthia, you're a helluvan actress," he would tell her. "But that's really all you are, a performer. You should've gone to acting school."

He didn't mean it, of course. It was his way to ride her, she told herself. But down deep, she resented it and longed for the day when she would compete against him head to head. She would show him what she could do. She felt the competition keenly this morning after the way they had made love the night before. Oh, Tony will be preening like a peacock all day because he made me come on his terms.

Power was the basis of their relationship. She understood that better than he. Yes, they had other things that bound them to each other, the same set of instincts that immediately pronounced something good, true, or decent, the same taste in friends, the same fundamental skepticism toward life. They also had a special chemistry, a blend of sexuality and competitive fervor, that kept them tuned to each other's moods. The health of their relationship depended on a certain equilibrium of more subtle forces, however, and nothing kept Tony confined to a wasteland of feeling more than a dry spell in his own reporting that corresponded to a string of successes by Cynthia. That was when Tony turned seriously to liquor to numb the sense of his own defeat at the hands of a woman, his woman. And Cynthia, intuitively aware of the source of Tony's malaise, would invariably bank the fires of her own ambition and succumb to boredom until she heard the siren call of the next good story. And then the cycle would repeat itself. Now Tony was riding high and it was Cynthia's turn to climb over his shoulders.

She sat in her cubicle down a long narrow corridor deep within the entrails of the television station and dialed Scooter Conroy's number. After ten rings, he picked up the phone.

"You're persistent," he said after Cynthia introduced herself. "O.K., you have me. What do you want to know?"

"Well, Scooter, I don't have any direct questions for you over the telephone. I'm a television reporter, you know. I would really like to get you on camera."

"Impossible."

"But, Scooter, I want to do a really sympathetic piece on a man who suddenly finds himself facing a prison term because he was obeying orders."

"I didn't say that, Cynthia."

"Oh, I know you didn't. But isn't it obvious? But please, I don't want to get into that. I just want to sit down with you and talk about your life and what's ahead, and what's in your heart and your mind. I'd like to come up with a package that's kind of a tribute to a man in crisis, a very special kind of man with an enormous number of friends in this city. It's not something I can do over the phone."

Now it was Scooter's turn to pause. "Look here, Cynthia? That's your name, right? Cynthia. I promised Tony I would talk to you even though my lawyer would kill me. No press, he tells me, no press at all. I made an exception for you because I like your boyfriend, but Jesus, now you're trying to take advantage of my good nature. You are, you know."

"But Scooter, if you can trust Tony, you can trust me," she said, her voice taking on just a trace of the Southern accent she had acquired one summer in a girl's camp in North Carolina. "It's really important to me," she said, quietly. Then, pausing artfully, she added, "It could mean my job, Scooter. It really could."

"O.K., I'll see you, but no camera. That's final."

"O.K. Where can I find you? I'll be right over."

☐

Cynthia arrived at the address on Dartmouth Street in the Back Bay shortly before noon. She carried a bottle of Beaujolais, two sandwiches, a six-pack of Budweiser, and a Sony tape recorder. An unshaved Scooter came to the door.

"I brought lunch," she said. "I thought you might be hungry."

Scooter hadn't been prepared for a woman as young and pretty as Cynthia. Suddenly, he felt embarrassed by his growth of beard and his rumpled trousers. For a moment, he hesitated before allowing Cynthia into the apartment. She headed immediately for the kitchen, where she pulled the food from the bag and yelled back to Scooter:

"Do you prefer beer or wine with your lunch?"

"I think I'll have coffee," he said, and headed for the kitchen himself. He put the kettle on to boil and excused himself. "Do you mind if I shave?" he said. "You got here earlier than I thought."

"I don't mind at all. I'll fix the coffee."

Within ten minutes, a shaved and freshly dressed Scooter joined Cynthia in the kitchen, where she had laid the sandwiches on plates and found napkins and silverware. She had also opened the bottle of wine and poured herself a glass.

"I feel sorry for you, Scooter," she said when he had taken his seat at the table. "You really deserve better."

She had worn a white silk blouse that buttoned down the front.

She had deliberately left half the buttons undone, and as she spoke she leaned over just enough to test Scooter's reaction. Later, she would take herself to task for her shamelessness, but for now she was having fun, enjoying the contradictory impulses of interest and embarrassment she was stirring in a man old enough to be her father. She also noted that he was not an unhandsome man. His face was rugged if prematurely worn, and his eyes were kindly and intelligent although red from booze and lack of sleep. She spotted a nearly empty bottle of J&B on the kitchen counter near the sink.

He stared at her and said, "If you weren't Tony's girl and I was a little younger, I wouldn't be so comfortable sitting here."

"You don't seem comfortable at all," she said and laughed. He joined in the laughter and she hit the record switch on the Sony.

"What do you want to know?" he asked, and this time his tone was cooperative.

"As I said, I want to know about you," she answered.

"O.K., Cynthia, I'll tell you this much. It hurts. It really hurts. We've been friends for all these years, not so much me and Connie. I mean not on a personal level. But Eileen and me. Jesus, we went through school together and we always stayed close. Her family and my family were like related. Not really, but I called her mother Aunt Aggie and she called my mother and father Aunt Honora and Uncle Frank. We were always together, growing up. And I did all I could to help out the family. You know who got Eileen's brother, Tommy Mannion, his first job? It wasn't Connie. At that time, he wouldn't have dared. It was me. And to this day, or until the other day, I should say, if Eileen had a problem, she would come to me. So it hurts. It's family, you see. Real family. I'll tell you something else. And people around here will have trouble taking it seriously. They all believe it's ancient history. But I know for a fact it isn't."

"What do you mean?"

He took a big bite out of the sandwich. "Hey, this is good. Where did you get it?"

"Rebecca's."

"Fancy schmancy," he said. "Let me pay for it."

"No. Are you kidding? It's on the station. Expense account."

"O.K. You could still put in for it even if I pay, you know. Reporters do that all the time."

"I don't."

"Neither does Tony."

"Tony has nothing to do with it."

He noted her sensitivity but said nothing. She then asked him to get back to the point he was trying to make.

"Oh, yes," he said. "To be blunt. I don't think I'd be in the jam I'm in now if I were a black or a Puerto Rican or a Yankee, I mean the right kind of Yankee."

"You mean you're being done in because you're Irish?"

"Well, yes and no. I'm not whining. I don't whine about the way things are. That's the way things are. An Irishman, an Italian, a Jew. They all face a different set of standards in this town. I don't know if you ever encountered it. What are you, Italian, Greek?"

"No, I'm Jewish. I mean I was born Jewish. I'm an agnostic myself. I don't pay attention to religion."

"Being Jewish hasn't got anything to do with religion, as far as I can tell," he said. "Unless you're one of those guys who wears a fedora around Coolidge Corner on Saturdays. It has to do with the tribe you belong to. So what you believe or not is beside the point. How long you been around here, anyway?"

"Not long enough, evidently."

"Well, talk to Tony about this. He understands. You should, too. But anyway, let me explain. If I was a black guy or a Puerto Rican, the whole thing would be swept under the rug. Connie surely would never have come forward. He wouldn't have dared. And the Yankees, they can't get in trouble if they try. No one believes it, not even the Irish, when you say one of them had his hand where it shouldn't be. And that's brainwashing, because in my experience the Yankees have the longest fingers of them all and they never pay, never. It's the Irish and the Italians and the Jews who take the fall because everyone expects them to be on the take and there's nobody to protect them."

"But Connie is Irish."

"Connie *was* Irish. He turned a long time ago, when he went over to Harvard. He isn't Irish anymore. Oh, he'll yell for the priest all right when he's on his deathbed, but he belongs to the other people body and soul, the people who put him where he is and who'll keep him there as long as he can do their job."

"Which is?"

"To cut the balls off the Irish in this state. Give the blacks their shot. As long as they take their orders from the same people who've been giving orders in this state since the Pilgrims came, and I don't mean the Indians."

"An interesting theory."

"Not a theory," said Scooter. "It's a shameful fact of history. Knock the Irish out of Boston and you take away their power base, spread the power around like chicken shit. It's nothing to dwell on, but it's a reality. You ought to go around and take a look at the old neighborhoods."

"I've seen."

"It wasn't an accident, what happened. That's all I'm saying."

She paused with a pencil in her mouth and stared at Scooter, watching to see if his eyes again descended to her cleavage.

"Scooter, what's behind the mess on Duncan Avenue?"

"How the hell do I know? Read Tony's column. Why are you asking that?"

"Because Tony went there because of something you told him, that's why."

He stared back at her, his eyes revealing nothing now but hard blue. "Then why don't you ask Tony, if you think that's true?"

"I did."

"And what did he say?"

"He said the mayor was involved."

"Did he really? He didn't write that today."

"Not directly, but the hint was there."

"A hint means nothing. A hint wouldn't bother Connie Haydon one bit. You know, you are a beautiful woman. If ever you and Tony cash it in, you know I'm available most nights and weekends."

"Scooter, I find you very attractive, but we mustn't mix up what we're doing here, don't you think?" She looked directly at him and smiled her warmest smile. The flirtation was beginning to melt him.

"I think I'll try some of that wine after all," he said.

He stood up and dumped what was left of his coffee into the sink. He then poured some wine into the coffee cup. "This will do fine," he said.

"Tony and I are unofficially partners, you know."

"Is that so? It's funny, I could have sworn Tony told me something different about that."

"Oh, he won't admit it, but it's true. If you trust Tony, you can trust me."

He took a long swallow from the cup and refilled it. "Jesus, Tony has his hands full," he said.

For a moment, Cynthia thought she had carried the flirtation too far and that Scooter was about to reach for her. His crude vitality appealed to her, and she tried to imagine what she would do if Scooter became amorous. She was surprised to find she wasn't sure. She didn't wait to find out. Instead, she stood up and walked to the sink and leaned against it, looking down with her smoky eyes at the red-faced Scooter.

"Are you corrupt?" she asked.

"Is that a serious question, lady?" he replied.

"Very serious. Because if you are, what the mayor did was right, and he should have done it a long time ago, whether you were Irish, Albanian, or a Virgin Islander. I mean, I know you're charming. I feel that right now. I'll bet you were devastating with the ladies. You still are. But seriously, how would you describe your attitude toward public morality? I know. Nobody in all these years has ever asked you that question, but remember, you've never been accused of a federal crime before, either. So I think it's fair."

"Well, what the hell do you expect me to say? You are serious. Right. You are serious?"

"Yes," she said, unsmiling.

"O.K. I think that's a dumb question, but I'll answer it. No, I am not corrupt. Public morality is very important to me. Morality is very important to me. I wouldn't fuck my friends or their girlfriends. And I wouldn't steal. No, I would never steal. I would lie only when I had a serious reason to lie. I believe in loyalty. I believe people should look after one another in a real way. I believe in protecting the weak. I think that's what a politician should be all about. I see a kid crippled with cerebral palsy and I want to take him in my arms and hug him and tell him that I know he is not that twisted body, that he is something special inside that body, that's beautiful and clean and made to last forever. No, I'm not corrupt. I'm a man who grew up in this town and loved the good that was here and the bad, too. I could recognize it. I knew from an early age where it came from. All the stupidity and ignorance and poverty. That's being poor, lady. Were you ever poor? I was. Piss poor. And from the time I was a kid I tried to do something about it for me, for my family, and for my friends. Sticking together. That's what I learned, and there was real glue holding us all together, holding this city together. Corrupt? Shit. I'll tell you what's corrupt, if you really want to know. And I have a feeling you aren't interested at all."

He stared up at Cynthia, who had a faint smile on her face, a smile that was a nervous reaction to Scooter's intensity but which he interpreted immediately as condescension. Suddenly, the intensity flared into anger.

"You know something?" he said. "You come in here and flash your little tits at me and that big smile of yours like you're here to get a story even if you have to give me a blow job, and then all of a sudden you change the rules of the game and start this superiority number over corruption. Well, Jesus, I don't know what your game is, but if you came here to get laid, you came to the wrong place. And if you came here to get a story, you went about it the wrong way."

Now it was Cynthia who was getting angry. "Hey, Scooter, hold it right there. I don't know why you suddenly blew up like that, but if I gave you any wrong signals, I'm sorry. I didn't mean to and I wasn't feeling the least bit superior to you. I was trying to get a sense of you and how you felt about your life and your work, and you gave it to me. Hey, you gave it to me beautifully."

"You people," Scooter said. "Tony is the only one of you people who's any good."

"I'm really sorry you feel that way, Scooter," she said, moving toward him and touching him lightly on the shoulder.

He pulled away sharply.

"What a terrible misunderstanding. You have given me so much feel for yourself and what happened to you. I would never put you down. I'm not that kind of person. Do you think Tony would go out with me if I were?" She looked at him with her lips drawn tightly downward, her eyes almost teary from sincerity. "Believe me," she said.

"Sorry," he said. "I can only take so much."

"I know," she said. "I don't think you're corrupt at all. I mean it."

"I appreciate that. The corrupt people are all those good-government creeps that keep the pressure on where all the little people are vulnerable, never on the big people."

"And Connie Haydon plays into their hands. At least he did with you."

"He's a bad guy, Cynthia," he said, and she thought for a moment he was going to cry. The prospect alarmed her more than the thought that he might try to come on to her.

"He's behind the Duncan Avenue business, isn't he?" she asked.

"He has to be," he said.

"Why?" she asked hesitantly, fearing that even a one-word question might stop the flow of information she sensed was on the verge of gushing forth.

"Look, I'll tell you, but throw that tape away. I'll tell you what I know and none of it can you use as coming from me. But the more I sit here, the more fucked up I get, the madder I get, and then I read all this shit this morning about the pope coming. I don't know if he's coming or not, but I do know that as long as people think he's coming there isn't going to be much attention paid to what I say or what happened to me."

She hit the off switch on the Sony and resumed her seat at the table.

"I'll tell you this and you can share it with Tony. I don't care. The same ground rules. O.K. But if you fuck me up . . . Well, you better not fuck me up. And you'll have to do some checking yourself. O.K.?"

"O.K.," she said.

"The guy in this up to his asshole is Tommy Mannion. He's been working with this guy I have never had any use for named F. X. McGivern. Tommy and McGivern have been running together for years. Anyway, they set up this phony company and very quietly began buying up land around Duncan Avenue with different straws, all pointing back to the same group. The problem when you do something like this is once the word gets around, it gets tougher to pull off. So these guys kept things pretty quiet for a long time, but sooner or later the word gets out. And the word got out in this case, and because of Tommy it was pretty much assumed that you-know-who was in the middle of it."

"Are you saying he wasn't?" she asked.

"Are you kidding? How could he not be, with his own brother-in-law involved? He had to be."

"What if he wasn't?"

"He was; he is."

"Why are you so sure?"

"I got a good source."

She was about to pronounce the name that came to her lips, but her professionalism stopped her. The name was Eileen.

□

Elmer Granger did not like Mayor Haydon. It was not a personal dislike. He didn't know the man and rarely encountered him except at civic ceremonies both detested: Haydon because he was bored by almost any occasion where someone or something else was the center of attention; Granger because whenever he ventured out of his office, he encountered fresh reasons for not doing so again. The condescension and the indifference he encountered each time he came into contact with the city's powerful nettled him. The merchant with the friendly smile wouldn't dream of having the *Bruise* delivered to his door, let alone advertising in it. The entrepreneur with the development scheme up his sleeve would cozy up to a flunky from the *Mammoth* before he would deign to pass the canapé tray to the publisher of the *Morning News.* And members of the banking elite would fix him with a knowing smile after asking the question that he had grown so sick of hearing in his years in Boston: "And how is your paper doing these days?"

No, Elmer Granger did not often venture forth into the greater world of the city, and he did not often invite that world to visit him in his office. So he was never more than a passing acquaintance of Connie Haydon's, which made it easier for the publisher to indulge and even refine his dislike. And Granger disliked politicians the way a small child dislikes peas — out of instinct only slightly reinforced by the experience of having tasted them.

And if Granger disliked all politicians, he especially disliked Boston politicians, with their sarcasm that passed for humor (oh, he had heard some of the barbs they tossed in his direction, calling him Elmer Fudd, for example), their disdain for the rules that bound most of the civilized world, their sense of superiority. He was bowled over when he found out people in Boston actually referred to their city as the Hub. Why, they'd steal the hub caps from a moving hearse. Hub, my ass. And Haydon was the worst of the lot. Not only was he crooked, he was a hypocrite, putting on airs as if he knew anything about the world outside his own precincts. He wouldn't last three weeks in Kansas. People would see through him like a piece of Saran Wrap.

And now he was outside his door, the mayor himself, with no call in advance to see if he could clear the time to meet, no preliminaries to negotiate, arriving in his limousine as if he were a Gridlock honcho.

"To what do I owe this honor?" said Granger as he followed his secretary back into the reception room where the mayor had barely had time to take a seat by a magazine table laden with that morning's editions of the *Bruise* and an old copy of *Arizona Highways*.

"Come on. I thought I'd buy you lunch," said Haydon.

"Oh, my," said Granger. "And I just made a lunch date," he lied.

"Well, you'll have to break it. This is important."

"I'm afraid that may not be possible."

"Well, if that's so, we'll just have to sit in your office and talk. I don't eat much for lunch anyway. What time is your appointment?"

"He'll be here any minute."

"Well, you can keep him waiting. I'm sure he won't mind. Do I know him? If I do, chances are he owes me a favor. We'll just let him wait."

Haydon grabbed Granger by the elbow and steered him back into his office and closed the door behind them.

"Take a seat, Elmer. Relax. I'm sorry we haven't gotten to know each other better, but we are busy men. I'm sorry. If you knew me better, you'd know I don't stand on ceremony."

The mayor settled into an easy chair alongside Granger's desk and waited until the publisher sat uneasily in his own chair by the window, which the mayor noted was streaked with grime.

"I'll get right to the point, Elmer. We both respect directness. You got to do something about that Tony Owen. He's on a cheap tear; he's been slandering me and he's got to stop. He's been implying, without the slightest shred of evidence, that I'm crooked. That's dishonest, that's unfair. But he's your guy and I expect that you are going to say to me, when I give you the chance, that I have a lot of nerve barging in here and telling you to put a leash on your star columnist. Well, that's just what I'm telling you to do. I want him off my ass right now."

"You're absolutely right, Mr. Mayor. I ought to kick you out of here. Who the hell do you think you are?"

"But you're not going to do any such thing. You're going to shut up and listen. I'm coming to you with a beef. A legitimate beef, like any reader has a right to do. Forget that I'm the mayor."

Granger stood up. "I don't like your tone," he said.

"Sit down, Elmer, and hear me out."

Granger moved as if to grab the mayor, who sat still and smiled disarmingly. "Elmer, please sit down," he said quietly. "Or I'll knock you on your ass."

"You'll do what?" bellowed Granger, who let out a strangled whoop and like a teenager back in the prairie leaped for Haydon's shoulders. Clutching them with his right arm and breathing hard, he tried to flip the mayor over his hip. But Haydon was too quick. He slipped the grip and buried his head into Granger's belly, and, driving forward, plowed him back into the carpet.

The racket brought Granger's secretary into the room. "I can't believe this," she said.

"Get the hell out of here," yelled the publisher from the floor, as he lurched forward and shook free of the mayor.

The woman withdrew as a breathless Haydon yelled after her, "Just playing."

Like tired Titans, they sat side by side on the carpet, breathing hard. Haydon was smiling. "We're getting too old for this sort of thing, don't you think, Elmer?"

Granger didn't smile. "If this ever gets out, we'll be a laughing-stock," he said.

"Are you kidding? People will love it, shows we're not pussies. Hope you didn't hurt your back."

"It would take a bigger man than you to injure me."

"O.K. I concede. You can almost throw me out of your office. Now that that's out of the way, let's talk."

Granger stood up and went back behind his desk, leaving Haydon still sitting on the floor.

"Take a seat," said Granger.

"I already have one."

"Then take a chair."

"O.K."

Granger leaned back in his chair, and for one of the few times since he came to Boston, he felt at ease in his surroundings. He had stood up to this bully and showed him some of the stuff he was made of.

He also looked at the mayor in a totally different light. He was tough after all. He also wasn't afraid to look foolish in defending a point of honor, although he wasn't quite sure now, as his excitement subsided, precisely what that point was.

Abruptly, Granger stood up once again and shot out his hand. "Let's shake," he said. "You know something? I have to admit it. I like the cut of your jib."

"Hey, and I like the cut of yours. You're all right in my book, Elmer." The two men shook hands and promptly sat back down.

"Now, tell me what this Tony Owen business is all about," Granger said. "I know what reporters are like. Sometimes they go off the reservation."

And so the two men talked: the mayor detailing what, from his point of view, was a long and dolorous story of one reporter's personal vendetta against him and his administration, and how his efforts to get across his side of the story had been consistently rebuffed over the years. He brought up the Duncan Avenue situation and insisted to the publisher that his own hands were clean on that score, and that he would resign tomorrow should anyone produce a scintilla of evidence linking him directly to the land speculation that he conceded had gone on in that precinct. As he talked, he indicated his appreciation for the publisher's point of view, and while allowing that he lacked any expertise in newspaper economics, he knew a bad situation when he saw one and recognized that it was to no one's interest, least of all the owners of a business, to throw good money after bad. He sympathized with those who would bite the bullet and make the hard and irrevocable decision to close the *Bruise.* Not once did he indicate that he had any information, although he had a great deal, that the publisher's main desire in life was to get out of the *Bruise,* out of Boston, out of the aloof and chilling Northeast. And when he dropped his actual threat, he did it almost casually, so that Granger wasn't immediately sure that he was hearing correctly.

Yes, he said, he had thought long and hard about the *Bruise* and the jobs that were involved at the paper, and particularly the jobs held by his constituents, good Boston people all of them. He knew that he could keep those jobs in place and embarrass the hell out of Gridlock. All he would have to do, he said — and he looked away so as not to give Granger the sense that he was reading his facial reactions, while noting them carefully out of the corner of his eye — was to declare a tax holiday, perhaps for five years, which would automatically pump two million dollars into the operation. He could also appoint a blue-ribbon commission of local merchants to recommend ways of boosting the paper's advertising revenues, which would be a polite way to hammer advertisers into line. He realized, of course, that even with these moves, and there were other steps he would consider, it would not push the *Bruise* anywhere near profitability. But he would create the illusion that profitability was possible and make it difficult for the people at Gridlock to abandon their baby in Boston.

As the mayor's message registered, a nerve in Granger's left eyelid began to flick out of control, and the publisher had to still the twitch with his hand. The gloomy vision of another five years in this barren place closed like a fog around his mind. This man could keep him from Kansas forever; this man could undo his dream. This man was a menace and there wasn't much he could do to stop him, except bend where he wasn't accustomed to bending. He had compromised often over the years, and in Boston he had made the biggest compromise of all, consciously working to diminish his newspaper's chances for survival. Though he did it for selfish reasons, he also did it because he believed that all hope for success was gone. But only rarely had he compromised that part of himself that was the man of news. He took pride in retaining a sense, no matter how small, that the news product should be uncontaminated by politics and politicians. Now that last vestige of pride was under siege, and he knew, before the words came out of his mouth, that even this last outpost of his integrity was about to fall. He would shut off Tony Owen. Of course, he would. The mayor left him little choice.

"I think you make a convincing argument," he said, rising up from his chair and escorting the mayor to the door. "You are a most persuasive man. If you have any further complaints, please don't hesitate to call."

"I'll make it a point," the mayor said. "And I'm delighted by this encounter. I didn't think you were a bad guy despite what I heard."

"And what have you heard?"

"That you are one tough hombre."

"I used to be," Granger said sadly.

□

Haydon arrived home to find the kitchen filled with silence and cigarette smoke. Tommy Mannion sat with Eileen at the kitchen table, sipping a glass of beer. A look of pain darkened Eileen's face. She looked old and cross. The ashtray in midtable brimmed with spent butts. Eileen was back to chain-smoking, Haydon noted with distaste. At that moment, he hated her and her brother and thirsted for confrontation. But he checked the impulse to lash out at them and, as the silence deepened, walked to the refrigerator and pulled out a container of milk. He drank deeply from the container itself, aware that he was sharpening Eileen's own irritation. She hated it when he did that. But she said nothing as he drank, staring at her all the while. He was poised for battle, and she knew that, just as he recognized the same signs in her. For if their marriage had failed in sustaining love, it had succeeded in forging intimacy. They were so close they could read with precision a world of meaning in each other's smallest gesture, the slightest sigh, as if they were instruments matched to mirror and record their tortured selves.

"O.K., Tommy, my boy," he said, finally. "How bad's the damage?"

Tommy smiled weakly, relieved that Haydon seemed to be joking. Eileen observed the smile and shuddered inside at her brother's obtuseness.

"It doesn't have to be bad at all," he said, pleased that his own voice was level and adult. "I haven't done anything wrong."

"Well, that's a relief," said Haydon, glancing savagely back toward Eileen. "That's a real relief. Because someone told me that you've been dabbling in land over on Duncan Avenue and using my name to get through the Zoning Board. I'm relieved to hear that isn't true."

"I didn't use your name," said Mannion.

"Hey, then there was no reason to invite you over here to thrash this out. Hey, I'm tickled. Eileen, let's see if we can get tickets to the ball game tonight or all go out to dinner. Terrific. City Hall in an uproar and for no reason at all."

"Connie, stop it," said Eileen. "I hate it when you're like that."

"Like what? Trusting? Believing that my brother-in-law is a man of his word? That he wasn't trying to make a fast buck at my expense over on Duncan Avenue?"

"Connie, why don't you hear him out, let him tell his side of it."

"I thought he had, Eileen," said the mayor. "O.K., Tommy, lay it out for me. Go ahead. I'm listening."

Mannion stood up and walked to the refrigerator to get himself another can of beer. Haydon and Eileen sat silently waiting for him to resume his place at the table. Mannion paused, groping for an opener, conscious of the mayor's eyes on his back.

"For God's sake, Tommy," Haydon sputtered. "That's a flip-top can. Open the goddamn thing."

"I know. I just pulled the tab the wrong way."

"Well, get another one, will you? You're acting like an idiot."

Mannion finally sat back down and said, "First of all, and so help me, I wouldn't lie to you, I never once used your name, Connie. Let's get that straight. O.K.?"

"O.K. Go ahead."

"O.K. I know how you feel about McGivern. But he's my friend; he's always been my friend."

"No, you're wrong," said the mayor. "He's nobody's friend. He's sick; he's always been sick. It's like being friends with a cobra."

"You just never gave him a break," Mannion said.

"Don't give me that, Tommy. He's been trouble all his life, as your sister knows. He's sick and his family's sick. Christ almighty, remember that sister of his, running through the streets tearing her clothes off? She was nuts, but he was psycho."

"I could never understand your fascination for that guy," Eileen said.

"Well, for once, my wife agrees with me," the mayor said.

"He was my friend," said Tommy. "I'm loyal to my friends."

"Oh, Christ," said Haydon, disgusted.

"Well, you only saw one side of him," said Tommy. "You never saw the good side."

"All I saw was the kid who used to set fire to cats," said Haydon.

"Well, he always stood up for me," said Tommy. "And he did pretty good for himself. He got no help from anybody and he put himself through college and law school and he built up a pretty good little practice in Dedham."

"I wonder who he ever got for clients," the mayor said. "And I'll bet he stole the bar exam."

"Give him some credit for brains," Tommy said. "Eileen, you tell him how smart McGivern is."

"He's always been bright, Connie. Give the devil his due."

"Well, he's been smart enough to know who to cultivate in this town, that's for certain," the mayor said.

"Anyway, while he was in Dedham, he got to know a few people who were dabbling in real estate, looking for areas that were in the path of an upswing. You know, buying cheap so they could sell dear. And they got pretty good at it. They bought a bunch of properties right on the edge of Route 128, and within a year or two someone came along with plans for a shopping mall, and bam, they all had cash in their pockets."

"Just like that," said Haydon. "Just happened to be at the right place at the right time. Marvelous."

"Shut up, Connie," said Eileen.

"Anyway, through F. X. I got to know these guys pretty good and they started talking to me about doing the same thing in Boston. Well, you knew I was doing real estate. I mean, that's what I've been doing since I got out of school. I mean, you never seemed much interested in the details."

"You have been doing real estate and insurance for years, that's right," said Connie. "And I was never much interested in the details because I thought I knew them pretty good. You were doing pretty respectable work out there on Centre Street. A few houses here, a few condos there, and you were doing pretty good with the auto insurance, too. And then you got greedy."

"Hey, what are you, the only guy in town with permission to make a buck?" snapped Tommy, the servility gone from a voice that now reached toward a tone of authority.

"Talk to me like that and you'll be out of here on your ear," said Connie matter-of-factly.

Mannion's head sagged on his shoulders and he nervously took a long sip of beer and reached for another cigarette. The pack was empty. "Here, have one of mine," said Eileen, sliding a pack of Winstons across the table.

"So then you formed Articulate, Inc., isn't that right? You and your friends. And began moving in on Duncan Avenue, isn't that right?" asked the mayor.

"It wasn't as simple as that. I mean, they talked to me for months about doing something, and I kept putting them off."

"Why? You weren't interested in a big score?"

"I put them off because I wasn't sure what we were doing was right."

"But there was nothing wrong with it. You told me that yourself."

"There wasn't. Or at least I didn't think there was. I felt a little funny about it because you know how people might talk. I mean, it was a good part of the city that was really underdeveloped. You told me that yourself. Remember? I mean, it was a slum — and if I didn't get involved, somebody else would. I mean, it was a prime deal. But I kept telling them no because I didn't think you would like me to get involved."

"Well, you were right on that score. So what made you change your mind?"

"Well, one day F. X. comes along and says he has a tie-in with this European company and once we got all the titles transferred, we'd just turn the whole thing over to them and they'd push ahead with the actual development, and I wouldn't have to have my interest made public at all. I'd stay in the background and they'd put my share of any profits into a bank account in Brussels. Nobody would ever know. All they wanted me to do was give the hint on the street that I had an interest in seeing things go smooth, and down the road I'd take my share."

"And how well did you know these other guys?"

"Not real well. I relied, as I told you, on F. X. He said he could vouch for them, they were all right."

"It never occurred to you that they were goons?"

"No."

"And so you never signed anything?"

"I never signed any papers saying that I was a principal in Articulate."

"Then what did you sign? You had to sign something."

"I signed one document for the Belgians that they said they'd keep locked up in Europe in a safe-deposit box."

"Why did you sign that?"

"They wanted some proof of good faith on my part. They said it was routine."

"And why did they want that? They already had what they needed from you, and McGivern was already their partner, wasn't he?"

"Yeah, but . . ."

"But what?"

"Well, they gave me some money up front."

"How much money?"

"They gave me twenty thousand."

"You idiot. And you took it. Where is it?"

"I've spent some of it. I took Madeline to Acapulco, remember? And the rest I have in a safe-deposit box."

"In Mexico?"

"No, here."

"And what was the paper you signed? Tell me precisely."

"I told you. It was a tender of good faith."

"Bullshit."

"It was a document that acknowledged my good faith in dealing with the Belgians after all the approvals were obtained."

"And acknowledging that you were already in the bag up to your ass, and that if you backed out at the last minute they'd have something to hold on to, like your balls."

"Connie, don't," said Eileen.

"And where did you say this document was?"

"I told you. In Europe."

"O.K., Tommy. I want you to get out of town. Take the rest of that twenty thousand and split, and stay out of town until you hear from me."

"Hey, Connie, I don't know why I should be running. I didn't do anything wrong. I'm not a public employee. I didn't break any laws. The only reason I stayed in the background on this was to protect you. I didn't want people to think . . ."

"You didn't want people to think it was my project. Not much, you didn't. Well, I don't know who the hell you're fooling. I don't think you're kidding yourself. I mean, I never thought you were stupid. But maybe I overrated you all these years. Maybe you did think these people were really interested in your business skills. You poor idiot, if that's what you believed."

"But I haven't broken the law. All I did was hide my interest in a real estate development firm."

"Oh, Christ, Tommy. You don't seem to realize that there's a dead body over there on Duncan Avenue. Don't you understand that you're in the middle of a homicide case?"

"Hey, I had nothing to do with that. Anyway, it was an accident. Nobody knew that bum was in there."

"Eileen, I always thought your family was a little slow, but this guy is absolutely retarded. Listen, Tommy, there's a dead body because somebody tried to burn down a building. That's arson and that's against the law. That's a felony and that bum lost his life as a result of a felony being committed. You don't have to be Clarence Darrow to know that you can build a case on that."

"But I had nothing to do with arson. I don't know anything about that."

"Well, you ought to talk to your old pal McGivern and see if his hands are so clean, and if they aren't, yours aren't either, because you are tied to him like a Siamese twin. And I'll tell you something else, Tommy. If the DA or, heaven help us, the U.S. attorney, starts squeezing your old pal McGivern, you think he's going to hold his hand in the fire for you? Like hell he is. He's going to place all the blame on you and hope for a deal, because they would be a hell of a lot more interested in you than in that two-bit hustler. And the only reason they would be interested in you is me. And don't play dumb. You aren't that stupid, no matter how you try to play it."

"No, Connie, he isn't stupid," said Eileen. "I think he's trying to be as candid as he can be under the circumstances with you all over him like an inquisitor. He needs your help, Connie, not your badgering."

"Well, Eileen, there isn't an awful lot I can do but urge him to get out of town as soon as possible and go someplace where no reporter can find him, just in case that document should see the light of day."

"And what if it does?" asked Eileen.

"Well, if it does, then I think Tommy is going to have to go see the DA and take his medicine. If he's lucky, he'll get off without going to jail, depending on how well he cooperates."

"That would ruin him," said Eileen.

"If he doesn't, that would ruin him and me both," said Haydon.

"Not if nothing ever gets out."

"Hey, Eileen, I'm trying to limit the damage. I'm doing everything I can. But whether you believe it or not, I can't control everything that happens in this town. And what I can control, I can't control without cooperation. I'm asking Tommy boy here to take a simple precautionary step and make himself scarce for a few weeks, and you and he are both dragging your feet." The mayor sat and stared coldly at Tommy. Then he asked, "What about McGivern? Any way to keep him from shooting off his mouth?"

"F. X. will be cool," said Mannion.

"Did he hire anyone to burn down that building, or did he do it himself?"

"I don't know anything about that fire. As far as I know, it was an accident."

"You're lying to me, Tommy. Eileen, your baby brother is a liar."

"Goddamn it, I'm not lying," said Mannion, now standing up and glaring at the mayor across the table.

"Then how come you said to me no more than five minutes ago that nobody knew the bum was in the building before it got torched?"

"Jesus Christ, I was surmising. That's all. Do you think if they knew they would have burned it?"

"It depends on the kind of mood McGivern was in, I suppose, and the pills he was popping. Oh, Christ, this isn't getting us anywhere. Tommy, go ahead and find a place you'll be comfortable. See, Eileen, how considerate I am? I could have picked the place for him to go. Tell your wife you have to leave town on business and you'll be in touch in a few days, and make sure no one knows where you'll be but me and Eileen."

"I don't like the idea of running like I'm a criminal or something," said Mannion.

"You're worse than a criminal," said Haydon. "You're a fool. And you need to get out of town for one big reason. If I have to look at you much longer, I think I'll kill you myself."

"Tommy, do what he says for now. Go ahead. Go home. I'll tell him the rest," Eileen said.

"Do you mean there's more to this sordid tale?" said the mayor.

"Go ahead, Tommy. We'll talk later."

He stood up and tried to move from the kitchen with dignity, but the effort was too much and he half stumbled at the doorway and might have fallen had he not caught himself in the door frame.

"Stay sober," said Haydon. He waited until he heard the front door close and then he turned to Eileen. "So there's more he was afraid to tell me."

"Yes," said Eileen. "There's more. You're not so innocent yourself, you know."

"Oh yes I am."

"No, you're not. You met with a guy named Jean Clerc in your office sometime last October. Clerc is the North American representative for the Belgians."

"How do you know that?"

"Because Tommy told me. I know it's all circumstantial. You meet with people like that all the time. But if Tommy is in trouble, so are you."

"Do you love him that much, or do you hate me that much? Which is it?"

"It has nothing to do with my feelings, Connie. It has to do with the evidence."

"And you think anyone would believe that I'd get myself tied up with creeps like McGivern and two-bit crap down on Duncan Avenue? Come on, now!"

"Your enemies would. And there's more."

"I'm beginning to think there's no end to this."

"Tommy was afraid to tell you, and I can't blame him. You are so cruel, Connie. McGivern didn't have his own money in this, but he has money, a lot more than Tommy got for playing front man at a few crucial times. And it's all wise-guy money."

"I can take care of the North End."

"Can you? Not if it looks like you're going down the drain along with my brother."

"Tommy told you all this?"

"Most of it."

"Who else have you been talking to?"

"Never mind."

"You knew Scooter was going to Tony Owen, didn't you?"

"I told him to," she said.

"Oh, God," he said. "What are you trying to do to me?"

"I want to see you squirm."

He stood up and leaned over the table and slapped her with all his might. "You bitch," he said. "How could you?"

The blow knocked her off the chair and left her sitting on the linoleum floor. She looked up at him defiantly and said, "Go ahead and hit me, Connie. Give me a black eye. And I'll tell everyone where I got it and I'll tell them what kind of man you are. What am I doing to you? You have some nerve asking me that. And what have you been doing to me for the last two years? Humiliating me with that little slut assistant of yours everywhere I turn and people looking at me so sympathetically. And then you turn on the people who made you. Even on Scooter, just to save your ass. Who do you think you are? Now you tell me, who do you think you are?"

He walked from the kitchen up the stairs to their bedroom and threw himself head down on the bed and tried to blot the anger out of his mind and get it back under control. He lay there for five minutes, suppressing the urge to demolish. He began taking deep breaths, trying to cool and clarify his mind.

He heard her coming up the steps, walking slowly and heavily. She walked into the room and sat down by the chair near the window, the chair in which he used to read when he was home in the afternoon and could catch the sunlight streaming in the window.

"Connie, I would like to destroy you. I would. But I don't want to destroy my brother. If you save him, I won't hurt you. But you have got to protect him. And after it's over, then we can go our separate ways. But let him get ruined in this mess, and so help me I'll do everything in my power to ruin you. Everything."

"It's a mess you helped create, Eileen," he said. "You didn't have to interfere."

She ignored what he said. "You should know a few other things, too, to help you sort things out. McGivern's investors are looking for a big payoff, and no matter how much they may like the mayor, they aren't going to kiss their money good-bye. And then there's that little matter of the document."

"You mean the one that's over in the safe-deposit box in Brussels?"

"Yes. Tommy also got a copy of it, of course. He gave it to me."

"So what are you going to do, blackmail me with it?"

"No. I don't have it anymore."

"What did you do, burn it?"

"No, I didn't burn it. I mailed it to somebody who might find it useful someday."

"Who?"

"Guess."

"Who, damn it?!"

"Scooter."

"You fool. And you say you want to protect your brother? You turned the only thing that can put your brother in jail over to Scooter?"

"He won't use it, unless I tell him to. He's loyal, you know."

"Loyal my ass. He's the one who gave the story to Tony Owen, with your help, of course."

"No. I told him to go to Tony Owen, but he already had the story. He's the one who told me about it. Tommy told me the rest after I confronted him."

"So you've known about this for a while?"

"No, only for a few days. Since they nailed Scooter. He called me after he knew you were going to screw him. He wanted to see if I had any influence over you."

"Why didn't he tell me himself?"

"He didn't want to hurt you. He still doesn't. He's loyal. I told you that. He's old school."

"So he goes to Tony Owen?"

"What would you do?"

"Jesus, I'd try to protect my own. You don't give a damn about your brother. That's clear now. All you want is to get me because of Corinne. You're sick."

"No, you're sick. Scooter won't use that document unless I tell him to. I can trust him. And what was I going to do? Tell Scooter to take his medicine when the only leverage he had on you was Duncan Avenue? Now, at least, you can see to it that the city gives him a good defense team. You can also use your influence in Washington to get him a lenient sentence, if it comes to that. And, you can make sure his pension rights are protected."

"Christ almighty. Scooter means more to you than I do."

"You are not my friend."

"And I suppose you want me to break up with Corinne?"

"No, I don't care if you break up with her. That won't restore my pride. I want something else."

"What?"

"I want you to fire her . . . for incompetence."

"That's preposterous."

"Suit yourself. That's what I want."

"And if I don't?"

"Then we'll see."

"Never before this moment did I realize just how hard you are. You are absolutely ruthless."

"I've never had power before. Now I have it. Why shouldn't I use it?"

"And all because of Corinne?"

"You are hooked on that, aren't you? But it isn't just Corinne. It was a dozen sluts like her before, and all your inattention and abuse and using me like I was an appendage of your ego, and never thinking for a moment of me and my life and what it was like sitting here in this empty house waiting for you and not being able to do anything on my own. Everything was for you, everything revolved around you, and what did I get out of this? A lot of lonely nights, sitting around the table with Charlie, just waiting, and thinking sometimes maybe I ought to give Charlie a tumble just to serve you right, but knowing how he would react, out of the fear of you, and not wanting to see that. So just sitting here and drinking and smoking and making small talk, and hoping some friends would drop in just to break the monotony. You forgot I existed. You really did. You not only forgot, you didn't care. And there was nothing I could do about it, before now."

"You could've left."

"And gone where? And what would you say to people? I could hear you, I could just hear you. 'And Eileen, well, you know how women get. Menopause. You know. She hasn't been the same since her menopause. And she took to drinking. And it was hell at home. So now everything is for the best.' Do you think I could have abided that? No, now you'll dance to my tune for a change."

"If I survive, you mean."

"Oh, you'll survive. You'll do right by Scooter. You'll do right by Tommy and you'll do right by me. If we go down the chute, we'll all go down together."

"You'll see to it that your brother gets out of town. I think I can get Tony Owen off the story. But I don't want Tommy around in case that McGivern connection gets out. You'll look to that?"

"Yes, I'll look to that. But first I want you to call Tommy up."

"For what?" he asked.

"I think you owe him an apology."

11

BOBBY BANTAM WAS INSANE. Tony Owen understood that now. It was a special kind of insanity, situational and temporary, but Gridlock, the *Bruise,* the mad publisher, and now the pope had finally shoved Bantam over the line into a land where reality and unreality blended, where everything was possible and anything true. It was a magical land, where contradictions ripened like exotic flowers and the guideposts pointed only to confusion. Here Bantam's wonderful instincts meant nothing. They worked as well as they ever did, moving toward the news like the mongoose toward the snake. But Bobby remained and insisted on remaining invincibly ignorant of one central fact: the snake had already struck and the lethal venom was en route to the heart.

And so Bantam seized on the pope story as if there were an endless stream of editions ahead, and an infinite amount of resources at his command, blinding himself to the reality that he was all but out of reporters and all but out of time. Tony told himself that he knew better, that the end was at hand, and if he was going to go down with the *Bruise,* he could at least work for the small satisfaction of taking an enemy or two down with him. And what better choice of enemy than Connie Haydon. But now, Bobby Bantam was going to deny him even that small final pleasure, and all Tony Owen could do was laugh, then follow orders.

But follow them creatively.

Doc D'Amato had shown him how.

"Don't sweat it, Tony. You already have a saint. Bernie. Bernie Kremenko. Why don't you hold him up as a martyr for our age? That way you might keep Bobby reasonably happy and still do your follow on Duncan Avenue."

Tony laughed. The idea tickled him. "Saint Bernie Kremenko, urban saint. Christ, my brother would love that one, but I'm not sure how it would play with Bobby. He'd think I was pulling his chain. But I'm going to play with it and see what happens."

And so Tony began the process of finding out who Bernie Kremenko actually was, first by tracking down the woman who claimed his remains from the morgue. She was his daughter, a woman named Gross who lived in Melrose.

She was reluctant to talk to Tony but melted enough under his persuasive powers to sketch the outlines of her father's unhappy life. Once he had had a little produce business, supplying about thirty mom-and-pop stores in and around Malden and Everett out of a panel truck he bought with a GI loan. But he was a mild man, too mild to run even a small business. One day, a competitor told him that he had taken down the names of all his customers and that beginning tomorrow they weren't his customers anymore, they were the competition's. So Bernie Kremenko took the panel truck and parked it in the back alley and never moved it again. He would never make another nickel, except what the welfare and social security people gave him. He got sent to a mental hospital, then, when they began closing down the mental hospitals, he ended up on the street, a derelict. His family had long since lost track of him.

The man who turned the other cheek, mild Bernie Kremenko, too good to survive. A nice column idea, Tony told himself. He could spin it through his typewriter in two hours. That gave him at least four hours to hit the street. Time enough, he knew, for a surprise call on F. X. McGivern, and time enough to make a sweep at City Hall to check on the status of the records kept from him the day before.

He grabbed his jacket and headed out across the city room. As he passed the city desk, John Walsh stopped him. "Hey, Tony. You might be interested in this. The Fire Department just issued a report on the fire that killed your bum. They said it was caused by careless disposal of smoking materials."

"Bullshit," said Tony.

"Bullshit or not, that's what they said. The bum fell asleep with a cigarette and set fire to material stored in the basement. No evidence of arson."

"The mayor is moving fast," said Tony. "It doesn't matter. We'll be able to prove it wasn't smoking."

"I'm not so sure of that," said the city editor. "Their report is pretty definitive."

"John, are you kidding me? This is an obvious cover-up."

"Maybe, but the burden of proof falls on us now, and I don't think we're going to come up with it. You're going to have to soft-pedal the arson angle."

"Sure, John, way to hang in there. You're a real ballsy guy."

"I'm just telling you, Tony."

Tony snorted and headed across the floor to the escalators and out the building. Bright afternoon sunshine greeted him; so did his brother.

□

"Oh, Christ," Tony muttered. "Malachy, what can I do for you?"

"Let's talk," said Malachy. "Just for a moment."

"O.K., but only in English," Tony insisted.

Malachy headed toward the *Bruise* entrance as if to go into the cafeteria, but Tony grabbed his arm. "No, not here. Let's go around the corner."

They walked together in silence. Tony walked a little forward, whistling to himself to hide his discomfort at being with this ragged stick of a man, this brother, the bum. Malachy, aware of his brother's embarrassment, hung back a little. At times, in the past, Tony's ill-concealed shame angered him and provoked him into outrageousness as the only weapon at his disposal. But today he was understanding, and his mind was suffused with love and pride in his brother. Within five minutes they reached the deli where, two days before, Malachy had been rudely ejected. The proprietor was about to toss him out once again, but seeing Tony with him, he relented after coldly staring at Malachy to show that he had not forgotten him. The two brothers sat in silence before their coffee cups. Malachy wanted Tony to talk first, hoping that perhaps he would bring up the papal visit, which was so patently providential it had to be foremost in Tony's mind.

But Tony wasn't thinking of the pope; he was thinking of Malachy's dirty feet breaking through the ruptured sneakers. "Tell you what, Malachy," he said, "if I give you some dough to buy yourself a new pair of shoes, promise me that you'll buy them and not give the money away to your pals. What do you say?"

"If you want me to have new shoes, if it's important to you, Tony, then, yes, I'll buy them. But they are not important to me. Why are you worrying about such things when I don't, and they're my feet."

He spoke sweetly and reasonably, and despite himself Tony's skepticism toward his brother eased. He reached into his pocket and pulled out a twenty-dollar bill, which he thrust into his brother's palm. "Here," he said. "Take care of yourself for a change, O.K.?"

"You don't have to do that, Tony, unless it makes you feel a little better about me. If it does, I'll be happy to take it. But it isn't important to me, except as it concerns you."

"Take the money and shut up," said Tony, gently.

"Thank you," said Malachy, and he pushed the money into the side pocket of his soiled trousers. "God is good, Tony, and so are you. You really are."

"Well, there you are, Mal, wrong on both counts. But my, you are feeling pious today."

"And why shouldn't I be? My prayers have been answered."

"And what prayers were they?"

"The pope is coming. I knew he would. I knew somehow somebody would listen."

"Don't tell me you're being taken in by the hype, too. It's all hype, Mal. I mean, he may be coming and then again he might stay home. The mayor is pumping up the story to keep everybody's mind off more pressing business, like who the hell is burning down Duncan Avenue."

Malachy looked hurt and Tony was immediately sorry. The sorrow followed the hurt as if by reflex. He had reacted that way to the bewilderment and pain on Malachy's face as long as he could remember, even before the day of their mother's death, the day that marked in Tony's mind the beginning of his manhood, the day that locked both him and Malachy into roles they would play for the rest of their lives. From that day on, Tony would live only with facts, and for facts. He would take his solace from the grubbiness of a narrow reality, and Malachy, with Tony's help, would survive through illusion.

Tony became a practical person. He helped Aunt Jenny pay the rent by finding odd jobs after school and in the summer, while Malachy burrowed deeper and deeper into books and into religion. Rituals fascinated him, and prayers and incantations. He studied the lives of the saints and found a kinship with the Catholic mystics and dreamed of the stigmata and utter abandonment to God's will. And after school, while Tony was working at a grocery store in Brighton Center, he would practice the movements of a priest at the Mass, standing before a mirror, holding a wine goblet covered with a silk scarf.

Aunt Jenny saw God's grace in Malachy's "vocation," and Tony saw in Malachy's radiance the protective film his brother would need to get through. Some people were born, he realized even then, without a kind of invisible skin to protect them from what life was really about. These were the vulnerables, born with every psychic nerve exposed, and the slightest movement, even the most benign breeze, brought excruciating pain, a pain that loved ones could not bear to see.

On that day when Tony came home from school and smelled the gas as he stood on the landing outside their third-floor flat, his first thought, even before he inserted his key into the lock and found what he sensed he was going to find, his first thought was of his brother and how he would spare him the pain. And as he opened the door and looked into the old-fashioned kitchen and saw his mother's lifeless body crouched by the open oven door, he began plotting a way to spare Malachy the pain that he could not bear, a pain that he himself refused to yield to, that he knew he would never yield to.

So he turned off the gas and got a pillow from the bedroom and gently moved his mother's body to the floor. Then, he ran to Mrs. Mulligan's flat on the first floor and told her to get an ambulance because something dreadful had happened to his mother, and he stood by the first-floor flat and waited until Malachy came up the street from school. And while Mrs. Mulligan got an ambulance and ran to get Aunt Jenny to take over, Tony took Malachy down to Murph's, the ice cream parlor on the corner, and told him that their mother had to go away with the angels and that she and Jesus and the Virgin Mary were now looking down on them, and that she had told Tony before she went away that he was to look after Malachy because he was such a special boy and that there was nothing to be afraid of. And that look of terrible hurt came over Malachy's face, and for an instant, Tony was reminded of the pain he himself was keeping squeezed inside, and a sob that was the last burst of his childhood rose in his throat and was immediately subdued. Malachy never knew that his mother had killed herself, never knew the sense of expectancy that Tony felt as he mounted the stairs, never suspected that there was any secret locked in his brother's heart. Later, as Malachy grew older, Tony and Aunt Jenny told him that his mother had suffered heart failure, and Tony felt that was literally true. Her heart had failed.

But still, there were times in the middle of the night when Tony would suddenly awaken, the odor of gas strong in his nostrils, the sense of his mother like a presence around him, and he would start from his bed to the kitchen to see if a gas tap was open. Recently, he startled Cynthia that way. "But Tony," she had reminded him, "you have an electric stove." And he had laughed and fallen back to sleep.

Now, he again thought of that day as he sat across the table and looked at Malachy. The illusion had ended in madness. He hadn't conceived of that.

"I'm sorry, Malachy. You're right not to be cynical. I'm sure he is coming."

"I know he's coming," said Malachy. "And Tony, you have been so good to me, I want to ask you another favor."

"What is it?" asked Tony.

"I want to change the terms of the deal we made the last time."

"You mean you won't talk to the people at the chancery?"

"No, I'll do that. I gave you my word. But I want you to do a little something extra for me, and then I'll do something extra for you. Is it a deal?"

"Wait a minute, Mal. Be specific."

"I want you to help me see the pope long enough to talk to him. I know he'll want to talk to me, and you can arrange it. I know you can."

"Oh, come on now, Mal. I'm just a newspaper guy working for a paper that's going to have the pope so pissed off by the time he arrives, I won't get within a mile of him myself. How can I do that for you? Come on, think a little bit. It's not possible."

"You once got me in to see Kennedy."

"That was different."

"Yeah, I know, I was a priest then, I looked respectable. Well, I'll look respectable for the pope, believe me. I'll dress up. I'll even go to the chancery's home."

"Mal, don't get your hopes up. O.K.? I don't think it's going to happen."

"Oh, it will happen, if it's God's will, and I think it's going to be God's will. And in return, I'll find out for you who's burning down Duncan Avenue."

"Hey, you stay away from there, Mal. There're some pretty tough characters involved. You can get hurt."

"Nobody will hurt me, Tony. I'll wash your back; you wash mine."

"Come on, Mal. I don't need your help. I got the story. It's almost ready to roll."

"Almost. You don't have it."

"Spare me, please. Stay away from Duncan Avenue. I'm telling you," Tony said.

"I can help. I will help. You'll be hearing from me. God is good, Tony. God is good."

□

At midafternoon, Tommy Mannion, flushed and frazzled, joined F. X. McGivern at a table in a secluded corner of the Parker House bar. McGivern, round as a marble, fitted into the captain's chair as if he were molded for it. He was perfectly at ease, any anxieties worn away by the two brandy Alexanders consumed while waiting for Mannion.

"Don't get too excited," said McGivern. "That's how deals get blown. We got a problem. We figure out the solution. There's always a solution. So your brother-in-law is pissed."

"He wants me out of town," said Mannion.

"So go," said McGivern.

A waiter who seemed fresh from Sardinia or Corsica glided up to the table and took Mannion's order ("Two Heinekens and another one of these for my friend"), half bowed, then slipped away toward the service bar.

"Why do the Irish always hire these ginzos?" said McGivern. "It must make them feel superior. It's like uppity Irish hiring English nannies. A crock of shit."

"I don't want to go," said Mannion.

"But go. Don't get the mayor in an uproar. Just go. Head for the West Coast. Lots of nice pussy. Get laid, gamble a little, get laid."

"Fuck it," said Mannion. The waiter returned. McGivern thanked him profusely, meanwhile sharpening the edge in Mannion's mood. "Hey, be cool. What are you trying to do, attract attention?"

"Hey, can't I sit down on a spring afternoon and shoot the shit with a lifetime friend? What the hell's the matter with you? Madeline isn't giving you enough."

"Get serious, for Christ's sake," said Mannion.

"O.K., I'll be serious. From what I hear, the only problem we got isn't really much of a problem. It's Tony Owen. He's the only reporter in this town who gives a shit about Duncan Avenue and that old bum. And from what I've seen of him, he isn't ten feet tall. I mean, he doesn't know the people he's dealing with."

"So what are you suggesting? Knock off a reporter? Is that what you have in mind? Jesus, you are going nuts, F. X. Then you'll have everybody on our ass, even the fucking *Mammoth.*"

"Hey, I'm suggesting nothing. I'm just telling you he ain't ten feet tall and he scares like everybody else. And don't give me that look, Tommy. I mean, you've been dealing with goddamn Europeans, Belgians, civilized fucks. You know who I'm dealing with? Well, it isn't the same thing. I may not show it, but I'm scared. I'm scared shitless when I think of what can happen to me if this deal falls apart for one reason or another. The Belgians might ruin you, embarrass you, knock your brother-in-law out of office. But they aren't going to pull your goddamn fingernails out. Do you know what the other guys are capable of doing? I do know, and I'm not fucking with my partners. A little fright can go a long way."

"Just don't muscle a reporter. It doesn't pay."

"How about somebody close to the reporter? You were telling me about that blonde in the Southie bar. Is he sweet on her?"

"They're friends."

"Maybe she'd carry a little message."

"I wouldn't advise it."

"But you're getting out of town, remember?"

"He's also banging that TV reporter, Cynthia."

"Hey, you just told me. You never mess with reporters. I listen. See?"

"I'm going to leave tonight. I think I'll go to L.A. Check into a hotel and think a while."

"Madeline know you may be leaving for a while?"

"I'll tell her later. She's getting worried."

"The more ignorant you keep her, the better. Tell her it's a big business deal."

"I know how to handle it."

"You know, Tommy, there really isn't much to worry about. It's a matter of a few days. Then the heat's off. The only thing we have to worry about is that Connie will get so ripshit he'll queer the deal."

"Eileen won't let him. She's behind me all the way."

"She ought to be, the way he treats her. They going to split?"

"That's all Connie would need. Nah, where would she go?"

"Who knows? Joannie left Teddy."

"Yeah, but national is different, don't you think?"

"Who can figure puss? I can't. Hey, Tommy, I got to be off. The lid is on. Let's keep it that way. We got some beautiful property and a beautiful development. We can't lose. Just be cool."

"You too."

"Always."

"I'll get the tab."

"Great. I'll get you next time." McGivern waddled off and headed around the corner to his State Street office.

□

Tony Owen was waiting in the reception room when he arrived. "Mr. McGivern?" he said.

"Do you have an appointment?" McGivern asked, and the voice was like the one Tony had heard on the telephone, gruff and bullying.

"I just wanted you to answer a few questions."

"Beat it or I'll call a cop."

"Just a question or two, if you don't mind."

Tony pushed into the lawyer's office and took a seat by the window. "You're not going to call a cop, F. X. That'll just get you in deeper."

"I'm not going to talk to you, Owen, so get lost."

"Listen, fat man. All I want to know is who your partners are in Articulate. Is Haydon involved?"

"Go fuck yourself."

"Is that on the record, fat man? What's your own interest on Duncan Avenue?"

"Go fuck yourself."

"That's no way to talk to a reporter."

"You can sit here all afternoon, but that's all I'm going to say to you."

"Good. You're on the record."

"Get lost, Owen, before I lose my temper."

"I'm going, pal. I have what I came for."

"And what was that?"

"Confirmation that you are the lowlife everyone says you are. You see, your reputation precedes you. Have a good day."

Tony was on full alert by the time he returned to the *Bruise*. He knew that he had a major story, that McGivern was involved, that the mayor had to be involved some way. He also knew he had a helluva column for tomorrow, a column that would write itself.

The phone call from Cynthia came just as he was sitting down at his desk to write.

"Catch me tonight, Tony," she said. "I've got a good one going on Duncan Avenue."

"What do you mean, a good one? You told me you were doing hearts and flowers on Scooter."

"That's what I intended. It got heavier than that."

"What do you mean, it got heavier?"

"The story is too good to hold."

"Hey, Cynthia, this is my story. What do you mean, it's too good?"

"Tony, I'm sorry. I've just been doing my job."

"Hey, you're going to be looking for a new boyfriend if you don't tell me what it is you're up to."

"Better tune in at six. I've got to go."

"Goddamn it, Cynthia, tell me."

"See you tonight. Watch me."

She hung up.

"Shit," Tony said. He reached for the phone and dialed Scooter's number.

"What did you tell Cynthia, old pal?"

Scooter hesitated, as if selecting his words, and said, "Tony, you've got a handful in that girl."

"Scooter, what did you tell Cynthia that she's putting on the six o'clock news?"

Again Scooter paused. "What can I tell you, Tony? Your girlfriend is a witch. She had my head spinning and the next thing you know I was telling her things I wouldn't tell a priest in confession. It was weird. You got your hands full. I can appreciate that."

Tony was becoming irritated by Scooter's repeated use of that phrase, but he was also aware of how irresistible Cynthia could be while intent on getting information. The surprise to him was not that she had gotten Scooter to talk but that she had tried to get Scooter to talk, that she actually set out to beat Tony on his own story with his own main source.

"Scooter, let me try once more. What did you tell her that I don't know?"

"I told her only one thing and I don't think she can verify it; surely she can't do it in one day. I told her that the mayor's family was involved in Articulate."

"Not bad, Scooter. Not bad. Why didn't you tell me?"

"Because I wanted you to find out on your own. You would have found that out on your own."

"I'm not having too much luck yet," Tony said. "I've gotten as far as McGivern; that's it, and I can't even prove his involvement, with Articulate anyway."

"Well, he's involved. And so is Tommy Mannion."

"Then the mayor is, too."

"No comment, Tony. No comment."

"Did you tell her you had proof?"

"No."

"Well, we both better watch the six o'clock news. Is there anything else new with you, Scooter?"

"Yeah, there is, as a matter of fact. Haydon is sending me messages, I think. I got a call today from his guy Stanley. He wants to see me tomorrow. I thought that was interesting."

"Who wants to see you, the mayor or Stanley?"

"Stanley. Connie won't come near me with a ten-foot pole. I'll keep you posted. Hey, Tony, don't be mad at me. She hypnotized me, she really did."

"Sure, Scooter. I didn't know you were such a sucker for the ladies."

"Now you know."

"Now I know. See you."

He hung up the phone and looked at the clock over the city desk. It was almost six o'clock. He walked into Bobby Bantam's office, where the *Bruise*'s only working television set was stored.

"Bobby, sorry to bother you, but I have to watch the news on Channel Four. Cynthia is doing a Duncan Avenue number."

"Jesus Christ," said Bobby Bantam. "What are you two doing, playing games? You got your girlfriend going on the story now? Now I've heard everything." He spoke with an irritability that surprised and unsettled Tony.

"Bobby, don't be ridiculous. You ever hear of the women's movement? It's arrived. I don't tell her what to do. She just up and stole my story."

Tony turned on the television set and sat down on the sofa alongside. He watched the opening fanfare that made every day seem like the day World War III started. He watched as the camera zoomed in on the anchor desk and caught the young and handsome anchorman looking grim and concerned, as if he were a surgeon about to give a patient the bad news about his biopsy. The anchorman ticked off the day's leading news events: the papal visit; a fire along the Chelsea waterfront; the governor's budget heading for heavy opposition on Beacon Hill; a coaching change for the Celtics; and — at this Tony hunched closer to the set — "And, a new scandal rocks Boston City Hall."

Five minutes into the show, they got to the scandal. There was Cynthia Stoler, looking bright and competent, standing in a trenchcoat.

"This is Duncan Avenue in Boston, not far from Symphony Hall. On this street since last September, eight buildings have caught fire, including this one, number forty-two, right behind me. Here, a vagrant by the name of Bernie Kremenko died three weeks ago in a blaze that the Fire Department today blamed on the careless disposal of smoking materials.

"Residents of the buildings that have not been hit by fire are living in terror, asking themselves when, not if, the flames will visit their homes."

The camera moved to a Puerto Rican woman named Anna Morales. Two children clung to her skirt and she faced the camera, looking every bit as grim as the anchorman and a lot more concerned. "I'm frightened. Me and my husband, we take turns sleeping in the night, so one of us will be awake if the fire comes."

"Why don't you just move?" Cynthia asked.

"Where would we go?" Mrs. Morales replied.

"The Fire Department blames the fires on vandals and accidents," Cynthia continued. "Squatters, they say, inhabit most of the buildings and they are vulnerable because they are part of the city's stock of housing of last resort.

"But the Fire Department had no comment or knowledge of the fact that buildings on both sides of Duncan Avenue, and some on Duncan Avenue itself, are being bought up by a single company, a company, our High Impact News team learned today, with close ties to an important Boston political family."

"Good God, she doesn't know that," Tony sputtered. "How the hell can she say that?"

"She said it," said Bobby Bantam.

"High Impact News also learned that all the city's records on land transactions involving property in the Duncan Avenue vicinity have been impounded by the administration of Mayor Cornelius J. Haydon as part of an ongoing internal investigation."

"Shit, I had that today," Tony said.

"She doesn't read your column, lover boy."

"High Impact News also learned that at a lightly attended meeting of the city's Zoning Board a year ago, a change in zoning in the neighborhood, permitting the construction of a major commercial complex that would include a hotel, was approved, creating the conditions for a bonanza for the people fortunate enough to own shares in the company quietly assembling land in the neighborhood.

"One local appraiser contacted by High Impact News estimated that the land is now worth at minimum about fifteen million dollars, even if no development is forthcoming. But should a development be approved by City Hall, the value of the land would quadruple overnight.

"Stay tuned to High Impact News later in the week for further developments. This is Cynthia Stoler reporting."

"Christ," said Tony Owen. "She's way ahead of everybody on this story, and I don't think she checked a fucking thing."

"It's a piece of crap anyway," said Bobby Bantam. "It doesn't matter. I don't think there's much of a story there. People are land speculating all the time. It's the nature of things in a big city. So what else is new?"

"Hey, Bobby, you got to be kidding me. This is a helluva story. She hasn't done all the homework yet, but she's on the right track. It happens to be my track, so I just happen to know."

"Tony, I'm not concerned. Duncan Avenue isn't going to save this paper. It just doesn't have it."

"Well, I think it's got it. I'm going to write about it again tomorrow."

"Like hell you are," said Bobby Bantam. "I thought we straightened that out this morning. You're supposed to be writing about a saint and the pope."

"I am. I'm doing both."

"That's not possible, Tony."

"Bobby, I'm telling you. Bernie Kremenko was a saint. I've talked to his family. He was a saint, who wouldn't hurt a fly. Don't get yourself worked up. I know what I'm doing. You'll like it."

"No, Tony. No Bernie Kremenko. No Duncan Avenue. No. No. No. That's it."

"Are you serious?"

"Dead serious. No more on Duncan Avenue, Bernie Kremenko, or the latest scandal at City Hall. No more."

"I can't believe that I'm talking to Bobby Bantam here. What the hell is the matter with you? After all these years, the heat is getting to you, or what? Bobby. Look at me. I'm your old pal and protégé, Tony Owen. Remember me, the kid from Brighton? The kid you discovered. Your pal, your confidant."

"Tony. I just talked to Elmer and he laid down the law. He says no more, nothing but the pope. That's our life preserver. There is no other. And to tell you the truth, the old man might be right on this one."

"Haydon got to him, that's all that means, and you know it."

"Maybe he did. I don't know and I don't really care, either. He was in there today, that's true."

"Bobby, this is a good story, a really good story. Don't you realize who the hell is behind all this stuff on Duncan Avenue? It's the mayor's brother-in-law, that's who, and that shyster McGivern. We're going to get that story. I know we're going to get it. I know it like I can't be wrong. You know when I feel that way I don't let you down. I never have. You know that. Come on now, Bobby, don't go the other way on me now. We got about two weeks to go on this adventure. Let's not throw our cherry away now."

"Tony, on this one I have to go the other way. I have no choice. It's orders from the publisher and I told him already I would. I'd make a deal with the devil if it would save this paper. This is my life, and from what I hear from Granger, that's what old Haydon has in mind, a deal to save the paper. He's working on it. I'm not going to fuck that up."

"So you know more than you're telling me."

"No, I know what I heard between the lines from Elmer, and he thinks it's really important to cool it for now. If that broad of yours gets some more shit, then we can go back to it. But she has nothing and you got nothing but a little tickle, another tickle. That's all you're doing with this thing from day one, and whether you accept the fact or not, you did blow the pope's story because of it."

"Bobby, I can't believe what I'm hearing."

"I'm sorry. You going to quit on me?"

"Jesus, you are taking this seriously. No, I'm not quitting, but I'm not going to give you a column for tomorrow. Kremenko was all I had. And I don't feel like going back to the drawing board."

"O.K., we'll skip you tomorrow. I'll call for the saint entries myself. Name your saint. Perform your own canonization ceremonies. The *Bruise* will sell you a do-it-yourself kit, complete with white smoke. They use white smoke for that, don't they?"

"No. Fuck it, Bobby. I'm going home."

"Sorry, Tony."

"Bobby, I got to keep remembering that you are my oldest friend."

"Maybe I'm saving you from yourself. And Tony, believe me, if I thought that chasing your scandal was going to make the difference in us building up the numbers and staying alive, I'd be all over it.

I really would. I'd tell Granger to get lost. I don't know if you believe that, but I know it's true. You just haven't got it yet, and we don't have time for you to get it. Maybe sucking up to Haydon might help, and maybe the pope will bring us a miracle. I don't know."

Tony stopped listening to Bobby Bantam. Instead, he found himself studying his eyes. The fatigue was there, the same look of wear that rode the eyes of all the people who kept pulling the oars at the *Bruise.* He also looked old, as if the years had suddenly seized him, hunching his shoulders, hollowing out his chest and coating over his eyes with a film of doubt, yes, that's what it was, doubt and fear. For the first time since he had known him, Bobby Bantam seemed unsure and afraid.

"I guess it is the end of the line for us, isn't it?" Tony said.

"It better not be," said Bobby.

"But you've given up. I can see it in you. You've thrown in the towel. You don't see any hope. They've finally whipped your ass. You're going on your guts, but your brain has clicked off."

Bobby Bantam said nothing. He walked over to the window. "Look, they've repaired that sign. How could I give up now? They've fixed that sign."

"Then why have you?"

"Tony, you're getting to be a pain in the ass. I haven't given up. I can't give up. I've got two shots. And one of them, in my professional opinion, just isn't very good. The other one isn't so great either, but it beats yours and I'm going with it."

"Tell me what the publisher said to you."

"The publisher didn't say anything to me but what I told you. But he did tell me if we have any hope at all, that help is going to come from the mayor."

"Bobby, where was the mayor all the years we needed him? If he could do something for us, why didn't he do it before? You don't seem to be thinking like Bobby Bantam. You're thinking like some scared overnight editor, like one of those honchos over at the *Mammoth,* sitting on their goddamn lead. What did Granger tell you that you didn't tell me? Did he promise you a job, another paper? And that son of a bitch, he doesn't want us saved anyway. All he wants, as you've told me a hundred times, is to get out of here. So what did he do, offer you a deal somewhere?"

Bobby Bantam turned from the window and looked Tony Owen

directly in the eye. Anger flickered across his features, then died out. "Anybody else talked to me like that, Tony, and they'd be out of here on their ass. But I know you care. And I care, too. This place is my life. You know that. When they close the door, I'm going to go into a room somewhere and shut the curtains and turn out the lights and stay in bed, and I may never get up. Because I'll have nothing to get up for, nothing. Nothing at all. And I'll tell you something else. I've followed my instincts all along on this paper and now we're a few days from closing the door. So now, I'm not going to try something different. I'm going with my instincts and, who knows, maybe there will be a miracle."

"We haven't even got a story, Bobby. Not even a story. We got a half-assed contest. Jesus Christ. Some instinct."

"And maybe the mayor will come through."

"And maybe Granger is lying. Have you considered that?"

"If he is, we'll know it soon enough."

"So your mind is made up."

"Tony, you're not listening too good."

"No, I'm listening and hearing just fine. I'm just sorry it's ending this way. I'm sorry for you; I'm sorry for me. And I'm pissed, too. After all these years, we've got that bastard on the hook and you want to cut the line and let him swim away. I guess things don't end with a bang. It's like the poet said. You're whimpering, Bobby."

"I'll be seeing you, Tony."

Tony Owen walked out, stopped at his desk to get his coat, ignored John Walsh, who came over to him to discuss something, and, head down, left the *Bruise,* feeling like a man who probably would not return. He stopped at the liquor store on the corner, bought a bottle of Beefeater gin, and headed for the subway that would take him home.

12

ON ORDINARY EVENINGS, Tony Owen prepared martinis with meticulous care. On this night, he put ceremony aside. He dropped the ice cubes into an ordinary drinking glass instead of into the melon-shaped goblet he customarily used and filled it halfway with gin cut with a dash of bitters. He drank deeply and the buzz hit him almost at once. In four swallows he finished the first drink and began readying the second. Tonight he had a legitimate excuse for hitting the bottle.

But as he sat at his kitchen table, working on the second drink, and the memory of what had happened that day began surfacing in his mind, he lost all desire to be drunk. Instead, he got to his feet, took his half-finished second drink, and poured it down the drain. "God-damn," he said to himself, "you are not going to sit here and get bombed and wake up tomorrow feeling that Bobby Bantam had a point. No, you dumb son of a bitch, you are going to face this sober."

He put the gin bottle up on the shelf by the refrigerator and filled the kettle with water. He was sipping coffee when the buzzer sounded. It was Cynthia.

"I wasn't sure you were going to let me in," she said as he opened the various locks barring entry to his apartment.

"I'm just letting you in so I can kill you," he said.

She had supper with her: two Greek salad sandwiches from the Aegean Fare down the corner.

"I thought you might be in your cups by now," she said.

"I am," he said, turning over his coffee cup so she could see the black liquid staining the bottom of the crockery.

"You're not even mad?" she asked.

"No, not mad, surprised. I might have been furious but they killed my column for tomorrow."

"You're kidding," she said.

"I wish I were. Bobby's gone totally overboard. He's gone."

"I'm sorry," she said. "And I'm sorry for what I did to you. Something got into me while I was interviewing Scooter. And the next thing I knew, there was this wonderful story."

"That I had told you all about."

"Hardly."

"You're right. You went off halfcocked with no names and no attribution. You were fucking bush. All headline."

"I thought you weren't mad."

She was smiling at him in a way that invariably made him smile back. It was a smile blended of confidence in his affection, an affection, and this the smile acknowledged, that condoned her outrageousness. It was a smile of a woman who knew she was beautiful and that her beauty mitigated a multitude of sins, including an unbecoming competitiveness. That aggressive aspect of her personality Cynthia never acknowledged in words. Her smile said all she ever would say to Tony on the subject.

"Super bitch," he said, and despite himself he smiled.

They left their sandwiches half eaten and tumbled into bed. And when she came, he stared down at the shifting patterns in her eyes and felt triumphant.

"Why is it always a power trip?" she asked when it was over and they lay side by side, smoking cigarettes.

"It wasn't," he said.

"With you it's never just sex. It's always proving something to me, to you, to somebody. Why can't we ever do it just to do it, can you tell me that?"

"Oh, Christ, Cynthia, lay off."

"I'm sorry," she said. "It's just that I wish we could do something together without trying to one up all the time. It really gets boring. I mean it."

"This speech gets boring."

"Well, tell me. What do we do as two people together, for each other, no strings attached? Name one thing. Go ahead, you can't."

He jumped out of bed and pulled on his pants. "I really don't understand this. I guess I can't do anything right. It just isn't my day. Why don't you go back to your own place?"

"Forget it, Tony. I'm sorry. You've had a tough day."

Now, he felt he needed a drink after all. He went into the kitchen and found the bottle of gin. This time, he didn't bother with an ice cube. He took the gin and poured a thumbful into a glass and downed it.

"I must threaten you a helluva lot the way you hit that bottle at the first sign of conflict," she said, walking naked into the kitchen. "Why don't you grow up, for God's sake?"

He poured himself some more gin, then grabbed his half-eaten sandwich from the table. "Thanks for supper."

"Tony," she said. "I have an idea. Hear me out, O.K.?"

"Go ahead. I'm not going anywhere. This is my apartment, I think."

She sat down at the table. He stared at her breasts and wondered why it was they looked so unerotic now, when just minutes before they were burning into him. His stare made her self-conscious and she crossed her arms over her chest.

"Let's work together on the Duncan Avenue story."

"You're crazy."

"No I'm not. The paper isn't going to let you do anything. So let me do it for you. They won't manipulate our people."

"It's not a television story."

"You don't know what you're talking about," she said.

"It isn't."

"You know, that's something I really dislike about you, Tony. You speak so emphatically about something you don't know a goddamn thing about, like what's a TV story and what isn't. It's a great TV story."

"You mean all pictures and no facts."

"Listen, Tony. We can nail this down. Working together, we can nail it down in just a few days. With the station going after those records, as well as the *Bruise,* we could force them free in just two or three days."

"And then what will we have?"

"Well, we can go to work on McGivern and Mannion. We can trace their relationship. We can put the spotlight on Articulate. We can talk to people on the Zoning Board. We can get enough circumstantial evidence to flush out the mayor. And I'll tell you something else, we can get the attorney general to look into the whole arson situation. And maybe find out why the Fire Department put out that phony report today. We might even get the *Mammoth* going on the story."

"That's not going to do a damn thing for the *Bruise.*"

"Don't kid yourself. The *Bruise* would be forced to get back into the ball game if everybody else is doing it, and you'd have the head start all along. And if they don't and the paper folds, so what's different? You'll still be looking for work."

"Bobby Bantam would never speak to me again. He thinks I helped you with that report tonight."

"Well, you did," she said.

"Like hell I did."

"You got me the interview with Scooter. Did you forget?"

"Oh, shit."

He sat back in his chair and closed his eyes. He remembered the conversation with Bobby Bantam, the look of despair in the man's eyes, the sense of defeat. He remembered the comment about the mayor's meeting with the publisher and he had seen those conferences before. They had been sold out. Bobby didn't believe it, but he knew. But working with Cynthia? Jesus, what an idea. He tried to sort out the alternatives, working patiently within the *Bruise,* helping Bobby get the coverage organized for the pope. So Bobby gets mad at him. He has as much reason to be mad at Bobby.

"O.K., it's a deal. We'll work together. But my rules."

"Oh, Tony. I'm so excited," she said, and he felt the warmth of her breasts on his back. "Your rules. Whatever you say goes. It will be our secret. Just you and me."

"O.K. A deal. We'll talk about it in the morning. Let's go back to bed."

They fell asleep in each other's arms, and Tony's sleep was deep and tormented. He dreamed he and Bobby Bantam were crossing a bridge over a wide body of water, more a lake than a river, and that the bridge had suddenly given way in a high wind and Bobby began falling through and Tony was trying to hold him with one hand while supporting himself with the other, and then Bobby had slipped into the darkness. He called his name repeatedly, and then there was a loud ringing of bells as if from the foot of the bridge. The bells kept ringing.

"Get the phone," said Cynthia. "Oh, no, that fucking phone. Didn't you take it off the hook?"

Tony fumbled in the dark for the receiver. "Hello," he said.

"Is this Tony Owen?" said a voice that Tony couldn't trace.

"Yes."

"This is Dr. Carruthers at City Hospital. A woman was brought in here tonight. She's injured, and insists on seeing you."

"What?"

"I'm sorry. I know it's late. But it's a police matter. She has to see you."

"What time is it?" Tony asked.

"It's two-thirty," he said.

"What's her name?" Tony asked.

"Louise Finnigan," he said.

"What happened to her?"

"Somebody beat her up in South Boston."

"I'll be right there. Where should I meet you?"

"Come to the emergency room. Just have me paged."

Tony was now wide awake, and he was half dressed before Cynthia could ask him what was going on.

"A friend of mine got beaten up tonight. I have to go."

"A woman?"

"Yes. Somebody you don't know. A Louise Finnigan from South Boston."

"You bastard," Cynthia said.

"Don't start now. I'll call you. I don't know what it's about. Stay here, O.K.?"

He didn't wait for Cynthia to say another word. Instead, he grabbed his jacket and disappeared out the door.

WHO IS
THE HUB'S
HOLY MAN?

Tony smiled despite himself when he spotted Bobby Bantam's headline on the *Bruise* rack by the cabstand. Maybe the little bastard was right, Tony thought. Maybe the pope is the better story.

He dug a quarter out of his pocket and bought a *Bruise,* then jumped into the one cab waiting at the stand. The driver was asleep. "That's a good way to get killed, Johnny," he advised the driver.

"Hey, man, when your number's up, it's up. You got to trust your karma. Where you headed?"

"City Hospital, emergency room."

The cabbie drove fatalistically, speeding through two red lights in Brookline Village and almost ramming a drunk as he headed up Tremont Street in Mission Hill.

"Slow down, man. I'm not an emergency room patient myself, yet."

"Sure, sure," the driver replied.

But he made no effort to slow down. Instead, he continued to press down on the accelerator, squeezing the last bit of sleep out of Tony, who slumped low on the back seat and closed his eyes to await the collision he thought imminent. It was clear that this cabbie was not trained in Boston. Boston drivers had a code of their own. Anarchy was the rule of the road, a rule that pedestrians, other drivers, even the police, recognized and accepted. While drivers in Boston had the élan of their counterparts in New York, for example, they had none of their discipline and skill. The Boston driver compensated with a becoming realism, generally driving at leisurely and sublethal speeds. The Boston driver might maim, but he seldom killed.

Tony, tonight, drew a cabbie with murder in his eyes. It was with great relief that he arrived outside the door of City Hospital.

"That was some ride," Tony told the driver.

"What are you complaining about? I got you here. You want me to wait?"

"Jesus, no." Tony handed him a ten-dollar bill and told him to keep the change. The tip was thirty-five cents.

"Fuck you, too," the driver said and sped off into the night.

A tall, thin doctor with eyelashes and brows that were so white they gave his blue eyes a pale quality stood at the reception desk, talking to a nurse and a young man with his right arm freshly bandaged. A policeman stood off to the side, half listening to the conversation and half reading the *Bruise* sports pages.

"I'm looking for Dr. Carruthers," Tony said as he approached the group.

"I'm Dr. Carruthers. Tony Owen? I'll be with you in a moment."

Tony took a seat and flipped through the first pages of the *Bruise*. On page six where his column usually ran, there was a little box explaining that Tony Owen was on vacation.

Some vacation, thought Tony. The ride had left him wide awake and edgy. He looked around for a Coke machine. It was out of order. He reached for a cigarette.

"No smoking in here," the nurse standing by Dr. Carruthers said, looking over at him. "You'll have to step outside."

"I'll only be a minute," Dr. Carruthers said.

"Take your time," said Tony, trying to hide the irritation in his voice.

The goddamn widow. Who would have beaten her? You never know in this jungle. No neighborhoods are safe anymore. The North End had gone to hell, except on the main tourist trails. The kids were telling the old Mafiosi to shove it. And here's Louise getting clobbered in South Boston.

Now a detective Tony recognized but couldn't place came out of a side office and joined the group around the young man with the bandage. Tony got up and joined the circle. The young man was explaining how he came to be stabbed, a story the officer reading the *Bruise* had obviously heard before or he was so jaded by reports of street violence that he didn't care to hear another one.

"Hey, Tony, sit down, we'll be with you in a minute," the detective said.

Tony took his seat and stared at the knot of people from a distance of about fifteen feet. The young man was gesturing with his free hand; the white-eyebrowed doctor was nodding. The nurse was trying to busy herself with the paperwork on her desk. Finally, the group broke up and the detective and Dr. Carruthers summoned Tony into the side office.

"That kid out there," said the detective, "and Tony, I want this off the record, O.K.? He got nicked in the arm tonight when he tried to stop two guys from stomping a lady in South Boston. A fireman's widow. I understand you know her, Louise Finnigan?"

"Yeah," said Tony.

"Anyway, Louise is all right. I mean she's scared silly and the kid got a pretty good description of at least one of the mugs, the guy who stuck him in the arm. Anyway, we're trying to make sure the descriptions he gave and the one Louise will give us when she settles down are the same. But I don't want anything in the paper about the witness. I don't want anyone going after him. So you understand?"

"Yeah," said Tony. "Where's Louise?"

"I'll take you to see her. Remember, she's scared. She said she had a message she had to give to you in person, and after she talked to you she'd try to talk to the police. She's mildly sedated and we're still running tests on her to make sure there are no internal injuries. But all her vital signs are good," the doctor said.

"Where did this happen, in her apartment?" Tony asked, wondering whether anyone was with the widow's son.

"No, it happened on the street, Broadway, right near her house. About two. It might have been worse if that kid hadn't come along," the detective said.

"She's got a little kid at home," Tony said.

"I know. We've got him taken care of," the detective said. "O.K., Tony, you go with the doctor now. And I'll be waiting here to see what she tells you."

"Let's go," Tony said.

Louise was sleeping when Tony and Dr. Carruthers entered her room on the third floor. A reading lamp on the bedside table supplied the only light in the room except for that which spilled over from the hallway.

"Mrs. Finnigan," said the doctor, "Tony Owen is here."

Her right eye was swollen and shut tight. Her left eye was a slit, and her cheekbone was blackened and probably broken. Her lips were puffed and a small swab of cotton gauze covered what Tony took to be stitching work on the lower lip.

Tony squeezed her hand. "Christ, you look like you just went ten rounds with Marvelous Marvin," he said.

She pulled his hand, drawing him closer to the bed. He bent his head near her mouth.

She moved her lips to make a word, but the sound she made was indistinct.

Tony reached in his jacket pocket and pulled out his notebook and a ball-point pen. He placed the pen in her hand and the open notebook on her lap. He watched as she scrawled one word.

"What are you writing? Match? Is that what you're writing?"

She shook her head and made another sound, this time two syllables that sounded almost like baby talk. Then, trying again, she wrote out two words.

"Watch out," Tony said. "Is that what you're saying? Watch out?"

This time, she nodded and tried to smile. Again she struggled to speak, but failing to be understood, she took the pen more firmly in hand and wrote, more clearly this time: "They are after you."

"Who are *they?*" Tony asked. "Who is after me?"

She shook her head and started to cry.

"It's O.K., Louise. It's O.K.," he said.

"We better let her sleep," Carruthers said.

The detective was waiting for them in the reception room when they got back downstairs.

"She didn't tell me much except that someone is after me. I guess maybe they beat her up as a warning for me. I don't know."

"And who do you think would be after you?" said the detective, a tall man with an overflowing belly and wise eyes. "I guess I could name half the pols in Boston. You sure give enough people a motive."

"I don't know. I'll have to hear more from Louise tomorrow. She'll be O.K. tomorrow, won't she?" he asked, turning to the doctor.

"She'll be sore as hell, but she'll be able to talk a bit more with less difficulty, I would guess."

"Do you work for Mayor Haydon?" Tony asked the detective, after he struggled in vain to recall his name. It was a point of honor with him never to ask a policeman his name. He liked to think he knew most Boston policemen on sight.

"Everyone works for Mayor Haydon," the detective answered.

"You going to report this to him?"

"I'm going to report this to the commissioner. What he does with it I can't say."

"I'd like to see the report."

"Come by my office sometime. I have no objections, as long as it doesn't get in print over my name."

Tony and the detective shook hands and Tony walked to the phone and called a cab, and as he waited the reality of all that had happened to him that day began to sink in, and for one of the first times in his career he felt more than insecure. He felt scared. He thought of Cynthia at home alone. He knew she wouldn't have bothered to refasten the locks after he left. He got back on the phone and got the dispatcher. He wished he had the same driver who brought him to the hospital in record time. He should have asked him to wait.

"This is Tony Owen of the *Bruise* again. Where is that cab? I'm in an awful hurry."

The dispatcher patiently explained that the cab was on its way, and as soon as Tony hung up the phone he saw it waiting outside the door.

"Get me to Cleveland Circle as fast as you can," he said. "There's a big tip for you if you hurry."

Only the main lock was fastened when Tony got back to his apartment. Cynthia was still asleep. He looked at the clock. He had been gone for less than two hours. He was too wired to get back into bed. He put water on the stove to boil and sat at the kitchen table, trying to think his way through what had happened. He tried to think of the number of people who knew that he was even acquainted with Louise, let alone that she had slept with him. He remembered the other night in the bar in Southie and the drunken Tommy Mannion. He knew; so did any number of other people in the bar that night.

But if they were going to beat someone as a warning to me, why wouldn't they have picked on Cynthia, lying here all alone? Too spectacular, too obvious. And they don't beat up on news people. It had to be Mannion! It had to be Duncan Avenue.

He remembered Scooter's warning. McGivern's paisanos. What a nest of worms. He listened to the sounds of the early morning. A few birds sang outside. A dog barked. An occasional car passed outside on Beacon Street. He heard Cynthia stirring. She was not sleeping deeply, perhaps she wasn't asleep at all, but just lying there thinking of the woman he had to rush out to see in the middle of the night. What the hell was he going to tell her? Maybe she wouldn't ask. Not that it was much of a relationship. A roll in the hay over in Southie. Getting back to his roots. Mother Earth. Jewish girls think too much, much too much. The bed springs squeaked. Cynthia was stirring now. No doubt. She was awake. He heard her feet hit the floor and soon she appeared in the doorway, wearing one of his bathrobes.

"Want some coffee?" he asked.

"Yeah," she said.

"You won't believe what happened," he said.

"Try me," she said. "And it better be good."

□

Connie Haydon fell heavily into his wide and empty bed and was asleep almost at once. In his deepest sleep he dreamed a dream that lingered in his mind when he awoke, sealing him in a mood of black and impotent rage.

It had begun a reassuring dream. He and Winston Churchill. That's the man to be like, his mother had told him. Be someone larger than life. Grand scale. Never fashion yourself after someone ordinary. If you decide to become a writer, look to be a James Joyce. If you're going to become an actor, then look to Olivier. And if it's a politician, then strive to become a Churchill. Be grand. Aim high, be first-class. And now in his dream, it was Churchill counseling him, praising him, reassuring him as he sat with the great man in the garden of a country home. His mother was there in the kitchen, overseeing the production of a great feast, and in the dining room the expansive table was set for company with the best silver and a white linen cloth. And while the two men sat and talked, a rat the size of a raccoon with its belly swollen and its coat foully matted came into the garden from the house and began nibbling on Churchill's leg. The statesman, cigar in mouth, stood up in shock, kicked the rat away, and then in fury turned to Connie and shouted: "You are not what you seem. You are filthy, small, and treacherous." Connie grabbed a broom and turned on the rat, whipping it with the wooden broom handle, but the rat seemed indestructible. It stood there withstanding the blows as they fell and staring up at Connie with beady eyes and a little ratty smile. And when Connie awakened, the black mood was gripping him like an angry hand.

He felt frustrated, powerless, at the mercy of forces beyond his ability to channel, let alone control. He had never felt that way before, and never expected to. He was born with a sense of the nature of power and his own superiority, and he knew that the two were complementary facets of his own being, that his claim to a station in life high above the herd was an empty one without the ability to impose his will on those below him, and that that ability meant nothing if it could not be demonstrated.

Admit doubt, display weakness, and you invite defiance: the kind of defiance that Eileen hurled in his face. It was a defiance that frightened him, at the same time as it left him shaking with rage. He had lost her respect. He had lost her love. He already knew that, long before the confrontation over Tommy Mannion and Scooter. But he had also lost something that he never thought he would lose in his relationship with Eileen — his capacity to intimidate her. He no longer frightened her, and now he was subject to her scorn, her ridicule, and her retribution. And there was nothing he could do to counter it. She didn't seem to care if she were no longer the mayor's wife, if she were suddenly faced with a life without a chauffeur to take her shopping or to the movies, or down to New York for a theater opening; she no longer cared if she never again entered a restaurant where the maitre d' fussed over her, or never again played hostess to the world's leading celebrities as they called on the city. His power meant nothing. He could offer her the world and it didn't matter. Because whatever he offered, she would have to share with him because it came from him. The idea stunned him. She was indifferent. She was married to the most exciting politician in the country, a truly historic personality (my God, he knew they'd be naming high schools after him long after he was dead), and she was prepared to dismiss it all.

But to him, whether Eileen stayed meant the difference between running for office again or surrendering all that he had. He could not run again if on the eve of the campaign, she decided to walk out. There just wasn't enough time to repair the damage. The public has to be prepared for these things. Look at how long it took Kennedy to prepare the way for his divorce. A politician with a bad or busted marriage could survive in Boston, but not a politician whose wife hated him so much she wouldn't defer the separation until after the election.

But Eileen was threatening not only divorce. She was threatening to ruin him, to make him look like all the other tired hacks that Boston had produced in abundance over the generations; she was prepared to make him look like just another Irish pol on the take. And who would believe otherwise with Eileen herself pointing the finger at him? Good Lord. She might not only ruin him politically, she might even get him thrown in jail. That would be the ultimate humiliation. Going to jail, and for what? For something that he hadn't done.

He winced at the idea. Over the years, he had skirted the edge of the law. On occasion, he even crossed the boundary, when he was reasonably certain that it made no difference, that no one was looking, or likely to look. Countless times, he had taken envelopes stuffed with cash and slipped them into his pocket, letting people like Scooter worry about the source. And later, when he was told which developers, which landlords in need of a tax rebate or abatement, which suppliers in need of a rich contract were friends of the mayor, he would be careful not to inquire which had kicked in the cash, and which were merely men of good will proud to lend him their moral and political support.

While it was true that Haydon accepted illegal, and untraceable, cash contributions, he accepted them in good conscience. If quid didn't know quo, a quid pro quo was out of the question. By the same reasoning, it was out of the question that there was anything corrupt about the award of favors at City Hall. The North End cigar-store owner with the flourishing bookie operation might be ignored by the vice squad for two years after he passed along $50,000 to one of Haydon's lieutenants. But so may the equally prosperous bookie three blocks away, who didn't do anything more than send the mayor a friendly greeting on his birthday. Of course, it never crossed Haydon's mind that those who heaped cash favors upon him had no idea that they enjoyed no special status on his list of good friends. Nor did he consider that if they realized how indifferent he was to their contributions, they might radically reduce their gifts or curtail them altogether. Under Connie Haydon, those kinds of assumptions were a one-way street, and he, for his own peace of mind, wanted to keep it that way.

He relished the freedom the arrangement gave him to award a contract, rebate a tax bill, designate a developer, without feeling that he was bribed into doing it. "I am not corrupt," he liked to say, and every time he said it, he actually believed it.

Nor was he bothered by the size of the slush fund his campaign accountant maintained for him in half a dozen foreign banks. He knew the sum was considerable, but he didn't know how considerable because he refused to allow the man ever to inform him of the actual figures. Someday he would retire and take an accounting. But any knowledge now would be guilty knowledge, and Connie Haydon was an innocent man. Besides, the money, no matter what the amount, was his due. As he saw it, the mayor of Boston was grossly underpaid, scandalously underpaid. Had his talents been put to use in the private sector, he would be a millionaire ten times over. The campaign funds were just one way to compensate for what was owed him. It was also a way to assure himself that the style of living to which he had grown accustomed while he was mayor would remain his style of living for the rest of his life.

Now Eileen could jeopardize even this small piece of security. Over the years, he had tried to shield her from any knowledge of his financial affairs. But she was a bright enough woman. She had to know that there was more income than that acknowledged in the W-2 forms. Out of anger, she may well have begun spying into these arrangements. He remembered seeing her on New Year's Eve chatting with the accountant. Could she have been prying? Could she know?

Christ, Scooter knew. Scooter knew everything. But if Scooter talked, he implicated not only the mayor, he implicated Scooter himself. No, he would never talk about this. It would do in too many people, too many people Scooter befriended, too many people who trusted him. Besides, they wouldn't believe him, and if they did, they would throw away the key . . . unless they granted him immunity. No, even with immunity, Scooter would keep his mouth shut. Of course he would, particularly with certain inducements.

He looked at the clock by his bed. It was 6:15. He reached for the phone and called Stanley. "Meet me in Waterfront Park in forty-five minutes," he said. A groggy Stanley mumbled something that the mayor took for assent before hanging up the phone and climbing out of bed.

He raced through his morning exercises the way, as a boy, he used to race through his morning prayers. He then showered, dressed, and called for his car.

A fine mist was in the air and the April wind was cutting. Haydon sat in the rear of his limousine and scanned the morning newspapers.

His black mood lifted somewhat when he saw there was no Tony Owen column in the *Bruise* and no reference to the Scooter case whatsoever in either paper. The pope dominated page one of the

Mammoth, which announced the start of a seven-part series on Catholicism in Boston.

"Got a saint for the *Bruise,* Charlie?" the mayor called to his driver.

"I thought I'd nominate you, Mr. Mayor, if you don't mind."

"Good choice, Charlie. I wonder how I'd make out running to head the community of saints?"

"I'd vote for you."

"What makes you think you'd be eligible?" the mayor cracked.

The phone buzzed under the dash. "The commissioner's calling," said Charlie, who was detached from the Police Department to serve as the mayor's driver and chauffeur.

"Find out what he wants," the mayor said.

"He wants to know where you'll be. He's got to talk to you."

"Tell him we'll be at Waterfront Park," said the mayor.

The limousine edged around Charles Circle and nosed its way up the ramp onto the expressway. The early morning traffic was thin as the limousine headed down the elevated highway that sliced through rows of old warehouses and factory buildings, tenements reshaped for expensive condominiums, old wharves with new facing wearing the look of suburban chic.

The peddlers were out in force as the mayor passed the Haymarket, where his limousine curled down the ramp, cut through the shadows under the roadway, and headed toward the waterfront.

Stanley was sitting slumped forward on a bench facing the harbor as the mayor drove up. "Come on, Stanley. Get out of the rain," yelled the mayor as he swung the heavy gray door open. Stanley, his trench coat damp from the mist, climbed into the back.

"Connolly is looking for you," he said. "He called me right after you did."

"What's on his mind?"

"Something happened last night in Southie. Tony Owen is involved. I wasn't clear on the details. Some woman got beaten up outside her home."

"By Tony Owen?" said the mayor.

"No, I don't think so. He's involved in some way. I didn't get the details."

"Didn't you think it was important enough?" the mayor asked coldly.

"I was half asleep. He said he'd get to you first thing."

"Stanley, you never get anything right, do you?"

Stanley said nothing. He was accustomed to being kicked around by the mayor, and he was smart enough to recognize that being the vent for the mayor's frustrations was one of the reasons he was so richly paid. He offered the mayor a form of psychological release and the abuse, although directed at him, wasn't personal. At least, he didn't take it that way.

"I'm going to see Scooter at eleven," he finally said.

"Fine," said the mayor. "And what are you going to tell him?"

"Just what you said to me yesterday: that I think you are concerned, that no matter what happened you feel you can't wipe out the debt of loyalty you owe him for his years of friendship, and that in my opinion you still consider him your friend and would like to know precisely what it is he needs."

"Yeah, but be careful the way you say it. Make sure you put everything at a safe remove from me. You don't mention that we talked. He'll probably be wearing a wire."

"I'll be careful."

"Fine. And what else is happening today?"

"We might get some word today on the pope. It looks like it's going to be happening pretty fast now. Foley wants to see me this afternoon with some Italian monsignor who got in last night. Bertalami or something like that."

"You are vague this morning."

"Give me a break, Connie," Stanley said. "You just woke me up."

"Everybody wants a break," said Haydon. "O.K. I hope the pope doesn't come too soon. I'd like to string this out."

"This we can't control."

The mayor laughed hollowly. Stanley had no idea how things had deteriorated, no idea that his mission to see Scooter would likely prove an empty exercise, that even if he made the most outlandish demands, and they were met, he wouldn't be out of the woods. Eileen had the upper hand with an agenda all her own.

"Let's get out of the car. I feel like walking," the mayor said. That was why he came to the park. He loved the smell of the waterfront early in the day, the sense he took in the empty expanse of park and harborfront that this was his city, his place. People spoiled that, the noxious crowds that later in the day would move like a pastel-and-polyester army through the park, into the concourse leading to the marina, down through the pathways to Faneuil Hall Marketplace, and to the government buildings beyond City Hall. They used his city without any sense that he was sharing it with them, without any real sense of him. He was like an artist who produced paintings so in sync with the times that people looked blindly through them because they so perfectly reflected reality. He was not just another pol any more than this was just another city. This was special and he was special. And someday all these fools would stop in their tracks and realize what a man they had, and what a man they lost.

"Mr. Mayor," someone shouted.

Haydon turned. Behind him, about fifty yards away, had pulled up a police car. Commissioner Connolly climbed out of the front seat and walked toward him.

The mayor stood still and waited. The commissioner, a stocky man, moved heavily across the pathway toward the water, waving a manila envelope in front of him. "I've got to talk to you," he said.

The sun was warmer now and the mayor, Stanley, and the commissioner moved to a bench at the water's edge.

"I think you ought to know about this," he said, taking a seat on the still-damp bench. "It's about Tony Owen."

"What is this Tony Owen business all about?"

"Well, I told Stanley. This woman . . . Here it is" — he pulled the report out of the envelope — "Louise Finnigan, white, female, widowed, date of birth three/eighteen/forty-four, was accosted by two white males outside the premises at three-forty-four Broadway, South Boston, approximately two A.M., four/seventeen."

"Come on, Commissioner. Cut the jargon. Put the report away and tell me what happened."

"Well, from what I gather, and it's all in here, if you want to see it," he said, waving the report emphatically, "this woman was beaten up by two punks. I don't think they were from the neighborhood. Anyway, they did a good job on the lady, who, from what I hear, was a friend of Tony Owen's. She's going to be all right. But on the way to the hospital, she insisted on seeing him. He got called and came to the hospital. He talked to the lady and apparently, from what I can gather from the report, she told him that they beat her up as some kind of warning to him. They want him to lay off something or other."

The mayor's face reddened. "You got to be kidding me," he said.

"No. It's in the report. Here, I brought you a copy."

"No, no, I believe you. Keep the goddamn report. Did she get a look at the guys?"

"I don't know. She was all shook up. She should be a lot better later today and we'll run some mug books by her. Maybe we'll have some luck."

"Keep me informed," he said.

The mayor felt rattled. He turned and walked briskly toward the Aquarium. Stanley and the commissioner followed him. He turned again and quietly asked them to leave him alone. "I want time to think," he said.

At the Aquarium concourse he sat on a bench, looking down at the water. It had to be McGivern. It was just his style. Reflex. Lash out. Never worry about the consequences. Somebody else will sweep up the mess. He cursed Tommy Mannion. He cursed Eileen.

And I had it all set, he thought. Bobby Bantam was laying off. Tony Owen was silenced. He weighed the impact of the beating on the *Bruise* and winced inside.

He could see Bantam's headlines. Granger wouldn't be able to stop him. Now only one thing could possibly save him and it was probably too late for that. He was out of time and out of moves. He sighed and headed back toward the limousine. He, at least, knew what he had to do. It came down to a matter of timing. That was the only element of choice left him.

"Charlie," he said when he returned to the car, "drop Stanley wherever he wants to go and then take me to the office. I've got to think."

□

John Walsh didn't wait to be announced. He just dashed into Bobby Bantam's office, excitement overriding his laconic demeanor. "I think we've got a good one, Bobby," he said. "Just heard from the cops that some hoodlums beat up a lady friend of Tony's in Southie early this morning."

"Yes," said Bantam, showing a trace of irritation that Walsh would just barge in on him, as if he were Tony Owen or Granger himself.

"The guys who beat her up said they wanted her to get a message to Tony to lay off, and a few minutes after she got to City Hospital, Tony came over in a cab to see her."

"Where's Tony?"

"I don't know. He called in to say that he read in the paper that he's on vacation. So he said he's on vacation and he'll be in when he's rested up."

"That son of a bitch. Who's the lady? I didn't think Tony had any ladies in Southie."

"She's a fireman's widow. Louise Finnigan."

"Anybody talk to her yet?"

"I sent Stella over to the hospital just now."

"You send a camera, too?"

"No. Nobody's around."

"Send a camera. Get the works. Get the scene. Interview neighbors. Get the full police report."

"I'm trying to get Tony."

"He'll call. But make sure you got every base covered. Pull some people in from the State House if you have to."

Walsh hesitated. "I'm short-handed today. There may be some developments on the pope's visit, and I need people to find the saint."

"Don't tell me your troubles. Just cover the bases on this beating. This may be the story we've been looking for."

"What if it's connected to Duncan Avenue?"

"What are you talking about? Of course it's connected to Duncan Avenue. It's got to be."

"But I thought we were dropping that story."

"Hey, since when are you getting paid to think? That was yesterday. Today we got a story. A real story. Hoodlums beat hero's widow, try to silence *Bruise*. The *Bruise* won't be silenced. Never."

Bobby dismissed Walsh by turning his back and grabbing the telephone. He dialed Tony Owen's number. No answer. He called Cynthia at Channel 4. She came to the phone.

"Hello, Cynthia. Bobby Bantam. How you doing? Good? Just great. Hey, Cynthia, I've got to reach Tony. Urgent. Really urgent. You don't know where he is? You're kidding. No, I'm not calling you a liar. Hey, come on now. Hey. Are you kidding? Hey, you little bitch, I don't care if you are Tony's girl, don't you talk to me that way."

He slammed down the phone. Walsh was still standing there.

"What the hell do you want?" he asked.

"I wanted to see if you could reach Tony. Guess not, huh?"

"He'll call. He'd better, the ungrateful bastard."

13

"DO YOU REALIZE," Cynthia asked with reasoned calm as she and Tony Owen sat at the kitchen table, "that you are no longer simply Mr. Trained Observer? In this one, you're part of the story. Whoever beat up your girlfriend did you a favor. They made you just like the people you've been writing about for years."

Tony was in no mood for one of Cynthia's excursions into his unconscious. It was already dawn. The sunlight was streaming into the kitchen through the drawn window shades, and Tony was bone tired.

"You amaze me," Tony said. "I never know what Cynthia I'm going to be talking to. I really thought you might have been furious at me. I'm glad you're handling this so maturely."

"And why should I be angry? You yourself just told me the woman means nothing to you . . . I'm not sure that's true. But still, even giving you the benefit of the doubt, maybe now you'll come out of hiding."

"What is this hiding crap? Come on, Cynthia. Give me a break. I'm awfully tired."

"I am giving you a break," she said. "You thought I'd be in a rage. You see, I'm not. I'm being nice. But before you fall asleep, I think you should consider what I'm saying. You can't hide behind anybody now because you are in the story. You're part of the scene. It could be a turning point for you in terms of your growth and development."

"Oh, Christ, I'd rather you were in a frenzy than lecturing me on my goddamn growth and development. I'm doing just fine."

"But you're a participant, maybe for the first time in your life."

"What do you know about my life?" he said with sudden savagery that cut into Cynthia's feelings.

"I'm sorry. I thought we were closer," she said.

"Oh, shit," he said, reaching for her shoulders. "I didn't mean that the way it sounded."

He lit a cigarette and went to the kitchen window, drawing aside the shade and looking down into the garbage-strewn alley below.

"I think it's time to move," he said. "This place is beginning to depress me."

"Maybe it's not the place," she said.

"Baby, please. I know what you're trying to say. But you're wrong on this one. I'm in the story not because I'm a player but because the two of us are getting too close to someone's comfort zone. Don't you see the difference?"

He didn't want to argue the point. He wished she would let it drop so he could pop back into bed. But she was too persistent for that and the point was too important to her.

"That's irrelevant," she said.

"Then what's relevant?" he said. "You tell me."

"Your feelings count in this one."

"Don't they always?" he said.

"No, you use your feelings. It makes better copy."

"I'm a real son of a bitch. Is that what you're saying? Then why the fuck are you hanging around with me? Why don't you go out with some asshole who wears his heart on his sleeve and cries all night over the fucking whales? Why don't you?"

Now it was Tony who was getting out of control, and despite his exhaustion, he was almost ready to bolt out the door. And he would have, had Cynthia not softened her approach.

"I know how tired you are," she said. "I'll not press the point any further. But all I ask, and I don't think I'm being unreasonable, is that you think a little about what I said when you wake up."

"O.K.," he said. "We'll talk a little later."

Had Tony wanted to face what Cynthia was driving at, he could have conjured up a hundred examples to shore up her case. His memory brimmed with images of people mired deep in one form of misery or another, people Tony studied, talked to, manipulated, and in the end exploited without feeling much of anything about them.

He was good at getting at the way people felt who were engulfed in the flow of news. Once he had gone to a hospital to interview a young man whose bride had died in a car wreck ten minutes after they left on their honeymoon. The groom learned of the death just a few hours before Tony appeared at his bedside, and was in a state of near-shock. A sympathetic Tony got him to talk about how he had met his bride-to-be, and once the tears came, Tony moved quietly off — his column already written in his head, telling himself that what he did was therapeutic, as, indeed, it probably was. It was, he told himself repeatedly, the nature of his work. He didn't do it to be callous; he wasn't callous. He was good at what he did not because he lacked feelings. He had feelings.

He used them. He directed them. He took his fine edge from them. But he never let them touch him. That would never do. They were like a light he could switch on or off, and Tony Owen found that was better for all concerned.

"And it's not a matter of hiding, Cynthia," he said as he headed toward the bedroom. "It's the nature of the business. One learns to bleed quietly and in private. And she isn't my girlfriend, by the way. She's somebody I know."

"Fine," said Cynthia. "In any event, she may have done you a great favor. I almost wish you were in love with her and then you would know what I'm saying is true."

"Don't start again, please."

"Would you write about the woman? Would you write about her relationship to you?" Cynthia asked.

"Yeah, I suppose."

"You suppose? But what if she doesn't want it in the paper, what if later when she's got her wits about her, she asks you to keep it out — then what would you do?"

"She's not going to ask me that. Besides, there's a police report," he said, standing at the bedroom door.

"That doesn't mean anything. You had a relationship of some kind with her, otherwise these creeps wouldn't have gone after her. I mean, what if they went after me and I asked you not to write about it, to let the police do their work quietly — what would you do?"

She stared at Tony, who looked away. Finally, he said, "You wouldn't ask me that, would you?"

"I might if I were scared enough."

"Then I would go along."

"And you'd have contempt for me after that."

"So what is it you're trying to get me to say?"

"I'm not trying to get you to say anything, Tony. I'm trying to remind you that being a reporter doesn't lift you outside the human race. You owe something to that woman. People are not on this earth to provide you with column material. You know that you owe something to the rest of us, too."

"Get off it, Cynthia, you're as much a reporter as I am."

"But I haven't resigned from the human race, not yet."

"O.K. Enough. I've told you I'll think over what you're saying," he said.

"And just one more thing. Let me remind you of something else," she said. "You can handle this story on your own terms. I mean, after what Bobby Bantam said to you yesterday, you don't owe the goddamn *Bruise* a thing. It wasn't Bantam they were trying to intimidate last night. It was you. You're out from under."

"I can work with you now. Is that what you're suggesting?"

"Not just me. You can still work with Bobby, but if they don't want to go heavy, I'm here."

"I thought you'd get around to that. But what if they come after you next? Won't you be too scared?"

"Not with you around."

"O.K. We're in this together."

"Together."

"O.K., but we're going to move slowly. In case you haven't noticed, we're dealing with some pretty mean people, and I don't want you blundering in somewhere over your head. You're not going to do anything unless you clear it with me. Is that understood?"

"Yes, sir," she said, standing up and giving him a mock salute.

"And today. Let's see now, it's Friday. Today we're going to lay low."

"Lay low?"

"Yeah, we're on vacation. At least I am."

"You mean you're not going to work the story today?"

"Maybe a little phone work. But no, we'll lay off until Monday. Let Bobby Bantam sweat. Let the people who beat up Louise think they've gotten away with something."

"But aren't you worried the *Mammoth* will pick up the story?"

"No, they won't react. It's just another beating in Southie as far as they're concerned. They'll just ride the pope all weekend. Besides, they can't cover two stories at once. It would be too taxing. They can't concentrate that hard."

"O.K., but I'm going to work. I'm not on vacation."

"Fine, but no Duncan Avenue stuff. Nothing till Monday."

"What about Louise?"

"What about her? She'll be in the hospital until Sunday night, Monday morning."

"Are you going to exploit her?"

"Oh, Jesus, are we partners or not? If we're partners, you got to drop that kind of talk."

"Partners."

She stuck her hand out stiffly. Tony took it and squeezed hard.

"We're partners, but I'm the boss."

"I understand," she said, wincing.

"You'd better."

□

After Cynthia left for work, Tony took the phone off the hook and slipped into bed, sleeping until it was past noon. Then he got up, threw on some old clothes, heated up the coffee left over from his talk with Cynthia, and sat down by the phone, notebook and pens at hand. He called Tommy Mannion's real estate office and got no answer. Then he called the Mannion home, just to confirm what he already suspected — that Mannion was incommunicado.

The elderly woman who answered informed Tony that Mannion was out of town on a business trip, and that she had no idea when he would return. It made no difference. He knew that Mannion would not speak to him.

He checked his watch. It was after one o'clock. Perhaps he ought to check in with Bobby at the *Bruise*. No, it was better to let him sweat a little longer.

He telephoned Scooter. "They're turning vicious," he said. "They beat up a woman I know in Southie last night."

"That's McGivern. He's a ratfucker. I told you that."

"Are you guessing or do you know?"

"I don't know anything."

Scooter's voice was neutral. Even the word *ratfucker* carried no emotional freight.

"Scooter, you can help me break this wide open and put some very bad people in their place . . ."

"I got to go now."

"What do you mean, you got to go now? Remember me? I'm your friend, Tony Owen. What's the matter? Is someone with you?"

"Got to go now."

He hung up. Tony reached toward the dial to call him again, then replaced the receiver in its cradle. It was no use. Scooter had gone as far as he was going to go.

Tony was getting nowhere. He put water on for more coffee and the phone rang. It was Bobby Bantam.

"What are you doing at home? Get your butt in here. We got a helluva lot of work to do."

"I'm on vacation," Tony said. "I read it in the paper."

"Get in here. Come on, now. You won your point. I was wrong. You've got a helluva story."

"Why do you say that? Did something happen that convinced you?"

"Don't be cute, Tony. I know what happened last night to that lady in Southie. Hey, if she means a lot to you, I'm sorry that this story got her messed up, and I hope it doesn't mess you up with the lady from Channel Four."

"Bobby, this may come as a shock to you, but I'm not at all sure I even want to do the story. And by the way, that lady has a name. It's Louise. I want to do Duncan Avenue. I'm not sure I want to do what happened to Louise."

"How can you not write about Louise?" he said, the irritation rising as he spoke.

"It's not much of a story, Bobby, if I don't write it and she doesn't talk about what happened. And I'll tell you straight out, I'm not going to write unless she says it's O.K., and I haven't talked to her about it."

Bobby's tone softened. "Hey, Tony, I can understand what you've been going through and that last night was an ordeal. But, Jesus, this is what we've both been waiting for. This could be our break. Goons beat up widow in bid to stop *Bruise*. Come on, now, Tony. We're not going to walk away from this."

"But it's Duncan Avenue, Bobby. You said no Duncan Avenue. No Bernie Kremenko. You thought it was all crap. All you wanted was the pope. You wanted to let the mayor off the hook, you and Granger."

"O.K., are you happy now? You've pulled my chain. I thought the pope was a better story. I was wrong. You were right. You want me to kiss your ass? What's the matter with you? The beating changed things."

"So now you're convinced we can do Duncan Avenue?"

"Hey, we've got only a few weeks, maybe days, to pull this off. Now we have a cutting edge. So get your ass in here."

"And what about Granger?"

"Don't you worry about Granger. I'll handle him."

"I'll see," Tony said.

"What do you mean, you'll see?"

"I want some time to think about it."

"You son of a bitch, what do you think you're doing to me?"

"Nothing. The story will hold. I'll see you Monday, maybe."

"Monday?"

"Hey, I'm on vacation, remember?"

"Tony, don't push me."

"Bye, Bobby."

Tony hung up the phone, pleased with himself. He had proven a point to Bobby Bantam. It didn't occur to him that perhaps Cynthia had also proven a point to him.

□

Monday morning, Bill Raleigh gathered his chief editors in the conference room across the city room from the editor's office. Sean Dugan was there, the executive editor who had trouble deciding whether he was a politician, like most of his friends, or a newspaperman. His political instincts were sharper than his news instincts, being more regularly honed. He was also a company man to the core, a safety-first bureaucrat who never forgot that there was no percentage in taking risks. At Dugan's elbow was William T. Bender, deputy executive editor. He was a stocky man with pebblelike dark eyes and a wisp of a nose, and his stock-in-trade was silence. He would sit at meetings and listen, his little eyes screwed up, an inscrutable look on his featureless face. And when it was clear that a consensus was emerging, he would succinctly summarize. Bender had a reputation for wisdom.

Cyrus Corning, managing editor, sat across the table from Dugan and Bender, his body tilted toward Raleigh at the head of the table at an angle that struck a comfortable compromise between aloofness and groveling. Corning kept his position by swallowing small insults for a decade or more, deferring to inferior men in the hope that ultimately justice would be done him. He was not especially popular around the conference table.

Finally, there was city editor Tom Curtis, a slum kid who had won a scholarship to Dartmouth, where he starred on the rugby team. Curtis, a talented man, had an innate sense of his own inferiority; he compensated by taking on the personality of a stage Irishman, back-slapping, joking, drinking too much, and allowing himself to be overwhelmed by long, deep fits of despair.

"We've got to make up our minds what we're going to do with that Duncan Avenue story," Raleigh told his editors. "It's getting to be a tough story to ignore."

"We're not exactly ignoring it," said Dugan. "We've got Horn-blower working it. He should come up with something in a few days. I don't think we should get shaken out of our game plan just because some bimbo gets beaten up on the street. What the hell was she doing there at that hour?"

"Well, the angle that's fresh is Tony Owen."

"Yeah, but we don't want to give him free publicity. They'll be pumping it up for all it's worth," said Corning.

"Let them," said Curtis. "It's still a horseshit story. And nobody is paying any attention anyway. There's only one story in town right now, and that's the pope and what he's coming for."

"I agree," said Dugan. "Even if there is something to Duncan Avenue, and I'm not at all convinced there is, nobody's going to pay much attention. Whatever the *Bruise* does, it's going to look like the desperate reach of a dying paper, and the silliest thing we could do, it seems to me, and I'm not closing my mind at this point, but the silliest thing would be to come out full blast on this and promote the *Bruise* by promoting the *Bruise*'s story."

Raleigh frowned, buried his head in his hands, and reached for the phone.

"Helen," he said to his secretary, "try to get me Stanley at City Hall. If you get him, get me out of the conference room.

"I'm not sure you guys are wrong," he said. "I'm just a little worried. I mean, we got the *Bruise* just where we want them. It will take a miracle to save them. I just don't want to hand them a miracle. Either by doing something or by not doing something."

"Look," said Curtis, "anything we do is going to give their story credibility. I say we do our own story at our own pace and pay no attention whatsoever to what's happening to them."

"How long will it be before Hornblower is ready to write?"

"How long do you want it to be?" asked Dugan.

"Let's wait awhile. In the meantime, it wouldn't hurt to run a three-paragraph story tomorrow on the beating in Southie. It is a matter of record."

"Just what I was going to suggest," said Bender. "I think we should put it back on about page five or six of the Metro section, just to show people we're aware of the incident and don't assign it a great deal of importance."

The phone rang. "I've got Stanley Blum on the line, Mr. Raleigh," said his secretary.

Raleigh excused himself from the conference room and walked back to his own office.

"What can I do for you, Bill?" Stanley asked.

"Two things, Stanley," Raleigh replied. "First of all, what's new with the pope?"

"I think they'll make an announcement today or tomorrow. It looks like he'll be here within two weeks. He'll be staying for two days at the cardinal's residence in Brighton, and the highlight of the trip will be a Mass at either Harvard Stadium or Fenway Park, depending on availability. And that depends on the exact date of his arrival. The Red Sox are a problem at Fenway, but the location is perfect. So everything depends on the timing. I was hoping to get to you sometime today."

"Fine, that sounds terrific. Any idea of the agenda?"

"Not yet. I'll let you know as soon as there's a hint of anything.

But it looks like he'll be heading for Miami and Chicago, too, maybe Los Angeles. Everything is so hush-hush. We'll never be sure until the last minute."

"O.K. Now, what can you tell me about the beating of that woman over in Southie? What kind of story is that?"

"Bill, I'll tell you what I know, and I think it's pretty accurate stuff. But Louise Finnigan — I think that's her name — from what the police tell me, is a woman with, well, how should I put it, with a reputation that isn't the best in the neighborhood. Tony Owen shacked up with her a few times, but so have a helluva lot of other people. She sort of fell apart after her husband died. Husband was a fireman. Well, he'd be turning over in his grave if he knew about her carryings-on. I mean, let's face it, Bill, she's a bit of a slut. I mean, I'm not judging her, and I really don't know the lady, but she drinks a little more than she should for her own good, and it was inevitable that she'd run into some trouble."

"Maybe so, Stanley. But from what I've been hearing, she got beaten up by some people who were out to stop Tony Owen."

"Stop him from what?"

"From banging the drum about Duncan Avenue."

"I'm telling you, Bill, and I don't know what the mayor's been telling you, but that story is a lot of horseshit. The *Bruise* hasn't even been touching it for days now. I mean, they were trying to hook the mayor on that one and they got nowhere, and now they'll probably seize on that street incident and try to pump it up some more. The story isn't there, Bill. It just isn't. That's all I can tell you. Of course, if we hear anything different about it, I'll get right to you."

Raleigh hurried back across the city room to the conference room. "That may not have been connected to Tony Owen after all, that beating in Southie," Raleigh said. "The woman is apparently a bit of a slut, pushing her luck out late after drinking too much."

"I'm not sure that's true," said Curtis. "I knew her husband and I met her once or twice. She always seemed sensible to me."

"I don't think Stanley would lie to us about this one, do you?" said Raleigh. "I mean, he'd be found out pretty quick if he's lying."

"Well, there's enough doubt raised to support our initial feelings," said Dugan. "Let's put it on the shelf until Hornblower is ready. In fact, let's have Hornblower incorporate the story, if there is a story there, into the main effort. Same timetable."

"Fine," said Raleigh. "Now for the serious business. The pope is going to be here within ten days. Still no agenda. Big outdoor Mass at either Fenway Park or Harvard Stadium, depending on the timing. We better have all hands cranking on the preparedness. How're we doing with the series on Boston's great monsignors? Jesus, do you realize that Saint Peter's alone has produced more than forty of them, including a dozen bishops. We ought to do a profile on that church. That's really special."

"We'll also need to start serializing the life of the pope. That book we bought should break down nicely," said Dugan. "We can sked it once we know the exact date."

"Who do we have heading the task force?" Raleigh asked.

"Carl Abrams," Bender answered.

"But he's a Jew," said Curtis.

"Better that way. He's more objective and he'll give us a fresh perspective on the whole coverage."

"Well, let's get cracking," said Raleigh. "There will be only one better story in town all year."

"What's that?" asked Bender.

"The death of the *Bruise,*" Raleigh said.

□

"She's a terrific woman," said an exuberant Stella Ferral as she cornered Tony Owen seconds after he arrived in the city room Monday morning. "I don't think I've ever met a braver human being. I mean, Tony, she's unreal."

"Who are you talking about?" he asked. "The saint of the day?"

"No, I'm talking about your friend who got beaten up in Southie," she said, more quietly now. "I took her home from the hospital this morning, and she gave me a terrific story, which Bobby says I should write in collaboration with you, if that's all right. I mean, I got to the hospital by nine this morning."

Tony bristled and stalked away, leaving Stella, who was anxious for conversation, stranded in the aisle. Bobby Bantam, who had just emerged from his own office, spotted Tony as he reached his desk.

"Glad to see you back, Tony. Not the same place without you, not the same paper. I mean it."

"I'm not happy, Bobby."

"So, what's happy? You see Stella?"

"Yeah. I got the news. You're preposterous."

"Well, she can feed you her notes and you won't have to be bothered after that. Better get to it. This could save our ass if we play it right."

"Cut the crap, Bobby. That was a rotten thing to do."

"You cut the crap," Bantam replied. "I wasn't even sure you'd show up here today. What did you expect me to do?"

"I told you I wanted to talk to her, didn't I?"

"Well, go ahead and talk to her. She'll tell you the same thing she told Stella. She wants the story out. She likes the *Bruise*; she likes you. She doesn't like being pushed around."

"I wanted her to talk to me, not to Stella. You'd have been better off using Molly Minton on the story."

"Molly Minton? Then you'd really go through the roof."

"Molly would play it straight, I think."

It was useless to continue the argument. For some reason, he and Bantam were at cross-purposes. That rarely happened.

"O.K., if Louise says it's all right, I'll collaborate with Stella on the story, if you want me to. I have to tell you something. I've cut a deal with Cynthia on this."

Bobby wrinkled his nose and peered up at Tony. "What does that mean?"

"Cynthia and I are in this together now, just in case Granger tries to knock the story down. It's too important to me. If the *Bruise* isn't going ahead on Duncan Avenue, then I'll work with Channel Four, or go back on vacation. By my calculations, I've got five and a half months coming to me."

Tony braced for a typical Bobby Bantam explosion. Instead, Bantam stared up at Tony, a small smile on his face, then said quietly, "That's O.K., Tony. Just make sure she gives us credit on any of your material whenever she uses it. We can stand the promotion. And wait till you see my front page for tomorrow. Come on into the conference room. I got to show you. You'll love it."

On the corkboard in the conference room, Bobby had already posted the dummy of the front page based on the story Tony Owen hadn't even begun to write.

"This'll be worth ten thousand copies all by itself. What do you think, Tony? Is that a grabber? We'll have 'em by the fucking balls."

Tony stared at the dummy. In capital letters, four inches tall, Bantam had come up with the message:

BASTARDS!

"And right down below we'll have the picture of your sweetie with her eyes swollen shut, and right alongside her picture we'll begin the story of how they're trying to scare us off the story, and inside we'll review the whole Duncan Avenue business and stack the stories around your column and refer to an editorial that Paddy is already putting together on how the people's paper won't be pushed around. And from then on, it will be a drumbeat."

Tony frowned. He knew that Bobby, when he was set on a page one, didn't like to listen to anything but enthusiastic approvals. He also knew that the display could have an impact, a big impact, on the town. For a moment, he could almost share Bobby's optimism that they had stumbled onto a story to save the paper. Still, he frowned.

"What's the matter? You don't like it?" Bobby Bantam said.

"No, it isn't that. It's Bobby Bantam at his best. I'm just not sure I can do this to Louise."

"Do what to Louise? She already gave us the story."

"Bobby, I'm just not sure she knows what she's doing."

"Fuck her. She's already talked to Stella. It's too late for second thoughts. She's ours, pictures and all."

"She hasn't spoken to me, Bobby."

"Go ahead, explain. Tell her the whole thing, you son of a bitch, but if she changes her mind, I'm going with the story myself, if I have to write it myself. And what the hell are you all of a sudden, a goddamn bleeding heart? You ought to be working for those stiffs across town, for Christ's sake."

"I'm still going to lay it all out for her, Bobby," he said.

Stella provided Tony the phone number where Louise was taking refuge. A woman answered the phone. At first she refused to concede that Louise was there, but she relented as soon as Tony identified himself.

"I'm sorry I put you through all this," Tony told Louise when she finally got to the phone.

"You didn't do anything, Tony," she said. Her words came slowly and quietly, so quietly that Tony asked whether it was still painful to talk. The question nettled her.

"Tony, you're making me very tired," she said. "I don't want to talk to you now."

"But I want you to understand. I know you talked to Stella."

"I do understand. I'm going to go now."

"I don't want to put you through more in the newspaper. Do you understand that?"

She sighed. "Tony, stop acting as if I matter to you. I told you. You owe me nothing. Now please, let me go back to sleep."

"But, Louise . . ."

She hung up. He reached for the dial to call her again, then had second thoughts. He sat with the phone still in his hand, staring at his paper-strewn desk. Bobby Bantam came over to him.

"Is it all straightened out?" he asked.

"I guess so," Tony answered.

"Good. Then let's start writing."

Tony bent to the typewriter, trying to suppress a feeling of uneasiness, but vagueness befogged his mind and he made three false starts. He was set to throw the column aside and take a long walk through the neighborhood when the phone rang. Cynthia was excited.

"Tony. I'm really scoring. I've gotten the records from City Hall and the art department is putting together a chart I can use on the air tonight to show the patterns of ownership, and wait until you see it. It's going to knock your eyes out. And I'm heading down to Dedham right now to see one of the secretaries in that law office. I have a feeling she's going to cooperate. She sounded very nice on the phone. How are you doing on your end?"

"Fine," he said. "Bobby sent Stella Ferral over to the hospital this morning and they got a good interview with Louise. Tomorrow we'll be going with the attempt to scare the *Bruise* off the story. It should be a helluva package."

Cynthia paused, then she said, "You didn't talk to her yourself?"

"I called her. She didn't seem eager to talk to me."

"What do you mean?"

"I don't know, maybe she was still doped up or something. Anyway, I asked about how she was feeling and she said she didn't want to talk to me."

"Are you planning to use her name and all that tomorrow?"

"Yes."

"And she's aware of that?"

"Yeah. I mean, I think so. Stella told her all that."

"I'll bet she did. You mean you didn't tell her what was happening?"

"I told you she didn't want to listen. She didn't want to talk. So get off my case."

"You just told me she was too drugged to talk. Which probably means, unless I've suddenly gone stupid, that she probably has no idea what's happening. You're taking advantage of her, Tony."

"No, I'm not. We talked about that," he said in exasperation. "She wasn't so doped up she didn't know that."

"So you did talk?"

"Good Lord, Cynthia, will you get off it? I thought we were trying to put a story together, and all you're doing is grilling me about someone who means nothing to me."

"Jesus, Tony, isn't that the problem? Aren't you putting your finger on what's the goddamn problem. She doesn't mean anything to you, and she's probably in love with you, which is why she's doing what she's doing, risking her neck and all, and you could care less. You really are a shit, you know that? I can't believe it."

"Cynthia, I can't believe you. Are we working on a story together or are we not? 'Cause if we are partners, we had better stick to the story or we'll end up not talking to each other ever again. You know, you have this funny habit of changing the ground rules of our relationship at the slightest whim. And to tell you the truth, it's getting to me. I want to do this story and all you want to do is toy with my mind. Well, let me tell you, Cynthia, you aren't my goddamn psychoanalyst."

"All right. I'll drop it, but I can understand why Louise won't talk to you. You know, you have a lot to learn about women — never mind women, people. You have a lot to learn about people, Tony, you really do."

"Drop it."

"It's dropped. I told you that. Anyway, watch me at six. I think I'll have a helluva piece. And try not to totally destroy your girlfriend. I'll be seeing you."

Cynthia's call left Tony infuriated. For the thousandth time, he told himself that never would he marry her, never would he subject himself to so much grief. He had made a sincere effort to communicate with Louise, and she had rejected him, refused to listen. What did Cynthia expect, that he try again, once more submit to the uncertain emotions of someone who obviously had no understanding of what he himself was all about? He had never pretended to be anything but what he was: a newspaperman living for the story, trying to hold body and soul together while pouring his guts into a no-account rag that reeled from hand to mouth, never knowing which edition, which payroll, would be the last. It was absurd to torture yourself with the subtleties of meaning under the circumstances. Life was rough-hewn; he was rough-hewn; yet here was this woman asking, insisting even, that he be delicate, and not just to her but to another woman, a woman she didn't even know, a woman he had slept with, for Christ's sake.

"The hell with it," he said, and reached for the phone. Again, the strange woman answered, again there was a pause as she went to Louise to find out if she cared to speak to him, and again Louise took the phone.

"I'm sorry, Louise," Tony said. "I don't think I was clear when we spoke before. I just wanted you to know that your name is going to be all over the paper tomorrow. We'll be using you for a front-page story on how the *Bruise* is standing up to thugs. If I were you, I'd think long and hard about whether you want to get involved in something like this. It could really complicate your life, and you might feel really exploited."

Tony waited, and in the silence before her reply, he found himself hoping that she would say no to the story. He could feel the confrontation ahead with Bobby Bantam, and for once he felt nothing within him recoil at the prospect.

"Tony, I know, or I have a pretty good idea of what the story will be like. Go ahead. I want the story out. I'm not ashamed of anything I did, and I know the cops in this town. They need a little pressure to do anything, and I really want them to catch those guys. I'm not afraid, I'm not ashamed, and I'm not going to hide."

"But people are going to talk, and you live in a very small town."

"Hey, I've tried to tell you before that I'm my own person. And what are they going to say: that I had a relationship with you. So I did, such as it was. But I'm not doing this for you, Tony, and you seem to have trouble accepting that. I'm doing it for myself. You're absolved. Go in peace. It's O.K."

"Why did you hang up before?"

"I don't remember that I did. Oh, I suppose I did. You can be a pain in the ass with all your concern. I don't think you really care all that much for me, and you don't have to pretend. You just make too much out of the fact that you went to bed with me once. I told you then, and I'll tell you now, it's no big deal. I wanted to do it, don't you understand? I'm a free adult person and I wanted to sleep with you, and I meant it when I said no strings were attached."

"O.K., Louise, I'll call you tomorrow," he said, and in his mind he wondered whether Louise Finnigan was really an Irishwoman.

He sat and stared at his typewriter for five minutes after he hung up the telephone. To his surprise, he felt flushed with desire for Louise. He found himself thinking of what Cynthia had described as the perfect woman for a newspaperman. "What you guys need," Cynthia had told him repeatedly, "is a woman who can't speak, see, or think, who is always available for the odd hours you want to get a little, who'll make no demands, and who'll have no needs beyond your own. You don't want a person; you want an abstraction with a pussy."

On reflection, it occurred to Tony that Louise was not that at all, but a woman who had turned to him at a difficult time in her life, who had used him, and was still using him, for some private purpose of her own, and that even the pain that came her way on the street and the humiliation that would follow in the wake of the *Bruise* — and he could hear the snickers now along Broadway — was part of a personal calculus whose elements had nothing to do with him. He comforted himself with the thought that once that inner score was settled, whether it had to do with the dead fireman or someone or something else in a lifetime of flawed feelings, she would never again so readily admit a drunken columnist into her bed, or allow others benefits from her personal hell.

But it was the fantasy of the undemanding, all-yielding woman that Tony accepted now, and despite himself, his desire stirred and all but blotted out the rest that was Louise. Now he was in a mode for work and the vagueness vanished from his mind and he began to write.

"Her only sin was this: she was a friend of mine and in the twisted logic of the underworld, they decided to use her to send me and my paper a message, and the message was this: 'Lay off Duncan Avenue.'

"O.K., you sick bastards, I've gotten the message and here's my answer, and the answer of the *Morning News*: You are going to pay. You are going to pay for what you did to Bernie Kremenko, and you are going to pay for what you did to Louise Finnigan."

"Keep it rolling, Tony, you're singing, really singing," said Bobby Bantam as he sat by Tony Owen's side, grabbing the takes as they came from the typewriter. "This is going to do it; this is really going to do it."

□

Connie Haydon took no calls all Monday afternoon and received no visitors. Utterly alone within his office, he sat behind the oak desk that once belonged to Daniel Webster and thought. He stood by the big picture window, looking down at the throngs moving in the marketplace, and thought. He thought while lying stretched out on the sofa and while pacing the floor like an imprisoned felon, and always he came back to the same conclusion that he had reached Friday morning in Waterfront Park. It was his only chance and it just might work; surely nothing else would. Outside his inner sanctum on his secretary's desk, the messages were piling up. Stanley had to see him, and Corinne, and the police commissioner, and Henry Hornblower. The cardinal had called and so had someone from the State Department. But Haydon wasn't interested. All that concerned him was the crisis he faced, and meticulously he picked at its components. Withdrawn from the distractions that went with his position, Haydon was capable of cold and merciless objectivity, even toward himself. He saw all the players on the board, and he could anticipate their next moves with a practiced judgment that seemed at times omniscient. And he used that anticipation to craft his own strategy. His judgment was buttressed by a sense of timing that few politicians possessed. When he acted, invariably, or so it seemed to his enemies, it was as if everyone else was moving in reaction to him and that they were on the defensive rather than the mayor. Long ago he had learned that the illusion of control could sometimes serve better than the real thing, and he was a master at the art of political illusion.

Shortly after five o'clock, he completed his calculations and summoned Stanley to his office.

"Make arrangements for a news conference tomorrow night just before the news and start getting papal flags ready. I want one on every street corner in the city. I don't care whether there are Catholics in the neighborhood. I want those flags everywhere as soon as possible, and get the merchants going so we have them in all the store windows. And I want a big one flying from the City Hall flagpole."

"Where are we going to get them?"

"That's your problem. Get them."

"Is the news conference going to be on the pope?"

"Tell them it's a general news conference on a specific theme. We'll let them all know tomorrow. Meanwhile, I'm going home and I don't want to be disturbed."

"What about all these people looking for you?"

"Deal with them; use your own discretion. Have Corinne help you. Just don't bother me any more tonight. I'll see you here in the morning, first thing. We'll have a busy day."

□

His strategy settled in his mind, the mayor was almost buoyant as he marched up the front steps of his home and pushed in the door. He had done his work, thought things through, and he allowed the small possibility that his plans just might work after all. Gone was the gloom and uncertainty of the morning. He was back in action. Defeat was possible, even likely. He couldn't delude himself about that. All those people clutching at his heels, trying to bring him down. They had all the leverage. But they'd know they were in a fight and a few of them would go down with him. At the very least, he'd see to that. Eileen, for one, she'd know, and she wouldn't long forget.

She was sitting on the sofa in the living room.

"How are you, darling?" he called, his voice mellow and bantering.

"Hello, Connie," she said, glancing up momentarily from a copy of the *Bruise*.

"Kind of late in the day to be reading the morning papers, isn't it? Unless there's a tidbit or two in there that bears closer scrutiny."

"No, there's nothing in here really. Not even a Tony Owen column today. I don't know why I buy this thing."

"Well, enjoy it while you can. It won't be around long."

He flicked on the television. It was 5:59.

"I hope I'm not disturbing you, am I now, my bride? I'd like to watch the news."

"No, not at all," she said, ignoring his sarcasm. "I'd like to watch it myself."

"I thought I'd watch High Impact News, if you don't mind. I really enjoy Cynthia Stoler, don't you?"

"That's fine with me," Eileen said.

He took a seat on the sofa beside her and watched. He was not surprised by any of the tease-ins: papal visit getting closer, still the mystery behind the trip; water contamination in Lynn; teenage lovers carbon monoxide victims in Stoughton; the Red Sox considering adding a second black player; and a special report from Cynthia Stoler on the Duncan Avenue arson situation.

"I think I'll fix myself a little drink while I'm waiting for Miss Stoler," the mayor said. "Would you care for one?"

"No, I've had one," she said.

"So I see," he said, looking down at the now-empty water glass that he knew had been half-filled at least once that afternoon with Jack Daniels. "You seem a bit edgy today. Did something happen that I might have missed?"

A star-shaped crystal ashtray, a wedding gift that had miraculously survived the years, was on the table in front of her, its interior an unsightly blend of gray ashes and filter tips.

"I don't know, Eileen, why you're so nervous. It seems you have all the cards in your hands. It would seem to me that you would be riding high by now, a woman in total control of her destiny."

"Be still," she said, barely looking up at him as he stood at the bar and fixed a dry Manhattan.

"O.K., not another word. I won't even comment on the dent somebody put in this quart of booze."

"Coming up next, a special report from High Impact News reporter Cynthia Stoler on the situation on Boston's Duncan Avenue," the anchorman announced. The mayor sat down on the sofa alongside Eileen, his drink sloshing in his hand.

Once more Cynthia was back on Duncan Avenue in front of number forty-two, the building where Bernie Kremenko died. The mayor was prepared for anything she had to say, and for a moment he leaned toward the screen and mugged, "Go on, give me your best shot, Cynthia. Let's see how hard you can hit."

Then he listened.

"For the past week, the administration of Mayor Cornelius J. Haydon has been sitting on the public records relating to the ownership of properties on and around Duncan Avenue, where arsonists have been on a rampage for the past eighteen months . . ."

"Be objective, Cynthia," said the mayor.

"Today it was clear just why . . . A firm called Articulate, Incorporated, a firm with direct links to powerfully placed city officials, has been the major mover of property titles in the area."

Cynthia disappeared from the screen and in her place was a chart with the properties owned by Articulate, Inc., represented in flaming red. The camera stayed fixed on the chart as Cynthia resumed her story.

"One of the principals in Articulate is Boston attorney F. X. McGivern, one-time counsel for the owners of some of the city's sleaziest properties in the Combat Zone. McGivern is a close associate, and some say an inseparable companion, of Mayor Haydon's brother-in-law, Thomas Mannion, who is in the real estate business.

"McGivern, reached in his office late this afternoon, refused to discuss his relationship to either Articulate or the mayor's brother-in-law. As for Mannion, he was said to be out of town on a business trip."

"That wasn't so bad now, was it?" said the mayor.

"Wait a minute. She isn't finished," Eileen replied.

"McGivern, meanwhile, has been playing an active role in trying to drive the few remaining residents of Duncan Avenue from their homes, going so far as personally to sign eviction notices against those harassed tenants. McGivern's precise role with Articulate could not be immediately determined, but clearly it is a major one. High Impact News learned that today when it interviewed three employees of a Dedham law firm that drew up the incorporation papers for Articulate.

"All three employees worked in the offices of Dedham lawyer Otto Otlowski until his death last year, and all three clearly remember the circumstances when they were asked to be listed as the 'straw' owners of the enterprise.

"All three said they signed the papers at the insistence of McGivern, who left little doubt that he was one of the men in charge. None of the three would agree to appear on camera, but all three willingly signed statements attesting to McGivern's involvement."

"Very interesting report, Cynthia," said the anchorman to her as the screen split in two. "But I don't yet see the links to City Hall. Maybe you could clarify that for us."

"Certainly, Walter," said Cynthia. "Members of the Zoning Board told me, on a not-for-attribution basis, that it was McGivern and the mayor's brother-in-law, Tommy Mannion, who sought the zoning change that will at the very least quadruple the value of the property, and that they had no doubt in their minds that the mayor knew of the request.

"And today I also — and I've been saving this up for a special report later in the week — spoke to the head of a Belgian development company with an option to buy the Articulate holdings. He told me that he personally had discussed the project with Mayor Haydon, and he left the meeting with the mayor convinced of his support."

"Very interesting, Cynthia. And what does the mayor have to say about all this?"

"I'm sorry to say I don't know, Walter. He wasn't taking any calls today. His press office said, 'No comment.' "

"Well, thank you very much, Cynthia. Now for other news . . ."

The mayor bounced up and turned off the set.

"Well, what are you going to do?" asked Eileen. "Have you decided?"

"Yes, I have, Eileen. Your demands were ridiculous. I'm going to do nothing about them, nothing at all. What I will do is tell the truth."

"You think you're going to do to my brother what you did to Scooter?"

"That's right, and that's why I could care less what Cynthia Stoler has to say or what Tony Owen has to say or what you have to say, because in this one my hands are clean."

She stood up and stared down at him as he sat on the sofa, his hands cupping his barely touched Manhattan.

"You're bluffing," she said, her green eyes fixed on his grinning face.

"Then you can call my bluff. By the way, do you have a nice gown to wear to the papal reception? I'm sure there's going to be one. Maybe you should run over to Bonwit's tomorrow and pick out something appropriate."

He kept the grin locked on his face, mocking her, infuriating her. But she bit down the anger, fighting off the impulse to lash out at him. As she regained her poise, he let the grin fade from his face.

"Somebody beat up a girlfriend of Tony Owen's."

She ignored the remark, her mind turning on what he had said earlier. She knew him as well as he knew his opponents, but even she wasn't quite sure what he intended to do.

"I'll have Scooter turn over that document. That would put you in a sorry mess now, wouldn't it?"

"Scooter is a toothless tiger. He'll turn over nothing, not that it matters if he does."

"You've gotten to him?"

"Call him and see for yourself."

"I've warned you, Connie," she said. "I'll see to it you're ruined. Don't pretend you don't care. I know how much you care."

The grin remained on Haydon's face, but his eyes turned hard and cold. By now he was reclining on the sofa, staring up at Eileen, deliberately making himself vulnerable to her, knowing full well that he had, for now, disarmed her. "Eileen, why don't you wait until tomorrow and see what I'm going to do and then you can make your plans. Do what you want to do after that. But don't jump to conclusions. Things are never as bad as they seem, and you may have some leverage left after all. Right now I can't see any, but who knows?"

He rolled over on the sofa as if to go to sleep. She stood by the sofa, staring at his back. If she had a knife in her hand, she might kill him. She could see herself reaching for a blade like the big carving knife hanging in the kitchen, then bringing it down right between the shoulder blades, and she could imagine him turning toward her with that madman's grin painted on his face. She shuddered and reached for the cigarettes on the coffee table, and walked out of the room. Yes, she told herself; I will wait and he will pay, one way or the other.

□

Bobby Bantam was humming, a low, barely audible hum that caught people by surprise, especially people who didn't know that humming in a monotone that resembled the sound of an electric mixer was just one of Bobby's idiosyncrasies, one of the sound effects designed for the theater of his mind when that mind was racing full tilt. Bobby didn't know he was humming. On nights like tonight, he was oblivious to everything around him except the object of his concentration, which was the production of the *Bruise.*

"Goddamn," he shouted to John Walsh, "get a hold of the general manager and tell him they better up the press run by twenty thousand. No, make that twenty-five. This one is going to break the bank. Jesus, we might save this goddamn tub of a newspaper in one edition. Would you believe it?"

He stood by the city desk, Tony Owen at his side. It was midnight, and the first edition had just come up from the press room. "Tony, this one is a collector's item. Perfect."

It was one of those rare editions that emerged almost exactly the way Bobby Bantam had conceived it, down to the closely cropped picture of Louise Finnigan propped up in her hospital bed, looking the worse for wear despite an odd smile that must have hurt her swollen lips.

"It's nice, Bobby. It should sell a ton."

"Never mind a ton. Just give me fifteen thousand. That will open the eyes of those blind bastards out in Kansas. Wait till the mayor sees this; he'll be heading for refuge in Costa Rica. Terrific."

"I wonder how long it will take Granger to see this."

"It depends on how good our circulation department is."

"Then I guess we'll never hear from him," Tony cracked.

They were still laughing when the phone rang.

"What the hell do you think you're doing, Bobby? I have every right to come in there right this minute and wipe the floor with you. In fact, if you were standing here in front of me this moment, I think I would strangle you, absolutely strangle you, you miserable, lying, disloyal little son of a bitch."

"Elmer," said Bobby, "hold on a minute. I don't think I can hear you very well. You caught me at the city desk and it's no place to carry on a conversation. Let me get back to my office."

Without waiting for the publisher's reply, Bobby Bantam switched the call back into his office, about one hundred fifty feet across the newsroom floor. Tony Owen followed.

"Now, what is it you were saying out there?" said Bobby. "I don't think I heard a word."

"You know just what I said, you little snake. I'm telling you I'm just about set to put on my shoes and come down there and deal out some prairie justice."

"You mean you're going to hang me?" said Bobby.

Tony Owen could hear the slam of the publisher's phone from where he was standing almost ten feet away.

Bantam looked at Tony and said, "I think he's going to come down here and try to horsewhip me. Would you believe that man?"

"You keep saying you can handle him."

"Well, maybe I can, but I'll tell you something. I'm not going to wait around here to find out. Hey, he'd order a replate if he thought that would make the story go away. Now he's stuck with it and he knows it."

"For this edition."

"For the whole press run. After that, we'll see. But my bet is that he's stuck with the story now, especially after the piece that Cynthia did tonight. Now all the TVs will pick up the story, leading off with the Louise Finnigan piece, and if things break right, we could make our magic number, or be right at it just before the pope comes, and wait until I tell you what I have planned for the pope. You won't believe it. Special zones for each neighborhood. Even Roxbury. How do you like this one: Here comes Jay Pee Deuce."

"What are you going to tell Granger?"

"Hey, you can tell him. You think I'm going to wait around here till he arrives? He just might try to beat me up, right in front of the troops. I'm splitting."

Within seconds, Bobby Bantam had cleared off his desk, throwing into the trash basket every item he had failed to get to during the day. Grabbing his jacket and keeping his head down, lest he see something or someone that might detain him, he steamed toward the escalator and whatever refuge awaited him.

Tony was about to follow when someone shouted over from the city desk that he had a phone call. He walked to his own desk to answer it.

"Tony Owen?" a polite voice said, a voice polite enough to belong to a telephone solicitor.

"Yes," Tony replied.

"You're playing with dynamite, you realize that, don't you? Do you want to end up like Don Bolles? You will, you know. Please lay off and pass the message on to your girlfriend. It's just not safe what you're doing."

The caller hung up before Tony could say a word.

"Who was that?" the night city editor asked.

"Just some crank," said Tony. He said it emphatically, but the caller didn't sound like a crank at all.

14

CONNIE HAYDON went to bed early, snapped off the lights, and gazed into the darkness. For an instant, he thought of Corinne and how he had abandoned her. But his mind raced on, groping for solace. There was no point in self-reproach, which merely sapped the energy he would need for tomorrow. Yet the islands of consolation eluded him and he could not sleep. Eileen was to blame. She had planted the seed of doubt in his mind, unsettling him. And now, as hard as he tried to blot out all but the most pleasant thoughts, the idea of his political end surfaced in his mind. The idea shouldn't be unsettling, he told himself. He had always recognized that one day he would face the ultimate defeat, the loss of all the dreams he had nourished since childhood, and that prospect had never bothered him. But as he lay in the darkness, he realized that he had never before confronted defeat, only the idea of defeat, an abstraction so unreal that it neither terrorized nor startled. What Eileen had done was tear that abstraction down, forcing him to confront not the idea of the end but the end itself. He had to consider a possibility, yes, even a likelihood, that he would soon be powerless.

Power had been his shield from the start, defining him, protecting him as he rose, someone special from the start. Oh, he'd be governor someday, they had said of him, even while he sat on the City Council. And when he was a progressive state representative, the pundits painted an even brighter picture. He'll be a U.S. senator someday, surely. And when he became the celebrity mayor, the still-young man who spoke for the forgotten people locked in the cities of America, they were saying anything was possible for Connie Haydon. Even Bill Raleigh assured him it would happen, and why not? Kennedy had done it; so why not Connie Haydon? Why not, indeed?

But it never did happen. Other men, lesser men, moved up, surpassing him, elbowing him aside as they rose. And the glamour of the rediscovered cities, a glamour concocted by liberals out of the ashes of long hot summers, began to fade as their accountants added up the costs and found that helping poor people was impossibly expensive and personally ungratifying. In fact, they discovered, poor people were the problem with the cities. Get rid of them and the cities were a wonderful place to live. And Haydon got that message, and his politics began to change, and his city began to take on the glitter of the richer suburbs and the cash began to run in torrents, carving a golden mask onto the aged face of downtown. The silver and gold jingled in the pockets of a new crowd, and Haydon's power grew. But no one talked about him as a young man anymore, and no one suggested that one day he would move up.

He was still powerful, of course, more powerful than ever. But it was not the power of almost infinite possibility; it was the power of the ruthless and entrenched, and its face was no longer young but as old as compromise.

Now, even that power could soon slip away, and as Haydon stared into the darkness, he could see, for the first time, the emerging outlines of ordinary life. He began to wonder how it would be. Would people stop greeting him on the street, let him walk on by, let him pick at his meals undisturbed in a restaurant? Would he still be shown to the best tables? Would he have to stand in line at the airport? Would the invitations still come in to the best dinners? Would women still look at him in the same way? What would it be like to drive a car by himself, to reach out and plunk a quarter into the coin machines at the tollbooths? He tried to imagine, to make the prospect real. He tasted the unpleasantness, the nastiness, the bitterness that seemed to be ahead, and he wanted no part of it. He had to survive. He would not be driven out of office, out of power, and, he told himself, it was not because he lacked the strength. No matter what Eileen said, he knew he was strong enough to stand up to adversity. It was not a matter of character. It was a matter of likes and dislikes, of what he was used to.

Gradually, he began to feel pleased with himself, and he thought ahead to his news conference. He would show them tomorrow the stuff that he was made of; he would show Eileen. He would show those creeps over at the *Bruise.*

His head settled deeper into the pillow and soon he was conscious that he was dreaming, and he thought how odd to be dreaming that he was dreaming, and he sighed in relief that he wasn't dreaming about rats.

It was dusk and the mayor was on stage before a vast throng on the Common. He was dressed formally, as if it were Inauguration Day, and beside him on the platform was Sir Winston himself and Connie's own mother, looking regal, and John Kennedy was there, smiling in the background. Standing beside Churchill was the pope. It was not the Polish pope but the pope of his youth, Pius XII, with an aristocratic smile on his severe face.

Off to the side in the crowd stood a gang of boys from the old neighborhood, and they were smiling up at him. The smiles were not friendly. They were mocking him. He stared down at them, with a hard glare. But their mockery was even more blatant. He motioned to a police superintendent, indicating the troublemakers with a nod of his head. Except for the gang under the tree, the throng was silent. The superintendent turned his police face toward the punks but did no more than stare.

Now it was time for the ceremony, and the mayor moved toward the battery of microphones. The silence deepened. The multitude spreading out as far as the eye could see on all sides of the great stage seemed locked in stillness, as if each member of the audience was afraid that the slightest motion, the faintest sigh, might trigger a flood of noise that would wash over the assembly in a chaotic tide. Did everyone know something that Connie Haydon didn't know? He looked over at the boys once more. They too were silent but still smiling, insolently, certain of their place, disdainful of his.

And then Connie Haydon spoke. "Fellow citizens of our special city," he said. And then, before he could utter another word, one of the gang shot his arm forward and an egg splattered on Haydon's chest. He looked up and now the boys were laughing, and the crowd, inexplicably expressionless until now, was grinning up at the mayor. And now another egg came, and then a tomato, and the missiles came not just from the boys under the tree but from every part of the crowd, and the laughter now had broken through. Sir Winston was apoplectic. He came forward, arms upraised, and his voice rang out with the command: "Silence!" And there was, for an instant, silence, almost as impenetrable as before. But the instant didn't hold, and soon the eggs began to fly once more through the air. One hit Sir Winston on the forehead. The knot of distinguished guests upon the platform began to recede to the safety of an underground shelter. "By God, you should have warned us this was apt to happen," Churchill told the mayor, and Haydon was mortified. He awoke with the dawn, still shaken from his dream, and he went through his morning calisthenics with savage determination.

□

Tuesday morning's *Bruise* hit the city with even more impact than Bobby Bantam had imagined. Bantam knew the extent of it within five minutes of awakening as he turned the radio dial and heard each of the local AM stations pounding away on the story, quoting the *Bruise,* of course, but also borrowing liberally from the Cynthia Stoler reporting of the night before.

He reached for the telephone by his bedside and called the general manager.

"It's a good thing I asked you to go up last night. I should have had you take it to thirty-five. I think we could sell them all. How did we do?"

"Same as normal."

"What do you mean, same as normal? That's impossible. We hiked the press run."

"Same as normal, Bobby."

"Didn't we sell out?"

"Quite likely," the manager said.

"Then we had to go up."

"Bobby, we didn't run any extra papers. Elmer absolutely forbade it."

"What do you mean, he forbade it?" said Bantam, incredulous. "How did he even know about it?"

"I told him. Would have been my ass."

"You incompetent little bastard. You trying to save a paper or save your ass, you no good . . ."

He began to splutter. Finally, in frustration, he just slammed down the receiver. "I don't believe it," he said. "I just can't believe it."

Walter Griswold read the *Bruise* at his breakfast table in Pride's Crossing and reached for the telephone.

"Bill, this is Walter. Have you read the *Bruise* this morning?"

"I'm reading it now, Walter. It's Bobby Bantam at his best, or worst, depending on your point of view."

"Well, I've read it, Bill, and quite frankly I'm not thinking about Bobby Bantam. I'm thinking about the *Mammoth* and wondering why we've gotten skunked like this."

"Oh, I don't think that's at all accurate, Walter. We haven't been skunked. I mean, we know all about the story. We just don't think it's quite the story the *Bruise* is presenting. And we've been watching it very closely with one of our best reporters."

"Well, Bill, perhaps my news judgment isn't as trained as yours, but it seems to me they have a helluva story there, *Bruise* or not. My God, man, they have a neighborhood being burned down by a consortium with ties to City Hall. They have an attempt by mobsters to silence them and an attractive young woman being beaten up on a city street. I really don't understand your reluctance to jump on this story with both feet."

"Well, you've used the right word, Walter. I am reluctant, deeply reluctant, to lend our authority to a story that's obviously designed just to build circulation and keep them in business a little longer. And the heart of their story, although they haven't come flat out and said so, is that the mayor is behind the changes going on in that place, and I just don't believe it, and I can't believe that you believe it about Connie Haydon."

"Who did you say we had working this story?"

"I told you. Henry Hornblower. You know, Billy Hornblower's son. A fine, thorough, and meticulously fair reporter."

"Bill, don't you think we might have someone on this story a little faster and more aggressive?"

Raleigh said nothing. He was stunned. Never before had young Walter gone this far.

"You're off base, Walter. I think you're getting a bit beyond your area of competence, if you don't mind my saying so."

But young Walter did not back down. "I think I'm competent enough to read the morning papers and to recognize when we've had our socks beaten off."

"I would like to remind you, Walter, that we are not putting out a scandal sheet. We have a bit more restraint than to chase after every trashy story that comes our way."

"I disagree with you, Bill."

"Well, when you have been around a little longer I'll take your disagreements more seriously."

"Bill, I'm not calling you to get involved in an argument. I'm sorry it's come to that."

"All right, Walter. I accept your apology. But try to understand one thing. I do not believe that Connie Haydon is a crook and an arsonist or goes around ordering women beaten up in South Boston. I don't think you believe that, either. I believe he's our kind of fellow, and that he has been very good to our newspaper. I think it is wise to keep that in mind before you would authorize me to embark on a campaign that would bring him down, open the floodgates to a number of people who do not share our values, and perhaps throw a lifeline to the *Bruise*. It is no time to become impulsive."

"Good day, Bill."

"Good day, Walter."

□

Elmer Granger was still fuming when his alarm went off. He fumed through breakfast and fumed as he walked to work, ignoring each of the *Bruise* boxes he passed en route and knowing without looking that each was already sold out. He fumed as he sat at his desk and read the *Times* and the *Wall Street Journal.* He was still fuming at ten o'clock when he picked up the phone and called the big boss in Kansas.

"I'm just calling to keep you informed. A little snag seems to be developing here. Bobby Bantam's crew has come up with a pretty good story."

"Well, what does that mean?" the boss asked.

"It means there could be a burst in circulation."

"More than the target figure?"

"It's possible."

"It must be one helluva story," the boss said.

"It's complicated. I'll send you today's editions."

"Can the circulation be sustained? It would look dreadful if we hit the target and had to close down anyway."

"That's the problem. I don't see how it can be sustained. I think the story is a one-week wonder, and if we're not careful we'll get ourselves locked into an even worse situation."

"Well, Elmer, I don't know what to say. You are the fellow, I believe, who kept insisting on that target figure. You were the one who said if we set it too high, it wouldn't be believed, and that twenty thousand was just high enough not to be attainable."

"Well, I'm trying to control the press run."

"Well, we're counting on you to control the entire situation. I want us out of Boston, but I don't want to have the president of the United States calling me up and lecturing me on my duty to the First Amendment, and I don't want union trouble, either. You stay on top of the situation and keep me informed. Maybe the story will fizz out."

"I hope so," Granger said.

"I hope so, too. I want an exit from Boston, but it must be graceful. No other way is acceptable. We spend millions of dollars a year on our corporate image. It's very, very important to me, Elmer. I'm sure you understand."

"I understand."

□

A call from the attorney general himself awakened Tony Owen, who had to extricate himself from Cynthia's arms to reach the telephone. He wanted to announce to Tony personally that his office was undertaking an investigation into the whole Duncan Avenue fiasco. Tony politely advised him to hold up the announcement until the evening to allow the *Bruise* to break it as an exclusive.

"Well, what about Channel Four? Cynthia Stoler has done a lot of good work on this story, too."

"She won't mind," said Tony, "believe me."

"What won't I mind?" asked Cynthia as she emerged from sleep.

"That I take an exclusive on the AG's investigation."

"Like hell, I don't mind. Give me that phone."

"Too late," he said. "He's hung up. Come on, give me a break, it's my story."

"Not anymore."

She climbed out of bed, immediately awake and ready for work. "Oh, I don't care about the AG. If you want that one for yourself, go ahead. I'm after bigger fish today. I'm going to get McGivern."

"We'll get McGivern together."

"He won't see you, Tony. He'll talk to me. I can make him."

"Like you made Scooter?"

"He's got to talk to me. He's got to give his side of the story. And he will."

The sunlight filled the room, accentuating their nakedness. It was the kind of light that made Tony reach for his bathrobe, but even in harsh light Cynthia was beautiful and her hair took on an almost golden hue. She was a woman without flaw or blemish, Tony thought. He reached for her, but she whirled away into the shower.

"No," she called back. "Today I'm tracking down McGivern. You are covering the mayor's news conference."

"I never go to those, you know that."

"You're going to this one; I'll get you on camera. We've got to keep the heat on."

"I don't want to be there if the bastard squirms out of this."

"If you're there, maybe he won't."

"Maybe he will."

"I'm going to try to find McGivern. If I get him in time, I'll head over to the news conference," she said, her head sticking out of the shower.

Her insistence began to alarm him. "I don't want you seeing McGivern without me around. He's a dangerous man," he said, fleetingly recalling the voice on the telephone the night before.

"Listen, my little Boy Scout, I don't know if I'll find him, but if I do I'll have my crew in a truck outside wherever it is we meet. Those guys can protect me a helluva lot better than a broken-down newspaper bum. Give me a break from your chivalry, Tony. And be professional. What I'm saying is the professional way to work, O.K.?"

For a moment he thought of insisting. "Hey, didn't we have an agreement?" he said. "I thought I was the general in this army."

"Yeah," she said, smiling broadly. "But we didn't agree to be unreasonable, did we? I promised to be careful. And I will be."

"You promised to follow orders."

"Tony, nothing can happen to me. I'll be careful. I'll stay in touch. I'm a professional, too, Tony. Give me some credit."

Reluctantly, he dropped the subject, thinking at the same time that he would take his own crack at McGivern before she got a chance to corner him. That will teach her to try to steal a march on the old master, he thought. For all his guile, he was slow to see guile in women, particularly the women in his life. Had he paused for a moment and considered the ease with which she surrendered the attorney general's story, his suspicions might have been aroused. But he was still coasting on the story he had written last night, and he suspected nothing as he kissed Cynthia good-bye and bounded down the steps, heading for Mike's and his morning coffee.

□

Mike Goukas spotted Tony coming through the door and for the first time since Tony knew him, he came out from behind the counter and shook Tony's hand. "A masterpiece. That story this morning was a masterpiece. I hope they get the bastards. I'd like to get them myself."

Tony dropped Mike's hand and tried to head toward his customary seat at the counter.

"Oh, no, not today. No seat at the counter. For Tony Owen this morning, we have the white-tablecloth treatment."

Tony followed Mike's gaze to the rear of the deli and there a table was set with a white tablecloth and a linen napkin. "This morning you drink your coffee in style."

The other patrons now joined in the congratulations, leaving their stools to clap Tony on the back, to grasp his hand. "Hey," Tony protested, "you guys are acting like I won the Pulitzer Prize. All that happened was a friend of mine got beat up. Give me a break, will you?"

He spoke with a grin pasted on his face, and as he sat down with Mike, he told the deli owner, "I love it, Mike. I love it. Maybe we'll stay alive after all."

"Maybe you will, Tony. I think you will. I really do."

The reaction in the newsroom that day was also unprecedented. As Tony walked into the room, what seemed like the entire crew of the death ship was gathered near his desk. And as he approached, they applauded. Tony tried to brush the people away, but he was moved.

"It's nice to win one, isn't it, Bobby?" he said to Bantam, who had come out of his corner office.

"Oh, it's nice, all right, but wait — I'll tell you how these bastards are conspiring to fuck us anyway. Come on in here."

He sat in his customary place beside Bobby's outsized desk, impatient to get on with his hunt for McGivern, but it was clear that Bobby was on the verge of explosion. So he settled into the chair and listened.

"You know how many extra papers we sold today? Take a guess, go on. What do you think, ten thousand, fifteen thousand? I mean, we turned out one of the greatest damn editions in the history of this city, and I've been around here a long time. So tell me. How many do you think? Well, I'll tell you. We didn't sell more than a few hundred more. And do you know why? You can't buy a paper in this town today. You just try. Everywhere you go, it's a total sellout. And do you know that Granger refused to increase the press run? He absolutely refused. He's dying for me to walk out of here, to take a hike, and I ought to, I ought to just go and deliver a blast that will take Gridlock's socks off. But this is a fixed game, Tony. We can't win, no matter what you do, no matter what I do. There's no way we can bring up the numbers. We could have the copyright on the cure for cancer and we wouldn't make that magic number, because Gridlock has made up its mind to close this place and the number is just a charade, a gimmick. The whole thing is a farce."

Tony looked sympathetically at Bobby Bantam, who sat coiled on his chair as if ready to spring at the first opportunity.

"Why don't you call Gridlock?" he asked.

"I've been trying for the past two hours. They haven't let my calls get through to anybody but the flunkies. I have to talk to the boss."

"Then why don't you walk out with a blast?"

"And why don't I go on unemployment for the rest of my life? You don't do that if you want to run another newspaper, and if I don't have a newspaper, Tony, I'm not breathing. I'd dry up. You could zip up the body bag and throw me away."

"Have you spoken to Elmer this morning?"

"We're avoiding each other."

"Then I guess all you can do is be the good soldier. Keep playing out the string. Isn't that what you told me yourself? Keep pushing ahead without worrying about what the other guy is doing? If we're going to go down, go down with the flags flying and the band playing. I think that's what you told me, Bobby."

"Is that what you're doing?"

"That's all any of us can do. Enjoy a paper like today, and don't worry about how many more shots we're going to be able to take."

"It's different for you, Tony. Sometimes I'm not even sure if you care whether we make it."

"You're wrong, Bobby. I care. I care a lot. I just want it to end. The caring can kill you. I don't like to have to care. I just wish they'd stop screwing around. I can't get too excited about the number. I never believed the number bullshit anyway. I'm surprised you did."

"You need hope, Tony."

"Yeah, and you need your daily fix, Bobby. I don't think, even if you believed in the number, that it affected you that much. You're right. You need the action. The publisher messing with your head is a kind of action, too. Straining for a number that isn't real is action. You're just a junkie who looks in his medicine chest and sees he's almost out of fixes. You'll get another one."

"You think I'm that cynical, you, my best friend in this whole place."

"Yes. If you weren't, you'd quit on the spot and take an honest job."

"Hey, I think that applause out there went to your head."

"No, I'm just getting ready for the end by throwing out all my illusions, and you, Bobby, you are one my last illusions. So enjoy today's paper. We ought to have a good one tomorrow, too."

"What will we have besides the mayor?"

"I don't know. I'm trying to track down McGivern."

"Great. See if you can come up with Martin Bormann, too. I hear he's in town."

"See you later, Bobby."

"Yeah, and thanks for cheering me up. Excuse me while I cut my throat."

□

McGivern had reached Cynthia Stoler the night before, just before she left the studio after the six o'clock news. He had promised to talk to her under certain conditions: that she tell no one, not even Tony Owen, about the meeting, that she arrive alone and by alone he meant without a crew waiting in the street. To assure privacy, she was to go to the Grasshopper Lounge in Quincy Market at noon, when she would be given instructions about a rendezvous. If there was the slightest breach in the arrangements on her part, the interview would be canceled. '

"Aren't you frightened? From what you've been saying about me, I'm a pretty bad guy."

"No, I'm not afraid," Cynthia said. "You'd have to be a fool to harm a reporter."

"I'm disappointed," he had said. "Fright can be delightful."

She ignored the remark, went back over the terms of the agreement, and hung up. Her lips would be sealed from Tony Owen; her mind would be sealed from fear. "He wouldn't dare hurt a reporter. He's too smart for that," she told herself, and at the time she believed it.

15

CYNTHIA WAITED for fifty minutes at a table near the bar, studying the faces of the men drinking there while keeping a copy of the morning *Mammoth* open in her lap. A few businessmen, a couple of architects from one of the firms in the offices overhead, a tourist or two. One of the businessmen tried to pick her up. She discouraged him with a cold stare and glanced back down at her newspaper. She tried to hide the irritation that was rising in her as the minutes passed. By one, it was obvious now that she had been stood up. She left a five-dollar bill on the table for the two Campari and sodas she had sipped during her vigil, folded her newspaper, picked up her purse, and walked out into the sunlight. She got three steps from the front door when someone approached her from behind and took her arm.

"Don't turn around and don't look up at me," he said. "I'm taking you to your interview." His hand clamped down hard on her arm.

"Not so hard; you'll bruise me," she said, her voice so even that she herself was surprised at her control.

Her companion relaxed his grasp, but the grip remained firm as he steered her toward a car parked on Federal Street in front of the United States Trust Company. "Be calm," he told her, "and you'll get the interview."

He spoke softly and the softness reassured her. This man was no hoodlum. She had nothing to be afraid of. The car was a silver Impala with four doors. Her escort opened the back door and guided her inside. She didn't notice the second man until her head was inside the car. She tried to back out, but her escort held her buttocks and with a quick push sent her tumbling toward the second man, who grabbed her by the shoulder and pulled her head down toward his lap.

Unseen now from the street, she tried to scream, but no sound came from her throat. She smelled the chloroform at the instant it did its work. And when she awoke, she was in a totally darkened room, lying sprawled on a hard wooden floor, her hands cuffed to a radiator.

Her throat felt scratchy and her head ached. Her hands were numb from the cuffs. She moved her hips and the cloth of her skirt and underpants rubbed against her skin. She was relieved to realize that she was clothed. She tugged at the cuffs and succeeded only in hurting her wrists. She twisted her head to read the time on her watch, but darkness enveloped everything and she regretted not having bought a luminous dial.

She lay still once more and tried to listen. She could hear the sounds of traffic on the street. The traffic was regular but it wasn't heavy, and from the sound she guessed she was on an upper story. The room itself was utterly still. She swung her legs in an arc, straining to touch an object that would give her a clue about the room that contained her. She could touch nothing and noticed that one of her shoes was missing. She tried to remember which shoes she had worn that day. She wasn't sure; she wasn't even sure of the outfit. She nudged closer to the radiator to take some strain off her arms and succeeded only in adding to the discomfort of her head and neck. She didn't scream for several more minutes, not until she heard the scratching a few feet away. The scratches were hard and almost metallic. They'd begin, intensify, then die away. When she felt the brush of soiled fur near her cheek, she threw back her head and bellowed like a soul who had seen the face of death.

□

Three hours before Cynthia Stoler was pushed into the rear of the Impala, Tony Owen walked down the hall of the State Street office building housing the legal suite of F. X. McGivern, Esquire. He pushed open the door and found McGivern himself sitting at the receptionist's desk, reading a copy of the *Bruise*.

"So you're back again, Owen," he said, looking up from the paper. "After what you wrote today, I'm amazed you would show your face around here." Tony stared at him, expecting to see the truculence that marked his face at their last meeting. Instead, McGivern was smiling. "I've got to hand it to you. You may not have brains, but you are a gutsy little guy."

"I don't see why I should be afraid. It's women you like to beat up on, isn't it?"

"Hey, don't you start accusing me of anything. For all your innuendo, and I'm sitting here trying to decide whether I should sue, I had nothing to do with what happened to that lady in Southie. From what I hear, she ran into some street kids. Look at this shit." He slapped his hand down over Tony's column. "You've got some imagination, that's all I can say. To tell you the truth, Owen, I don't care what you write. Write anything at all. You're like a little bug. You don't bother me at all."

The smile remained on his face, to some extent disarming Tony, who was prepared for a confrontation, a confrontation that he hoped would get physical. He stared at McGivern's fat face and wanted to smash it, but the smile held him back.

"I want to talk to you," Tony said.

"Talk to me? Friends talk to me. You are not a friend. I don't want to talk to you. But if you want to interview me, that's something else. I don't have anything to hide."

"O.K.," Tony said, returning the smile with his toughest stare. "I'll interview you." He pulled a notebook out of his pocket and sat down opposite McGivern.

"No, not here," McGivern said. "Come into my office. I want this one on tape. For my own protection. I know how you guys can fuck up quotes, to suit your purpose."

They walked into the inner office with its rental furniture and Woolworth's decor. A big bristly cactus stood in a corner and two imitation Remingtons hung on the wall.

"You like the Wild West, huh?" Tony said.

"Oh, the paintings. Something my secretary brought back from a vacation."

"Where is she?"

"Day off."

"She wasn't here the last time I came, either."

"Another day off."

"Tell me about Articulate. When was it formed?"

"You read the incorporation papers; it's all there," he said, pushing his fat fingers at the controls of the tape recorder.

"Does the mayor have a piece of it?"

"Stupid question."

"I take that for an affirmative."

"Get off it, Owen. Look, we're wasting each other's time. Let me just make a statement and we'll forget the questions. O.K., let me make a statement?"

"Go ahead," said Tony.

"Here's all I have to say. Yes, I did incorporate Articulate. I acted in behalf of a group of clients. I am not at liberty because of the confidential nature of lawyer-client relationships to discuss those clients or their interests in the corporation. Yes, we are buying up land in the Duncan Avenue vicinity. No, we are not burning buildings down. We have made generous relocation offers to tenants in that neighborhood, and if you cared to inquire, you would verify that fact."

"Who staked you in this deal? Before Articulate, you didn't have two nickels to rub together."

"That's not true. And I'm not going to comment on that. You don't even know whether I'm one of the investors."

"It's going to come out."

"If it ever does, we'll know, won't we?"

"O.K., I guess that does it, Mr. McGivern. But first, I want to make a statement of my own, as a man, not a reporter." Tony stood up and tucked his notebook into his jacket pocket. Suddenly, the adrenaline began to flow and he felt his heart pumping, the blood running hot at his temples. His hands were clenched into a tight fist and he could feel the sweat in his palms. "First of all, I have no doubt that you had Louise Finnigan beaten up. Secondly, I have no doubt that you are the maggot who had me threatened on the phone. I want you to know that I'm going to see to it personally that you end up back in the swamp you came from. And if anything more happens in my life, I'm coming after you."

Tony paused and glared, thinking for a moment that he'd better warn McGivern not to see Cynthia. But no, he told himself, Cynthia would never forgive him if he cut her out of a McGivern interview while seeing the slug himself. She would misunderstand his motives. Besides, he didn't want personal considerations to interfere with professional ones. No, he would keep Cynthia out of this.

"I'm glad I have all this on tape because you are threatening me and demeaning me," McGivern said. "I ought to have you arrested."

"Here, I'll give you something to hang a charge on," Tony said, lunging forward with his left hand and cupping the back of McGivern's head. With his right hand, he chopped down on McGivern's nose. He dropped his head, shoved him back into the chair, and backed toward the door.

"You're going to regret that, Owen. You're going to regret that more than you can imagine." He was shouting, but his voice was muffled because as he shouted he held his hand to his nose, trying to stop the flow of blood. "I've got a weak nose, you bastard. You don't treat me like that, no one treats me like that."

Tony backed out the door and took the stairs to the ground floor. He didn't notice the Impala by the curb in a no parking zone. He noticed nothing but the pounding of his heart.

On one level Tony felt exultant as he cut through the crowds at Downtown Crossing and headed back toward the paper. But on another level, a deeper level, he felt frazzled and ashamed at his loss of control. He could hate, and he recognized that. But he had trouble accepting the violence that ran deep on the underside of that hatred. I could easily have killed that man, he told himself. And he knew that he was indeed capable of homicide. It was an aspect of himself that he rarely acknowledged. Now it left him shaken, even as he celebrated the look of shock and then pain on McGivern's face.

By now, McGivern was probably telephoning Bobby Bantam, reporting the assault, telling him to have Tony Owen available because he would be sending the cops around to arrest him. He wondered what Cynthia would say. And as he reached the paper and rushed to his desk, he rehearsed how he would tell her of the encounter and speculated to himself on her reaction. She would be angry, of course, that he reached McGivern, particularly if she failed to confront him herself. And she would be dismayed by his violence.

But she probably would be delighted that he had set aside the Gardol shield and let his feelings flow.

It was noon when he reached his desk and began flipping through his telephone messages. He looked for one from Cynthia. None was there. But there was a note from her news director. He wanted Tony to call.

"Do you have any idea where Cynthia is?" he asked. "We haven't heard from her all morning."

"Hey, the day is young."

"Yeah, but we've got a crew waiting, and she's more reliable than that."

"Maybe she went on a secret shopping spree," he joked.

"Look, if she calls . . ."

"Yeah, I know."

Tony felt a twinge of anxiety. It was unlike Cynthia to leave her crew hanging. She had assured him her crew would be with her if she tried to see McGivern. Perhaps she had tried to see him and was rebuffed, as she certainly would have been after his own nasty brush with the lawyer. But would she have gone to see him alone? No, he couldn't believe she'd be that reckless. Still, he wished now that he had warned McGivern about her specifically. A few words might have made a difference. It was also possible that she had tracked down McGivern and he had told her about his meeting. That would have infuriated her, perhaps to the point where she wanted to stay away from everyone until she cooled down.

He looked at his watch. It was nearly lunchtime. Time to see Bobby. He'd probably had an earful from McGivern by now. He walked into Bobby's office.

"Would you believe it?" Bobby said in greeting. "Those idiots out in Kansas haven't returned my call yet. They won't talk to me. How do you like playing in a game that's rigged against you? What a bitch."

"Bobby, there's something I got to tell you. I slugged McGivern this afternoon."

"Good. You get a story out of it?"

"Hey, I slugged the guy, made his nose bleed."

"So let him sue. Gridlock is good for it."

"I didn't get much of a story."

"Columnist steps on maggot. That isn't bad. He must have provoked you pretty good. How'd you get that close to him?"

"He was sitting in his office, like he was waiting for me."

"Good, then he expected to get popped. You owed him one."

"It doesn't bother you that I lost control? I mean, I didn't act too professionally."

"Don't worry about it. You're doing the news conference, right?"

"I hate that idea. Connie's going to make me throw up."

"Oh, he'll surprise us all. Be a professional and cover him good. Not that it makes a helluva lot of difference. We're just playing out the string. But do it good anyway."

"You talk to Granger yet?"

"No. He's avoiding me, too. He can't squelch me now and he knows it, not the way everyone's going wild with this story today. Do you realize the calls I've gotten? Look at this."

He handed Tony a sheaf of telephone messages: the *Columbia Journalism Review,* the *New York Times,* NBC News.

"That Finnigan lady knew what she was doing. From Southie housewife to media celeb, all because she took a few chops to the choppers. I'm sending all the calls to the publisher. Let's see how he handles them. This paper is going from a death ship to a battle wagon overnight, and the son of a bitch is dying inside. He's dying. Why don't you go and take a poke at him as long as you're in a fighting mood?"

☐

Connie Haydon stretched out on the sofa in his inner office and closed his eyes, concentrating on nothing but the darkness. Everything was in readiness. He had spent the day rehearsing his statement, polishing it, and parrying mock questions from his staff. Like a prizefighter, he had avoided all intimate contact with women, emotional as well as physical. And while Corinne took part in the rehearsal, she didn't linger behind after he dismissed the staff. This was time alone, time to feel the energy surging, time to clarify the mind, time to relax the body. He breathed deeply, trying to increase the supply of oxygen in his brain. Five minutes before he was to appear in the news conference room, his secretary knocked on the door. "It's time," she said. It was six o'clock.

He stood up, stretched, dabbed water on his face and neck from the washroom tap, changed into a crisp white linen shirt, adjusted his silk tie, combed his close-cropped hair, donned his suit jacket, and rang the buzzer for his top aides.

Stanley and Corinne flanked him as he walked into the news conference room, blinking under the glare of the television lights.

He stood at the walnut-paneled rostrum and peered out at a crowd even bigger than he expected. The *Mammoth* had a full complement of reporters, six in all, including Hornblower. And he noticed to his slight surprise that Dugan himself was there, standing in the background against the rear wall. He frowned as he spotted Tony Owen, sitting next to the *Bruise*'s City Hall reporter. At least they spared me Cynthia, he thought, noting that a young man he didn't recognize was with the Channel 4 camera.

Normally, he would crack a joke at the start of his news conference, and he was tempted to for a moment when he saw the *Times* man, an earnest young reporter in a seersucker suit, sitting in the front row with his notebook and tape recorder balanced on his lap. Instead, he stared at the *Times* man and smiled just enough to transmit a flattering sense of recognition. Then he stared down at his prepared text.

"Good evening," he said gravely. "First, I have a statement which I will read to you. And then if there are any questions . . . A text, of course, will be available to you. I'm sorry they were not available in advance."

Tony Owen opened his notebook. A technician from Channel 4 turned from his camera and whispered, "Hey, where the hell is Cynthia? Nobody's heard from her all day."

Tony blanched. He looked around the room, checking the doorways to see if perhaps she had just arrived and was poised there, afraid of inflicting her tardiness on the others awaiting what the mayor had to say. "I have no idea," Tony said as the technician turned back toward the camera.

"I have been following, for some time now, various accounts of the unfortunate situation on Duncan Avenue. At first, I must confess, I did not take it too seriously, nor did there seem much reason to. The Fire Department had assured me that the incidence of arson in the neighborhood was no higher than it would be in any other area with a similar history and similar problems. Yet, to be sure that there were no grounds for administration concern, I personally ordered an investigation into the patterns of sale, resale, and demolition, and I instructed fire officials to re-examine each and every fire in the area over the prior eighteen months to make certain they were not overlooking a pattern of willful destruction for profit.

"I ordered the investigation even as the energies of this administration were concentrating on a coming event of great importance and historical significance to this city — the imminent visit by His Holiness, the bishop of Rome. And by the way, ladies and gentlemen, it is my understanding that His Eminence, the cardinal, will have an announcement of great importance at the chancery later this evening."

Immediately there was a stirring in the press rows as half a dozen reporters led by the AP and UPI rushed from the room for the telephones.

"That goddamn Connie doesn't miss a trick," said the City Hall man to Tony, who was so intent on Cynthia he barely heard a word the mayor was saying. "He's having the cardinal wrap him in papal bunting."

"Now, getting back to Duncan Avenue. A few days ago, I began getting the preliminary results of that investigation. I will share them with you today.

"A corporation, Articulate, Incorporated, has been the prime agent of change in the Duncan Avenue area, buying up over the past two years eighteen parcels of land either on or bounding Duncan.

"One of the principals in Articulate, Incorporated, is a member of my family, Mr. Thomas Mannion, a real estate agent normally operating in the West Roxbury–Roslindale area.

"Another principal is attorney F. X. McGivern of Sixty State Street.

"Articulate, Incorporated, has insured each of the acquired properties in sums up to four million dollars each, and has been the beneficiary in sums totaling two and a half million dollars as a result of fires in that area over the past eighteen months.

"Only one of those fires has been deemed to be a possible result of arson. That is the fire at number forty-two Duncan Avenue, in which a man identified as Bernie Kremenko perished. That fire is now being reinvestigated by a special task force comprising the top arson investigators in the city and state, with the cooperation of the governor's office.

"That the four-block area, including and bounding Duncan Avenue, has been rezoned to permit hotel and high-rise apartment construction is a result of action by the Zoning Board last March 8.

"I had no knowledge of either the pattern of land acquisition or the involvement of Mr. Thomas Mannion in Articulate, Incorporated, until a few days ago. Nor was I aware of the significance of the rezoning action in affecting the value of the parcels involved.

"I stand before you today shocked and appalled at the situation. There is little I can say in my own defense, except that once again I trusted unwisely, acting, as I suppose most people do, on the assumption that those near and dear to them share their basic values and aspirations for their families and for their city.

"Throughout my public career, I have tried to live up to the highest standards of personal integrity. I am not going to stand up here today and tell you that I am an honest man. If I haven't demonstrated that to you by now over the years, then I haven't effectively communicated what I feel inside about the seriousness of the public trust. But I am going to tell you that I am a trusting man. Gullible, I suppose, some of you would say. Naive. Inattentive to the details that to some of you seemed to shout out for attention.

"But I think that trust is part of the open-mindedness that my mother instilled in me. And that inattention to detail is an unfortunate by-product of what I think is the prime responsibility of the mayor of this city: to keep his eye on the big picture, the overall face of the city, its hunger for new sources of enterprise and commerce, its image before the nation, and indeed, the world. I think I have done that and done that well.

"It doesn't excuse me from responsibility for this scandal. And, indeed, it is a scandal, and the *Bruise* and Channel Four are to be commended for bringing it to public attention. The buck does stop here. Blame me, but try to understand the nature of my failure, the extent of my responsibility.

"The attorney general informed me this morning that he intends to convene a grand jury to begin hearing evidence in the Duncan Avenue matter as soon as possible. I informed the attorney general that he can be assured of the utmost cooperation on the part of the City of Boston in the investigation.

"I have also taken two further steps on my own. I have instructed the police commissioner to begin an intense and immediate investigation into the beating in South Boston of Louise Finnigan, and I have arranged to post a fifty-thousand-dollar reward for information leading to the arrest and conviction of those responsible for the attack.

"I have also instructed the corporation counsel to look into the possibility of eminent domain proceedings in the Duncan Avenue area after a suitable public purpose is found for assuming ownership of the parcels in question. It is my hope, and it may be premature to announce this, that the land can be put into the hands of a public or quasi-public corporation, which can develop the area for low- and moderate-income housing as well as urban parkland. I should have a sense of the feasibility of both strategies within the next seventy-two hours.

"My basic point is, I want to stop the profiteering and the destruction right now, and I don't want any doubts on that score.

"Are there any questions?"

"Mr. Mayor," said Henry Hornblower, vigorously shaking his hand in the air, "have you any information on the pope's arrival?"

"That son of a bitch," said Tony Owen.

"Would you believe that guy?" said the *Bruise*'s City Hall man.

"Well, I don't want to overstep my authority. I mean, we are all forced to bow to higher authority," he said, casting his eyes skyward. A few reporters laughed. "But you'll have to talk to the cardinal about that. And he'll be expecting you all at about seven, from what I understand. I would like to say, now that Henry has brought it up, that it is unfortunate that the Duncan Avenue mess happened. But it is also unfortunate that it has happened at a time when it could so easily mar the magnificence of the moment ahead when the pope sets foot in our city. That is one reason why I decided to clear the air tonight, so we can start looking forward instead of backward."

The *Times* man raised his hand. "Mayor Haydon, sir, you have now had two major scandals breaking in the past two weeks, and in the Bernie Kremenko matter . . ."

"You don't mean Bernie Kremenko, I don't think, do you, Mr. Hearns?"

"No, of course not," said the *Times* man. "I was referring to the case of Scooter Conroy. In both cases, you pleaded an excess of loyalty. But do not both cases indicate a rare blindness to corruption carried on directly under your nose?"

The mayor flinched. He hadn't expected the *Times* man to ask that kind of question. "I think, if you'll recall what I said . . ."

"But I haven't finished the question, Mayor Haydon, if you will. And if it does indicate that, how can you possibly seek re-election with such a burden?"

Haydon grew testy. "I was expecting a reporter's question," he said, "not a political speech. But let me tell you, Mr. Hearns, that the question of my candidacy remains unresolved. I hope to have an answer within a few weeks, in my own mind. As for those two instances of corruption, I don't think that's a very bad batting average for a man who has been in office for twenty years. And no one, may I remind you, has been convicted of any crime. Conroy has been accused, and I believe, politician or no politician, that he is entitled to a presumption of innocence, even by so august an institution as the *New York Times.*"

Tony Owen sat back, his temper barely under control, as he listened to the mayor. He had questions, lots of questions, but he was reluctant to ask them because each question, no matter how it was phrased, no matter how surprising it came to the mayor, would be hammered back into the questioner's throat. Besides, he had only one question that was pressing on his mind: Where was Cynthia, how was it possible that she hadn't called him or the station, or showed up at the news conference?

Now the mayor, stung by the man from the *Times,* was going to the radio and television reporters for questions. The radio crew was a raw lot, most of them kids just out of Emerson College or BU with as much news sense as one of Mike's waitresses. They came to the conferences hoping that perhaps they'd be picked up by one of the television cameras and be able to ask their girlfriends whether they caught them on TV.

"Mr. Mayor," one of them asked, "how does your wife feel about her brother being involved in Articulate?"

"She is, of course, quite surprised and, like me, upset."

Tony Owen couldn't let that one slide. "Mayor," he said, adding a cutting edge to his voice, "how does she feel about you throwing her brother to the wolves, just like you did her friend, Scooter Conroy?"

The mayor ignored the question and tried to recognize another member of the radio crew.

"Mayor, I asked a question," said Tony, shouting over the radio man's blather about papal flags.

"And I'm not going to dignify it with an answer," said the mayor, glaring at Tony with the kind of hatred he had seen earlier that day on the face of F. X. McGivern.

"Are there any more questions?" asked Stanley, who was standing off to the mayor's side.

"Thank you, Mr. Mayor," said Hornblower, and almost as suddenly as he appeared, Haydon was back in his inner chamber.

"Bastard," Tony muttered after him. "Bastard."

"He turned Duncan Avenue into a one-day wonder," said the City Hall man.

"We'll see," said Tony Owen.

□

Cynthia screamed until her voice had all but given out. Then she fell back into the darkness and whimpered, her knees up against her chest as if she were a small child. She had never known such terror. And now her throat burned with thirst and her arms and back ached with a dull pain she knew would worsen. She had already soiled herself and had to twist her body until it was almost parallel to the radiator to get away from the puddle she had left on the floor. She tried to count to get a sense of the time, but she kept losing track as she reached the eight hundreds.

"Someone help me, someone get me out of here," she called, but her voice was so feeble, it only reminded her of her helplessness. She was in a situation she had spent her entire adult life trying to avoid; she was at someone's mercy, and she wasn't even sure who that someone was. She assumed it was McGivern, but she had never seen the man and she was certain it wasn't McGivern either in the car or on the street. It was probably the pair that had done the number on Louise Finnigan.

She tried to remember how long a person could live without water. She couldn't remember. She didn't think it could be more than a day or two. She tried to pray, but all she could remember were little-girl prayers. She concentrated on trying to send a telepathic signal to Tony, and then it occurred to her that even if she did, she couldn't tell him where she was because she didn't have any idea. All she knew was that it was in the city. Maybe somebody will find my shoe, she thought, and began trying to construct a scenario. But then she thought of all the times she had seen shoes in the street and how little curiosity a shoe evoked in the passer-by.

She had dozed off into a fitful sleep when she heard the sound of footsteps on a stair. Mustering all her strength, she shouted, "Help me, help me. I'm trapped, I'm trapped."

She heard the sound of a moving door handle. She heard the door open and was amazed that it admitted no light. She thought for a moment that she must be in a tunnel connected to another tunnel. Then she saw the beam of a flashlight.

"Help me, please help me," she said.

☐

Tony Owen took a cab back to the paper, ignoring the cabbie, who was anxious to get the real story behind the beating of Louise Finnigan. But Tony could not respond to him and when they got to the paper, he had to be reminded to pay the man, so anxious was he to get to his desk to see if there was word from Cynthia.

But the only messages were from readers. He tried Cynthia's apartment, then his own. He called the station. No word at all. He tried McGivern's office and got no answer there. McGivern had an apartment in Charles River Park but the phone was disconnected. Tony decided he'd head over there. She had to be with him. Nothing else made sense. He kicked himself for not asking McGivern about Cynthia when he was with him, but he tried to keep her as separate from himself as possible when he was working, and although the question had occurred to him, he didn't ask it.

He got up from his desk, his face ashen, and walked into the conference room where Bobby Bantam was laying out page one. "How do you like this one, champ? Mayor Says In-Law Outlaw."

Tony didn't respond.

"What's wrong?" asked Bantam. "Somebody kill your cat?"

"Cynthia. I don't know where she is. She didn't report to the station."

"She's probably chasing an angle somewhere and lost track of the time. It's not even seven-thirty. I wouldn't worry."

"I'm very worried, Bobby. There's been threats."

"That's cranks."

"They weren't cranks who worked over Louise Finnigan."

"Jesus, you are worried."

"Bobby, this isn't Cynthia. She's blown her news show tonight, one of the biggest nights of her career. I can't work, Bobby. I've got to find her."

"Wait a minute, Tony. You've got to work. We're on a roll here. Calm down. Where are you going to look? I mean, I'll send Kerrigan out. He's a better detective than any Boston cop anyway. Tell me where to send him, and he'll go. You sit down and write."

"I can't. Not until I find her. I wouldn't be any good if I tried."

"Where do you want to look?"

"It's that bum, McGivern. He's got her. If I find him, I'll find her."

"Hey, Tony, he's a bad guy all right, but he's not a kidnaper, for Christ's sake. He wouldn't dare. I mean, you're talking about big-league nerves, and he ain't got them."

"Oh no? He's vicious and he's beaten."

"Well, look, let me call Superintendent Ryan at police headquarters. He'll have his guys quietly looking around for McGivern. Where does he live?"

"Charles River Park. Emerson Place."

"Hold on here a second, Tony. Let me get the superintendent. He owes us a favor or two."

Bobby reached for the index file of phone numbers on his desk and quickly punched a number. "He's coming. He's getting up from the supper table," Bobby said.

"Hey, Frank, this is Bobby Bantam. Need a favor, a big one, and I need it now. You know that guy McGivern, the lawyer? We got to talk to him tonight, which means we got to find him. Hey, I know, I'm not asking you to do our job. Come on, give me some credit for a few brains anyway. Look, there may be a crime here, but I don't want to sound a false alarm. So be cool, but I'll explain."

Tony looked out the window just as the hotel across the street turned on its night lights. The sign had been repaired, and like an omen brooding over the city, it read: HOTEL CONGRESS. But the sign hardly registered. A wave of barely familiar feelings was beginning to rise up out of a part of Tony he had forgotten ever existed. Fear was one of the feelings, a sense of dread, like the feeling he had had years ago as he walked up the steps to his mother's apartment and hesitated to open the door even before he smelled the gas. But he also felt something else, something that he never knew he could feel, not this way, not this desperately. God, I love her, he said to himself. I can't bear it.

"Look," said Bobby Bantam to the superintendent. "I know you've got your hands full with the pope, but the son of a bitch isn't even here yet. I'm telling you this could be a matter of life or death. For Christ's sake, you can be a hero."

Bobby was silent for a moment, but he looked at Tony and gave him the thumbs-up sign. "O.K., send a car by the front door and he'll be waiting for you. Yeah, he knows what he looks like, certainly. And he never forgets a face. O.K., thanks, Superintendent. I owe you one."

Bantam hung up. "O.K., Tony, here's the drill. The cops are going to come by and get you, and they'll get you inside McGivern's office and apartment. If he's there you'll get a chance to talk to him. Meanwhile, if she turns up or you find her, you come back and write. If she doesn't, well . . ."

"You mean you're going to go without me for tomorrow? You changed your mind?"

"Yeah. You convinced me. This could be a better story."

□

"Let's go," said Connie Haydon to Corinne, as he caught her by the elbow and moved, with her in tow, toward the door to his private elevator. The news conference had just ended, but he was indifferent to the critique of his performance, which Stanley and other staffers were poised to provide. He didn't want to see his staff right now; he didn't want to hear what they had to say about how he handled his antagonists in the press. All he wanted now was what he had been denying himself as he prepared for the news conference — a moment with Corinne, a moment to breathe free of crisis.

"Where are we going?" she asked as they descended toward the underground garage and his waiting cars. His driver, Charlie, was standing by the limousine.

"I'm taking the Ford out tonight," Haydon told him. "She'll drive. Take the rest of the night off. I'll see you at my place in the morning."

Not a word was spoken between the two as she headed the car out into the traffic at the rear of City Hall, then turned right onto

Cambridge Street and headed toward Cambridge. As they neared the
Longfellow Bridge, where the turrets stood like an honor guard at
attention, the mayor motioned forward with his hand.

"You want to go to Cambridge?"

"Yes, anywhere," he said. "I just want to get out of Boston for a
moment. Cambridge, anywhere. Just drive."

She wasn't sure of his mood, and the uncertainty contributed to
her own anxiety. She thought him magnificent at the news conference; she wasn't sure that he agreed. She had seen him triumph
before, only to be filled with despondency afterward — as if the
victory were flawed by the ease with which it was attained and the
recognition that the effort that went into it somehow lifted him into
a realm of utter isolation.

If she waited, the nature of his mood would reveal itself, and it was
infinitely preferable to endure the silence than risk the repercussions
of guessing at what was going on in his mind and guessing wrong.

She drove down Memorial Drive toward Route 2, and as they
neared the turnoff to Harvard Square, she felt his hand on her thigh,
stroking it possessively under her skirt. She waited to judge the
nature of the caress and found it more a gesture of reassurance than
a sign of desire; she ignored it, keeping her eyes fixed on the traffic
in front of her. As they neared Buckingham, Browne and Nichols,
he spoke for the second time. "Turn in there," he said, gesturing to
the empty and dimly lit school parking lot. "Keep the motor running, just in case an MDC cop comes along and sees us."

She pulled into a parking space and put the car into park. They
sat side by side in the front seat of the Ford, staring at the traffic
moving along in front of them. His hand now was between her legs,
his fingers brushing her panties. He detested pantyhose.

"Thanks for not talking," he said, and removed his hand. "I didn't
want to hear another voice, especially my own. I just wanted to be
with you. I wanted to think what it would be like, pretend a little.
It isn't over yet, you understand?"

She turned toward him and looked into his eyes for a clue to what
he meant. They seemed sad.

"You mean with us?"

"No, I mean the crisis. It isn't over."

She was eager to talk about them, and now she was embarrassed
that her eagerness showed. She was always doing that, letting her

own feelings, her own needs, stand in the way of more important things, like the future of Connie Haydon. Not the man, as he had told her so many times, the man wasn't important. It was the symbol, the symbol that in truth represented the future of Boston. That's what she had to consider, that's what he considered. And when he behaved coldly toward her, she shouldn't think for a moment that she was a woman being ill-treated by a man. It wasn't as simple as that, Connie had said, while wishing, with all his heart, he assured her, that it only were. Ordinariness, he told her, that's what he craved, the limitless and unappreciated freedom of the ordinary person, with no responsibility beyond himself and his family. She remembered how once they had sat alone in the rear of a big North End restaurant and how Haydon studied the face of all the customers as they came in the door, seeing in each signs of simplicity and ease and contentment. How lucky they are and they don't realize it, he said, and she nodded. Yes, he was paying the price for being special, and if she was to love him, she would have to pay the price, too, and she accepted that, even now, as he relegated her feelings, her very being, into a subcategory of a large and impersonal political problem.

"You did well tonight," she said. "Poor Tony Owen. You took his toy away."

"He's only part of the problem. It's not hard to put him down. But he's already done his damage. Controlling it. That's what I was trying to do. Did I succeed? Yeah. I kept the water out of the engine room. The ship is still floating. And not too many people could have done that, under the circumstances. But, hey, let's not kid ourselves. We've taken some heavy shots. I'm not the same guy anymore. I'm still alive, but I'm bleeding. I can clean up the blood all right, and if I do it and I don't take any more hits, I'll be all right. People forget. They have short memories. The point is to keep the crisis short, compress it. If you let it get drawn out, if you take another hit a week from now or a month from now, then it's sayonara. It's the death of a thousand cuts. So did I end the crisis? No. I limited the damage, for now. But there's still some mines in the water."

"You mean Eileen?"

"That's a big one. I've got to face her tonight. I've called her bluff. I've got to hope she doesn't have enough pride left to go through with what she's threatened to do. I'm not at all sure about Eileen. Could I keep her in check for a week? Maybe. A month, maybe. Longer than that? I'm not too hopeful. But who knows? Maybe she'll understand that I did the only thing I could do. I mean, she knows me. She knows I'm not just going to lie down and die."

Corinne looked away and stared at the traffic moving on Memorial Drive. She stared as if transfixed, not wanting to look on Connie Haydon, not wanting to ask the question she knew she had to ask, not wanting to hear the reply, which she knew would come.

"What about us?" she said, finally, and tried to close her ears to his answer.

He surprised her by taking her hand, then reaching up and taking her face between his hands and kissing her on the tip of the nose. "I could lose everything," he said. "I know you realize that. I'm not at all optimistic. And then what? Would you throw away your life for a broken pol? No power, no glamour. I don't know if I can handle it. I really don't, and I think you have to ask yourself whether you can handle it."

"But I love you," she said. "I don't love the other things. Just you. You don't believe that, do you? I've not convinced you of that?"

"And who is it that you love? Those 'other things' may be all there is."

"I don't believe that."

"Thank you," he said. He took her in his arms and held her until his arms ached from the strain. "Come on, we've got to get back. I have a date with Eileen," he said, finally.

"Thank you," she said, and resumed her seat behind the wheel.

Ten minutes later, she dropped him off outside his home.

☐

A uniformed cop and a plainclothesman were in the front seat of the police car that picked up Tony Owen ten minutes after Bobby Bantam hung up the phone. He didn't recognize the patrolman. The detective was Billy Curry, a round and rumpled veteran of the vice squad. Curry was a good cop. Tony felt better just seeing him.

"If McGivern is around, we'll find him," Curry said. "He's about as easy to spot as a honeydew melon on a pool table."

Curry got the key to McGivern's apartment from the building superintendent, and while the patrolman stayed in the car in case McGivern happened to show up outside, Tony and the detective rode the elevator to the eighteenth floor.

Curry knocked three times, loudly, so loudly that a neighbor stuck her head out of the adjoining apartment door. When there was no sound from inside, Curry used the key. The apartment was in darkness.

Curry hit the light switch by the door and called once more for McGivern. Again, there was only silence. Tony and the detective moved into the living room, which was bare except for an Oriental rug in the center of the room and an overstuffed sofa. A half-empty bottle of Jack Daniels was on the floor by the couch, along with crumpled copies of the day's newspapers. They walked into the bedroom and found only a rumpled bed, a portable television set, and a dresser. The dresser drawers were open. Curry looked under the bed and in the closet.

"If he owns a suitcase," he said, "he's taken it."

In the bathroom, there was a soiled white shirt and a towel with traces of red stain. "He came here after I hit him this afternoon," Tony said. "You can see the blood from his nose."

"O.K., let's check his parking place."

They took the elevator down to the underground garage. The Impala was parked in McGivern's spot. Curry tried the doors. They were locked. He shined his flashlight through the car's windows. The beam caught a woman's shoe half-hidden under the front seat.

"Interesting," he said, and reached into his pocket. "You didn't see this," he said. With his blackjack, Curry smashed the side vent window, then opened the car door and picked up the shoe. "This look familiar?"

"Yeah, it looks like one of Cynthia's shoes. But I can't be sure."

"Well, we'll compare the size with the shoes in her closet at home, O.K.?"

"Yeah, but let's head over to his office. He may still be there."

"O.K., I'll get the fingerprint guys over here to check out the car. See what we got."

Curry worked the radio to headquarters while the patrolman drove the squad car down behind City Hall and up to State Street. Again, they got a key from the building superintendent, who insisted on accompanying them to McGivern's office. Again, they found a darkened suite of rooms, with no signs of the counselor.

"She's got a couple of pairs of shoes at my place. Why don't we head there?" Tony said after they left the law office.

Fifteen minutes later, Tony had located a pair of Cynthia's shoes on the floor of his closet. They were the same size: eight and a half. "Well, that's not conclusive," Curry said. "That's a pretty common shoe size. Let's see what the fingerprint guys come up with."

"Can you call me?" said Tony. "I think I'm going to stay here for the night in case the phone rings."

"You ain't going back to work?"

"No."

"O.K., but we'll have to get a tap on your phone, just in case."

Once the detective left, Tony called Bobby Bantam, who said he'd have the City Hall man handle the news conference. And they'd do without the column. He said the station had called several times, and was thinking of perhaps putting an announcement on the eleven o'clock news that Cynthia had disappeared, but they were afraid of looking foolish if she suddenly turned up.

Tony barely heard him. He was convinced that she was gone, that McGivern had taken her, and the idea that he would never see her again began to flood his mind and his heart.

As his feelings rose, he regretted begging off his column, kicked himself for choosing to stay at home by the phone rather than hit the streets, searching for McGivern himself. He felt a tightness in his stomach and chest, a sense of need for air, for movement. But no, it would be absurd to go out; he wouldn't find McGivern who, plainly, by now didn't want to be found.

The pressure in him kept building. He went to the cabinet and pulled down the bottle of gin, then abruptly pushed it back. No, he had to stay sober, just in case he was needed. He had to be sharp. But he felt the need to run out of the apartment rising in him like a compulsion, a command. But he couldn't. He was a hostage to the telephone; he had to stay near, he had to wait.

He stared at the phone, an old-fashioned black telephone on the old-fashioned cradle. He liked the way the receiver folded into his chin and shoulder, allowing him to talk and type at the same time. It sat there on the table, its silence no longer neutral but ominous. Tony stared at it blankly, becoming almost catatonic, and then it rang, and he reached for it savagely, ripping the phone from the cradle before the echos of the first ring faded from the room.

"Hello," he said.

"Hello, Alice?"

"There's no Alice here, you fucking asshole," he shouted, and ferociously slammed the receiver back into its cradle. He hadn't realized how angry he was — at himself for endangering Cynthia; at Cynthia for not taking precautions; at McGivern. But the anger was even deeper than that. It was at everything in his life that conspired to leave him at age forty-two, alone and hopeless, and fearful, in a bachelor apartment by an ugly old telephone.

"You can't count on anyone," he said to himself. "You just never can."

16

MCGIVERN WHIRLED his light around the room, purposely keeping the beam away from the direction of Cynthia's voice. "I hear cries and whimpers," he said. "I just can't seem to find where all the commotion's coming from."

Cynthia immediately recognized his voice, and felt more relief than fear. Now, at last, this insane charade will be over. He'd had his fun; now it was time to go home before the little game got more serious.

"F.X., come over here and free me. Enough is enough," she said, calmly trying to convey the sense that she would be willing to forget the whole thing.

He aimed the flashlight beam directly at her face, then let the light tease down to her ankles and slowly up her skirt and blouse.

"Cynthia," he said. "What are you doing here fastened to that dirty old radiator?"

"Please," she said, "help me. My wrists are hurting."

"Help you? Are you in pain? Now how could that be?" He walked up to her, his feet straddling her hips, and shined the light directly down into her eyes. "I don't see any pain in your face, Cynthia," he said. "I do see fear. You are afraid, aren't you? Well, let me see."

He knelt now by her tousled hair and checked the handcuffs. "They're not too tight," he said. "I don't know why you're complaining."

"F.X., enough. Come on. I'll forget the whole thing, but let me go right now. I promise. No one will ever know."

"But, Cynthia. It doesn't matter if people know. The police are probably looking for me right now. I'm sure they've missed you at the station by now. It's after seven o'clock."

He sat down heavily against the wall about six feet from where Cynthia lay. "Please. I can't stand being tied up. What do you want? Do you want anything from me? Do you want money? Do you want me to promise you something? Please let me go. I'll do anything, but I can't stand being tied up. And there are rats here. Please."

"Are you propositioning me? Is that what you're doing? You really are not in any position to do that, are you? I mean it isn't a question of what you want to give me. I think it's more a matter of what I want to take."

"Oh, God," she said, suddenly angry. "You bastard, let me go."

He smiled. "Don't worry. I'm not going to rape you. I mean, I have some standards. I think there might be an element of duress in any proposal you make. That, I suppose, would constitute rape."

He drew a pint flask from his pocket, unscrewed the cap, and drank. He then, without standing again, crawled like a lumbering sea turtle toward Cynthia and pushed the silver flask against her lips. She pulled away.

"You had better drink. It could be a long time before the next one."

The brandy trickled over her lips and tongue, then in a gush washed down her throat. She gagged and most of the liquid trickled down her cheeks.

"Don't waste it, Cynthia. It's precious stuff, especially for you."

"Are you going to kill me?" she asked. "If you are, do it and get it over with. I think you're scum."

"Aha, no more fun and games. Now it's all so serious. Now somebody is likely to get hurt. Now it's not just a story, is it, Cynthia? But don't worry. I'm not going to kill you. Not directly anyway. I may let you die. But I'll give you a sporting chance. Whether you live or die is immaterial to me. You wanted an interview. I came here to give it to you. It's as simple as that. You see, I'm a man of my word. I told you you'd have an interview. So go ahead. Ask me some questions."

"Please, let me get up."

"That's not a question."

"I'm aching all over."

"That's not a question either."

Cynthia suddenly screamed as loud as she could and then, lifting her legs, she lashed out with all her strength toward McGivern. Her feet missed, and as her scream subsided, she heard only his laughter.

"This place is boarded up as tight as a banker's purse. Nobody can hear you. Do you know where you are? No, you have no idea. Well, I shan't tell you. That will be a little surprise for another day. If you get out of here. If you don't, well, then the angels will tell you."

Cynthia began sobbing quietly now, her body shaking, her breaths coming in little gasps, like those of an infant left crying too long.

"No questions? What kind of reporter are you? I really thought you were made of sterner stuff. Well, you just lie still and listen, and I'll tell you what you wanted to hear, even though you don't seem the least bit interested."

He took another drink from his flask and leaned back against the wall once more.

"I almost changed my mind about this whole plan this very day, but your boyfriend came by to see me and he did something that just wasn't very wise. He punched me. Right in the nose. Now, I'm not a man of violence, but I am a man of great pride, and he hurt my pride. He really wounded it. He also drew blood. Ruined a new shirt and a perfectly good suit. Anyway, I took his attack as a sign that I should go ahead with my initial impulse, have you abducted, taken here, and then abandoned after I got a chance to complete my end of the deal. You see, I have a sense of honor."

"You creep."

"I'll ignore that. And I'll tell you the truth. It's very simple. I have as much right as Connie Haydon or anyone else in this town to make a little money in the grand American style. And that's how I got involved in Duncan Avenue, in a pure, and for the most part legitimate, enterprise that I couldn't have gotten into at all were it not for the family of Connie Haydon and some of my friends from the North End. Now that's the shorthand version. If I had more time to dally here with you, I'd tell you the long version, and I'd tell you all about how poor I was growing up, how I wore the same shirt and pair of pants all through high school, how there was never any food in the house, how my drunken father used to beat me, how my sister went nuts. But I don't think you'd feel much sympathy for me, would you?"

Cynthia was lying now with her eyes tightly closed. Her sobs had stopped. She was trying to will herself into unconsciousness. McGivern aimed the flashlight directly into her eyes. She closed them even tighter.

"Would you?" he asked again, this time nudging her hip with his shod foot.

She didn't answer.

"Would you, I said, bitch?" he repeated, and this time his foot hit her hip hard. She rolled over away from him and again started to sob. The pain in her wrists intensified but she wouldn't roll back to face him.

"O.K. I borrowed a lot of dough for this deal and I made some dough back from the insurance. But I'm a high roller. One night I blew fifty thousand — would you believe? — at the track. Just like that. Do you know the thrill of blowing fifty thousand bucks in one night at the track? Do you know the excitement that runs through you while you're watching those horses come around the bend and you know if that one horse comes in, you are almost gilt-edged? You could live like a sheik for a year. You can pay back money you borrowed. You can buy all the broads you ever wanted, ever dreamed of. You can live anywhere, do anything, say anything, be anybody. Totally free, like you parasites on a limitless expense account. I wasn't worried. This deal was too solid. It couldn't miss. I'd be a millionaire.

"And then all of a sudden, that fucker Tony Owen comes along and I could see it coming. Poof. Everything gone, every hope gone. And by the way, the mayor killed the whole deal tonight. I heard it on the radio. He made it official. I knew he'd do what he did, even before he did it. What choice did he have? A foregone conclusion."

"You didn't have to beat up Louise Finnigan. That was pretty stupid."

"It didn't matter. That just brought it to a head faster. I'm like you. I like to see things get resolved fast. Once Haydon knew there was mob money involved, he had to do what he did, and he would have known in a matter of days. At least I got the satisfaction of counterpunching your boyfriend."

"Why didn't you go after him directly?"

"To tell the truth, I like hurting women. You didn't know that, did you?" He laughed. "Just couldn't stand my mother, I guess."

Cynthia kept her face turned away, her body braced for another kick. It didn't come.

"But what's happening to you is nothing compared to what will happen to me, if the mob gets hold of me. They won't only be mad about the money; they'll be mad as hell over all the investigations that are coming down on this. I talked them into it, you know. They would have been just as happy doing coke and numbers and whores. But I talked them into becoming legitimate housing investors. And look what's happening.

"So I'm going away. It will look like I disappeared. They'll all be hunting for me. They'll all be looking for the two of us. But you won't be with me. You'll be right here."

Despite herself, Cynthia turned back toward him. "Please," she said, "please don't leave me here to die. I couldn't stand that. Kill me now, but don't leave me here like this."

"I'm sorry, Cynthia, but that I can't do. You see, it wouldn't be sporting, and I couldn't do that any more than I could rape you. That, you see, would be murder, and I'm not a murderer. I mean, I really felt bad about that bum Bernie whatever his name, for that very reason. You see, I am an officer of the court, and I take that quite seriously. I mean, I might beat you to within an inch of your life, but no, I couldn't kill you. I have my ethics, you see.

"Did you know, by the way, that I am firmly opposed to capital punishment? I was on a committee. You may have seen that in the files, if you looked. No, I have a plan and I'm going to stick to it. I am going to put you in the hands of God. I am going to leave here and begin a journey I've been thinking about for a long time now."

"You'll let me starve to death?"

"It's not an absolute death sentence, Cynthia. Really, it's not. I'm leaving you in a place often frequented by derelicts. In fact, to show you how fair I am, I put you in a suite that has been used, and used very recently, by squatters. You can see the junk over in the corner."

He pointed the flashlight across the room, and Cynthia could see a pile of clothes and discarded tin cans. "You see, signs of human habitation. Perhaps you'll be saved by a tramp, and just to give you a running start, a leg up, so to speak, I'm going to leave you this little flask." He shook it first. It was nearly empty.

"You'll have to ration it, a drop at a time. It might save your life. Who knows?"

He climbed back up to his feet and bent down and placed the flask within reach of her grasp, and left it there.

"You'll never get away," she said. "You are so repulsive, someone will spot you."

"It doesn't matter, Cynthia. Don't you understand? If I stay here, I'm dead in any case. I had a dream and it's gone. You destroyed it. You and your friend, and you can't say I didn't warn you. I warned you repeatedly. You just didn't listen. Now you can think about your mistakes for a few days, and soon, one way or another, it will be over. Good-bye."

He moved away. The beam of the flashlight disappeared and she heard the sound of his heaviness descending on the stairs.

□

Stanley was waiting in a city car parked up the street from the mayor's house when Corinne and Haydon arrived. He hopped out of the car and came running down the sidewalk toward the mayor as Corinne drove off.

"I've got to talk to you," Stanley said.

"O.K.," said the mayor, taking a seat on his front steps. Stanley sat down beside him.

"Good show, by the way, really good," Stanley said.

"Go on, tell me what's so important," the mayor said impatiently.

"Two things. One, the pope. He'll be here in three days. The Mass will be Friday night in City Hall Plaza. That's what the cardinal wants. He says it's more symbolic for what the pope has in mind. Besides, the Red Sox people are being bitchy. This will be better and the commissioner says the security is better."

"O.K., that's pretty much what I expected. Where else is the pope going?"

"The rest of the itinerary isn't official, but it will probably be Baltimore, New Orleans, San Francisco, then up to Montreal."

"So we got to share him. Too bad. I wonder how the hell Baltimore got into the mix. Two-bit town."

"Catholic tradition would be my guess."

"Maybe. Too bad the man's living in the past. O.K., we'll be ready for him. What else is on your mind, Stanley?"

"Well, I don't know what this means, but the commissioner just called, and he says it's too early to tell for sure but it seems that Cynthia Stoler has disappeared. Her station hasn't heard from her all day. Tony Owen went out in a cruiser tonight with Billy Curry. So far, they got nothing. They're looking for McGivern."

"Jesus, that bastard is capable of anything. Did they pick him up yet?"

"They can't find him. There's no formal alarm. It's too early. They like to wait twenty-four hours before pushing the panic button. But the station is getting a little bananas. She's a flake, but she's never done anything this bizarre before."

"It's McGivern. He's flipped and he's trying to scare the hell out of her. Get back to the commissioner and tell him to pick him up right now. The hell with twenty-four hours. This is all we need with the pope coming. So you think I did well, Stanley. You liked the news conference."

"I thought you were a master. Best yet."

"Shows how little you know, Stanley. Keep me posted. Don't forget, bring in McGivern and have the commissioner call me as soon as they find him."

Haydon pushed open the front door. The hall light was on, but he could feel the emptiness in the big house. He called for Eileen from the bottom of the stairway and wasn't surprised when he got no answer, nor was he greatly surprised to find an envelope on the kitchen table propped up against the cut-glass sugar bowl. The pale blue envelope was from Eileen's personal stationery, and his name was written in her distinctive free-flowing script.

He held the envelope in his hand, tapped it a few times against his palm as if to judge the weight of its contents, then walked upstairs to his study.

He was relieved in a way that she had decided against confronting him. He had dreaded the prospect and now, perhaps, it could be postponed for a day or two. He disliked scenes, not enough to shy away from them. But they were unpleasant, particularly when they involved issues of emotion. He felt unsure dealing with women on those terms, their terms, women's terms. It was so much easier to deal with men; their strengths and weaknesses were so much more apparent, their reactions so much more predictable. With men, it was all pride, appearances, and power. But women were more subtle, more volatile. One had to manipulate them with extreme caution, while not forgetting for a moment the different values they placed on things. For a man, he didn't do all that badly dealing with women.

Until recently, Eileen had been no problem, really. She was unhappy. Their marriage was a sham, if truth be told. And the baby thing; after all the years, that was still an open wound. But never before had she even hinted at jumping the traces. True, she didn't have a lot of love in her marriage. She had other compensations. She was one of the most envied women in the city, and how many women her age still had love? She had freedom, he left her alone, there was nothing tangible she might want that she couldn't have. And she had more friends, real friends, in the city than he had. All told, it was a pretty good life, and if it wasn't for Corinne he wouldn't have heard a complaint that he would have to take seriously.

But now, as he sat in his study with the pale blue envelope in his hand, he knew in his bones that it would take weeks, months, to appease Eileen. He also knew that it would take great energy and concentration on his part, energy and concentration that he was no longer sure he could muster. It would be so much easier just to walk away, if only he could, if only he dared. But he couldn't imagine that. He couldn't imagine being anything but what he was. He couldn't imagine a new life. He couldn't imagine being happy just with himself and Corinne. No, he would appease Eileen, no matter how long it took. He would come up with something good for the short run. She wouldn't, she couldn't, stand missing out on the pope's visit. And after that, he'd send her and her family off somewhere, to Florida maybe, or the Caribbean, to get some perspective on why he was forced to do things, even unpleasant things. For all of her talk, for all of her new-found pride, she wasn't going anywhere; she wasn't going to do anything. In the crunch, she'd compromise as she always did.

He tore open the envelope. He expected to find a long and tortured letter. Instead, he found three pale blue sheets of paper, two of them blank. The middle sheet contained a three-line message in Eileen's handwriting. It read:

> Shithead,
>   You're going to pay.
>   Eileen.

□

The telephone in Tony Owen's apartment rang only once more before Tony fell into a fitful sleep. Scooter Conroy called to inform Tony that Eileen Haydon was with him and she wanted to talk.

"To be perfectly honest with you, Tony, I've been trying to talk her out of it. She's all upset, and in another day or two she's going to see things a lot differently. But she begged me to get hold of you. I told her that's all I'm going to do. Hey, right now I need Connie Haydon a helluva lot more than he needs me. I tried to tell you that on the phone the other day."

"Oh, is that what you were trying to say?" Tony answered.

"Well, will you do something?"

"Scooter, you got me at a bad time. Something's happened to Cynthia. She's disappeared."

"What do you mean, she's disappeared?"

"She went out this morning to try to meet McGivern and she never came back."

"You're shitting me."

"Scooter, do you have any idea what could have happened to her?"

"You mean you let her go out alone to meet McGivern?"

"Hey, she's a big girl, Scooter."

"Let me make some calls. Christ almighty. Tommy Mannion will be back in town tomorrow. Maybe he can help. Jesus, Tony, I'm sorry."

"Don't be sorry. See if you can do something."

"What do you want me to do about Eileen?"

"Send her to Stella Ferral or Bobby Bantam. I can't deal with Eileen right now."

"Do you want me to call?"

"Yeah, just call Bobby. Tell him you spoke to me, he'll handle it. I don't want to tie the phone up anymore."

"The cops got a tap on it?"

"I presume so. Just in case McGivern or somebody calls."

"Christ, now Haydon will know the whole gig."

"Some things can't be helped. I got to hang up now. Good-bye."

□

It was three-thirty Wednesday morning when Commissioner Connolly telephoned Connie Haydon. The mayor was still awake and he answered the phone immediately, as if his hand were poised over the receiver.

"I'm going to drop over and see you, if you don't mind. I have some information," the commissioner said.

"I'll be up," said the mayor.

☐

Tony Owen awoke before dawn, his mind reeling like a tape recorder, shuttling fast forward toward a terrifying future without Cynthia, then pitching back into the clutter of a past where his life was like a photo album torn out of sequence. Patches of things danced before his eyes. Aunt Jenny. His mother, her eyes sad and harassed. The kitchen. Always that kitchen. Cynthia. The time they met at the abortion doctor's trial. How he watched her walking back and forth from the water cooler. Legs and ass. He knew them before he knew her. Did he really know her? Malachy. The same eyes, their mother's eyes. Cynthia's eyes. Cynthia. He could see her now on a slab in the morgue. Eyes open. You failed. Scooter was right. How could you let her go alone to see McGivern? Why didn't you ask? He could see himself at the funeral. Eyes dry. He didn't care. Eyes wet. He really cared. Trying not to observe himself. Trying to be. Would Haydon be there? What would he say? I'm sorry, Tony. And what would he say to Haydon? You son of a bitch, it's all your fault. I'm going to kill you. And the commotion as they tried to hold him back. It's O.K., it's O.K. He's upset, Your Honor. You know. He's been through a lot. But why did he have to observe the scene? Why couldn't he just live it, endure it, without self-consciousness, without criticism of his own performance?

Tony got out of bed at the usual time, showered and dressed quickly, then looked at the clock. He was right on schedule and that pleased him. He had heard or read somewhere that it was important in these circumstances to adhere to one's routine, and so at nine-thirty he left the apartment. But he skipped his customary morning coffee at Mike's; he didn't want to face people if he could avoid them. *Bruise*-bound, he boarded the Beacon Street trolley.

Along Beacon Street at every intersection, papal flags were hanging. At ordinary intersections, the flags were bunched and fastened high up on utility poles, safely removed from the clutching hands of neighborhood kids. At major intersections, like Kenmore Square, the papal yellow flew in a wide ribbon of nylon across the width of the avenue.

Public Works Department crews seemed to be everywhere, scraping and washing and dusting and clearing away in a civic imitation of the virtuous housewife, bent on rubbing out the slightest signs of dirt and disorder as if they were reflections of a guilt better obscured. And in store windows, portraits of a smiling pontiff emerged like campaign posters. At discreet intervals, the pope's portrait and that of Mayor Haydon were pasted up side by side, as if the mayor were the pontiff's impresario in the city's biggest pageant since the return of the regiments in 1865.

Tony's eyes caught the twin posters and he nearly gagged, and for the first time since it was clear that Cynthia had disappeared, he thought of something other than himself and Cynthia. He thought of Haydon and how everything and everyone seemed to be conspiring to prop him up. He thought of the press conference yesterday, and without having yet seen the morning's papers, he knew the mayor had gotten his way. "I'm letting that son of a bitch off the hook," he muttered to himself.

He recalled the phone call last night from Scooter, and he thought of his own indifference to what was obviously a story that could at last bring down Connie Haydon. He winced at the thought of himself, a wimp sitting immobilized by the telephone, unable to act, unable to fight back. There was so much to do, and here he was in a crisis, fast losing sense of who he was. Cynthia was to blame. She was turning him into mush. Feelings, he reminded himself, were a luxury for people with lots of time and lots of money in the bank. He couldn't afford feelings. They were out of his line, and if he didn't watch it, the way he was carrying on, he'd end up like Malachy, muttering to himself in the street.

He'd tell Cynthia that, the next time he saw her, and he'd see her again. To think otherwise was just another way to give in to this incredible weakness, and he wouldn't give in.

So on that morning he strode into the *Bruise* newsroom, looking to all the world like a man ready for a day's work.

"What a pleasant surprise," said Bobby Bantam. "I thought you might sit today out. You have it coming, you know."

"There's too much to do," said Tony. "The mayor got away with murder this morning."

"Don't worry about your friend Connie Haydon. It's only a matter of time. The bum's all washed up, Tony. But anyway, come on into my office. A lot has been happening."

Tony hesitated. "What do you want me to do today?" he asked.

"First, let's talk, O.K.?" Bantam said, and steering Tony by the elbow, he guided him into the corner office. "Come on, let's sit down and talk this over."

Bobby pulled a copy boy aside, handed him a bill, and sent him on a coffee run. "And bring back a couple of Danish. Anything but raspberry. I hate their fucking raspberry."

Bantam yelled to his secretary to hold the calls and took a seat on his sofa. "Come on, Tony, sit down over here. Make yourself comfortable."

Tony sat down alongside Bobby, feeling a little uncomfortable at the intimacy. He preferred Bantam when he was being Bantam.

"Tony, I was hoping you would stay away today. I think you're a little spacy. I bet you can't feel your feet on the floor."

"I'm all right. I let myself indulge in a little self-pity last night. But today I'm myself. I got to work this story, and the story is Mayor Haydon."

"Hey, you're right, in a way. You know, Eileen called me last night, and she's with Stella Ferral right now, I believe. If this works out, we're going to have a three-part series — "Eileen Haydon's Nightmare," the wronged wife fights back. Great stuff. I think I'll begin moving it just in time for the pope. You think that son of a bitch will ever get to be a Knight of Saint Gregory? No way. Forget him. I think he'll be through in a week."

"I'd like to write that."

"Tony," said Bantam, who reached out and patted Tony on the shoulder. "That kind of stuff isn't for you. It would be beneath your dignity. You go after the hard stuff. When you're ready."

"Now, you wait a minute, Bobby," said Tony, slowly getting to his feet, "what's this 'when I'm ready'? I am ready. What are you talking about?"

Bobby sat still, his face a mask of wise concern.

"Tony, I don't know what's going on in your head this morning, but you may not be up to date on the facts. So let me just tell you quickly. First of all, the mayor and Commissioner Connolly are planning a news conference at noon on Cynthia's disappearance to outline the steps they're taking to try to find her. Channel Four is leading with the story. They're asking the FBI to come in because it's a kidnaping case. We, of course, are going to go big tomorrow, even though the pope is just about ready to get on the plane. In fact, I'm going to have the city desk try to get a statement out of the Vatican, appealing for Cynthia's return.

"And you won't believe this, but ten minutes after the story went out on the AP this morning, who the hell calls but Kansas, wanting to know what the hell is going on."

"Fuck Kansas."

"Sure, fuck Kansas. Just two days ago, we were heading down the chute. They wouldn't take my calls. Now they're calling me."

The copy boy walked in with the Danish. Bobby unwrapped them, and turned to the young man. "You've got to be kidding me. You're putting me on. Didn't I just tell you anything but raspberry, and what the hell is this?"

"It's raspberry, but it's all they had left. I thought you'd think it was better than nothing."

"Get out of here, you turkey. On another day, I'd fire your ass."

The sentinel walked out. "The nerve of that kid. Here, Tony, you eat two of them."

"Sorry, I'm not hungry."

"See, you're not hungry. That's what I mean. Here we have this big story. Let's face it, it's the biggest we've had over here since what? What was the last one that was our story that really shook everybody out of the trees?"

"I don't remember."

"It was the North End building collapse. Twenty-two dead. Lousy cement, lousy steelwork, bribed inspectors. Shit, you were still a kid."

"We've had better stories than that since I've been here."

"Go on, name them. Go ahead. Go ahead. Have that Danish. Good for you. Sugar. Energy. You probably haven't eaten in twenty-four hours."

"Bobby, stop playing mother. My mother is dead. I don't need another one."

"Oh yes you do, Tony. Because you don't know what you're doing to yourself. You've lost your perspective. Hey, it's understandable. I mean, hey, I like Cynthia a lot and I'm not . . . you know what I mean."

"No, I don't know what you mean," Tony Owen said.

"Look, all I'm telling you is that you shouldn't try to work this story. You can't help. You're not in shape to help. You're too involved, and I'm telling you, the longer you stay around here, the more questions you're going to have to be answering, and it's too painful. Reporters can be bastards, you know. Maybe you don't know. Maybe you never stopped to realize."

"I stopped to realize lots of times, and I can see right through you, Bobby."

"Oh boy," said Bobby Bantam. He settled back against the cushions. "Look. You think I just want you out of here so you won't be in the way while I pump this story up like the goddamn Goodyear blimp. You think I think you'll inhibit me by your presence and that's why I don't want you around. Well, you're wrong, because this story is so big there is no way you or anyone else can inhibit me. If anything, I need someone to inhibit me. Otherwise, I might go overboard. I don't know how, but it's possible. No, Tony, listen to me. I care about you. I really do. That's all."

"Then let me work. That's what I need."

"Remember the Patty Hearst kidnaping? You know who got hurt in that one. It wasn't Patty Hearst. She got identity she can use for the rest of her life. She was just a poor little rich girl when she got grabbed. Afterwards, she became a personality. She grew up. No, the one that got hurt was her boyfriend. Remember the poor sap she used to live with? He's the guy that got hurt because he cared. The news just ate him up and spit him out. I don't want to see you end up like that guy."

"My name's not Weed," said Tony.

"That's right. That was his name. Weed. Well, he wasn't Steve Weed either before the roof came down on him."

"I'm going to work. That's it. And I don't want your sympathy, concern, or hovering. I can't stand it when you hover. O.K.?"

"O.K. You win. Do what you want."

"Fine, that's all I ask."

Bantam sighed, stood up, moved back behind his desk, and began flipping through his messages. "There's no sign of McGivern. He's just vanished. The cops got one of their alarms out for him. And with all the publicity, he might turn up. Presumably, he's got Cynthia with him, wherever the hell he's gone."

"I think I'll just sniff around town and see what I can come up with, unless you want me to do something specific."

"I told you what I want. And that's a dead issue. You have a free hand. Of course, you can handle these if you want." He handed Tony a sheaf of messages from reporters wanting interviews.

"Fuck them," said Tony.

"That's the first sensible thing you've said all morning," Bobby Bantam allowed.

□

John Walsh watched Tony Owen leave the newsroom, then walked into Bobby Bantam's office. "Is Tony going to be all right? The cops don't have too much hope of finding Cynthia."

"He'll be fine, John. Let him work it out in his own way. He's learning something."

"That he's not as tough as he thought he was."

"Nah, he's learning that there's a good reason why people like us don't get involved. We're fucked up, and that's why we're in this business. You got to be fucked up to be any good. We're like shrinks."

"And whores."

"And whores. Good whores."

"I thought Tony knew that."

"He did; he just forgot. Next time, he'll remember."

Bobby's secretary interrupted. "Kansas is on the phone again, Bobby."

"Terrific," he said. "If you'll excuse me, John."

Bantam rushed to his desk and picked up the phone. This time it was the big boss himself. "Well, you finally got back to me," said Bantam. "You know we have a little miracle on our hands, and the pope hasn't even arrived yet."

"So I understand," the boss said.

"We can sell everything we can print. I kid you not. I've never seen such a news break."

"You are to be congratulated, Bobby. For better or worse, you have proven a point. I'm sorry that it seems, shall I say, tinged with tragedy."

"We all are sorry about that, sir. But what the hell. It's the breaks. We're in a tough business and I guess you can't complain when what happens to others happens in your own family."

"How does it look for her?"

"Well, it doesn't look good right now. Nobody can find the lawyer who ran off with her, and he's a little unbalanced to begin with. But Cynthia isn't the victim type. I mean, she can make life miserable. I suppose it's a question of how much he can take, or she can take."

"And how is Tony Owen holding up?"

"Like a trooper. He was in here on time this morning, ready to work."

"Amazing."

"Well, he's an amazing guy."

Bobby waited, anxious for the boss to get back to the point Bobby proved. An awkward silence developed. Bobby had the impression that perhaps the boss was talking to someone else who was in his office.

"How are things in Kansas?" he asked.

"I'm not sure, Bobby," the boss replied. "We're in the midst of a major reconsideration."

"Is that so?" Bobby replied.

"Yes. As you might have imagined, it would be extremely awkward right now to close our Boston operations, especially if we make, and maintain, our target numbers. And from what I understand, you will easily exceed the target for the rest of this week, at least, and probably longer, depending on how long that woman is missing."

"That's true, and with the way I plan to showcase things over that time, we should win a lot of friends for the paper. The *Mammoth* has been out to lunch on this whole story, you understand."

"But this is not a clear-cut victory, Bobby. If we don't add advertising gains to circulation gains, we're just going to end up losing even more money on production costs. And we are in a situation, quite frankly, that I hoped we would avoid. I mean, we are a wealthy corporation, but our resources are hardly infinite."

"Hardly, sir. But if we can't capitalize on all the good will we've been building and will keep building over the next few weeks, we never will. It's just a matter of getting out there and making the same effort from the business side as we're making here on the news side. And you won't have anything to worry about."

It was the first time in Bobby's career that he had ever criticized an associate to a superior, and he winced as he spoke. He hated disloyalty, and good reason or no good reason, he had just sold out Elmer Granger.

"We are considering some changes up there, maybe realigning the command structure down the line," said the boss.

Bobby's spirits dipped. "You have to do what you think is right," he said.

"We are giving serious consideration to naming you publisher."

"Publisher?" he asked.

"It's something I would like you to think about in the next few days. I have already spoken to Elmer."

"I'm sorry," Bobby said.

"No need to be," said the boss. "He took a position. Events didn't support him. That's life."

"I hope he feels the same way."

"He will, eventually. And, of course, remember, if you take the job we're talking about and things don't work out, there'll be no second chance."

"Things will work out."

"We'll see."

"I guarantee it."

"See you next week. And please tell Tony we're all praying for Cynthia. Such a lovely girl."

□

On most mornings, the *Mammoth* city room bore a striking resemblance to the actuarial annex at the John Hancock Insurance Company. Reporters and editors sat at their desks in a sullen torpor that endured until noon, when irregular knots of people would break away from whatever newspaper or magazine they were reading and slowly walk down the hall toward the company cafeteria for a leisurely lunch. Now and then, one of the city desk lieutenants posted near a telephone would signal to an intern or a novice reporter that there was an obituary to be taken and written. And after one of the unending succession of story conferences, a senior editor would summon the senior reporters into a cubbyhole for a discussion on the stories they would cover for that day.

Frequently, a story assignment was seen as an imposition, an unfair intrusion into a reporter's private time — time that he granted the *Mammoth* only on condition that it be used in conformity with the reporter's views on the nature of reality and his social standing within the newsroom. A story conceived by the city desk did not, as a result, always get past the assignment stage, because in the wrangling between editor and reporter over whether it was worth doing, reporters would often come up with an alternative idea of their own. The hard-pressed editor would seize upon the new idea as a compromise; the reporter would then bend to the task. In the course of the next two or three weeks, he might or might not produce a story for publication. Meanwhile, he would be insulated from any fresh assignments, always having the ready-made excuse: "Don't you remember? I'm already working on something."

Inevitably, the day-to-day paper was produced not by the high-priced, multitalented staff recruited from the sons and daughters of America's gentry, but by grinds recruited from working-class colleges like Northeastern, who believed that a position with the *Mammoth* represented deliverance into a higher order of being. Later, when they learned that the class distinctions within the *Mammoth* were every bit as oppressive as those outside, they rebelled and sank into cynicism. But that process took years before it extinguished all hope. Meanwhile, they worked like dogs, looking for the big news break that would make their reputation, while carrying the *Mammoth* on their shoulders.

This morning, the dogs were in their traces, as usual. But so were other members of the *Mammoth* staff, including Bill Raleigh and his cadre of editors.

Raleigh worked crisply but sullenly, choking back the fury that was building inside him, fury that he could not display because it was directed at the head of young Walter Griswold, who had broken all *Mammoth* precedent that morning by sitting in, in person, at the major news conference. And then, he had had the effrontery to remain and listen to every word as Raleigh ticked off the assignments. As far as the *Mammoth* staff was concerned, the presence of the publisher signaled the significance of the news before them that day. Today there would be no back talk, no ninety-minute lunches in the cafeteria, no browsing over magazines in the *Mammoth* library. Today everyone worked.

To Bill Raleigh, though, young Walter's presence in the newsroom was to be read not as the outcome of the extraordinary news developments. It was an unforgivable intrusion into his territory, a gross challenge to his authority. It was just not done, ever.

But he kept his emotions hidden behind brusqueness as he doled out the workload.

"Here's what I want," said Raleigh to Dugan. "I want the sharpest possible profile on Cynthia Stoler and her relationship to Tony Owen, everything we can get on the two of them, singly and together. I'd prefer to tell it through Tony Owen, and if he won't talk to us, get hold of his friends. Who do you have to do that?"

"What about Hornblower?" Dugan replied.

Before Raleigh could answer, Walter Griswold interjected, "I don't want Hornblower. Keep him on the pope. He's been screwing this one up for two weeks."

Raleigh, despite himself, glared at Griswold. "You're out of line, Walter," he muttered.

"Perhaps," he said, with an alarming trace of insolence, it seemed to Raleigh. "I don't want Hornblower."

Raleigh considered for an instant taking on the publisher in the middle of the city room; then he conceded the point. "Put O'Brien on it. You need a high-energy kid," he said.

"He's working the main story," said Dugan.

"O.K., then try Katzer."

"He hasn't worked anything like this before."

"I don't care; he's good."

Griswold turned to Raleigh. "Let's run this down from A to Z. Give me the stories we're going after on the Stoler case."

Raleigh bristled. Then he looked directly at the publisher and said, "O.K., but let's go and sit down again in the conference room. I have the list there."

The two men, accompanied by William Bender and Cyrus Corning (Dugan stayed outside to handle the assignments), returned to the glass-enclosed conference room, where Raleigh picked up a clipboard and began reading off the assignments, his voice unsteady as his emotions began rising in his throat.

"Main story — the disappearance, the kidnaping, the profile of McGivern, the mayor's news conference at police headquarters: O'Brien and Mickwell, with six interns, to be assigned by the main reporters, depending on the breaks," he said.

"Sublead — the Duncan Avenue story, with notes from Horn-blower." Raleigh stopped, stared up at his publisher, and said, "He's been working this story for weeks. He has some information. He'd better dump it, O.K.?"

"Fine," said Griswold, who by now had settled in a proprietary way into Bill Raleigh's chair.

"This will bring us up to date on the whole mess. Lange will work that with Jack Cabot pitching in."

"Fine," said Griswold.

"Then there's the Stoler profile. We already talked about that, with Katzer the writer."

"No women. We ought to have a woman working that, too."

"You're right," said Bender, who for his pains got a cutting look from Bill Raleigh.

"Yeah, I'll put Eaton on that with Katzer," said Raleigh.

"Is that it?" said the publisher.

"That's pretty much it for the main pieces," Raleigh replied.

"Nothing on the mayor. I think we ought to have a separate on him. Here's a man in the middle if I ever saw it, with the pope coming and this mess on his hands. How's he holding up?"

By now Raleigh was losing his self-control. "Sure, great. Let's do a piece dumping on him, and while we're at it, why don't we do a piece on what this story does to the *Bruise* and its chances of survival."

He spoke sarcastically, but Griswold ignored the barbed edge in his voice. "That isn't a bad idea, Bill," Griswold replied evenly. "Why don't you have someone from the business pages get Gridlock to see whether this mess is going to cause any reconsideration. I wouldn't be surprised if it did."

"Bender, you do it. I'm going for a walk," Raleigh said as he slapped the clipboard onto the table and walked out the door, trying to hide his feelings behind a forced smile that made them more obvious. He entered his office, closed the door, and took no phone calls for the next half-hour. When he emerged, Griswold was still sitting in the editor's chair.

"Hey, Bill," he called to Raleigh in a voice that could be heard halfway across the city room. "You got the best job in the whole place. I haven't had this much fun in years. Get in here. We haven't completed the assignments yet on the pope's visit, and your man Bender tells me we're running out of reporters."

☐

Commissioner Connolly had a number of things to tell Mayor Haydon when he rang his doorbell in the middle of the night. The mayor would have to think of an appropriate response quickly, because it was now apparent that Cynthia Stoler had been abducted. The mayor should also know, the commissioner said, with all the subtlety his manner allowed, that there was reason to believe that Eileen was in the company of Scooter Conroy and seemed determined to do the mayor the maximum possible harm.

"And what harm might that be?" asked Haydon.

"I think she plans to talk to Stella Ferral."

The mayor's apprehensions now turned to alarm. And once the commissioner left his house, Haydon was on the phone to Scooter Conroy.

"You bastard. What the hell are you doing with my wife?"

"I'm not doing anything, Connie."

"Where is she?"

"I honestly don't know. She left here an hour ago and didn't tell me where she was going."

"Is she meeting Stella Ferral?"

"Not at this hour. It's five o'clock in the morning."

"You arranged it, Scooter. I'll never forgive you if she talks to that witch."

"Connie, what can I say? It wasn't my idea."

"O.K., Scooter, but if she talks to Ferral, our whole deal is off and you'll die broke."

"Connie, you don't seem to understand. The lady is a free agent."

"I understand perfectly. I hope you understand."

"I can't help you, Connie."

"And I can't help you, either," said Haydon, and he placed the receiver back on the cradle.

17

CYNTHIA LAY in the darkness. Her body ached, particularly around her shoulders and neck, and her hands and wrists were intermittently numb. She wanted desperately to rub them, but the handcuffs and the nubby leg of the ancient radiator left her with only limited movement of her hands. She was able to reach the flask that McGivern had left behind and she rationed the brandy, taking just a few drops at a time. McGivern had left less than an ounce to begin with. Occasionally, she lapsed into sleep, but the sounds of traffic outside jarred her back into wakefulness, as did the sporadic noises of the building in which she was enclosed.

By the intensity of the traffic sounds, she was able to distinguish, in the darkness of the room, between the predawn hours and the daylight. It was her only gauge of the time. She also knew she was somewhere in the city, probably in an abandoned building, judging from what she had seen in the beam of McGivern's flashlight. She welcomed the traffic sounds. They were her only link to the reality outside the room. The building noises terrified her, particularly the scurrying and scratching in the walls not far from her head. When I die, the rats will come and eat me, she thought, and began to sob. Slowly she drifted back into sleep. This time it was footsteps on the stairs that awakened her. Someone pushed open the door and lit a match.

McGivern had returned to kill her, she thought, and she stayed quiet, trying to push herself into the floor as if she could disappear through the floorboards.

"You're in there somewhere. I know you are," someone said. And immediately her heart lifted in hope. It wasn't McGivern. It had to be a friend.

"I'm here," she called. "Please come and help me."

The man with the match trudged toward her. The match he was holding burned his fingers. He cursed and lit another one. Then, following its flickering light, he approached Cynthia and stared down into her face.

"So you are here," he said. "He told me you would be."

"Thank God," she said. "Please free my hands. They're hurting."

He stared down at her with a dim sense of wonder. Cynthia returned his stare, pleading with her eyes while trying to read in his some sign of a shared humanity. To her dismay, his eyes were blank and bloodshot.

Again she appealed to him. "Please, I'm in pain. Go for help. I'll make it worth your while. You'll never have to worry about money again. Please."

"He told me you'd say that," he said.

"Who?" she said.

"This fat man who told me you'd be here. He said if I went to this apartment, it would be finders keepers."

"Oh, God," she said. In the light of the match, his toothless face with its sunken eyes and white stubble looked like a Halloween mask. But Cynthia's defenses rose to reject what her eyes took in. She saw only an old man down on his luck, who would soon be rushing to help her. Now it occurred to her that she was deluding herself, that this was not a rescuer but a derelict hand-picked by McGivern to continue her torment.

"Where did the fat man go?" she asked.

"How do I know? He gave me fifty dollars. What do I care?"

"I'll give you a thousand."

"For what?" he said.

He sat down beside her, his back leaning against the radiator. He did not bother now with any more matches. Instead, he pulled a pint of whiskey out of his jacket. She listened to his breathing, heavy and wheezy, and despite herself smelled all the odors of the street as his sweat mixed with the filth matted on his clothing, encrusted in the pores of his ruined body.

"My name is Sailor," he said.

She refused to surrender hope. "My name is Cynthia. I'm a television reporter. I've been kidnaped. Everybody in the city is looking for me. I'm sure the mayor has offered a big reward. Rescue me and you'll be a hero. You'll be all over the newspapers and television, and you'll be rich."

"I know who you are. He told me," he said.

"Then you're going to help me."

"Have a drink," he said, and poured the brandy (it was Laird's applejack) down Cynthia's throat. This time she didn't gag. She was going to fight. She drank greedily, so greedily that he pulled the bottle from her lips roughly. "Hey, save me some, you," he said.

He drank what was left in the bottle, then curled up beside her and, to Cynthia's dismay, fell sound asleep.

□

Tony Owen dropped in at police headquarters, which was swarming with FBI men. They eyed him quizzically at first, then with barely concealed annoyance. He was a double nuisance — a reporter who was also connected to the case. They couldn't ask him to leave because he had a stake in the investigation, and they weren't on their own turf anyway. But they could make him feel uncomfortable and they did by ignoring him after asking a few perfunctory questions and giving a few perfunctory answers to Tony's own queries.

Finally, Tony stood up in Billy Curry's little office, which was the nerve center for the investigation, and announced abruptly, "You guys aren't getting anywhere." As he spoke, his frustration gave way to anger. "You probably haven't even looked down on Duncan Avenue. That would be just the kind of thing a sick prick like McGivern would do. Stash her right under our noses in one of those burned-out hulks he's been playing around with for months. And I'll bet you know-it-all bastards haven't even looked."

One of the agents, a tall man with eyeglasses and a jogger's wiry frame, looked up from the folder he was examining and stared contemptuously at Tony.

"Hey, everything that can be done is being done. We've had a team of people down at Duncan Avenue since the crack of dawn, for Christ's sake, and they haven't found a thing," he said.

"Are they your guys or Boston cops?"

"Hey, it's the Boston cops who know the territory."

"They couldn't find a coal shovel under the bed," Tony said.

"Well, they are looking."

"Maybe I'd better look myself."

"Maybe you ought to stay the hell away from there. You goddamn amateurs. All you can do is get in the way. Why don't you go somewhere and get some sleep. That way you might really help."

"Fuck you," said Tony.

"That's an intelligent comment," the agent said, and resumed his examination of the folder.

Tony turned and stalked out. The agent was right. He would get in the way. For now, he would let the cops do their work, but he had little confidence they would find Cynthia in time. He headed back toward the newspaper, cutting down Berkeley Street into the South End.

The morning was warm and bright and the sunlight fell harshly on the broken sidewalks, the filthy gutters, the abandoned and smashed automobiles that littered the streets near the newspaper. Tony walked aimlessly, trying to keep control of himself. Repeatedly, he told himself that what was happening wasn't real, that it was likely a runaway prank that Cynthia herself had helped concoct to test his affection. He remembered how once he had interviewed a woman whose husband was on the crew of the lost submarine *Thresher*. The navy had not yet officially given up on the doomed boat, but everyone knew that all aboard had perished. He remembered how that freshly minted widow grew angrier and angrier at her dead husband as she talked. And at the end of the interview, she was actually blaming him for the whole episode, blaming him as if he were actually sitting on the sofa beside her. "That dumb son of a bitch knew everything but to listen. I told him, 'Now you get out of the submarine service,' and he said, 'Sure.' My ass, he'd get out. Now I'll bet he's sorry." But Cynthia isn't dead. She'll be back.

He was one block from the paper when he encountered Malachy, moving hurriedly up the sidewalk toward him. Tony couldn't look at him, nor could he bear to listen to his voice. But had he looked, he would have seen a different Malachy. For one thing, he was wearing shoes, and his suit, though worn and ill-fitting, was clean. His face was shaven and his hair, dark and overgrown, was combed.

But Malachy did look searchingly at his brother.

"Tony, you should be so happy and you look so sad."

"Let me be, Malachy, I have to go. I'm late."

Malachy reached out and grabbed his brother's arm. "Something's wrong, Tony. You haven't been able to get me the audience. Is that what's the matter? Well, if it is, don't worry. I'll get through. I have faith, enormous faith."

Tony pulled away and began moving forward along the sidewalk toward a block cleared years before for an industrial park and now nothing more than a clearing where rats fed on the garbage tossed there by residents of the housing project across the street.

"I talked to Johnny Weissmuller yesterday, Tony," Malachy shouted after him. "You might be interested in what he had to say."

Tony kept moving, head down now, his legs pumping as hard as they could to escape from Malachy.

But Malachy came chasing after him, clinging like shame.

"He said it doesn't matter whether he's free or not, because a greater one is coming to tame the furies of this place. He's done his work. It doesn't matter now, he said. And you should have seen the look in his eyes. It was like the Old Testament, a prophet. What eyes, Tony. You have to see that man's eyes. I didn't know if he knew about the pope, so I told him and he didn't say a word. He just stared."

All the while, Malachy tugged on Tony's arm, until Tony had enough. "Leave me alone," he said. "Just leave me alone. I really don't give a damn about your Johnny Weissmuller, you crazy loon. Why don't you go away? Why don't you just die?"

The words were hurtful, but Tony spoke them quietly and pulled himself free, leaving Malachy standing on the sidewalk gaping at him, as if he were staring at a stranger.

"You don't mean that, Tony. You're just upset," Malachy yelled after him. By now, Tony was running across the street, his legs moving like a child running home after a bad fright.

He kept running for three blocks until he was startled by the heavy pumping of his own heart. And breathlessly, he struggled for composure and pulled a handkerchief from his pocket to wipe the sweat from his face and neck. God, I'm cracking up, he said to himself. What is the matter with me?

He found himself near the cathedral, where workmen were on ladders outside the main door, placing in position the papal coat of arms.

An impulse seized him. He saw an open door to the right of the main entrance and walked inside. He found the interior busy. A boom mounted on a Jeep labeled CLIMBING SIMON hovered high overhead, where a string of red hats representing the cardinals of the archdiocese was suspended. A workman in the boom was dusting each of the hats, one by one. At the altar, a man and a woman were scrubbing the marble steps, and cleaning machinery cluttered the aisle on the St. Joseph's side.

Tony ingested the details impersonally, mechanically, unaware that he was seeing or hearing anything. He entered a pew in the middle of the side aisle, stepping over a giant vacuum. His eyes took in a young boy helping the two adults at the altar. The boy was turned toward Tony, staring at him. The boy's image filled Tony's eyes but made no impression on his brain, and when Tony began shaking with sobs, he didn't know that the boy was looking at him with a cold curiosity, wondering what grief had brought him to this place at this time.

□

Malachy was momentarily bewildered by the uncharacteristic abruptness of Tony's departure, but nothing was going to put a damper on his spirits this day. Something extraordinary was at hand. He knew it. He saw an omen in the brilliant sunshine, a sign that providence was bathing the city in a special glow of anticipation. Perhaps Tony had seen it and it scared him. He would have to try to see him again later in the day, but first there was so much work to be done. He had to get his people as ready as he was for the great day.

He walked up Harrison Avenue toward City Hospital. He found Sewerplate Man in the middle of the next block, stretched out full length in the gutter on his stomach, peering through the grate into the muck below. Malachy crouched down by his head and looked down through the grate to try to see what held his interest. Sewerplate didn't stir. Finally, Malachy tapped him on the shoulder. Sewerplate looked up at him with vacant eyes, then peered back down into the sewer.

"Pope's coming. You got to start getting yourself together. Big day is Friday. That's the day after tomorrow. Got to get ready."

He continued to stare down at the sewer; then he reached out with one of his hands and grabbed a few stones and bottle caps from the gutter and dropped them one at a time through the grate.

"Well, I guess you're not going to talk to me today. But keep it in mind so you can start getting your good clothes together. Got to look nice for the pope."

Malachy stood up and continued his walk. From the time he awoke at the shelter and donned the clothes he had been readying for a week, he had not thought once of taking a drink. But now, as he came to a doorway by the Do Drop Inn where two bag ladies were sharing a bottle wrapped in a brown bag, Malachy could smell the Thunderbird from twenty paces.

"Hey, Father, you look like a priest today. Where you heading, for church?" called the older of the two, a thin, small woman whose dark complexion seemed ashen under the coating of grime. She had slept the night before in the hallway.

Malachy approached, and glanced at the bag. "The pope is coming. I'm trying to spread the good news and get everybody ready."

The women didn't react. The smaller woman tilted back her neck and took a deep swallow, while her companion, who might have been anywhere from thirty to sixty, reached anxiously for the bag.

"Save me some, you pig," she said, and pulled the bottle from her.

"Who's the pig, Nora?" her companion said. "Why don't you see if the Father will have some?"

"No, I'm staying dry for the pope," Malachy said.

"There's not enough left in her to matter," said the woman of indeterminate age. She handed the bottle, bag and all, to Malachy.

The bottle felt reassuringly hefty in his hand. "Well, a little pick-me-up won't hurt any more than altar wine," Malachy said, and tilted the bottle into his mouth. He felt surprisingly refreshed.

"Thank you, ladies," he said. "And don't forget the Holy Father."

Malachy walked into the tavern. Three street people he knew from the shelter were sitting at the end of the bar near the men's room. They looked up when Malachy entered, but neither accepted nor rejected his company.

Malachy approached the three, who looked at him as if he weren't there.

"Try not to drink too much for a day or two," Malachy said. "The pope's coming the day after tomorrow."

"Fuck him," said the man in the middle, who was clad in a World War II–style army overcoat.

"But it could change things. It will. Johnny W. says so."

"Fuck him, too."

"Buy us a drink," said a tall, slim man with one tooth left in the front of his face.

"I'll buy you a drink if you promise you'll walk with me when the pope comes. I've got three dollars in my pocket and it's all yours if you promise."

"I don't walk with nobody," said the man in the army coat. "Buy me a drink."

"We ain't much for walking, Padre. You know that?"

"We won't walk far. Just out to where the pope is coming, so he can see us and bless us."

"Anything you say, Padre," said the man in the army coat. "Just buy the drink."

The bartender was staring up at the television on a shelf over the bar.

"Would you bring these men drinks? I have three dollars," he said.

The bartender waved Malachy away and turned back to the television set. "Wait until I hear this," he said.

He was watching a newscaster telling of the disappearance of Cynthia Stoler. Malachy waited for the bartender, and while he waited he heard the name Tony Owen.

"What did he say about Tony Owen?" Malachy asked.

"What do you care?" the bartender replied.

"He's my brother."

"Yeah, and I'm Buffalo Bill."

"What happened to him, can't you tell me?" Malachy asked.

The bartender looked at him, saw that there was a change in Malachy, that his face and clothes were clean and the madness was not in his eyes.

"Nothing happened to Tony Owen. Somebody snatched his girlfriend, a television lady."

Malachy's heart leaped in elation. It was as if all his prayers were being answered at once. The pope was coming. And, at last, Tony Owen was suffering the way he suffered. I must pray for him, he told himself.

But first he waited for the drinks, and when they came he downed his, and with the change bought himself a small beer as a chaser.

"I need to brace myself," Malachy explained to his companions. "It isn't every day the pope comes, and I don't want to get too nervous."

☐

Bobby Bantam's feet barely touched the ground as he hung up the phone and danced out his door, turning briefly toward his secretary to say as he passed, "Tell Elmer I'm on my way to see him."

Within two minutes, he had barged past the publisher's secretary and into the inner sanctum of Elmer Granger, who glared at him from behind his desk.

"You knock before you come into my office, you little sneak."

Bobby just stood in front of the desk, his short legs planted far apart. He looked like an elf posing as a conquistador. He stood defiantly as if to say, "You, sir, have fucked up; you, sir, are finished." But his actual words were milder.

"Gridlock is keeping us alive," he said. "As I'm sure you know."

"For the time being, Bobby."

"Time being, nothing. I just talked to the big boss himself. He's bought the miracle."

The publisher stood up and came out from behind his desk. His face was red. Bobby thought he was going to hit him or, perhaps, pitch him bodily out the door. But he stood his ground and the publisher walked past him and called out to his secretary to hold all calls and visitors.

He returned and held out his hand. "Congratulations, Bobby. You've won this one. Gridlock isn't going to close us down, not now anyway. And you're right. We do have a miracle on our hands. Circulation should be up by thirty thousand, at least for the next week. And Kansas is very pleased."

The anger faded from the publisher's face. Now he was perfectly composed and at ease, the distinguished executive in the three-piece suit, jut-jawed and in control.

"So you came running in here to rub it in my face, did you?" he said, smiling.

"No, I'm not that kind of guy."

"You mean you're not a vindictive prick?"

"Yeah, you're right. I am a vindictive prick and I came in here to gloat."

The publisher grimaced, as if he had just smelled rotten cheese. "Just spare me the speech, Bobby, if you don't mind."

"No, I think I've heard enough of your speeches to give you just one of mine."

"Oh, Christ, why do you inflict this on me? Please, just go away."

"Then kick me out, you fucking bully. You just try."

The publisher stood up and came out from behind his desk. For an instant, Bobby retreated toward the door. The publisher smiled and sat down on the corner of his desk.

"You're a coward as well as a sneak."

"I'm going to tell you about newspapering in this town, you fucking hog slopper." He advanced a foot, as if to take back the psychic territory he lost in backing up before Granger's advance. "I'm going to tell you what the *Bruise* can be, if only it had a little help from people like you. It could be the paper that cuts through all the bullshit in this town. That cuts through that big gassy cloud of bullshit that the *Mammoth* chokes everybody with every morning while it keeps everybody locked into their own little middle-class cells. And most of them aren't even middle class anyway. It's all let's pretend. Let's pretend we're tuned into reality, that we belong to the rest of the rat race, that we're going to get our kids into the best schools, the best jobs, the best neighborhoods. All we have to do is go to the right stores, wear the right clothes, feel the right way about all the issues, and suffer the pomposities of all the boring politicians they try to put over on us because they follow the *Mammoth* line. It's nerve gas they put out. Goddamn psychological nerve gas that puts this town to sleep. And you let them get away with it."

"You're raving, Bobby."

"Damn right. Because I'm angry. Really angry. Because nobody will fight them. Nobody will tell people the truth. Nobody will say that a politician like Connie Haydon is a sellout to the big lie around here. And do you know what that lie is? I'll tell you and you can take it back to Kansas with you. The lie is that it's an honest game around here. The deck is so stacked it's sickening. And if I had the money I could hire people who would start hitting this society with a bucket of cold water every morning and shouting, 'Wake up, you dumb bastards. Look at what's happening to you. It isn't pollution and broken bottles and beer cans and fucking handguns. It isn't nuclear threat or the goddamn crooks in the legislature. It's unfairness. That's the problem. The game is rigged.' "

"I wonder if Gridlock knows you're a flaming Marxist."

"Me, a Marxist? That's bullshit. I'm like Tony Owen. I'm a goddamn monk, that's what I am, a flaming crazy monk who wants to sell newspapers by telling the goddamn truth, and I've never been in a position before to do it."

Bobby Bantam danced out of the publisher's office, paused for a moment by the secretary's desk to smile and say, "Don't you worry about a thing. Bobby's going to take care of you," then hurried out into the city room. "Hey, John," he called to the city editor, "come into the conference room. I got an idea for tomorrow's page one I want you to see."

He sat down at the conference table and grabbed a make-up pad from inside the drawer and hurriedly sketched a page one, limning the bold headline in red grease pencil.

"Here's what I want, John: This little overline, then the sell line. Like this. Now all we need is the story. I'm counting on you, buddy."

Walsh looked down at the dummy sheet. The overline read: POPE'S PRAYER. Then came the brass; it read: SAVE CYNTHIA.

Walsh seemed dumbstruck. "Now, Bobby, how the hell am I going to get that story? You think I can get the pope on the phone? Come on, give me a break."

"Sometimes, John, you haven't got the imagination you were born with. For God's sake, it's easy. Just get a hold of someone at the Vatican press office. They got to know what's going on. Ask them if the pope has heard about Cynthia and whether she's in his prayers. It's as simple as that. They'll be happy to give us a statement. Try it. You'll see. It's like getting rosary beads. The same thing."

Walsh grumbled and walked out into the city room. "Hey, cheer up," Bobby Bantam called after him. "Pretty soon you'll be hiring a few more reporters around here. Things are looking up. I'm on a roll."

"Sure, Bobby, sure," he said.

"The trouble with you, John, is you can't see what's in front of your nose."

□

In the dim light of the cathedral, Tony gave way to his grief and soon he was sobbing into his arms, which were folded on the pew in front of him. For all his sorrow, he could not bring himself to kneel. He sat, leaning forward in a crouch, in what for him was a great concession to divinity. And as his emotions overcame him, he forgot for a time who he was and what he was, and for the first time in his life he was without quibble or reservation just another part of humanity with as much claim to God's mercy as anyone who had ever lived. Love had made the connection, a love he had eluded so long, and even that morning had denied, a love that was profoundly threatening, that was, even as he accepted its reality, certain to shatter him because it was a love that ended, as did the only other love he had known, in cruelty and death. And now it was as if something frozen for so long inside had snapped under stress and the sorrows of all the others mingled with his own and he was no longer outside and protected, no longer a man with a white armband behind the screen of his own indifference. He was out there now with the others, without immunity, without defense, without distinction. The strength of his feelings frightened him and he tried to choke them off. But it was too late now. He was beyond self-consciousness. After a time, he realized that he was grieving not just for Cynthia, not just for his mother whose tormented eyes loomed before him like a dream before waking, but for himself, for all the years of his flight from his own end.

And he began to pray, mouthing the words at first from the formulas of his childhood until his memory failed, and then talking directly to God, haltingly, then with mounting coherence. He didn't ask for forgiveness. He had too developed a sense of justice for that. He did ask that Cynthia be returned to him alive. He made no promises; he was too much of a realist for that. He did say he would reconsider the way he lived his life. He felt he had no choice anyway. And when he finished his prayer, he stood up and felt a bit sheepish, especially as the boy on the altar caught his eye.

At least I wasn't a hypocrite, he told himself as he headed back to the street.

□

Sailor snored and his smell was sickening. Still, Cynthia, despite her discomfort, felt hope returning, and for no better reason than that he was there and hadn't yet harmed her. And out of hope rose her resourcefulness. Sailor would free her, she told herself. She would persuade him to. She decided against wakening him. Better to deal with him after he had slept off the booze. Whatever rationality was left in his ravaged mind could better be appealed to then. As the hours went by, she even began to welcome the pain that bit into her hips and shoulders. The pain, like the sounds of the street, was another link to reality. So she followed it as if it were a lifeline leading her out of the limbo into which she had fallen. For now, there was no chance that she would let herself sink back into that dangerous state where she lacked both will and consciousness and was drifting toward a surrender to death. Now, this dreg by her side gave her back her courage, her resolve. She began to spin out various approaches likely to enlist him on her side, and in the darkness all took on a plausibility that lifted her hopes nearer to a certainty. And then, it was she who fell asleep.

She was awakened by Sailor crouching by her side, stroking her hair, face, and shoulders. He touched her as if he were in a reverie. "Please don't," she said, when his hand slipped beneath her blouse and ran over her breasts. But he didn't seem to hear her, nor did he move when she tried to twist away from him, turning her back on him as completely as she could. His hands, still under her blouse, kept up their stroking on her back, returning to her breasts only when, after the pain in her wrists became excruciating, she was forced to turn back toward him once again. She took small comfort from the fact that there was no sexual urgency in his touch. It was not enough to fight off the panic that was building within her.

She had not been prepared for this. Now she was afraid that if she rebuffed him too sharply, he might turn on her with savagery, and her situation would be hopeless. But his touch was beyond bearing. She fought for calm but she wanted to scream, and before she knew it the scream was roaring from her throat.

And he stopped and sat back against the radiator.

"Don't do that," he said matter-of-factly, minutes later.

"Don't you do that," she said, her voice like a reproving school-teacher angry and sure of her authority.

"Finders, keepers," he said.

"Finders, keepers, my eye," she said. "You have no right, mister. And you better help me get out of here."

She could feel and smell his presence; she couldn't see him. Unable to read his face, she had to read his voice. She had to get him talking. Then she would know what to do.

"Please tell me why you don't seem to want to help me."

He continued to sit still, a bundle of foul-smelling rags over a living scarecrow.

"You won't talk? Are you afraid of me?"

"No," he said. "I'm not afraid of no broads."

"Then what's the matter?"

"It's what he said."

"You mean the fat man?"

"He didn't send me. I live here, most of the time. I met him out back."

"What did he tell you?"

"He told me if I let you go or brought the cops, they would blame me and send me away again. I'm not going back, never. I'm not sick. Why should they lock me up?"

"He lied to you."

"He gave me fifty dollars."

"So what? I told you what I'd give you."

"He told me you'd fuck, too."

"That bastard. He lied to you."

"You feel good, like my Julia."

"And where is Julia now?"

"Out fucking the mailman."

"I'm sorry."

"Put the welfare on me, the little whore. Wanted to take all my money and fuck the mailman."

"You've had a hard life," she said. "Maybe I can help you."

"Give me a fuck?"

"Well, maybe, if I knew you better. We just met, and you really haven't done anything to help me."

His hand returned beneath her blouse. She tried not to shudder.

"Now, Sailor, that's your name, isn't it? Don't, please," she said. "Let's talk some more."

He ignored her.

"Please," she said. "I'll scream again."

Again, he ignored her threat, and seemed to be sinking into the reverie that held him before.

"Look," she said, "it's no good this way. You won't enjoy it. Free me first. Let my hands get free. Then I'll be able to show you a good time."

He did not respond.

"Good Lord," she said. "Don't you have any idea how to treat a lady? What kind of man are you, anyway?"

His hands stopped. He sat back against the radiator.

"O.K. I'll let you do it. But first, I have to get something to eat. I'm starving. And you have to free my hands. I can't get away. You'll still have me here. But it will be so much better. You'll feel like you used to feel with Julia. You'll see."

"The same way?"

"Just the same way. You just tell me and I'll do it, whatever you say. But I'm a lady. I can't do it this way. You can understand that."

"I haven't got no food. I haven't got no tools," he said, and his voice had in it just the trace of little boy.

"Well, goddamn it, hurry out and get some," she said. "Whatever is the matter with you?"

☐

In the midst of the excitement of trying to handle two extraordinary stories on the same day, Bill Raleigh found himself in a snit. Not only was young Walter maintaining his presence behind his shoulder, but his business reporter had relayed disquieting news, news that he had not yet passed along to Walter Griswold.

The *Bruise* would be around after all, like an uninvited guest at the banquet, jeering, gibing, and costing the *Mammoth* money, lots of money, just to protect its flank, money that Walter Griswold hadn't planned on spending because Bill Raleigh had assured him that the *Bruise* was dead. It couldn't be possible, this sudden turnabout in Gridlock policy. He asked the reporter to go back and recheck the story and find out why. There had to be more to it. Meanwhile, he kept the development to himself and hoped it would fade away.

If it were true, he would have to resign, of course. Perhaps not right away, but soon, after a discreet passage of time, perhaps two months, perhaps after a leisurely working trip around the world.

"This McGivern is a real maniac; the things we're finding out about him make you wonder how the guy survived this long," Dugan told Raleigh as they stood in the middle of the city room, which was transformed by the energy of that special news day.

"Why? What did we find out about the guy?"

"For one thing, he was married once. Neighbors say they used to hear the wife screaming all the time. Anyway, she walked out on him after he used her as a punching bag one night. She divorced him back in 1972. Carney is over in Probate Court, trying to get the records. The neighbors say she was terrified of him."

"That hardly makes him a monster. Lots of people beat their wives."

"O.K., but he also beat up a prostitute in the Combat Zone. He got picked up for that, but she withdrew the complaint."

"What about the mob connections?"

"Hard to say. His closest friend is the mayor's brother-in-law."

"Interesting," Bill Raleigh said, but he wasn't really that interested. He had only one story on his mind — Gridlock and the *Bruise.*

Myron Rubin, the business reporter, came toward him. Walter Griswold was a few feet away. Raleigh did not want Griswold to overhear the conversation. He moved toward Rubin and took him by the arm. "Let's chat over in the business department," he said. But Griswold had spotted Rubin and he had a special interest in Rubin's story, since he was the one who asked that it be done.

"How are you making out with Gridlock? Are those people talking to you, Myron?"

Rubin, flattered at being approached directly by both the editor and the publisher, lit up with self-importance. "I think we've got a helluva story here. They say they're going to keep the *Bruise* going, and they're even going to pump more money into it."

Griswold said nothing, but his jaw tightened.

"I asked you to find out why," Bill Raleigh said.

"You knew about this, Bill?" Griswold said.

"Just for a few minutes. I wanted Myron here to confirm things before I told you about it."

"I'm still not sure of the why. But this is what they said when I talked to them: that the last few days have proved that the *Bruise* is a peculiar institution," the reporter said.

"Christ, so was slavery," said Raleigh.

"They said the vigor of the reporting showed that it was a peculiar institution within Boston and an organic part of the community. A newspaper of that importance had to keep in business, but it would have to be refinanced and reorganized. And the boss was coming east in a few days to discuss the situation in person with *Bruise* executives and union representatives."

"It sounds like they want the unions to renegotiate their contracts."

"That won't happen," Bill Raleigh snorted.

"Who knows?" said Griswold. "Their numbers are going to go through the roof for the next two weeks. Gridlock has brains enough to recognize that and to try to come in with something that will let them hold on to some of their gains. I don't know. But it's obvious the paper isn't going away for a while. Well, thank you, young man. You'd better get back to work."

As the reporter walked off, Raleigh said quietly to the publisher, "I didn't anticipate any of this. I still don't understand it."

Griswold frowned. "I don't see anything particularly complicated about what happened. We did what we have done repeatedly. We let the *Bruise* run wild with a story of their own with no serious attempt to match it or, better yet, to top it, and we finally got burned."

"It wasn't our kind of story, Walter. I thought you would have recognized that."

The publisher said nothing. He knew that Raleigh was seething inside even before the news out of Kansas. He also realized that he was humiliated and that if it were not for the news out of Kansas, Raleigh would have been fighting back with sarcasm and innuendo, trying to drive him out of the newsroom.

"You've changed the ground rules on me, Walter," Raleigh said quietly, without looking at the younger man. "I think that's terribly unfair. You're not altogether unhappy with what's happened, are you?"

Griswold was surprised at Raleigh's directness and did not want to respond to it, not now. But finally, he said, "If you are referring to the survival of the *Bruise,* no, I am not happy. It makes a mess out of things, and it could get a bit troublesome down the road. But

I am not displeased in one way. We'll be a better paper now. We'll have to be."

"It's your paper, Walter," Raleigh said.

"Precisely," said Griswold, icily.

□

Tony Owen walked out of the cathedral. He felt more gathered but he was still not focused. He knew he had to act or be overwhelmed by his emotions, but he had no idea what to do. So he walked, letting his legs carry him where they would, relying on some internal beacon that communicated nothing to his conscious brain, and as he walked, memories popped willy-nilly out of the untended garden of his mind, memories so unfamiliar that Tony wondered whether they were memories at all or the product of some psychic conjuring job out of his fantasies, not his past.

He walked faster, cutting down streets without noticing which streets they were, past faces that had no character to him. It was hot for April but he didn't notice the heat, nor could he tell whether he was hungry or thirsty. He felt no anger now, just sorrow for everyone he had loved and failed and managed until now to forget, and their faces appeared before him as he walked. And the one face that kept returning was that of his mother.

He was in the middle of Downtown Crossing on Washington Street, standing in the midst of the lunch-hour throng. I let my mother die, he told himself, and now I've done the same thing to Cynthia.

He saw a tavern across the street, a dimly lit basement business where the lunchtime regulars had taken all the seats at the bar. Tony ordered a double Irish whiskey and sat down at a table and buried his head in his hands. He had to think. He had to deal with how it happened; he had to deal with the memory of that face and those anguished gray eyes. He felt momentarily nauseous as the whiskey hit his empty stomach. He leaned his head back now against the wall and let the vision have full play. He couldn't run anymore now. And for more than an hour, he sat wrapped in his own little hell, unwilling and unable to touch the wellsprings of his own mercy. Finally, he drained his tumbler of the last of the whiskey and moved back onto the street.

On impulse, he headed up Tremont Street until he reached City

Hall Plaza. Directly below City Hall, crews of workers were assembling a vast platform, and the hall itself was bedecked with papal flags.

Tony walked into the building with its raw concrete façade and took the elevator to the mayor's office. A policeman was standing outside, chatting with the receptionist.

"I'm Tony Owen," he said. "I'd like to see the mayor."

"The mayor is very busy, I'm afraid," the receptionist said. "You don't have an appointment."

She was uneasy, and the policeman looked at Tony with a mixture of misgiving and contempt. Tony's eyes were wild, his clothes were disheveled, and his breath was boozy.

"He'll see me," Tony said. "Ask him."

The receptionist looked at Tony, saw the seriousness in his face, and went into the inner office.

Tony and the policeman stood together silently. Within three minutes, the mayor himself came out into the reception room.

"We're doing all we can, Tony. I hope you realize that. Our people are working around the clock. We have forty men assigned to this case and the FBI is working it, too."

"I want to talk to you," Tony said.

"Talk to me? Hey, you look a little rough. Kathy here," he said, nodding toward the receptionist, "thinks you might be a little dangerous. Are you dangerous, Tony?"

"No, I'm not dangerous," he said.

The mayor looked at him intently for a moment, as if to make that judgment himself. Then he said, "O.K., I'll see you. I hope you realize you're interrupting an important meeting."

"On the pope?" Tony asked.

"No, on Cynthia as a matter of fact."

The mayor escorted him into a small room off to the side of his main office. The room held only a desk and two facing chairs and was apparently designed for prompt resolution of interruptions like this.

"O.K., Tony, what do you want to talk about?"

The mayor sat down in one of the chairs in front of the desk and motioned to Tony to take the other.

Tony sat down. "I think you know what I came for," he said. "I want you to find out from your brother-in-law where he thinks

McGivern is hiding, and what he thinks he did with Cynthia."

"You don't think I've tried that? He doesn't know. He says he has no idea."

"Then let me talk to him."

"Tony, that I wouldn't do, even if I had the power, and I don't, for reasons that you might be able to guess, since you have played quite a role in screwing up my domestic relationships."

"You run the Police Department."

"So what? You want me to have the boys give him the old third degree? So much for the goddamn tribune of the people. I'm sorry. I'm doing all I can. And I can assure you, I'm not letting my feelings about you affect in any way the search for Cynthia. As a matter of fact, as I said at my news conference, we are bending over backwards. Good Lord, Tony, I want to get Duncan Avenue out of the papers, not keep it there."

"Tell me where Tommy Mannion is hiding."

"He isn't hiding. What for? He doesn't know a thing. You think McGivern confided in that idiot? He used him. That's all."

"Did you talk to him yourself?"

"As a matter of fact, I did."

"Then tell me what he said."

"Tony, you don't know how rough you look. Really, you ought to lie down somewhere and get some sleep."

"Tell me what he said."

"I told you. He doesn't know anything. Now you better get out of here before I call the cop."

Tony stared at him. The politician's eyes gave nothing away, just impatience.

"He told you he thinks he killed her, didn't he?"

"You know something, Tony, I hate your act. You think you're the only person who counts in this town; the only person who's clean. And you come barging in here making demands on me, of all people. You think I owe you anything? Christ almighty, you're dealing with the mayor of Boston and you better act with a little respect. I don't give a damn how much you're hurting now."

"Answer my question."

"Get out of here."

The mayor stood up and opened the door. The cop was standing on the other side. Tony looked at him blankly, then turned back toward the mayor, who was just disappearing through the door into the conference room.

Tony walked out of the office toward the elevators that would return him to the street. He had accomplished nothing but he felt better. He at least had acted.

The mayor resumed his seat at the conference table.

"What was that all about?" Harold Hooper asked.

"Tony Owen wanted to know what Tommy Mannion told us about McGivern. I must be getting soft. I didn't have the heart to tell him."

□

Connie Haydon presided over the meeting, but the details of the discussion — fresh public appeals for information, interrogations of the entire network of McGivern's associates, coordination with the FBI — buzzed by the mayor. Nor did he become more involved when the discussion switched to the pope's arrival and the security arrangements during his motorcade from the airport. The mayor's thoughts were about Eileen. He couldn't believe that she would make good her threats; he couldn't believe the report from the taps on the Tony Owen phone. If he could only sit down with her, he could stave off that folly, but he had no idea where she was, and all his attempts to reach her through relatives and friends had failed.

"There is a possibility that the president may fly up. It depends on how the budget debate shapes up in the Senate," Corinne said.

Haydon barely heard. Finally, he stood up and told Corinne to take over the meeting. "I have to make some phone calls," he said.

He walked back to his private office and telephoned Bobby Bantam.

"Hello, Bobby, this is the mayor," he said.

"Yes, Mr. Mayor," Bantam replied. "And to what do I owe this honor?"

"I'm just touching base, Bobby. I personally want to make sure you are up to date on the news conference we held before and the pope's timetable, and to see if you're having any trouble getting credentials for your people."

"No trouble at all," Bantam said. "And I think we got everything there was to get in the news conference. Are you sure that's all that's on your mind?"

"Yeah, I think so. No, since you brought it up, there is one thing. Somebody told me you were interested in talking to my wife, some kind of profile, is that true?"

"We're always interested in talking to people like Eileen. She's a very lovely and intelligent woman."

"Well, if you do, I'd like to sit in on the interview."

"You'd be willing to do that for us at this dirty, little, dying rag? Well, that is news."

"Come on now, Bobby. We're two grown men trying to make it in a tough world. We don't have to bullshit one another. Yeah, you can talk to both of us. Maybe next week would be good. With the pope here the next few days, it looks a little impossible. But next week you can have all the time you need. You can do a nice at-home piece on two lovebirds, a little the worse for wear after thirty-five years, but still plugging along. What do you say?"

"Sure," said Bantam. "Next week."

"I'll arrange it with Eileen this afternoon. I think the two of us together would be unique. It would be a real coup for you, don't you think?"

"Fine."

"Meanwhile, Bobby, you wouldn't fuck me, would you?"

"Fuck you, Mr. Mayor? Why would I do that?"

Haydon detected just enough malice in Bobby's reply to confirm in his own mind that Eileen had already talked to the *Bruise*. He shuddered at what she might have said, and hoped that perhaps no matter how much she damaged him, the *Bruise* might be willing to hold off the interview for at least another week. He would still be humiliated, but he wouldn't be taken down with the pope, and possibly the president, looking on. And even if she did talk, he wondered at the conditions she might have imposed on the *Bruise* for printing the interview. Surely she was smart enough to give him a chance to bargain before she destroyed everything. But if she wanted to bargain, why hadn't she called? He had to find her.

He decided to play a hunch and began to call the managers of three downtown hotels she favored. He hit on the second try.

"Henry, this is Mayor Haydon. How are you doing today? . . . Well, I'm just great, waiting for the big day . . . Well, Henry, has my wife checked in yet? She's trying to get away from the pressure for a day or two. So much confusion. You know how it is . . . Oh, fine, room ten-twelve . . . Mrs. Farrell, of course . . . Thank you, Henry. I'll be calling her in a few minutes."

Within ten minutes, Connie's limousine had pulled up outside the Copley Plaza and he was dashing across the lobby toward the elevators.

"I should have known better than to try to hide from you in this city," she said, finally admitting him after letting him cool his heels for three minutes. It was useless to fight now. The war was over, although Haydon didn't realize it.

It was the kind of room he would normally enjoy, with muted light and austere furniture, elegantly angled, functional but subtly so. Prints of nineteenth-century English racehorses hung over the double beds.

Eileen's suitcase, opened, was on one of the beds, and she had already made use of the breakfront bar by the window. A bottle of Scotch sat on the night table by the telephone.

"I hope you didn't give away the store, Eileen."

"What do you mean?" she answered.

He sighed and fell wearily into an easy chair by the television set.

"Thanks for the love letter," he said.

"You're welcome," she said.

She sat heavily on the bed and they stared at each other. He tried to read her emotions, but her round face was as blank as that of a passenger on a subway car.

"You understand the pope will be here Friday. There's a reception at the cardinal's residence, and I was hoping you would accompany me. See me through the next few days, and then next week we'll talk and see where we go from there. I don't want to lose you, Eileen. You know that?"

She stared at him and said nothing. Her silence was beginning to infuriate him.

"So what is this?" he asked. "Passive resistance? Say nothing, let the fool stand there and wave his arms and maybe he'll go away. Well, I'm not going to go away. I want an answer. Will you come with me to the reception?"

She reached for her drink.

"Goddamn it, say something!" he shouted.

"I really don't know what to say to you, Connie. I really don't. You knew how I felt and you didn't care. You don't care now. And you come bursting in here asking something of me."

"Only that you try to be responsible for another few days."

"For what? For you, so you can avoid a little embarrassment? It's too late for that now. You don't seem to mind embarrassing me. What the hell am I to you, anyway? You couldn't even give me a kid."

"Don't bring that up now."

"And why not bring it up, and everything else, too? No, you're right. That isn't the issue now. What happened between us doesn't mean a thing at this point."

Haydon's eyes focused on one of the prints over the bed. The jockey and the horse were out of scale. The horse seemed immense.

"I'm sorry it's come to this," he said. "You're like a stranger sitting there who resembles somebody I knew once."

"No, I'm not the stranger," she said. "I'm the same person I always was. That's the difference between us. You've changed and you don't realize it. You've turned into some idea you have of yourself. You're like one of Stanley's image concepts. You're so lost you don't even realize what you're doing to people or what you've done to yourself."

"What have I done that's so bad, except to tell the truth?"

"And you think what you said at that news conference was the truth? I didn't hear you say anything about the truth, which was that you weren't destroying Tommy, you were trying to save yourself. That was the truth. You were trying to save yourself at the expense of Tommy, of me, of what was left of our marriage. You didn't say anything about that. You didn't say anything about Corinne, and you certainly didn't say anything about the money you've been salting away for years. That would have been the truth."

He walked to the window and looked out into the street. A traffic jam had developed by a construction site and Haydon watched as the stalled traffic began to choke off movement in the surrounding streets. He felt calm, but he knew that it wouldn't take much provocation before he exploded.

He looked over at her sitting on the bed, her legs crossed under her. He had always marveled at how she could sit that way for hours without feeling uncomfortable. She was crying.

"You shouldn't be sad, Eileen. You're in the driver's seat. You can destroy me, if that's what you're after."

"I'm not crying over you. It's that poor girl on the news. She's dead. I know she's dead. Tommy said that's just the way McGivern would do it. Take her with him. He was such a cruel bastard. Tommy was always afraid of him, ever since they were kids. You don't know what that's like, do you, to be afraid of someone?"

"Sure, Eileen, I'm made of Kryptonite. I should open this window and fly out around the city, show the folks the kind of mayor they really have."

He moved toward her with a handkerchief he pulled from his back pocket and handed it to her as if it were a flag of surrender. She wasn't appeased.

"I said you did it to her. You drove McGivern over the brink just like you did me. You took away everything. You were cruel and you were stupid. All you cared about was yourself."

He sat on the bed near her and took her in his arms. "I'll make it up to you, Eileen. I will. I'll get rid of Corinne," he said, surprising himself with the ease of his betrayal. It had gotten so easy to let people go.

She leaned away from him and struggled to her feet. Her knees creaked and she felt the lack of circulation in her legs. She was getting old. The future would be hard to bear. She had to be tough and strong.

"It's too late, Connie. It really is. I went to the *Bruise.*"

"I know you did," he said.

"And you don't care."

"I care, but it's not too late to stop them or to ask for a re-interview. You can always say you changed your mind. I'm sure you didn't tell them anything that would jeopardize your own future or embarrass yourself. You didn't do that, did you?"

He was afraid to betray his own anxiety lest he throw away his last hope of salvaging something from the situation, some room to maneuver. His voice stayed cool, almost soothing.

"Of course, I did," she said. "Why else would I have bothered?"

"And you talked to them with no strings attached?"

"None at all."

"And what did you tell them?" he asked, his voice beginning to take on an edge.

"I told them the truth," she said, using the word like the weapon he had used against her.

"Specifically, what did you tell them?"

Now the edge in his voice was becoming so pronounced it alarmed her. It was time to break off the conversation.

"I think you'll have to read about it in the newspaper. I'm sorry, Connie, you have to go."

"I'm not going anywhere until you tell me what you said. Don't you know — oh, I guess you know perfectly — what those maggots can do with smut. You'd better tell me."

He reached for her and started shaking her by the arms, his face now distorted and red, the tendons popping furiously in his neck.

"I wouldn't do that, Mr. Mayor," said Stella Ferral as she stepped from her listening post in the bathroom. "You're just lucky I don't have a photographer with me."

18

BY MIDAFTERNOON, Malachy's sense of special mission was as keenly felt as before, but now it was fueled not only by spiritual ardor but by an inordinate amount of bad whiskey and cheap wine. Malachy was quite drunk. He was also in need of another drink.

Now he prowled the streets of the South End with a double agenda: to recruit more souls for the papal visit and to find himself fresh means to continue drinking. Getting bagged to Malachy was not a matter of just getting drunk. That was an early stage in a process that ordinarily ended in the swamping of all his senses. Once he started drinking, Malachy could stop only when he fell unconscious, and as long as even the dimmest sense of awareness remained alive in his brain, it could focus on only one object — the quest for the next drink.

Gone by now was the crisp and clean, almost clerical, look with which he began the day. Now the red and rheumy cast had reglazed his eyes and his clothes were as besotted as he was. Instead of the purposeful stride that marked his advance from the shelter that morning, he was reeling, desperate for an infusion that would keep alive the excitement with which he started the day.

He wandered without mooring from drinking place to drinking place, and as he headed toward Reggie's Tavern, he almost collided with Sailor, walking purposefully down Massachusetts Avenue, his worn heels digging into the sidewalk, his eyes looking straight ahead.

As Sailor breezed past, Malachy reached out and caught his shoulder.

"Let me be," Sailor said. "I'm in a hurry."

"Let's see who's in Reggie's."

"I'm busy."

"Can't you buy me a drink?"

"How'd you know I have money?" Sailor asked, his paranoia suddenly engaged.

"You got money?" asked Malachy. "How much?"

"Fuck you. I've got to go."

"Where?" asked Malachy, trying hard now to focus.

"Got to get some things."

"What things?"

"Tools and things."

"You got a job?" asked Malachy, incredulous.

"I got to fix up my room."

"You got a room?" asked Malachy, confused now, and thinking for a moment that maybe Sailor was someone else, someone he had never met before.

"You know. You seen it."

"Damn," said Malachy.

"I showed you."

"Damn, buy me a drink."

"Can't. No time," Sailor said, trying to pull away from Malachy's hold, which had now settled on his elbow.

"Got to. I've got to tell you about the pope."

"No way," Sailor said, and pulled away. Malachy lurched after him.

"Where you going?"

"To the shelter."

"Not your room?"

"I need tools."

Malachy was totally confused. He moved, breathless now, after Sailor, who was as sober as he'd been since the weekend he spent in the Charles Street jail before they repealed the drunk laws.

But Malachy, despite his condition, kept close behind his quarry. And as the two men passed in front of Johnny's Red Top Tavern, he managed to catch Sailor's sleeve.

"Let's go in here," said Malachy. "I can't walk no more."

By now, Sailor's own thirst was building. "O.K. One fast one," he said.

"God love you," said Malachy.

"But no pope."

Inside, Sailor discreetly pulled out a ten-dollar bill. Malachy could barely believe his eyes.

"Where'd you get that?"

"Never mind," he said.

The tavern had new management: three athletic-looking young men only a few years out of college who decided to take a flyer on an inner-city business geared to young people just like themselves. Sailor and Malachy were caught by surprise when they walked into the front door and found the customary dark brown decor gone, replaced by a bright yellow so fresh that the paint smell remained.

"Let's get out of here," said Sailor when he saw one of the new owners engaged in arranging a pot of geraniums on a stand near the men's room.

"No, stay," said Malachy. "We've got money."

The young man with the plant stood up and wiped his hands on his white apron.

"No hanging around here," he snapped, his voice surly.

"We're not hanging around," said Malachy. "We can pay. Show him our money, Sailor."

"Fuck this place," Sailor said.

"Show the man the money, Sailor," said Malachy.

Sailor dug deep into the pockets of his soiled pants and, to Malachy's amazement, pulled out even more money in a crumpled wad of bills and change.

"Where did you get all that?" asked Malachy.

"I don't care if you guys have money. You're not welcome. Beat it or I'll call a cop," said the young man with the apron.

But Malachy would not be moved. He had waited too long for a drink. "Call a policeman," he slurred. "I'm a priest, you know."

Sailor was becoming agitated. He had a mission of his own on his mind. He pulled at Malachy's sleeve. "Let's go," he said. But Malachy persisted, insisting that at the very least they be served a beer.

"Get out of here before I throw you both out on your ear," the man in the apron said. Now he was joined by his two partners, both mean-eyed and burly.

"Wait a minute," said the biggest of the three, a mustached hulk with an Eastern European look. "The man wants a beer. Let's give him a beer."

He went to the bar, leaned over from the customer side, and drew a small glass of beer. Then, just before he handed it to Malachy, he spit in it. And when Malachy handed it back, he took the beer and poured it on Malachy's head.

"Now get out of here, and I never want to see you bums again," he said, as his two partners rocked in red-faced laughter at the sight of the bedewed Malachy.

"You'll pay, you fuckheads," Malachy said and moved, defeated, toward the door.

"What a way to talk, and I thought you were a priest," said the man in the white apron.

"Let's go somewhere else," said Malachy as they stood on the sidewalk, trying to orient themselves.

"I'm going to the shelter," said Sailor.

"First a drink," said Malachy.

Sailor didn't reply. Instead, walking more slowly now, he shuffled toward Dover Street. In the shadow of the elevated, they found a hole in the wall filled with derelicts of all kinds, winos and mental cases, dropouts and psychos, bag ladies and men who simply lost their way. There was also a little bar serving beer and a shot of Old Forester for a buck.

"Just one," said Malachy.

Sailor followed him in and turning his back to the other people in the room, fished his money from his pocket, separated ten dollars from the total, then put the wad back. Malachy went to the bar and got the specials and the change.

"God will reward you," said Malachy.

Sailor took back the change before it could disappear into Malachy's pocket, downed his drink, hitched up his pants, and moved toward the door with his peculiar rolling gait. Malachy called after him.

"Where you going?"

"Got to get my tools."

"One more," Malachy said.

Sailor turned, frowning, and walked back to the bar. Again he dug into his pocket and pulled out his money, which he again tried to hide. But his attempt at discretion only signaled everyone else in the barroom that he had made a score. Soon he was the center of a cluster of people, pushing at his pockets, begging, insisting.

"No," he said, with sudden authority. The cluster opened like a dirty hand.

"Just one more for us," he said to Malachy.

As he sipped his second beer, he leaned forward toward Malachy's ear. "Julia's at my house," he whispered. He said it proudly, trying to hide his pride and pleasure, yet trying to reveal it at the same time.

"Julia," said Malachy. "Who's Julia?"

"Julia's my woman."

"You got a woman?" asked Malachy, as yet another wonder was revealed to him.

"A real woman," he said, his toothless lips moving like the mouth of a fish. "She's waiting for me."

"She look like her?" asked Malachy, pointing to one of the bag women, sitting dazed and defeated at the bar.

"Like that," he said, pointing to a *Penthouse* calendar on the wall over their heads.

"And what would you do with a woman like her?" asked Malachy.

"I'd do this," said Sailor, humming. He pushed a finger back and forth into a ring made of his thumb and index finger. "I'd do this, and this, and this," he said, his humming louder and more animated.

"Such terrible thoughts," said Malachy. "And the pope is coming."

Sailor knocked back the last of his whiskey. Malachy's glass was already empty and so was his beer, and he still felt thirsty. He didn't want to let Sailor go, not while he still had all that money.

"O.K.," Malachy said. "Let's go get the tools."

"No," Sailor insisted. "No, just me."

"I'll help," said Malachy.

"No," said Sailor. He downed the last of his beer and bolted out the door, leaving Malachy with no money and a thirst that burned in him like grace.

Abandoned by his friend and cut off by the bartender, he had no choice. It was panhandling or going dry. He headed for a stretch of sidewalk that had proven fruitful the week before — a stretch near Jake Wirth's on Stuart Street.

For an hour, he worked the street and took in no more than

thirty-five cents, not even enough for a beer. He was about to give up and head for another sidewalk when a group of Japanese tourists came out of the barroom and almost knocked over Malachy, who was slumped against the edge of the building.

One of the tourists apologized profusely, steadied Malachy on his feet as best he could, and pressed a dollar bill into his hand.

"God bless you," Malachy said, and rushed toward the nearest barroom that would serve him, the Grotto Inn. He put his money on the bar so the bartender knew exactly what he could afford and ordered a whiskey and a short beer. He downed them both before the bartender could return the bottle to its berth behind him.

"Hey, you're a priest, aren't you?" the bartender asked.

"Yeah," Malachy said, the thought embarrassing him now through the haze of alcohol.

"Your brother is Tony Owen from the *Bruise,* right?"

Malachy nodded.

"He was in here a while back looking for you."

Tony in the Grotto? Malachy couldn't imagine it.

"Have another one on me. Your brother left a helluva tip that night."

He poured Malachy a generous shot of whiskey and another beer. Malachy downed them directly and headed out the door. He had to find Sailor.

Thoroughly drunk, he staggered through the streets of Chinatown, headed for the shelter. Sailor might still be there, with all that money in his pockets. As he neared the shelter, he ran into Sailor, who had just emerged from the front door.

"Look it, here," he whispered to Malachy, pointing down toward his belt. The blunt heads of a hammer and a Stilson wrench pushed against Sailor's belly. "I hooked them."

Malachy was disappointed. He hoped Sailor had tucked a bottle in his pants.

"Let's get a drink," Malachy said.

"No, I'm going home. Got to see Julia."

Sailor scurried away, with Malachy lunging after him. "Then give me some money. Till tomorrow."

"No," he said. "Get away. It's mine."

Sailor turned his back on Malachy and ambled off. And Malachy, seeing him retreat, saw him as the last hope for getting enough to drink to allow his brain to sleep. He staggered after him. Although falling farther behind with every block, he kept up the pursuit. At the corner of Columbus Avenue and West Newton Street, Sailor lurched to the right. Malachy, despite his drunken state, had youth on his side, and he managed to stay close enough to keep Sailor in sight. Down West Newton Sailor hurried, laboring up over the railroad bridge, down into St. Botolph Street, into a slice of newly fashionable territory reclaimed from slumdom.

Malachy wasn't sure where Sailor was headed. He knew that he had been squatting somewhere in the Fenway. One night he had gone home with him, and all he remembered was crawling through ruins into a darkened room where they shared a bottle of cooking sherry and fell asleep. But he knew he could never find the street again, let alone the building.

"Sailor," he hollered as the dark-jacketed old deckhand neared Massachusetts Avenue, where Malachy feared he would lose him in traffic. "Wait."

Sailor stopped and waited. His eyes narrowed in anger. "Go home."

"Just give me money for a drink. That's all."

"No, I need it. Go." He swung his fist and struck Malachy high on the head. He turned now and half-ran across Massachusetts Avenue, headed toward Symphony Hall. It was dark now and the concert crowd was gathering outside on the stone steps.

The blow startled Malachy. It also somewhat sobered him, as did the long run through the South End. A remnant of pride stirred. He thought of the pope and the reality of the visit began to meld in his mind with the notion of the next drink, and his pursuit of Sailor began to take on a different aspect. It was not just a drink he was after now; it was Sailor's miserable but still immortal soul.

"Come back, Sailor," he yelled and began running after him.

Down the dark streets, the two derelicts, wheezing, slipping, sliding, advanced into the night until Sailor hit the darkness of Duncan Avenue, then vanished from Malachy's view.

The building at the corner was partially demolished and the walls had collapsed within. A red dump truck was parked up against the rubble, its rear piled high with bricks and scrap wood. Behind the truck was an alley, even darker than the dimly lit street.

Next door was another burned-out building, not yet demolished but tightly boarded with plywood covering the windows and the doors. Now Malachy remembered. This was where he came that night with Sailor when they sat and drank the cooking sherry. Down the outside stairs leading to the basement, there's a door with the plywood loosened.

Malachy cut across the rubble-strewn lot toward the alley. He got to the rear of the dump truck when he saw Sailor. He didn't see the hammer in his hand until it flashed and came thudding down on his head.

□

Tony Owen returned to the *Bruise,* his inconsolability around him like a cloak that kept his colleagues away. He sat at his desk, so piled with old notebooks and newspapers and telephone messages that there was barely room to set down a container of coffee. He glanced disinterestedly at some of the telephone messages, which included several from the *Mammoth.* He didn't want to talk on the phone. He sat there, blankly staring down at the clutter, for several minutes before Bobby Bantam came over.

"The cops have been getting tips all day from people who say they saw Cynthia. The commissioner called to say they were checking out each and every one of them."

"They're all bullshit," Tony Owen said.

"Come on, let's go for a walk," Bantam said.

Tony followed behind listlessly as Bobby Bantam headed out past the city desk where he informed John Walsh that he would be back within half an hour.

"Will we be able to talk to him?" Walsh said, looking at Tony.

"Hey, I'm right here," Tony Owen said. "Why don't you ask me?"

"O.K., Tony, you want to talk to your own paper?"

"I don't know."

"That's just what I figured," Walsh said.

"We'll be back," said Bobby Bantam.

"Tony, I had you pegged wrong," said Bantam as they walked toward the coffee shop around the corner. "You really love that lady."

"Yup," he said. "And I lost her."

"Hey, you didn't lose her. She was doing her job," Bobby Bantam said.

The sky was beginning to darken and a brisk late afternoon wind was scattering scraps of paper in the street.

"It might rain on the pope's parade," Bantam observed.

"That's what you want to talk about, the weather?" Tony said.

"No, I didn't want to talk about the weather."

They pushed open the heavy door of the coffee shop. Two policemen were sitting at the counter, awaiting their take-out. In the rear, Chinese kids were clustered around a video game.

Bantam ordered two cups of black coffee and the two men sat at a table by the window. Bobby examined a news rack and found it empty. "I wonder whether we sold out or whether they never delivered the paper today."

"What do you want me to do, Bobby?"

"You think that's what I brought you out for?"

"Yeah."

"Well, I wanted to tell you a few things. It looks like we're going to be all right. Gridlock is going to give us a reprieve. All this national attention, they don't have the nerve to do anything else."

"Congratulations."

"Congratulations? Jesus, you're acting as if you didn't have anything to do with it. You're the guy who did it."

"You mean, Cynthia."

"Her, too. I think they're going to make me the publisher. Granger is going, of course."

"You think or you know?"

"I know."

"Well, congratulations. You deserve it. You'll be good."

"Thanks."

"What do you want me to do?"

"Now or later?"

"For tomorrow."

"Tony, I'm not sure you can work, and I don't want to see you embarrass yourself."

"Maybe I have to work. You think of that?"

"Well, maybe we can do something in between. Maybe you'll let Walsh have some of the guys working the story talk to you, get some guidance."

"You mean interview me?"

"Well, yeah. Jeez, I'm getting hungry. You want something? I think I'll grab a sandwich. What do you say?"

"No, nothing for me."

Bobby jumped up, hustled over to the counter and ordered a ham and cheese on rye, then hustled back to the table.

"What's the matter, Bobby? You afraid to leave me sitting here alone?"

"Come on, Tony. I'm concerned about you. For that, you should give me a hard time?"

"Bobby, I think I want to have a news conference, invite everybody in, the TVs, the *Mammoth*. I'd like to make a public appeal for Cynthia."

"No, Tony. You'd look like a schmuck. The mayor's already done it, anyway."

"Not the way I'd do it. Besides, politicians turn people off, people who might listen to me. Hey, I'd do just what a lot of people do in my situation. Maybe somebody would see me who saw something."

"Tony, you're not like a lot of people. You're different; you're a newspaperman, and you're still working for a newspaper. You don't want to look like some ordinary schmuck."

"But that's the point, Bobby, don't you understand?"

The counterman yelled over to Bobby that his sandwich was ready. Bantam jumped up again, dropped a couple of dollars on the counter, and ran back with his sandwich.

"No, I guess I don't understand," Bantam said on his return.

"That's what's wrong with you, with me, with all of us. We never have to do anything. We never have to stick our necks out."

"Tony, how can you of all people say that? You're always sticking your neck out. For Christ's sake, that's why Cynthia is in this jam."

"No," said Tony, shaking his head. "It was never my neck. It's my paper's neck. Sure, we're personalities. But not really. We're extensions of what we work for. What happened here is peculiar. Some sick son of a bitch hit back at the individual. But how often does that happen? It almost never happens. I'm the voice of the goddamn *Bruise* in this town. It's the *Bruise* that protects me. I never have to take the risk; I'm insulated. All the while we can look brave as hell, but we're never really on the line, not as people we're not. For Christ's sake, who the hell are we as people anyway? Do we exist? We don't even vote."

"Speak for yourself, Tony."

"O.K., when was the last time you voted, Bobby?"

"I voted for Stevenson."

"That's what I'm talking about."

"Well, that's what I'm talking about, Tony. We make sacrifices and . . ."

"Perfect, Bobby. You hit on it. We make sacrifices, just like priests, and we sit and hear everybody's confessions and we always have the last word on what's wrong and what's right, and as long as we stick by the book we don't have to worry about a goddamn thing until the day we pick up our pension. We're like parents who live through their kids, except we don't have kids. We just have the schmucks, as you call them, taking all the risks and making all the news, and we never do anything but watch."

Bobby Bantam sighed, pulled out a cigar, and soon was wreathed in a cloud of blue smoke. "O.K., so now you're in a crisis and you want to flash your feelings to all creation. So why don't you write your column? That'll give you all the exposure you want, and you won't make a fool of yourself."

"Except it may not help anything, either. Don't you see? I want to do something; I don't just want to sit around and watch and wait. I've got to act, Bobby. Why can't you understand that?"

Bobby blew a cloud of smoke up over Tony's head. "I understand what you're saying. I just want to protect you a little because I think you're getting a little unraveled."

"Well, thanks, Bobby. I wish I was so sure that's all you're thinking about."

"You think I have something else in mind?"

"Maybe you're afraid I might be giving some help to the competition. I mean, now you're thinking like a publisher, too."

"Oh, boy, Tony. I'm not even going to respond to that one. Look, you talk to our guys first, and we'll see how that goes. That way you have some protection."

"Protection from what?"

"From saying the wrong thing and making an ass out of yourself."

Tony bristled. "Hey, I'm not a fucking ingénue. I'm forty-two years old and I know a little about myself and I know a little about the news business. I'm not going to make an ass out of myself. That isn't your concern. You just want to make sure that we get all the cream there is in this story. That's your only concern. So get off it, Bobby."

Bantam took a bite out of his sandwich, and bits of the bread and filling flew like specks of shrapnel out of his mouth as he tried to explain himself.

"Lookit, Tony. Here's what we got for tomorrow. We got the pope praying for Cynthia. It just came in a few minutes before you got back to the paper. Yeah, the pope is praying for your girlfriend. How do you like those apples? We got the mayor's press conference, the police search. They're even tearing up Duncan Avenue. We got McGivern and the role he played on Duncan Avenue. You can help us on that, too, if you care to. And we also got an exclusive on the mayor, that he's about to go into private life."

"He told you that?"

"No, he didn't. But if you saw half the shit we got from his wife, you'd know he could never get elected state rep around here. He's through. Shoe boxes. You know something? She says he's got shoe boxes in his closet loaded with dough. Shoe boxes. Not to mention the screwing around."

"I'm not surprised."

"He's going to be. And then he tries to browbeat his wife into backing off the story. The son of a bitch doesn't know when he's finished. And goddamn Stella Ferral is hiding in the bathroom during the whole scene."

"Pictures?"

"No pictures."

"I still want a news conference, and if you don't hold it in the building, I'm going to hold it myself on the sidewalk outside."

"Tony, Tony, Tony, what am I going to do with you? O.K., what are you going to say? Give me some idea what you're going to say."

"I'm not sure. I'll tell the truth. Whatever they ask me. It all depends on what they ask me. I just want to talk about it and make my appeal."

"Then, for Christ's sake, talk to me about it. I'm your friend."

"No, I want to do it my way."

"O.K., we'll call the fucking news conference and it's your ass. You're going to see how some poor sucker feels when he's thrown to the lions."

"That's the point."

"Tony, you are not yourself, that's all I can say."

□

Bobby Bantam arranged the news conference for eight o'clock in the cafeteria downstairs near the front entrance. He asked Tony for only one favor — that he talk to his own paper first, so there would be no deadline scramble, should he say something startling.

"I'm not going to say much that's startling," said Tony Owen. "Just how I feel."

"Just don't forget who you are," said Bobby Bantam, who decided he'd rather not sit in on the news conference himself.

Doc D'Amato, the medical writer, was assigned to interview Tony privately. "They talk a lot anyway," John Walsh explained to Bantam.

"Aren't you afraid Tony will think you're treating him like a psycho case?" asked Bobby.

"So what? At least he'll be talking to a friend."

Doc, who liked to work as informally as possible and always had his eye out for opportunities to use his expense account, suggested to Tony that they head over to the Athens Olympia for an early supper or a late lunch.

Tony, who had no appetite, declined, and the interview was conducted at Molly Minton's desk in the rear of the city room.

"Maybe this will help you get ready for the news conference," said Doc. "I feel funny talking to you in this situation; so if I ask you anything stupid, let me know, O.K.?"

"O.K.," said Tony. "Go ahead."

Doc opened his notebook and flipped on a tape recorder. "You don't mind if I use this, Tony? I don't want to misquote you."

Tony did mind, the soft whirring seemed loud enough to distract him; he also wasn't sure he wanted a permanent record. He hesitated. Doc said, "You might as well get used to it. Everybody's going to be using tape later on."

"O.K., go ahead."

"O.K., Tony, first of all, you must be pleased to learn that the pope is praying for Cynthia."

"That's a lot of bullshit and you know it. Some flunky monsignor has put out a press release. I doubt if the pope even knows about Cynthia Stoler."

"O.K., Tony. How did it happen? Could you tell me, to the best of your knowledge, what you know about Cynthia's disappearance?"

"Yeah. We weren't married, you know. I don't know if we ever would have been. It never came up. We weren't living together, either. Not technically, we weren't. You know, I'd stay at her place two nights a week; she'd stay at mine three nights. That sort of thing. But in the last week, we were closer, a lot closer. Because we were working on the Duncan Avenue situation and, as you know, I was having some trouble with Bobby on this story."

"You don't have to go into that, Tony," said Doc, who was hoping that Tony would be more direct. "Let's start over again, so we don't have a lot of repetition. Let's just stick to what happened the last night you were together and what you knew about her plans. I think it goes without saying that you had a relationship."

"No, I don't think that goes without saying."

"O.K., what kind of person is Cynthia?"

"What can I say? Tough, smart, brave as hell. That's what happened to her. They couldn't scare her off. She's also a little naive. I'm not sure she appreciated the danger."

"You tried to warn her?"

"That's what bothers me so much now. I'm just not sure how hard I did try. I mean, I told her to stay away from McGivern, that he was an animal, but she had this thing about reporters being invulnerable. Nothing could hurt them. I'd like to appeal to anyone . . ."

"You knew she was going to see McGivern?" Doc asked, cutting off Tony's pitch to possible witnesses.

"Yes, I knew she was going to try to see McGivern."

"And you tried to stop her?"

"No, I felt there was no stopping Cynthia when she made up her mind. So I really didn't. What I did do was go to see McGivern myself."

"That was your way to protect her?"

"That was my way to get the story."

"What do you mean?"

"I mean we were partners but I was competitive. Getting McGivern could have made the story. We knew he was in the middle of the whole thing."

"O.K., I'm pretty clear on McGivern. You saw McGivern on the day Cynthia was kidnaped."

"Yes."

"And you told him to stay away from Cynthia?"

"No, I didn't say anything to him about Cynthia."

"Why not?"

"I brought up Louise Finnigan."

"Louise?"

"Yes, I blamed him for having her beaten up, and I punched him. I gave him a bloody nose, but I didn't ask him about Cynthia."

"Well, you couldn't be expected to anticipate that she would be abducted — Cynthia, I mean."

"I'm not sure. I may have had an inkling. I'm not sure."

"Tony, do me a favor. Don't say that downstairs. It won't play too good."

"Doc, would you believe it if I told you I don't give a damn how it plays? I don't give a shit about the story. That was what happened to Cynthia. That's why she may be dead now. I only cared about the story. I didn't think about her. And it's like you now. You are my friend. Bobby Bantam is my friend. And you really care about me. I know that. You'd mortgage your house for me, if I asked you. I know that. And for all you feel about me, what you're really interested in is the fucking story, the story that saved the *Bruise* and Bobby and you and me, too. I guess in a few weeks, I'll be coming around and understanding that. But that's what's wrong. That's what's wrong with me. I can't absorb that right now, do you understand what I'm trying to say to you?"

Doc was growing more uncomfortable. He flipped off the tape recorder and excused himself. "Tony, wait right here, will you? I've got to make a phone call."

Tony waited for a few minutes, and when Doc hadn't returned, he wandered into the wire room to read the news from the AP and UPI wires.

He was reading the AP dispatch, which began:

"FBI agents, supported by a special forty-man detachment of Boston police, pressed their hunt Wednesday for vanished television newswoman Cynthia Stoler — believed a victim of retaliation for her exposé of an arson ring with links to the underworld and Boston City Hall."

As Tony was scanning the wire, Bobby Bantam walked into the wire room, accompanied by Doc D'Amato.

"Tony, I'm not going to let you do it. You're not yourself. I'm sending you home and calling off the news conference."

"Bobby, I'm going to tell the truth."

"Fuck the truth. You don't know the truth from a hole in the ground. Come on, I'm having Molly Minton drive you home. Now."

"You're going to use my stuff, you son of a bitch," he said, lunging at Bobby Bantam.

Doc D'Amato grabbed Tony by the arms. Walsh ran into the wire room from the city desk.

"Run downstairs and get the guard. Tony needs a sedative. Call the ambulance," Bantam said.

The next few minutes were a blur in Tony Owen's mind. The brief struggle with Doc and Walsh. Lashing out at the beefy guard from the lobby. The two Boston policemen who tried to talk to him quietly. The EMTs, the stretcher, being wheeled down the corridor and carried down the stairs, the drive to City Hospital, to the emergency room where he saw the same faces he saw the night he had come to Louise Finnigan's side, the needle in the arm, the vision of the woman in anguish, and finally, sleep.

□

Sailor felt savage and exalted, and the memory of what it was to be a man flooded his being. In his drunken frenzy, he experienced a sense of strength and daring. He had defended what was his the way a wolf would defend his den, and the bloody hammer jammed back into his trousers was a trophy of honor. Remorse would come later, and with it a terror of the consequences, unless his memory mercifully failed. But now, as he mounted the stairway toward Cynthia, he was the male back from the hunt, eager for his reward. He had the foresight to steal a flashlight along with the other tools from the shelter, and in his jacket pocket he had shoved a few slices left from a loaf of white bread.

"Julia," he called, as he pushed open the door and shone the flashlight at the dozing figure of Cynthia.

She moved abruptly, forgetting at the instant of wakening that she was fettered, and a sharp pain cut through her wrists and arms.

"Oh, you're back. Thank God. And you have the tools."

He moved toward her, shining the flashlight down into her face.

"Free me now, you promised," she said.

"Later," he said.

"Now, please do it now."

He bent toward her, placing the flashlight on the floor and dropping the tools heavily onto the hard wood.

He pulled the bread out of his jacket pocket, then threw the jacket down, and bending over her, he pushed a slice against her lips. Cynthia devoured it. He pushed another slice at her. She ate that, too, with just a few ravenous bites.

"Now, free me," she said.

"You'll run away," he said.

"Free me," she said, her voice stern and betraying none of the fear she felt beginning to build inside.

He moved closer toward her, his smell so nauseating she felt she was going to lose the bread she had just eaten. His hand again moved inside her blouse, and this time it moved with none of the hesitation of before.

"You're hurting me. Stop it this minute," she shouted.

But he became even more insistent, and then, to her horror, he began to moan in a deep unearthly way, like a dead soul tormented by the sum of all the pain he had ever endured, all that he had ever inflicted. And as he moaned, he began to rock back and forth convulsively as if he were in a state of ecstacy outside of time, outside of the bag of wizened flesh that was his body. His hands tightened on her, and with all her strength she tried to throw him off, but she had little strength left, and then he hit her hard with his fist and began tearing away her clothes. She screamed as he fell upon her, and when her screaming stopped, she noticed he was still and his toothless mouth was fixed upon her breast.

19

THE POPE'S PLANE touched down at City Airport at 9:00 A.M. Friday and Bobby Bantam was ready. He had been ready since 2:00 A.M., going over the coverage plans again and again in his head until it was impossible to sleep. Finally, at 5:00 A.M., he had stopped trying, and climbing out of bed, he quietly dressed and came down to the paper to set up his command post, which consisted of a chair set up before three television sets arranged in a row alongside the city desk and within an easy shout of the photo desk. There, at the long-awaited hour, Bobby sat and watched the pageantry, or rather he tried to sit, but his energy was running so high, he could use the chair only as a springboard, bouncing up as each new image flashed before him.

"Look at that," he yelled to Molly Minton, who stood by his side. "The goddamn vice president. The wimp, pushing ahead of everybody. Look at the governor, elbowing him for position. Would you believe grown men? Where's the mayor? Where's our guy?"

"There he is, behind the governor," said Molly.

"Oh, Christ, the guy must be steaming, just steaming."

The door of the Air Italia 747 opened. Two flight attendants peered down at the portable stairway, then made way for a team of security men, who ran down the ramp, taking positions at the edge of the crowd, which strained against the security ropes. There was a gradually swelling murmur, and then applause, as the pope, clad in white, came through the door, pausing artfully like an actor before descending from the plane. Now the applause rang out and the murmurs became shouts of greeting.

The pope walked surely down the steps, kneeled, and quickly kissed the tarmac. As he rose, a girl of about six or seven, wearing a country costume and carrying a bouquet of flowers, was urged by adult hands toward the pope.

"Welcome to our city, Your Holiness," she said, and handed him the flowers.

The pope reached down, took the girl in his hands, and lifted her, flowers and all, high into the air. Then he drew her into his arms and kissed her on the cheek.

"Get that kid with the flowers. Where's Walsh? Find out who the hell that kid is and where she got the flowers and what he said to her."

Walsh picked up a walkie-talkie and yelled instructions to Arnie Albanian, who was running the reporting crew at the airport.

"Hey, Molly, lookit. All the pols have their wives with them. All but the mayor. Eileen's hanging tough. Connie must be steaming."

The pope moved through the reception line of politicians, stopping to chat briefly with each one.

"Look at the attorney general. He's kneeling down to kiss his ring. Would you believe that hypocrite? Walsh, get somebody to find out why that turkey did that. What's he doing, going for the humble vote?"

The pope moved steadily through the ranks of greeters. Bobby took his eyes off the screen momentarily and spotted Earl Evers standing over by the water cooler.

"For Christ's sake, Earl, you're my main rewrite man. Come over here and watch this, will you? It's history, for Christ's sake."

Earl ambled over after pausing to pick up a notebook from his desk. He sat in the chair Bobby just vacated and began taking notes.

Collie Wallace, the chief photographer, stood by Bobby Bantam.

"Jesus Christ, Collie, where are our guys? I see the *Mammoth* guys all over the airport. Where's our guys?"

"We got everything covered."

"Bullshit. Did we get that little girl?"

"I'm sure we did. Leo's out there."

"What's he, the invisible man? You better double-check."

"Relax, Bobby. There he is. See him, over there. Right by the pope's elbow."

The pope walked over to a bank of microphones.

Now, the smile was gone from his broad face, and he looked grave. "May God be with you," he said, and blessed the crowd of dignitaries and media and security people. "And my greetings to this historic and holy place."

"Holy? That's a new one," said Molly Minton.

"I come to you with the peace of Christ."

"Say a prayer for Cynthia, turkey," said Bobby Bantam.

"I come to you humbly, prayerfully, that the peace I bring to this special place can, perhaps, touch the heart of this great and good nation, this citadel of liberty, which is the hope of the world. I thank you for the warmth of your greeting and for the generosity of your hearts. May the peace of the Lord be with you."

"Well, we still don't know what he's here for," said Bobby Bantam as the pope headed into the open van that would take him on a motorcade through the city.

"Sure we do," said Molly Minton. "He's come to bring us peace."

"That will sell us a lot of papers, won't it?" Bobby Bantam replied.

Bantam turned away from the television sets. Nothing would happen now except for the motorcade, which wouldn't get under way for a few minutes.

"How's it look, John? You got all the troops in place?" Bantam asked the city editor.

"Sure, all the troops," Walsh replied. "All ten of them stretched in a thin line from the airport to the North End. Then they got to run like hell all over downtown, through the Back Bay, down into the South End, then up through the Fenway and over to Allston and Brighton. But don't worry, they all have good legs, and they know how to do interviews and take notes while running four-minute miles."

"John, all I'm asking you is a simple question. Are we ready?"

"Yes, Bobby."

"Good. I'm glad. And is anything else new in the city today?"

"Yeah, one thing is new. It probably doesn't mean much, but it happened on Duncan Avenue. Another stiff. Murdered. No identification."

"Another Bernie Kremenko?"

"No, no fire. This guy got bludgeoned. But he may be a bum, too. Cops aren't sure. A little better dressed than most alkies. But the people from the shelter are checking him out to make sure."

"What else you got?"

"Everything else is the pope. An old lady in the South End has been at work for the past two days getting a dinner ready for the pope. She's been praying he's going to show up. If he doesn't, she's going to feed the whole neighborhood."

"How did she send the invitation, through Saint Peter?"

"Something like that."

"Anybody check the hospital to see how Tony Owen is doing?"

"Not yet."

"Well, do it, right now. I sure could use Tony today. And while you're at it, check the cops on Cynthia."

"I already did," said Walsh. "They said nothing is new."

Now, another roar came from the three television sets, and Bobby turned to watch the progress of the motorcade. The streets of the North End were packed, as were the apartment buildings along the route. Women leaned far out of their windows, waving papal flags.

"Find out who the hell put together those papal flags. They must've made a killing. Get somebody going on that from the business page, O.K.?"

"O.K.," said Molly Minton.

"And Molly, have somebody check police headquarters. Somebody's going to be falling out those windows or having a heart attack. Get all the ambulance calls."

"Got you, Bobby."

Bobby Bantam felt someone tap him on the shoulder.

"You got a lot of fucking nerve, Bobby. I ought to beat the holy piss out of you, rushing me off like that like I was some kind of basket case, you son of a bitch."

"Tony, Jesus, you're out. Great to see you," Bobby Bantam replied, only half taking his eyes off the television screens. "They let you out, huh? I was just checking."

"Why did you do that, Bobby?"

"Not now, Tony. Jesus. Here, grab a chair. Sit down. Help me watch this. Can you work? Shush. O.K.?"

Bantam, still watching the televisions, pushed a chair at Tony Owen.

"Walshie, get a hold of the library and see if you can find out when the city last had a turnout like this. This is really something. I'll bet crime is down. Molly, have somebody check headquarters to find out what kind of crime is going on today. Better yet, pull out all the reports for today and compare them to yesterday. You know, the incident reports."

"Hey, Bobby, where you going to get all the reporters?"

"Hey, can't you see? Tony just walked in."

"I'm not working," said Tony, taking Bobby's remark literally.

"Of course you're not," said Bobby. "Not until you're ready."

A young man carrying a sign that Bobby couldn't read rushed from the curb toward the papal caravan and was met by half a dozen security people and knocked roughly to the ground.

"Everything on that kook, Walshie. Everything. Get his sign, too."

Tony Owen fidgeted in his chair. Bantam noticed. "You miss the action, maybe a little bit, Tony?"

"No, Bobby. We've got to get a few things straightened out."

"Sure, Tony, later. How'd you like that little piece on the mayor? Right on target. The bum is through."

"I haven't been reading the paper, Bobby."

Bantam was getting exasperated. "Look, Tony, I'm trying to make sure we don't miss out on this. Why don't you go sit down in my office and wait for me? I'll be in as soon as the motorcade is over. Go on, please. Hey, look at that midget on the street corner carrying the cross."

"That's no midget," said Earl. "That's a kiddo."

"A kiddo with a beard? I thought you were smart, Earl."

"Oh, I was looking at the wrong midget."

"That isn't a midget you were looking at, you dummy. That was a kiddo."

Ten minutes later, Bobby came into his office where Tony Owen was standing at the window.

"He's stopping for lunch at the State House. Then he'll be going to the cathedral for a benediction. Is that what you call it, a benediction, with all the priests in North and South America? And then he's off to the cardinal's place for rest. Then there's the big Mass tonight, and then the next stop in the papal cavalcade. You don't much care, do you?"

"No."

"Well, forgive me. It's not that I'm as insensitive as it seems. I'm just trying to get your mind off Cynthia."

"Don't bother."

"I'm sorry about the other night. It was something I think I had to do. You were so upset. You would've made a fool of yourself if you went ahead with the news conference. A Tony Owen news conference. Oh, Lordie."

"Bobby, I'm hurting."

"Hey, don't I know it?"

"I don't think I want to do it anymore, after this is all over."

"What do you want to do? Be a gentleman, go to work for the fucking *Mammoth*. Is that what you want?"

"No, I don't want to do that."

"Well, look at yourself, Tony. How old are you? Forty-two, forty-three? What the hell are you going to do? What else do you know? You're a newspaperman, a goddamn good one, the best. So we're in an unusual situation. You think I enjoy it?"

"I think you love it, you son of a bitch. I think you love it."

Bantam smiled. "Yeah, you're right. I'm a sick prick. I love it, even this. Forgive me. It's true. But you know something? In other circumstances, you'd love it, too."

A whoop sounded in the newsroom. And then another.

"Holy Christ, what the hell is happening? They must have heard the paper is saved."

Bobby Bantam moved toward the door of his office and was almost knocked over by John Walsh, who came storming breathlessly over from the city desk.

"They found Cynthia, Tony. They just found her. She's alive. She's alive."

"I don't believe it," said Tony Owen. "I don't believe it."

"Yeah, the commissioner just called. A rookie cop. He'll tell you in a minute. He's on his way over. He's going to take you to the hospital."

Bobby Bantam, smiling and expansive, reached in his pocket for the biggest cigar Tony had ever seen. He lit it, threw the match into a wastebasket, and walked over to Tony, who had turned to the wall to hide his emotions. Bantam slapped Tony on the back and said to him, "I told you everything was going to be all right, now didn't I tell you that?"

□

ROOKIE COP IN MIRACLE RESCUE OF TERRORIZED TV STAR, read the inside headline over the *Bruise*'s account of Cynthia's emancipation, a development that tore Bobby Bantam in two. "Why does all the news have to break on the same day?" he lamented as he tried to decide how he was going to devise a front page to include the pope's remarkable day in the city, his unusual remarks outside City Hall, and the Cynthia saga. And when he learned that the death of Malachy Owen was the key to Cynthia's deliverance, he was beside himself.

He hadn't even begun to find a spot to display the three-part series: EILEEN HAYDON'S NIGHTMARE: SCENES FROM A ROTTEN MARRIAGE. When he tried to find one, he realized he had only one choice. "Walshie, tell Stella to hold off for a day. Eileen's nightmare will get lost tomorrow."

And so, the mayor got a day's reprieve. Not that it made much difference to him, so embarrassed was he already by the *Bruise* story predicting his retirement from politics, and the way he was pushed into the ranks of lesser pols at the airport reception.

Now he knew what was ahead of him. In the short run, it was humiliation at the hands of Bobby Bantam and the *Bruise*, with its fathomless reservoirs of bad taste and ill will. And in the long run, it was a life filled with ordinary days, a life without Corinne, whom he could not face, perhaps not ever again, now that he had betrayed her so shamelessly before Eileen. Love had to be stronger than that, and his had failed the test. Perhaps he would move to another city, New York, or possibly Los Angeles, and try to start again. But his energy was diminished now and he worried whether he had enough left even to ward off the jackals at his heels.

The *Mammoth*, with its standard broadsheet format, had an easier time packaging the day's momentous events, dividing page one between the pope and Cynthia, while downplaying the death of Malachy Owen and the miraculous nature of the rescue. But the *Mammoth* was hampered in one respect. When it was clear that young Walter Griswold planned to sit in on the story conference for the third day in a row, Bill Raleigh decided it was time to take his leave and left the supervision of the paper entirely in his publisher's hands.

"I'm going for a walk," said Raleigh.

"As you like," replied Griswold.

And so ended Raleigh's long career in journalism.

For Tony Owen, who wouldn't learn of his brother's death until later in the day, the news that Cynthia was alive and as well as could be expected struck like a sunburst, leaving him dazzled and disoriented. At first, he couldn't believe the news, so complete was his despair. But the joy on John Walsh's face and in the newsroom could not be denied. It had to be true; it was true. He remembered his prayer of the day before, and while his skepticism remained, he mumbled a thank you in the face of it. God had relented. Perhaps it was his prayer; perhaps the pope's. Yes, the pope had prayed for Cynthia after all.

But Tony didn't have much time for thought or thanksgiving. The police car was on its way to take him to Cynthia. He literally raced across the city room, past his smiling colleagues, and took the stairs at what normally would be a perilous clip.

In the back seat of the car sat the police commissioner and a patrolman, Joseph Gyenes, whom Tony had never met. Commissioner Connolly took care of the introductions.

"Here's the man of the hour, Tony. Just on the force for six months."

"Eight, sir."

"Eight months."

"Thank you," said Tony. "How is she?"

"She's going to live," the policeman said. "She was a little hysterical."

"You couldn't blame her. Jesus, I think we were just in time," said the commissioner. "Tell him how you found her," the commissioner said.

Tony had taken a seat next to the driver and he twisted around so he could see Gyenes's face, which was open and eager and uncorrupted, the face of a young Officer Friendly.

"Well, sir, I was assigned to help at the murder scene on Duncan Avenue. The homicide people were working around the body, trying to find a weapon, and working with the coroner to try to fix the time of death. I was asked to check on the periphery."

"Where on Duncan Avenue was this?" Tony asked.

"Do you know Duncan Avenue?" the officer asked naively.

"Yes," said Tony.

"Well, it was on the corner right by number forty."

"An empty lot?"

"Yes, we found the body of an unidentified male in the weeds. He was roughly thirty-five to forty, about six feet two, one hundred fifty pounds, dark hair, brown eyes, with severe wounds at the top of the skull. He had been dead for approximately thirty-six hours when the body was found by some students cutting through the lot on their way to class. He appeared to be a derelict. You know a lot of them just move into those abandoned buildings and crash there."

"I know," Tony said.

"Well, I started looking around the lot for a blunt instrument. It appeared that the victim succumbed to a blow from a pipe or bat of some kind, something heavier than a bottle. But I couldn't find anything on the immediate periphery of the homicide scene. So I decided to look a little beyond the immediate vicinity of the body."

"And then what happened?" asked the commissioner, turning to Tony and winking, as if to say, "Isn't he something?"

The car was cruising along the expressway toward the Storrow Drive exit.

"What hospital is she in? I never even asked."

"We took her to MGH. It was my decision," the commissioner said. "I wanted to make sure she had the best treatment."

"My God, what happened to her?" Tony asked.

"She's going to be fine, sir. Don't worry," the officer said.

"Go on," said the commissioner. "Tell him what happened."

"Yes, sir," said Officer Gyenes. "I proceeded along the edge of an alley that runs to the rear of Duncan Avenue. I found nothing in the alley. So I decided to check the building at number forty, which seemed to be completely secured.

"As I checked the rear of the building, I noticed a garbage-strewn stairwell leading down into the basement. For some reason, I decided not to walk away but to inspect that stairwell, even though I could see the doorway leading to the basement was boarded up, as was all other ingress to the structure."

"God works in mysterious ways," said the commissioner. "Would you believe it, Tony, he almost walked away without trying the door? A less conscientious officer would have, you know."

"Thank you, Officer."

"Well, there was a big rat that came scurrying by me and I have to admit to you that I hate rats. But once he was past me, I figured that any other rat down there with him would have run away, too. So I guessed it was safe. Anyway, I tried the door and the wooden sheeting was just leaning there. Somebody had pried it away. So by now, I figured I'd gone this far, I might as well go all the way just in case the suspect was hiding in the building or dropped the blunt instrument there."

"You're a good man, Officer," Tony Owen said. "Then what happened?"

"Well, it was pitch dark in there. So I took my flashlight and I flashed it around the cellar, and it was all cleaned out. And I saw the stairway leading upstairs. So I told myself, I've gone this far, I might as well see the thing through.

"And then I heard this moaning, this real low moaning, like a person was really hurt, really suffering. And I wasn't sure, to tell you the truth, whether it was an animal or a human sound. I really wasn't. I don't think I've ever heard anything like that."

"Poor Cynthia," said Tony. "Oh, God."

"So I walked up as quietly as I could to the third floor where the moaning was more distinct. And there was a door closed. I wasn't sure what was inside. So I took out my gun. I didn't know what I was going to run into, and I knocked on the door and I said, and I'm not sure why I said this . . . I could have gotten myself killed if there was a man with a gun behind that door."

"You'll learn," said the commissioner.

"I said, as I knocked on the door, and pushed it in, 'Officer Joseph Gyenes, Police Department, don't move, I'm investigating.' "

"He's investigating, would you believe it?" said the commissioner.

"And there was the female victim, manacled to a radiator, and this derelict was sitting beside her, beating his head against the radiator. He was the one who was moaning, saying this gibberish I couldn't make out."

"And Cynthia, what about her?"

"She was unconscious, sir. I thought at first she was dead."

□

Cynthia was asleep when Tony Owen was led into her room. The commissioner had posted a guard there, and someone (Tony learned later it was Bobby Bantam) had already sent flowers, which arrived just before Tony made his own entrance.

Tony was relieved that she looked so good. The only sign of violence on her face was a bruise below her left eye. One of her hands was thrown back against the pillow by her head. Tony lifted it gently and sorted a few strands of hair from between her fingers. Gauze bandages were wound about her wrists. Sedated, she slept soundly for almost an hour before she began to stir, mumbling at first in her sleep, then becoming more distressed, and finally crying out, "Help me. Will somebody help me, please?"

Tony took her hand and tried to quiet her. A nurse came into the room and took her pulse. "The sedative is wearing off a little," she said. "She should wake up any minute now."

"Maybe she needs another shot," said Tony.

"The doctor will be by soon. He'll decide," she said.

Tony was alone once again with Cynthia. Again, as he sat by her bed, the vision of his mother's face confronted him as he stared at her, and again he was face to face with the memory of the night long denied.

Now he let the scene play remorselessly in his head like a newsreel from beginning to end. Yes, it was he, sitting there in the kitchen, watching the pain on her face, the despair in her eyes, watching it from a distance, although he was sitting within easy touch of her sorrow, and all he had to do, all that was asked of him, was to reach out, touch her head with his still childish hand, touch her own hand, which trembled before him like a small animal, dying. And he couldn't move, couldn't or wouldn't. Not that it mattered now. She was asking him to save her, to pull her back from the edge, by some word or gesture to give her a reason to go on, and he couldn't, or he wouldn't, move.

They were alone in the kitchen. Malachy was already asleep in the bed in the adjoining room. "You have to be the man of the house now," she had said. "I'm counting on you."

Her speech was slurred and her breath smelled, almost always did now, of the Heavenly Hill that she kept hidden under the sink, as if he would never see it. And then she went off, as she always did, talking about his father and how he was to blame for the ruin of all their lives, and he didn't want to hear it — this wail of hers about his father, a wail that froze his heart, not because of any love for the man who had deserted them, but because long ago he had made his peace with that. As far as he was concerned, his father was a veteran who died in the war. He had not really known him, except as a shadow moving furtively at the edge of his memory. Why not the fiction of his death in combat? That was when he went away, after all, and he had never come back, never written, and never called.

Now it was her weakness, not his, that he had to deal with. The bottle under the sink, the meals never prepared or allowed to burn away, the clothes that were never mended, the bills that were never paid, the men who would slip out the door at the crack of dawn, moving as quietly as mice by his bedroom door.

No, he would not be, could not be, the one filling that bottomless void in her spirit, assuring her that everything was going to be all right. What difference did it make if he was going to be called upon to take over the family? Hadn't he already taken it over? It was he, after all, who was already raising Malachy; it was he who was already working after school in Morris's Delicatessen to put the food on the table. It was he who had to endure the embarrassment of Morris slipping him a neatly wrapped package of chops or hamburgers along with his fifteen dollars a week and saying to him, "You're not eating enough red meat. You got to get more flesh on your bones. Now bring this home to your mama and tell her to cook it nice."

And his mother, unaware of the weekly humiliation of having to take what others paid for, began to accept the handout as the family's due. "The old Jew is ripping you off anyway," his mother would say. "Imagine, fifteen dollars a week for all you do." And it was useless to explain to her that Morris didn't need his labor, that his own children who lived upstairs were available for all the stock work and deliveries that he performed. "He feels sorry for us, Mama," he told her once. And she had laughed at him. "Then why doesn't he pay you real money instead of yesterday's hamburger?" she asked, and laughed at him for being a baby in the world.

But she was the baby, she and Malachy, and maybe she had begun to notice his resentment, the hardening of his heart. When she tried to kiss him, he would pull away, avoiding the whiskey smell, avoiding the feel of her failure, the family's failure, his failure. He was barely twelve years old and already he was choked by a sense of indifference.

So she sat with him at the table and he knew what she planned to do, that she had in her own mind reached the limits of endurance, and she could go on only if he encouraged her, only if he told her that she was his mother and he loved her. But instead of reaching toward her, he pulled away, his heart a thing of ice.

"I'm so unhappy, Tony," she had said. "I'm so unhappy I could die."

He looked at her with the impenetrable blankness of neutrality, a look more quizzical than concerned, and changed the subject, or thought he had, although now he realized that what he said probably, as much as anything, pushed her over the edge.

"Malachy's teacher, Miss Morrison, wants you to come in and see her this week. She stopped me today in the corridor. She said to tell you it's important."

"What is it about?" she asked.

"I don't know, but I think she thinks Malachy is neglected. I heard her talking to another teacher in the office yesterday. Miss Morrison told the other teacher that Malachy looks like nobody's claim, and she doesn't know what to do. She got all flustered when she saw me standing behind her."

"Oh, God," she said. "I can't take it anymore." Then she buried her head in her arms and began to sob. And as she sobbed, Tony got up from the table and went to bed. When he left the house the next morning, he knew what he was likely to find when he got back home, and his heart was already prepared.

☐

As Tony Owen sat by Cynthia's side, he knew, or felt that he knew, that he had caused the death of his own mother, and that he would have to accept the blame if he was to go on. He also knew, or felt that he did, that he had come close to causing the death of Cynthia, and that her survival was, without a doubt in his own mind, a confirmation of what he had always known but never acknowledged. The universe was not altogether barren. Within its cold vastness was contained a saving grace — the trace of mercy that endured as ageless as the stars.

Finally, Cynthia opened her eyes and saw Tony.

"Where have you been, you bastard?" she asked, and slipped back to sleep before Tony could think of a reply.

☐

It was Bobby Bantam who would give Tony the news about Malachy later that afternoon. Tony was stunned to see Bantam himself standing in the doorway of Cynthia's room, his black derby in hand, a look of some discomfort on his face.

"What the hell are you doing away from the paper on a day like today?" Tony had asked him.

"Don't ask," Bantam had replied. "I'm dying inside. But I have to talk to you. Let's go into the lounge."

And so they sat on a plastic-covered sofa down the hall from Cynthia's room. "I don't know how much more you can take," he said. "But it was your brother who led the police to Cynthia."

"My brother? You're kidding."

"He's dead, Tony. They just identified him. He was murdered in that empty lot. The people from the shelter knew him."

"Heaven help him, the poor lost soul," Tony said.

"He was apparently on his way to where Cynthia was found. The killer knew him. I guess from what the shelter people say, they sort of hung out together. I thought I'd let you know."

"What are you going to do with this tomorrow, Bobby?"

"To be perfectly honest with you, Tony, I'm in a quandary. The pope hasn't even spoken yet and the stories are flooding the place. I really don't know."

"Don't make a carnival out of Malachy's death. Would you promise me that?"

"I don't know what you mean by carnival, Tony. But it's a helluva story. A priest. Your brother. Saves Cynthia's life. It has a lot of the elements. And the pope did pray for Cynthia. It has all the makings of a miracle."

"Where's the body, at the morgue?"

"Yeah. It's waiting to be claimed. I can deal with that if you want, tomorrow."

"No, I'll take care of it tonight. I want to see him."

"Tony, I've got to run. I'm sorry."

"Bobby. I want to see the body; then, if it's all right with you, I think I want to come down the paper and do a piece on Malachy. I'm O.K. now."

Bobby hesitated, and finally said, "I'd love to have you."

"You're afraid I might cramp your style, aren't you? I know what you have up your sleeve. 'The Miracle on Duncan Avenue.' I know you."

"You wouldn't," Bantam answered. "You wouldn't cramp my style, I mean, would you?"

"I might. I don't know. If I know Malachy, he wasn't on a rescue mission. He was looking for a drink. The pope had him pumped up like nothing you ever saw. Anyway, Bobby, I need to think and you need to get back to the paper. I'll see you tonight."

"Sorry again, Tony," Bantam said.

"Sure, Bobby. Thanks."

Bantam turned and headed down the hall toward the elevators. Tony called after him, "And Bobby, would you do me one more favor? Have somebody call out to Mattapan and see if there's a patient out there named Johnny Weissmuller. Find out what you can about him, if he's there."

"Tarzan? Johnny Weissmuller, as in Tarzan?"

"Yeah, just have somebody make the call, if you don't mind."

"O.K., I'll take care of it," Bobby Bantam said, his mind already clicking with possible headlines for the next day's page one.

□

Tony Owen looked down at the blood-flecked face of his brother, sighed, said, "That's him," and gently touched his cold forehead, as if in comfort; then he walked into the office and signed the necessary forms.

Afterward, he headed slowly back to the paper. He would mourn Malachy the best way he knew, by doing it in print. But he wasn't sure what he would say, or how he would say it. He felt no grief at Malachy's death, only a sadness that encompassed not just Malachy but their mother and Tony himself. They had all endured so much pain, more in his case than he could feel, more in the case of Malachy and their mother than they could bear. He had been the survivor, the one person in the family who learned early on to seize hold of the lifeline and never let go. The others never could get the knack, although Malachy tried — oh, how he tried. And who was to say that it wasn't God who finally released him, finally brought him to his reward for trying so hard to be what he could never be, a priest.

When Tony got to the paper, he said nothing to anyone in the newsroom. He just headed for his desk and rolled sheets of paper into the typewriter and began to say his good-byes to Malachy and to the shambles of their lives.

And as he wrote, he didn't much care how his words sounded or how they would strike whatever audience they found. He was writing a column, but he was writing it as a real person, to a real person, and for a real person. All he could do for his brother now was to try to make people understand him. And so he sat down and wrote the truth in a column that began:

"He was my brother. I claimed him yesterday at the city morgue. I was the only one who could. I was the only one he had, at least on this earth. He ended where I knew he would end, where he, I'm sure, knew he would end, even though he was a priest, a real priest. And partly because he was a priest, a real priest, the Reverend Malachy Owen, Father, Padre.

"He's being hailed as a hero today, as a man who laid down his life for his brother, literally, to save the life of Cynthia Stoler.

"So remember him as a martyr because, in a way, he was, long before he got mixed up in the Cynthia Stoler case.

"He was destroyed by his illusions. They made him what he also was: a drunk, a mental case, a derelict.

"Faith, hope, and charity. He believed it. The imitation of Christ. He lived it. Sacrifice, love. Those were his bywords, long before he became a bum on the city streets. A priest was to be selfless, so was he; a priest was to be chaste, and so was he; a priest was to be poor, and he lived with the simplicity of a sparrow.

"He lived like a twelfth-century saint in a world of bingo, and Buicks, and Tuesday on the golf course, and he was so out of place in the rectory that no pastor would have him for long because he'd screw up the works whether he was working in the suburbs or the inner city. And he didn't have the strength to fight off the pastors who complained.

"I can't blame them for complaining. I was his brother and he embarrassed me. I dreaded seeing him. The last time we met, I told him I wished he would go somewhere and die, and when I said it I meant it. Not that I didn't love him. I did."

Bobby Bantam came and stood over his shoulder. Tony knew from his silence that Bobby didn't like the piece one bit. He walked away and Tony kept on writing, realizing as he worked that he didn't really care whether the piece saw the light of day. He wasn't writing it for anyone but himself anyway. Then he finished, and he finished by blaming himself as much as anyone for what happened to Malachy, who was shaped so much by the death of his mother.

"Is she really with the angels?" he would ask years after she died. And Tony would reply, "She's with them this moment, looking down on you, Malachy."

"No, let's not bury him with any more illusions," Tony wrote. "For once, before his body is placed in the earth, let everyone look at him as he was, as he lived, and as he died. He fought for life, for joy, for meaning, and in the end he died in a raw junk heap on Duncan Avenue, more than likely while looking for a drink to sleep away the night."

"So what's your schedule now?" Bobby Bantam asked as Tony handed him his copy, copy that Bantam glanced at, then put down by his side, holding it as he might hold a cub reporter's memo asking for overtime.

"You want to know when you can start doing what you wanted to?" Tony replied, grinning slightly at his old colleague.

"No, I just wanted to know if you were heading back to the hospital, going home, or what you wanted to do."

"I might head back to the hospital soon. Cynthia's probably still conked out. They really shot her up."

"Well, maybe we should sit down and talk. I got some ideas I want to bat around with you, if you don't mind."

"O.K., sure."

John Walsh came over, bouncing on the balls of his feet. "It's great to be in a winning clubhouse for a change, isn't it, Tony?" he said.

"It sure is," he said.

"I'm sorry about your brother."

"Yeah, thanks."

Bantam retreated to his office, then came out, without Tony's column in his hand.

"I see you're not anxious to show me tomorrow's dummies," said Tony. "That's sure a change of character."

"Too early. Have to see what the pope says. I'm still struggling."

Bantam asked when the pope was going to speak. Walsh advised him it would be any moment now.

They gathered in front of the three television sets and in silence watched the ceremonies.

"Look at all those costumes," said Bobby, "and all those priests and bishops. God almighty, I didn't know there were so many of you people out there."

A temporary pulpit with a bulletproof screen was off to the side of the temporary altar. Bobby stood impatiently, waiting for the pope to move away from his escort of robed attendants and get behind the rostrum.

"We better sit down for this," said Bantam. "He might be all night."

Bantam, Walsh, and Tony Owen pulled up chairs and the pope finally began.

He spoke in a strong voice, his English heavily accented, his eyes glancing downward at the text, peering out at the vast audience. He was a big man, a physical man, but on the television screen he seemed shrunken behind the bulletproof glass as if he were encased in an overcoat many sizes too large.

The cameras focused on his plain face, only occasionally sweeping the front rows for quick shots of the well-placed and powerful in the audience. Mayor Haydon did not seem to be there, but perhaps the cameras had just not caught him.

The pope spoke of modern man, and his estrangement from the divine and his insistence on sin, as if sinning or not sinning were a test of his personal freedom. And he said why he had come to this city, of all cities, as the first stop in his tour. Because, he said, it was the city in America closest to the old world, the city that symbolically bridges what was and what will be.

And he spoke of the city that was rooted in time as well as place, that helped men mark where they were in an otherwise unfamiliar and hostile universe, that helped men know who they were and what they believed, which gave them a sense of values and standards. But now, he said, the city is no more the rock and reference point. It has become like a great train station where people pass through while flitting from stopping point to stopping point. And around the world, the ones who stay are the very rich, who have found in the city a way to profit from the impermanence and the very poor, who are tossed willy-nilly into the great cities of the world and cling there as a last hope for survival.

It is these poor, these urban castaways, these countless millions pressed against the walls of privilege and power who must be addressed, and what better place to begin to address them than in Boston, where the cultural memory of what a city is and can be remains alive.

"And, by the way," he said, his eyes lifting from his text, "I have long been struck by the simple proofs of faith, by the reality that rarely a day goes by when the ways of God are not manifest to His people on earth. Before I came to Boston, I asked that the Lord in His mercy consider my humble prayer and spare the life of your television personality, Miss Cynthia. And today I learn that my prayer has been answered and that the instrument of her deliverance was an urban priest, a man who, I am told, had dedicated his life to the spiritual needs of the homeless and discarded."

That was all he had to say about Malachy, but no sooner were the words out of his mouth than Bobby Bantam was out of his chair, dancing in the newsroom. "A miracle. The pope has just proclaimed a miracle."

"That isn't exactly what he said," said Tony Owen.

"That's exactly what he meant, even if it isn't exactly what he said," said Bobby Bantam. "Hey, Tony, you're going to have to rewrite your column now; it just doesn't play anymore. The pope just canonized Malachy."

"Oh, shit," said Tony Owen. "You don't need me anymore, Bobby."

Tony Owen was now standing in the middle of the newsroom. Bobby was a few feet in front of him, trying to talk to Tony but at the same time wanting to run across the room to his office and begin doing the mock-ups of tomorrow's page one. He had the headline now, the headline that would allow him to tie everything together into a beautiful, commemorative package.

"I need you, and more than ever," shouted Bobby Bantam.

"I've got to go see Cynthia."

"What will our readers think if they don't see you in the paper again tomorrow?"

"Tell them I went on vacation again."

"Hey, why don't you just do a little rewriting up at the top of your piece. You don't have to rewrite the whole thing. Just don't make Malachy look like such a bum. He's a hero, for Christ's sake."

"Yup, maybe he is," said Tony. "You do it, then."

"Hey, what the pope said is right, Tony. He was out there trying. Who the hell knows what he was thinking when he was killed? Maybe it was a miracle. Maybe God was just using him. Who the hell knows?"

Tony Owen didn't answer. He had only Cynthia on his mind. It was nearly nine o'clock. The Mass had resumed and on the television screen the thousands there were lining up to receive communion, and the pope was just one of a score of priests distributing the hosts. Yes, Tony Owen thought, nobody knows what was on Malachy's mind. Maybe the pope's prayer was answered, maybe his own — and maybe they both spoke into the same void, the void that swallowed up Malachy, that one day would swallow them all. It didn't much matter. Malachy would have liked what the pope said, would have reveled in it. With just a few words, he had justified Malachy's entire life, endowing it with a certain nobility, but more important, with a protective coating of myth. He was reordained, and now and forevermore he would be as splendid a priest as he was on the day of his first Mass, that glittering day that he thought could never be recaptured.

Malachy was reborn. The stubble was off his face; the rheumy lines were erased from his eyes, the slur from his speech, the sad drunken shuffle from his gait. It was as if he were back again in boyhood, practicing the priestly gestures before the mirror, purely, serenely, theatrically.

"How's this?" asked Bobby Bantam. "Slain priest a saint: Pope."

"You're slipping, Bobby. Where's the miracle?"

"You're right. I got to work on that."

"I've got to go," said Tony.

"But what about your column?"

"It's all yours. You want to change it, change it. I've written it. Now it's yours."

"I'll just fiddle with it a little, Tony, just to make it conform."

"Sure," said Tony.

"Then you trust me?" asked Bobby Bantam.

"Trust you?" replied Tony, and now he smiled and looked at Bobby and said, "No, but Malachy would like that. And if he is a saint, it's better to be on his right side, don't you think?"

"There's politics everywhere, isn't there?" said Bobby Bantam.

As Tony walked out of the building, Bobby accompanied him down the hall and escalator and out the front door. For a moment, the two old friends stood in the night air.

"Tony, I want you to take some time off, maybe a week or two, head down to the Bahamas or Saint Martin or somewhere with Cynthia, get some sun and some rest. What do you say? The *Bruise* will pick up the whole tab, let you think through what you want to do. What do you say?"

"Hey, it sounds like the best offer I've had in weeks. Thank you. You're going to be a great publisher."

"And when you get back, we'll sit down and talk. Maybe we can find something else for you to do. Maybe you'd like to be editor after a while. Two jobs. That's a lot of work. I mean I'm going to need somebody I can count on working for me."

"Thanks, Bobby, that sounds good. Cynthia will be happy to hear it."

"Just let me know when you're going and where."

"Sure."

"And one other thing, Tony. Just in case. You wouldn't mind too much if Stella looked in on you for a day or two?"

"Stella? You've got to be kidding."

"Well, you two are kind of a hot ticket these days, and I just thought — if it wouldn't be too big an imposition — you know, a little piece about the lovebirds from the islands . . ."

"Shove it, Bobby."

"Shove it?"

"Shove it."

A cab pulled up. "So long, Bobby," Tony said as he stepped into the back seat.

"So long, Tony. I'll be hearing from you soon."

"Sure."

"You'll be back, Tony."

The cab pulled away. Bobby Bantam watched it head down the street and cut over toward the expressway. "Oh, he'll be back, all right," he said to himself. "The son of a bitch has never had it so good."

As Bobby Bantam turned to re-enter the building, the lobby lights went out, and the streetlights behind him were suddenly dark as night. The guard inside the front door had reached for a flashlight, and it was the only illumination Bobby could see anywhere.

He groped toward the escalator, now silent and still. He heard footsteps on the second floor, then saw a second flashlight and heard the voice of John Walsh, who was standing at the head of the stairway.

"Bobby, you down there?"

"Yeah, what the hell is going on?"

"There's a blackout. I hear it's citywide. The Edison is working on it. That's all they'll say. Meanwhile, we're shut down."

"How long they going to take to fix the son of a bitch?" Bobby Bantam yelled into the darkness.

"They aren't giving any guarantees. All they're saying is they're working on it."

Suddenly, the implications of the blackout dawned on Bobby Bantam, and he stood stunned.

"Walshie, you get back on the telephone and you tell those hooples over at the Edison that we've got a fucking miracle on our hands and that a miracle isn't worth much if we can't get our presses rolling. In fact, you tell them it ain't worth a goddamn thing, you hear me?"

"Yeah, right away," he answered.

"And Walshie, you see if you can get a hold of the pope and tell him he'd better start praying again. It looks like the last prayer didn't take all the way."

"Sure thing, Bobby."

"Would you believe that son of a bitch?" Bobby Bantam said, and he began groping in the dark toward the stairs.

☐

Connie Haydon sat in the darkness of his City Hall office. He had been there for hours, locked so deeply in thought he had not even

noticed when the lamp atop his desk went out as if someone had
yanked the cord from the socket.

Outside, the crowd on the plaza had dispersed and the crews were
at work under portable lighting, stacking up the wooden chairs and
disassembling the temporary altar.

Haydon's mind was intent on wrapping itself around his problem,
but the task left him weary. He had never faced anything this vast,
this insurmountable. Everywhere he turned, he saw only humiliation
and defeat.

But he didn't give up the task. He wouldn't; he couldn't.

From time to time, he reached down and grasped the envelope
that was on his desk, the envelope containing Corinne's letter of
resignation. It was just as well; it wouldn't work. He wondered for
a moment whether he really loved her. Love, he said to himself,
what is love anyway? She gave to me, I gave to her, and then the
circumstances changed. They always do. That's what life is,
isn't it? Changing circumstances. Greatness lies in being able to
adapt. And when do men stop adapting? When they lose their
nerve.

And who had snapped his nerve? A pack of mental midgets,
morons running a third-rate tabloid; his wife, a woman he should
have left in the old neighborhood where she probably would have run
off with the goddamn milkman; the pope, coming in here like a
ringmaster at a media circus.

Connie Haydon beaten by these turkeys?

He reached for the telephone and dialed Stanley's number.

"Get in here," he said. "I want to have a strategy session. I have
a plan."

"But, Connie, it's three o'clock in the morning and there's a
blackout."

"I told you, Stanley. Get in here."

"Is Corrine coming?"

"No, she's through."

"Are you O.K., Connie?"

"Never felt better. Pick up a couple of hamburgers on your way.
I'm starving."

"Is that all?"

"Yeah. And a Thermos of coffee. This could take all night. We've got a lot of work to do. We're going to have a news conference at noon. And bring the commissioner. We're going to turn this town upside down."

"What are you going to say, Connie?"

"Stanley, don't you worry about that. By the time you get in here I'll think of something. Haven't I always?"